THE DOUBLE TENTH

TENTH

George Brown

ARROW

By the same author
RINGMAIN

This edition published by Arrow Books Limited 1993

1 3 5 7 9 10 8 6 4 2

Copyright © George Brown 1992

The right of George Brown to be identified as the
author of this work has been asserted by him in accordance
with the Copyright, Designs and Patents Act, 1988

First published in the United Kingdom in 1992 by
Century

Random House, 20 Vauxhall Bridge Road, London SW1V 2SA

Random House Australia (Pty) Limited
20 Alfred Street, Milsons Point, Sydney,
New South Wales 2061, Australia

Random House New Zealand Limited
18 Poland Road, Glenfield
Auckland 10, New Zealand

Random House South Africa (Pty) Limited
PO Box 337, Bergvlei, South Africa

Random House UK Limited Reg. No. 954009

A CIP catalogue record for this book
is available from the British Library

ISBN 0 09 992760 8

Printed and bound in Great Britain by
Cox & Wyman Ltd, Reading, Berkshire

For Terence Daley – gentleman

Acknowledgements

Dr C.E.D. Hearn of Overton and Dr A.P. Baranowski of St Thomas' Hospital, London, for their generous advice on 'psycho-amputation' of the hand.

Captain Dan Huntington, 2/2nd King Edward VII's Own Goorkhas, who couldn't have been more helpful and, for his sins, nearly had a dead author on his hands on Crest Hill, overlooking Shenzhen.

Captain David Wombell, 10th Princess Mary's Own Gurkha Rifles who, as always, went to great lengths to put me right on the technical military aspects of 'border watching', and whose threat to call in for a drink one day, by way of repayment, fills me with trepidation.

Only trust information that is stolen, or obtained by means.
Information given is suspect automatically.

Deng Xiaoping, *Power*, 1978

PROLOGUE

Johor, Malaya, 1953

Lieutenant Peter Fylough stared down the short barrel of the M1 carbine balanced between his knees and centred its sights on the misshapen footprint in the mud a few yards in front of him. Only his eyes moved. The rest of his body hadn't moved since he'd slipped into position and propped his back against a tree over three hours ago.

It had been pitch-black then, but now, as dawn broke, it brought with it a momentary lull in the teeming rain and the shy beginnings of a waterlogged sun began to turn the bone-chilling night jungle back into its daytime stifling, overladen, stuffy, putrid-smelling hothouse.

The insects had been awake for over an hour and their screams of triumph at surviving another night rent the unmoving air. In the distance a tiger cleared his throat and a wild boar panicked through his patch of jungle – just penetrable – whilst a parliament of gibbons from the safety of their high canopy whooped encouragement.

Fylough twitched a persistent fly from his lips, took his eyes away from the gunsight and glanced to his right. Corporal Togom, just visible through the undergrowth, squatted, Malay-fashion, on his heels a few yards away. His senses were active. His almond-shaped eyes swivelled towards Fylough and after a second's interrogative stare his lips parted over yellowing buck teeth and the straggly wisps of black hair over his top lip spread like an underdeveloped caterpillar beneath his nose – Togom's version of a grin – but it died before reaching his eyes. He pursed his lips in warning and stared over Fylough's shoulder.

Fylough turned his head slowly in the direction of Togom's stare. As he did so he reached out and gently touched the shoulder of the man squatting beside him nursing the butt of a Bren gun. His eyes narrowed as he tried to pierce the sticky gloom of the

1

narrow animal track that vanished into the undergrowth on his left. He had a broken, partly obscured vision of about fifteen yards – jungle-dark but highlighted every so often by sharp, knife-like shafts of sunlight that lanced through the overhead canopy.

Something had moved.

A branch? No wind here, no air even. No noise – just a feeling. Togom had seen it. Or had he sensed it? No. There it was again. Fylough swivelled his eyes again briefly. Togom stared inscrutably past him and along the track. Fylough moved his eyes beyond Togom and searched without success for signs betraying the fourth man of the team. He would have a clearer view from the other side of the small stream and, chin resting on the wooden butt of the second Bren gun, he'd be able to see further up the track. He was totally invisible. Fylough hoped he hadn't gone to sleep, lulled by the warm sun on his back.

But the damp, mist-laden warmth was short-lived.

With an eerie silence the clouds gathered themselves together and closed over the sun like a great velvet curtain. Without warning, the sky opened up again and the rain crashed mercilessly through the thin covering of leaves, drowning all sound and reducing visibility to a few yards.

Fylough blinked the rain from his eyelids and blew a dewdrop off the tip of his nose. For the hundredth time, he quickly studied the stream, roughly dammed and threatening to overflow its banks, and the white, silvery upturned bellies of a score of hand-sized fish stunned by powdered *tuba* root. Eight miles inside the jungle – three days' slow march from the nearest brick wall – somebody was killing fish for breakfast.

Kim Cheong opened his eyes and listened to the rain thundering onto the plaited fronds which made up the roof of his bamboo-framed hut. Beside him, on a crude platform made of split green bamboo strips, Ah Lian moaned quietly in her shallow half-sleep, half-awake state and pulled her sarong covering tighter around her to keep out the cold jungle air. She tried to disguise her shivering and prayed for the first signs of daylight. For with it would come the life-giving warmth, then the heat, and then the sticky, merciful sweat. She shivered again. And then the work – and the fear. The daily fear that started with the dawn and went on

2

until dusk, continuing into the night in the subconscious until a fitful sleep deadened it, but didn't banish it. Ah Lian was still enjoying her fear – even in her dream.

Kim Cheong pushed aside his thin cotton blanket and stretched, without disturbing the sleeping girl. There was nothing to tell him the hour – it was too dark to read his watch – but he sensed the time from habit, not yet dawn, but not far off. Ten minutes to stand-to and the camp was silent. But there'd be fifteen men like him, lying awake, waiting, listening, and another three nodding into their fear on the perimeter, their bodies sparsely protected against the penetrating rain, their eyes red-rimmed from the strain of peering into a black, impenetrable, wet nothing. He stood up and tightened the cord of his blue underpants. Even with the bulge of a filled waterproof body belt there was not much waist to tighten the cord around.

Kim Cheong was skinny, hungry skinny, with no bulge where his stomach should be, and his pale, grey-coloured skin was stretched over his light frame, showing up the blotches of malnutrition and the unhealed ulcer craters from protein deficiency. At twenty-five he was never going to get any older in appearance, he was going to look the same for the rest of his life – the jungle war would see to that. He unhooked the worn Sten from the projection by his bed and tucked its oiled covering cloth between the gaps in the wooden wall. It was cocked. In the dark he felt for the long slim magazine and gently tapped it to make sure it was firmly home. It was unnecessary. He slipped its strap over his bare shoulder and squatted in the corner while he swilled his mouth out with cold water. He spat it into the mud at his feet, then took another mouthful and, without tasting, swallowed it, stood up and walked to the side of the bed. There was no need to say anything. The girl was wide awake.

'Is it time?' she asked in a whisper. She never spoke any other way. She was fourteen now, she'd lived in the silent world for almost a year, and she knew no other way to speak.

'Ssssh . . .' Kim Cheong's acknowledgement barely carried over the striking rain and, as if on cue, a handful of fingernails scraped along the bamboo door-post. 'Get dressed.'

Ah Lian slipped out of her sarong and pulled on a pair of black baggy trousers. She tightened a crude cotton band round her puny breasts, flattening them against her chest, and pulled a black loose shirt over her head. She was without sex – not that being a girl would have made any difference when the soldiers came. She picked up a loaded single-barrel shotgun and followed Kim Cheong out of the hut to take up position on the camp perimeter. She rested the barrel in the 'V' of a small tree as Kim Cheong had taught her. It was necessary. The shotgun had only a metal frame for a stock. She was tiny. A slip of a girl. When she fired it – God forbid she had to – the rebound would just about cut her in two. Nobody told her, though. She had been taught to rest it in the crotch of a tree. She did as she was told.

They stood in silence, staring into the fading night as they'd done every day since they'd made this new camp several months ago, and waited, shivering, until the new day pulled the dark screen slowly upwards and replaced it with a wet, grizzly greyness. And then, as if by magic, it was broad daylight and for a blessed moment the rain drizzled to nothing, a thin sun crept briefly out of the leaden clouds to open up around them the familiar, untrustworthy jungle and the insects and birds celebrated the passing of another twelve-hour night.

As the camp came to life Ah Lian took her turn in the routine daily cycle. She relieved the river sentry at the foot of the hill, on the side of which, as if held in place by the clinging red mud, stood the scattered permanent huts of the 7th Platoon of the 5th Regiment of the Malay Races Liberation Army – eighteen men, all Chinese, plus one fourteen-year-old girl.

Relieved in turn, Ah Lian washed in the waist-deep running water and took her place in the queue for two handfuls of cold rice – cooked the previous evening before the rain put out the fires – half a small fish and a soggy wad of tapioca dough. Kim Cheong joined her in the corner of the communal hut and squatted on his heels beside her in the gloom as the rain, blotting out the sun's brief appearance, returned, bursting with increased intensity out of the black clouds above them. There was no comfort. No warmth. The rain drove in at an angle, cutting across the small open area that was used as a parade ground and driving across the slope of the hill, beating to the ground the sparse growth of the vegetable garden beyond the camp perimeter.

Kim Cheong draped a torn, dirty towel shawl fashion across his

4

shoulders, but it did nothing to remove the goose pimples from his skinny arms or reduce the chatter of his teeth.

'I'm fishing this morning,' he whispered in a stutter to Ah Lian. 'The river's full. There'll be plenty to eat tonight. You're in the garden . . .' he glanced sideways at her without turning his head. 'Stay on the upper slope. Just in case.'

Ah Lian pulled a face. 'I'd rather come with you and collect fish – I hate the garden.'

'You'll do as you're told!' he snapped, but there was no venom in his voice. He touched her leg in a gesture of affection. 'Anyway, you wouldn't be able to carry all the fish I'm going to collect.'

'Don't boast, you'll probably come back empty-handed again and it'll be my cabbage and chilli you'll be eating.' Ah Lian stared at the ball of cold rice she'd shaped with her fingers, then looked up at Kim Cheong. There was no hint of amusement in her eyes, her expression was blank. If she'd ever known what amusement was she'd forgotten all about it, as she'd forgotten how to laugh – and crying wasn't allowed. Laughing and crying! Ah Lian never gave them another thought. At the ripe old shrivelled-up age of fourteen and a bit, Ah Lian, a committed revolutionary, wasn't permitted proletariat emotions, even if she remembered them. 'What about the soldiers?'

'What about them?' Kim Cheong didn't look at her. Instead, he chewed on the unpalatable tapioca dough and stared across the mud floor at Hang Lee, the District Committee Member and Platoon Commander.

Hang Lee was an old man. He was forty at least. He'd fought the Japanese until they'd marched back the way they'd come but, as he continually told his platoon, they were easy meat compared with the British. They'd stuck to the fringes, they'd never bothered the real jungle soldiers – it had been a good People's War. But this was different, this was a war to the death – the Malayan Chinese people against the might of the British Empire. And they were serious – it was as if the British Army was trying to prove that it hadn't really been trying against the Jananese in '42. They were everywhere now – they, and their running dogs the Malays, sniffing their way into the deepest corners of even the safest jungle.

He must have felt Kim's eyes on him.

5

He looked up from his wooden bowl as if he'd heard Ah Lian's whispered question. He stared blankly at Kim Cheong, wiped a dribble of gravy off his chin with his finger, stuck the finger in his mouth and sucked it clean. He swallowed, then shook his head like a man absently shaking the rain from his face and went back to shovelling rice.

'We're secure here until we move nearer to Cha'ah village.' He parted his teeth, showing a mouthful of half-masticated rice and cabbage, and rested his eyes on Ah Lian. 'Think about it, Comrade. Chaah . . . food! Meat, eggs, chicken . . .'

'And killing?' whispered Ah Lian.

Another clap of thunder exploded over their heads and the rain intensified. It drew all eyes up from the food and removed the frown of reprobation from Kim's face. The crash of the metal rods of rain on the surrounding jungle and the rasping thunderous downpour thudding on to the *atap* leaves of the hut made further speech impossible. Hang Lee lowered his bowl from his face and pointed his finger at Kim Cheong. Kim Cheong nodded and wordlessly did the same to two other men. All three stood up, stared for a second at the torrent rushing off the roof and, like men resigned to jumping off the highest board, stepped through the waterfall and out into the rain.

Kim made a vague effort to protect the mechanism of his Sten from the rain but then, accepting the futility, tucked it under his arm and led the way out of the camp to join the pig track he'd used on the stream-damming operation two days previously.

He trudged head down, his two companions, one carrying a canvas sack made out of a tarpaulin taken from an ambushed lorry and the other with an old Japanese machine-gun slung across his shoulder, splodged in his footsteps. Every so often Kim stopped, and his two followers melted off the track. They were like ghosts. It was routine. That was why they were still alive. After a moment Kim alone moved on fifty yards, and waited. They joined him. And then they did it all again. He studied the ground and cursed the rain. The whole bloody British Army could have walked along here and left no trace. He stared about him, checked the undergrowth for snapped branches, listened, and smelled. No smoke; no aftershave; no cooking; no shit – fuck the rain! He retraced his steps, gave an animal-like grunt, and when joined

6

again by his companions moved toward the widening of the slippery track that dropped away to the dammed stream.

Fylough brought his eyes back to the track.

Kim Cheong was standing still, the rain pouring off his face and body as he studied the last stretch of track leading to the fish cachement area. His carrier and rearguard had done their disappearing act some distance behind him. To Fylough he looked alone, suspicious, and very, very alert. Kim Cheong frowned, then went down in a crouch with the fingers of one hand resting lightly on the sodden ground and brought the Sten to rest on his knee. It was pointing in Corporal Togom's direction.

It was pure chance. Kim had seen nothing except the slippery footmark, protected from obliteration by the slope of the track, and he recognised it as his own. He straightened up, his suspicion allayed and the warning tingle at the base of his neck ignored, then moved a step forward.

Togom and Fylough fired simultaneously and a fraction of a second behind them the two Brens opened up, splattering the track and moving downwards like powerful hoses to encompass Kim's writhing body.

Fylough leapt to his feet.

'OK! Leave him – he's dead!' he shouted at the Bren-gunners. 'You – on the track!' He pointed at the man who'd been squatting next to him. Then: 'Quick. Togom. Follow me.' He picked up Kim's Sten and threw it down the slope towards the stream. He lowered his voice and hissed to the unseen gunner. 'Stay where you are – cover the track. Tokachil . . .' He pointed to the other man who'd brought his Bren gun on to the track. '. . . come with us.' It had taken less than fifteen seconds.

With Tokachil and his Bren close in attendance and Togom bringing up the rear, Fylough slipped and slithered along the wet, muddy path. He knew that unless there was a sizeable camp nearby, any other terrorists would have melted into the undergrowth. Counter-ambush was unlikely. A fish-collection party would be lightly armed. They'd bolt. They wouldn't hang around. But watch out for some wild return fire.

He was right.

Kim Cheong's two companions were fractionally late in their

reaction. They broke out of their cover. The second bandit raised the barrel of his machine-gun and fired a long burst blindly in the direction of the ambush before joining the other man, who, discarding his canvas sack, ran crouched low back along the narrow track. But not before they'd seen Fylough's white face.

'*Dua orang, Tuan!*' 'Two men, sir!' hissed Togom and, still moving fast, exchanged his carbine for the other man's Bren. He squeezed past Fylough and in rapid bursts from the hip, moving the barrel gently from side to side, emptied the Bren's magazine along the track.

Fylough shook his head and gave a half-grin at Togom's set expression, then moved in front again, faster now, the footprints of the running men clear in the mud, filling as they were made with rain flowing down the track.

It was difficult to keep up the speed of the chase. Slipping, stumbling and gasping for breath, there was no sound save for the swishing of undergrowth against moving bodies and the muted splash of feet on mud. And then the gibbons, high up in the trees, recovering from the ear-shattering bursts of gunfire, found their voices again and rent the silent, rain-splattered air with their whoops, wailing like a village of Masai women heralding a death in the family. When they ran out of breath, Fylough stopped and listened. There was no noise ahead. No crashing of bodies through the undergrowth, no groaning from Togom's bullets, just an oppressive silence. They'd arrived.

Togom touched his elbow and crouched low, pointing ahead and above. Fylough joined him and, following Togom's pointed finger, peered ahead through the trees. There was a gap in the canopy that let in the light. They looked at each other. It was a camp. A large one. There'd be a rearguard posted.

Fylough tightened his grip on the carbine and nervously ran his finger over the safety-catch lever. It was off. He touched the bottom of the magazine – he'd changed it – it was new, full, and felt firm and solid in its home. He allowed a nervous tic under his left eye to run its course. He'd once had a magazine drop out of the carbine in the middle of an ambush – it was things like that that spawned idiosyncrasies.

Bang! Bang! Bang! Brrrrrr! Bang! Bang! It was the Japanese machine-gun. The shots rang out unevenly and hissed and crackled through the branches over Fylough's head. The two bandits had reached the perimeter of their camp.

Togom fired back – a quick burst of rapid fire from the Bren and then he dropped low on to the track. He didn't seek the safety of the undergrowth. He'd spotted the mark on the tree – the aiming point for the sentry. There'd be a shallow trench on either side of the track, full of knife-sharp, pointed bamboo waiting for the novice to throw himself into cover.

'*Tuan!*'

Fylough nodded without looking round and pressed himself against the trunk of a large tree. He'd seen it too. 'Come on,' he hissed and, crouched low, darted ahead of Togom.

Crack!

Another shot rang out. A different weapon. Only one shot. The machine-gun had moved on; somebody else was holding them up. And still no sign, only sound, the reverberation of the last gunshot echoing through the jungle and bouncing away like thunder from tree to tree.

Fylough broke through the shield of branches that blocked the path. They'd been discreetly half-cut and bent across the track to disguise the camp's entrance. A log across the track and more branches. A gap to the side – convenient – another pit. This one, full of three-foot-long sharpened bamboo, was a dual-purpose trap – wild pig or an Englishman. And beside it a stack of logs – the only barricade – a sentry's shield. No need for caution now. If they'd got this far it didn't matter. He leapt over the concealed pit. Togom followed, the Bren gun still tucked firmly under his arm, and behind him the other man, nursing his Sten gun, worked his way through the branches and over the log.

They were now in the open.

Across the vegetable garden that stretched up one side of the slope the two terrorists slithered, trying to hold their footing. The sentry had gone in another direction. The camp looked deserted. Mercifully the thunderous rain had softened to a fine, warm downpour. But it went unnoticed.

Fylough stopped, steadied himself and aimed at the leading figure.

Bang! Bang! Bang!

He stopped and peered over the sight. Then fired another four shots. Nobody screamed. Nobody fell. He changed magazines and cursed as the figure disappeared behind the first of the huts. The second man, a rapid glance over his shoulder, slipped, fell on all fours and scrambled wildly to his feet. He'd lost valuable ground. He cast another terrified glance over his shoulder, half turned and fired from the hip. The heavy .303 thundered but the bullet winged harmlessly into the trees. Fylough steadied himself again, blinked away the rain from his eyes and shook his head. It wasn't enough. His face streamed with water. It was difficult to aim. Beside him he heard the Bren thudding out short three- or four-round bursts and behind, from his left, the toy-pistol-like cracking of the Sten.

The Chinese went to his knees again, scrabbling in the mud in panic. He'd almost made it to the bamboo hut. He knew if he reached it he'd be almost safe. Under cover of the flimsy huts he'd race through the main area of the camp to the thick blanket of secondary jungle behind the last of the huts, and then he'd be into the first leg of the concealed escape route. Just another few yards . . . He glanced quickly over his shoulder. The white man was floundering on the muddy slope. His feet had shot out from under him and, like a still photograph etched on his brain, he could clearly see his feet slipping and scuffling as he struggled upright. He smelt safety. Then Fylough stopped, steadied himself, and, resting on his knees and elbows, stared with streaming eyes through the tiny ring sight. The Chinaman's back filled the aperture.

He'd almost relaxed when one of Fylough's hasty group of shots hit him in the arm. But the shock didn't stop him. He didn't falter. Then the second and third bullets thudded into his back and came out through the top of his shoulder. He stumbled, but he'd made it. He grasped the side of the hut, staggered, turned defiantly and sent another unaimed shot at Fylough, now on his feet again. It was a mistake. He should have kept running. He heard Togom's burst of Bren thud into the bamboo beside him just as he pulled himself round the side of the hut and out of sight. He was a fraction of a second too late. Fylough's next shot scythed through the flimsy covering of the hut and caught him in the spine, low down, and without realising he'd been hit again he found his face pushing into the mud. He tried to blink it away from his eyes and was vaguely conscious of the rifle, still gripped firmly in his right hand, being prised away. He heard it splash into the ground some distance away and then felt his arm pulled as he was dragged on to his back. A hand rubbed the mud away and the fine rain cleared it from his eyes. As yet he felt no pain – only fear.

Togom placed his foot on the Chinaman's stomach and peered into his face.

'Open your eyes, *bangkal*!' he said. Togom wasn't even breathing hard.

The terrorist did as he was told and looked up into Togom's toothy smile. But Togom's smile was only skin-deep – it never went beyond his teeth.

'D'you know him?' asked Fylough when he returned from inspecting the empty camp.

'Lam Lee,' replied Togom. 'Used to be the cook's scavenger in Ten Platoon at Geylang in '44 – he couldn't cook either!'

Corporal Togom bin Haji Hashim, GM, CPM, plus four Second World War medals from a grateful British Government, had fought the real war with the men he was now hunting. A Malay among Chinese he'd enjoyed fighting the Japanese. He was also enjoying fighting the men he'd lived and fought with for three years. It was all the same to Togom – he had a penchant for choosing the winning side.

'Sure?'

Togom nodded.

Lam Lee blinked at the mention of his name – Togom's face meant nothing to him. Then he grimaced, and a scream burned into his throat as the first wave of pain hit him. It didn't upset Togom. He put all his weight on to the foot pressing into the wounded man's stomach and when the scream died into a gurgle he said, conversationally, 'Where's the bolt-hole, Lee? How many of you? Where're you meeting?' Togom stuck the Bren muzzle into his neck and showed the bandit his teeth. It wasn't very reassuring. 'Come on, boy!' He jabbed the machine-gun in his neck with every word. 'Save your life. Quick!'

Lam Lee clenched his eyes and summoned up the strength to spit. It reached no further than his chin, but it didn't matter. He'd made his answer. He started screaming.

Fylough and Togom exchanged glances. Fylough hunched his shoulders, wiped the rain from his face, and, then, without

11

looking down at the man on the ground, walked into the nearest hut and lit a cigarette. He placed two dry ones on the crude table beside Kim Cheong's makeshift bed, sat on the bamboo edge and, as he drew smoke luxuriously into his lungs, gazed studiously at the open map on his knees.

Togom, still with his foot on the Chinaman's stomach, moved the Bren gun so that its conical muzzle rested on the wounded man's chest just below his collarbone. Lam stopped screaming. Togom wrinkled his nose, raised the muzzle three inches and, tightening his grip, squeezed the trigger. It was still on automatic. Five heavy .303 bullets ploughed into Lam Lee's heart, scooping out, as if with a large soup ladle, the top half of his chest. Togom stepped back and rubbed his bloody boot in the mud. He'd already lost interest in his former comrade.

The two Malays and the Englishman smoked their cigarettes as they wandered in and out of each of the fragile huts. They didn't expect to find anything. Hang Lee had had enough warning to evacuate – everything had been taken, even the invaluable cooking pots. A good bandit leader could clear a camp of everything moveable in five minutes; Hang Lee had been given enough time to have a bath as well if he'd wanted it.

The three met up on the far side of the camp and checked the escape route. It was quite obvious now; they'd left a gap as wide as a London bus, the mud churned up as if an army had stampeded through with all its gear. But there was no point in following. Hang Lee and his people would have split into small parties; in two days' time they would rendezvous and then make their way to the safe camp, converging on it from different directions. Retracing their steps the three joined up again beside Lam Lee's body. He'd finished flailing around and lay in the shallow depression in the mud he'd made in his death throes. They studied him for a few minutes while they finished their cigarettes. No revolutionary this but a hardbitten terrorist; a murderer who, curled up, looked like a scruffy boy who'd dropped off to sleep in a muddy pool. It seemed a pity to disturb him but, taking a leg each, Fylough and Togom dragged him across the vegetable garden and after flattening the bamboo spikes dropped him into the pit. There'd be no sign of him or the pit in a few months' time.

*

Kim Cheong's body lay exactly where they'd left it on the track.

Fylough and Togom squatted on their haunches and studied his features. His face, washed clean by the rain, was peaceful and untouched by bullets; he looked almost as though, bathed by the thin morning sun, he'd given in to the temptation of a gentle pre-luncheon doze.

'What's his name?' asked Fylough. His question remained unanswered as, watched by Togom, he glanced first casually and then with mounting interest at the documents in Kim Cheong's body belt. Suddenly he became aware of Togom's scrutiny. He folded up the sheath of papers before cramming them hastily into the canvas pouches of his own belt. He looked back at the body and then jerked his chin interrogatively at Togom.

Togom's attention was elsewhere. He frowned, crouched low, listening. He peered over his shoulder at the track behind him.

'It's a pig.' The Bren-gunner from the other side of the stream forestalled Togom's frowning query.

'After all this shooting?'

'I saw it.'

Togom wasn't happy. 'Come over here and move down that track until we've finished here. You,' he said to the other man, 'watch the flank.' He turned back to Fylough and shook his head as he stared hard at Kim's face. Kim Cheong's closed eyelids stared back. After a moment Togom pulled a face and sucked air noisily through the wide gaps in his large front teeth. He tried to close his lips but after a second the teeth won and they parted again. Fylough lit two cigarettes and gave one to Togom. Togom didn't try to hide his perplexity. He took Kim's chin in his hand and moved the dead man's head this way and that, frowning in concentration as he studied his features. After a minute or so he shook his head slowly, pulled deeply on the cigarette and, still staring into Kim Cheong's face, said, 'I don't know him, *Tuan*. He's different. I think he's special.'

'What d'you mean?'

Togom sucked in more air and whistled it out through his teeth.

'A ghost.' He touched his forehead and looked Fylough in the eye. 'A feeling up here. I'm not sure. He might be Chinese. He's not local.'

'China Chinese?' Fylough stared with renewed interest at Kim's face. 'You sure?'

'No, *Tuan*, I said only a feeling. Perhaps Sergeant Johari. . . ?'
Togom raised his eyebrows. He was going to leave it at that, and
then, realising what he'd let them in for, touched the body with his
foot. 'But it'll be hard going carrying this back to camp, and Johari
doesn't know everything. Or everybody!' He finished with a little
hiss and the hint of a smile. Fylough knew what he meant.

Platoon Sergeant Johari, pre-war regular police constable, ex-
lieutenant of the Japanese/Malay Army, the Hei Ho. Volunteer
for the Kempeitai, the Japanese Gestapo. All good friends now –
no hard feelings. After all, Johari had given the Communists a
hard time during the war – we were all fighting them now. Togom's
smile turned into a grin and he pushed Kim's chin away with his
forefinger. 'But he knows more than most of us!'

The three Malays lashed Kim Cheong's hands and feet together
and threaded a strong three-foot straight branch between them.
Kim Cheong weighed nothing. He was awkward rather than
heavy. Togom swept the stream clear of stunned fish and left them
on the bank to rot. His face settled into a scowl as he took the front
end of the pole and stared at the back of Fylough's head, who, with
the Bren gun strapped to his shoulder, led them back the way
they'd come.

At the first changeover Togom, rubbing his shoulder, exchanged his weapon for the rearguard's Bren and stepped over
Kim Cheong's body. He watched Fylough and the other man pick
it up, then, as he passed to take up his position in front, said to the
Malay, 'Did you hear anything behind?'

'Like what?'

'Like that pig you said you saw back there.'

'I heard nothing.'

'The pig's following us.'

'You're imagining things, Togom,' whispered Fylough. 'That
ghost's playing with you again!'

Togom didn't smile. 'Watch the rear,' he told the Malay. 'Don't
go to sleep – spend all your time listening.'

They reached the base camp just as night began to close in.

At half-past six the next morning Fylough lit his first cigarette of
the day, pulled on wet socks, and laced up wet, muddy jungle
boots over the top of wet, muddy trousers. It brought no look or

14

feeling of distaste to his sombre features. It was normal. There was nothing unusual in starting the day chilled to the bone in damp, sweat-soaked, jungle-smelling clothes. He accepted a metal cup of scalding tea, sweet, soup-thick with condensed milk, from one of the Malays, and carried it to the small, ineffectual, smoky fire near the centre of the camp. Three Europeans squatted there. It was an unusual gathering of white faces; there should have been only one other.

Fylough sat on his ankles, Malay-style, and tossed a solid fuel slab into the smoke. When the smoke intensified he threw in a match and the whole thing burst into flames.

'That's called instant fire,' he pronounced and raised the mug of tea to his lips. It was too soon, his lips refused to accept the scalding metal. He blew on it and kept it just below his mouth, every so often testing the heat.

'And a waste of a bloody tommy cooker!' Lieutenant Harry Kenning smiled to show he didn't give a bugger about tommy cookers, or anything else at the moment except getting some of the hot tea inside him.

Kenning, like Fylough, was Police Special Forces, 10th Federal Jungle Company. Two hundred Malays; a handful of Chinese; six officers – three English, two Chinese, one Malay. Half the men in the base camp were Kenning's, the other half Fylough's. By two weeks' seniority Fylough commanded the unit. But it didn't matter. After three years, most of it spent in deep jungle, Kenning and Fylough had no arguments left – it was like a marriage, except these two were the best of friends. The other two men by the fire didn't belong to the club.

After five weeks on this operation Corporal 'Dixie' Dean was beginning to feel at home. It hadn't been his choice, he hadn't volunteered – but he was awfully glad he came. Tall, thin and wiry, he sat on the other side of the fire, squatting with his back to a tree, running an oily cloth lovingly over the open breech of a well-worn Remington 'Wingmaster' pump-action shotgun. The barrel was sawn off so that only eighteen inches remained. Dixie had done the war – the proper one. Corporal, 22nd SAS Regiment, he'd 'come down' from colour-sergeant, Coldstream Guards, to help resurrect in Malaya the disbanded wartime SAS. It hadn't worked. The real SAS had all gone back to driving buses or digging coal, or back to parent regiments. The new people hadn't worked it out – yet. They could jump blindly into the jungle, but they had an awful job walking out. And they couldn't kill bandits. Their hearts were in the right place, though. Dean had been ordered to find out how Malays led by crazy Englishmen were doing it. He'd been forced on Fylough and Kenning but they were learning to live with him. He was their sort of man. And Dixie Dean was learning how to find and kill bandits.

He looked up from his oiling job and studied the two young Englishmen.

They were both of an age – early twenties – uncommunicative, taciturn, older than their years. Dixie Dean knew what they were, he didn't need to speculate: they were killers. It didn't show in their faces or their manner, but it was there under the skin: ruthless, intelligent killers both. And, after over a month, Dean could say, without having his arm twisted between his legs, that these two, and the men they commanded, could knock spots off the SAS as he knew it in its resurrection. This was what was needed, not regimental throw-outs. This was the breed: intelligent and hand-picked, linguists who spoke only Malay in the jungle. They lived off a handful of rice, a mug of tea, a wine gum when the going got tough. They were as much at home in the mud and swamps as they were in the Malay kampong and Chinese village. They had their own spy networks and agents, they ran undercover operations, ambushed without mercy and used the same manual of dirty tricks as their opponents. They were above all ruthless – prisoners were not welcome. They expected, and got, no quarter from their enemy – it didn't worry them. They made up their own rules of warfare as they went along, ignoring the British Army's gentle insistence that, for some strange reason, terrorists should be treated like soldiers. These men were winning – the terrorists were being killed out of existence. Dixie Dean logged his assessments, his findings, his conditions for the future, and stood up.

The fourth man sat apart, his legs outstretched. Another Englishman, he was from Special Branch and wasn't here by choice; he'd been foisted on to the party to 'find out what's going on at the pointed end of the sausage'. So far he hadn't discovered anything about the jungle that would induce him to volunteer for a second excursion, and he had no illusions – he knew he wasn't welcome. 'Was he carrying anything?' he asked.

'Like what?'

'Papers.'

Fylough shook his head. 'No.'

Dixie Dean broke the awkward silence. He looked up from his oiling job and glanced at the mound under the poncho on the edge of the camp. 'Why'd you bring the Chink back, Peter?'

Fylough managed to get a sip out of his mug. He pulled a face, then smiled shyly. 'Corporal Togom declined to name him. As he looked a grade more than a shithouse wallah I though we'd better have Sergeant Johari run his eyes over him.' He took another few sips of tea. 'I'd hate to shove one of the leaders of the Malayan People's Communist Party down the hole and let it go unnoticed.'

'What difference does it make?'

'Morale, Dixie, morale. The whole bloody lot might throw in the towel if we tell them the mountain's crumbling.' Fylough turned to Kenning. 'And talking about mountains, how far has Johari gone? I don't want this bugger going rotten on us before he sees him.'

Kenning continued sipping tea noisily from his hot metal mug. He lowered it fractionally. 'He'll have heard the shooting. He's in the wrong direction to ambush your runners so he'll come straight back. He'll know we'll want to get after them. He'll be here before lunch.'

Kenning underestimated him. Fylough had barely finished his tea when Sergeant Johari stepped through the trees on the camp perimeter.

Johari was a small man even for a Malay. Perfectly formed, with short stumpy legs, he was a good-looking man. No facial hair, like the majority of his countrymen, he had almond-shaped eyes which, unlike Togom's, occasionally twitched with a sort of hidden humour, although nobody had ever heard him laugh. It wasn't difficult to imagine Johari in a Japanese officer's uniform – shiny jackboots, a scruffy handkerchief hanging from the back of his cap and a long, curved sword dangling on the ground behind him.

Throwing off his heavy pack, he glanced curiously at the poncho-covered corpse as he strolled towards the four Europeans squatting by the fire.

17

'*Nasib, Tuan?*' 'Luck?' he remarked, and nodded over his shoulder at Kim's body. He accepted a cigarette from Kenning and a mug of tea from an orderly and squatted down beside Fylough.

'Two,' replied Fylough. 'We brought this one back for you to look at. Togom doesn't know him.' He didn't voice Togom's theory.

Johari lit his cigarette and placed his hot mug on the ground in front of him. He stared over his shoulder for a second at the covered mound again, then back at Fylough. 'Where's Togom now, *Tuan?*'

'In the river– having a bath,' interjected Kenning.

'Get him,' ordered Johari to the Malay who'd made his tea. 'Excuse me,' he told Fylough and Kenning. He didn't acknowledge Dean or the introspective Special Branch man – they weren't his people, they didn't count out here.

'We'll come too,' said Kenning.

Johari pulled the poncho away and turned Kim Cheong on to his back. He stared into his face for a moment, then squatted beside him. Togom appeared, a towel draped round his waist, jungle boots unlaced, flapping around his ankles, and his Sten gun hanging by its strap over his bare shoulder. His head was dripping wet and traces of toothpaste remained at the corners of his mouth like little white continuations of his straggly moustache.

Squatting down, he started a long, low-key muttered conversation with Johari, who listened intently, occasionally interjecting a question as he turned Kim's face first this way, then that. Neither man's expression changed as they studied the dead man. Johari drew heavily on his cigarette and stood up.

'A stranger,' he told the two lieutenants. 'I don't know him.' He stared down at Kim Cheong's face again. 'Maybe a courier. Maybe a visitor from outside – maybe Special.' He stopped in mid-sentence and watched Togom squat again, untie the string holding Kim's blue cotton underpants and pull them down below his hips.

'*Awak ingat dia-punya nama ada tertulis di-butoh-nya?*' Johari laughed outright and Togom's teeth parted in a broad, hissing grin. Both Fylough and Kenning joined in the laughter.

But the Special Branch man saw nothing funny.

18

Dixie Dean did. 'What's the joke?' he asked, and made a mental note to start getting to grips with the Malay language. He'd already decided to make overtures to join up with these two crazy bastards.

'Corporal Togom has a thing about penises,' grinned Kenning. 'Johari asked him if he thought he'd find the guy's name engraved on the tip of his cock, or words to that effect!'

Dean frowned doubtfully at Togom, then smiled. 'So why's he staring at it like that?'

Togom looked up at Fylough, his grin wider as his lips took a more comfortable position over his large teeth. He held his thumb up and ran a finger across the first joint, then raised his eyebrows interrogatively.

'What's that all about?'

'He wants the end of the Chinaman's cock.'

'Jesus! What in heaven's name for?'

'He'd have it put in a little bottle with some rose-water and blessed by somebody who specialises in these matters.'

'I'm not with you.'

'It's an aphrodisiac – very powerful!'

Dean couldn't tell whether Fylough was pulling his leg or not. Kenning lit a cigarette and grinned. Dean stared at the two of them. 'You mean the bugger would drink it?'

'Good God, no! He'd tuck it somewhere in the bedroom of some floozie who's tormenting the life out of him and – bingo! She won't be able to refuse him and he won't be able to stop!'

'It works?'

'I don't know, I've never tried it.' Fylough became serious. 'Johari, let's have one of his hands for fingerprints and then bury him. I want to be out of here in an hour.'

'Make it both,' suggested Kenning. 'Might as well do the job properly.'

'OK. Both hands, Johari.'

Togom slipped away and came back with a cigarette dangling from his lips and carrying a short but heavy parang of bright steel. He'd taken it from a dead Communist in the early days. It was a beautiful blade, balanced, and had an edge like a razor. He lifted Kim Cheong's penis with its tip, studied it critically, then raised his eyebrows at Fylough again.

19

Fylough gave the merest shake of his head. Togom wasn't surprised. But Bentley, the Special Branch man, was – he hadn't seen Fylough's response.

'Is this absolutely necessary?' Bentley looked as though he was about to throw up his early-morning cups of tea and looked green under his recently acquired jungle pallor. He turned away and addressed himself to the overhanging branches above them. 'We're not bloody savages, you know, Fylough.'

'Oh, aren't we?' Fylough allowed himself a wink at Kenning. 'Think yourself lucky it's not yours – I'd find it very difficult to refuse the good Corporal Togom such a prize!'

'It'll go in my report.'

'Fuck your report! Go and get your gear packed. We're moving at nine.'

Togom went to work on Kim Cheong's hands. He ran the blade lightly across the wrist, cutting well into the skin, about a quarter of an inch deep, then, placing the thick branch he'd been tied to under Kim's wrist, Togom bent the hand across it. He invited Johari to place his foot on Kim Cheong's arm, held the hand down with his left hand, and swung the parang. He could have been cutting a carrot. The hand came away as clean as if a surgeon had performed the operation.

'Did you say something?' Togom, expressionless, looked up at Johari and raised his eyebrows.

'No.'

'Funny – I though I heard words. Must have been *hantu*!'

'I don't think there are any ghosts stupid enough to be hanging around here! Although,' said Johari, philosophically, 'they say dead men sometimes feel pain. But enough of that. 'Gom, stop chattering and get the other bloody hand off and let's get on with it. Hey! You two!' He turned his head to a group of men, packed and ready to move off, who'd sidled up to watch Togom at work. 'Start digging a home for this guy, and don't make a meal of it. I don't want anything special; he's a bloody Chinaman, not a member of the royal family!'

They rolled Kim Cheong into the shallow grave and covered him with a sprinkling of soil and leaves. It barely concealed him. The animals would find him regardless of how deep they put him and how much they put on top. They filed out of the camp in a long, silent line. Nearly all trace of their habitation had been removed. Apart from a few cut branches and crushed undergrowth which would soon be obliterated by the returning jungle, it was as if no one had ever been there.

After the last man had slipped into the enveloping, sunless semi-dark, silence and still descended on to the former camp site. Nothing stirred. Shortly the animals would come, at first shyly, wary of the lingering smell of man, then, more boldly, the wild pig with its keen nose and the boar with the ivory razor tusks who would unearth the buried debris of human habitation. But, for the moment, only the branches of the tall trees moved in the gentle breeze. Only that – and a tentative, indiscernible movement of the soil over Kim Cheong's grave.

1

London, 1988

David Kent lowered himself into the oversprung armchair, reached forward, parted the net curtains by one finger's breadth and peered through the gap at the street below. A few parked cars, two women gossiping over a crying baby in a pushchair, absent-mindedly rocked by its mother without interfering with the conversation, and a Post Office van, its warning lights flicking and its front door wide open, obstructing the pavement. Nothing out of the ordinary. He placed his eye to the viewfinder of the Nikon camera, its long-barrelled telephoto lens mounted on a tripod in front of him, and stared with narrowed eyes at the end of the avenue. The camera was fine-focused. There was no need to touch anything. Down there nothing moved, except the shifting of weight from one leg to the other of the uniformed policeman on duty outside the Embassy of the People's Republic of China. Kent removed his finger and allowed the curtain to fall gently back into place.

'Bugger-all happening out there,' he said over his shoulder to the man lying on the camp bed in the corner of the room. 'Anything interesting in the diary?'

'Nothing. Not this morning, not yesterday, not the day before and not the day before that!'

'Thanks! You can go back to sleep now.' Kent moved his buttocks to a more comfortable position, lit a cigarette and continued to stare blankly at the Embassy gates in the distance. It came round twice a month. The boring, routine watching from the sparsely furnished room above the Agency-owned betting shop. It had been an observation point ever since the Chinese had come back into the fold and started talking again. It was a routine MI5 Watch. Nothing ever happened. Kent reckoned the Chinese knew they were there. But then Kent would. He was the new boy, this was only his second Watch and he was already bored with it.

Chinese-watching couldn't be anything else. After eight years in the Royal Hong Kong Police Force he should know more than most how the Chinese mind worked. A thirty-two-year-old sceptic, it took a lot to surprise him, least of all what he was doing in a scruffy room over a betting shop in West London. It was better not to think too much about it. MI5's jaundiced use of men with special talents had come up trumps – the ideal job for a fluent Cantonese-speaking Englishman was watching the Chinese Embassy from a lookout post above a betting shop. But Kent didn't hold it against them. Not much! He smiled crookedly to himself. It made all the difference; it was the sort of thing his face did quite well and softened it from a set, some would say arrogant, expression. It appealed to women, of all ages. It was probably the underlying hard edge, the casual grey-eyed stare that came down from his six foot two and his attitude of 'I don't care if you don't' that was the attraction.

He stubbed his cigarette out on the bare floorboards, studied for a second or two the pattern he'd made and looked up. He was just in time. A grey car had slipped casually down the road and pulled into the Embassy entrance.

Kent moved forward in his chair, stuck his eye to the viewfinder and just had time to study the single occupant's face through the telephoto and click the shutter before the policeman waved the car forward through the gates.

'What time did 513 D 7932 leave the Embassy?' he asked without taking his eyes from the viewfinder.

A grunt from behind him, a creaking of straining camp bed and, after a pause, 'Half-past eight this morning.'

'How many in the car?'

'Three – the driver plus two.'

'The third Secretary plus who?'

'Doesn't say. How d'you know it was the Third Secretary?'

'Check it.'

'You making work?'

'Check the tape at Clarence.' Kent sat back in the armchair, lit another cigarette and turned his head to watch his partner tap out the Clarence Terrace control-room recorder code. After a moment the phone was dropped back in its cradle. 'Third Secretary, plus Chin Xan Wah, senior correspondent of NCNA, and an Embassy driver – Chinese.'

23

'You sure about NCNA?'

'Yes. The New China News Agency it said.'

'That means Central Intelligence.' Kent frowned over the spiral of smoke from his forgotten cigarette. 'And the Third Secretary is Goh Peng. He's new, and he's a major in CELD. What the bloody hell are they up to?'

'What's CELD?'

'Central External Liaison Department. It's China's MI6.'

'So what's the big deal about a couple of Chinese Intelligence zombies taking in the sights?'

David Kent looked over his shoulder again. 'Nothing,' he grinned crookedly, 'except there's only one man come home – the Third Secretary.'

'So?'

'Wouldn't you think it somewhat unusual that the Third Secretary of the Embassy of the People's Republic drives himself home wearing a pair of dark glasses and a chauffeur's hat perched on top of his bonce? Log it. Here, let's change places for a second.' Kent squatted on his heels beside the telephone, checked through an index of numbers and punched out a Central London number.

'This is Reuter's, Far East desk,' he told the person who answered. 'Put me through to Mr Chin, please – urgent. No, sorry, Mr Chin only; it's special.' He held on briefly, then replaced the receiver and pulled a face at his companion. 'He's not in his office; he's not at home; he's not at the Embassy. They don't know where he is. What sort of head of bureau is that? Worse, what sort of bloody spy buggers off with his embassy's resident Intelligence chief and doesn't even leave a decent cover story?'

David Kent's suspicions and observations found their way in a direct line from Watcher HQ in Clarence Terrace to the head of Section K – Counter-espionage – at MI5 HQ. He, in turn, passed them on to his subordinate in Section K8 – surveillance of unfriendly (and friendly) diplomats, other than Soviet. Evelyn St John Woodhouse's request to have the Chinese Mission placed under full-time surveillance had thus come full circle. The priority of Kent's report was not sufficient to start the inter-departmental bells clanging, but it was enough to bring a frown of interest to the forehead of Woodhouse as he sipped his gin and tonic in the Pig and Eye Club in Leconfield House that evening. The frown dissolved into a thin smile when his deputy joined him at the corner of the bar.

'I was thinking about this Chink business,' he told him when the barman had slid out of earshot. 'Have you made anything out of it yet?'

Woodhouse's deputy scraped a handful of cashew nuts out of a bowl, threw two or three into his mouth and shook his head. 'I don't think there is anything to be made out of it. I thought I'd let it run.'

Woodhouse didn't seem disappointed. 'There's something I've been meaning to ask you. How the bloody hell does a Watcher from two hundred yards away tell the difference between a chauffeur and a Third Secretary? I thought these Chinese all looked alike.' He joined his deputy in the cashew-nut bowl and chewed a mouthful. Without waiting to finish eating he added: 'And the women have their thingumabob crossways instead of up and down?'

Woodhouse's deputy was not in a jocular frame of mind. He tapped the two ice cubes in his gin so that they bounced up and down, making the tonic froth over the rim of the glass. He frowned at the loss, dipped his finger in the spillage and sucked the finger dry. 'The Watcher's a China hand. Came from the Hong Kong Police. He can tell the difference – speaks the language too.'

'And do they?'

'Do they what? Who?'

'Chinese women – are they built differently?'

'It's a joke.'

Woodhouse looked mildly disappointed. 'So what's a talented fellow like that doing working as a Watcher? My charlady's grandson with his bib and rattle can do that sort of thing. Get him out of there.'

Woodhouse's deputy managed a bleak smile. 'Who, your char's grandson?'

'Don't be funny.' Woodhouse liked to be the one with the sense of humour. 'Have this Chinese-talker transferred to K. Tell Gerald we want to follow up the Chinese puzzle.' He paused for a drink and waited for his deputy's smile.

None came. Woodhouse's deputy sipped his gin without

25

betraying his thoughts. Woodhouse had gone round the bend. He'd seen the indent for a specialist on Chinese habits; it was an indent that came from above. Not heaven – nearly – but the initial below God's signature had been ESJW – Evelyn St John Woodhouse! The silly bugger had initiated Kent's Watching brief himself. But still, let's humour the poor bastard. 'Thine will be done!' he murmured unhumorously and put his glass back on the bar.

Woodhouse ignored the response. 'Find out what they're up to. Find out where this carload of Chink spies disappeared to and what the bloody hell they think we are to allow them to roam willy-nilly all over the bloody place – and then tell me how they were allowed to get away with it.'

'Official?'

'Definitely not. Just ear to the ground, eye to the crack in the door – you know the sort of thing. But keep it in the family. D'you want another glass of gin?'

Two days later David Kent was transferred to Department K8 and told to 'find out what the bloody hell the Chinks thought they were doing roaming willy-nilly over England's green and pleasant shores', and Woodhouse and his deputy were able to relax once more over their gin and cashew nuts.

2

David Kent filled his large cup half with milk, half with water, emptied it into a saucepan and brought it to the boil. He poured the liquid back into the cup, added a spoonful of Nescafé and two of sugar, stirred it, and lit a cigarette. That was breakfast.

While he waited for the coffee to cool he opened his pocket diary at the address section, ran his finger down the page and stopped at the name Stone. He dialled the number.

Stone must have been doing the same thing – waiting for his coffee to cool. The phone was answered immediately, albeit with only a bad-tempered grunt.

'Freddie,' began Kent, 'in your capacity as Police Liaison Officer can you find me the name of the guy who was on duty at the Chinese Embassy last Wednesday afternoon – say half-past four?'

'Sure. What d'you want him for?'

'I want him to look at a logbook. An official car went out of the compound on Wednesday morning and came back at half-past four. I'd like to know what it was booked out as and where it went.'

'It won't say.'

'And also the mileage covered.'

'That's better. But I can improve on the copper. There's a rum-drinker employed at the Embassy to wash cars. He'll look at the log for you.'

'One of ours?'

'No. But he'll do as he's told. He hasn't got a permit to live here. I'm just waiting for the West Indians to give us another hiding, then I'm going to hand the bugger over to Immigration just to get my own back!'

Kent didn't join in the fun. 'Where does he live?'

'Brixton.'

'Ask a silly question.'

Kent ran Fred Stone's rum-drinker to ground in an all-West

Indian pub off Coldharbour Lane. He was a thin-lipped, round-faced, below-average height Jamaican with the shifty, cross-eyed look of a born loser. The suspicious silence that descended over the motley crown in the stuffy, smelly lounge bar lasted until Kent and his new friend left by a side door.

Kent felt like one of the survivors of Rorke's Drift when he slipped over the boundary into white country and stopped his car with its untalkative passenger outside a well-lighted pub in Tulse Hill. Inside there was no suspicious silence. Nobody gave them a second glance.

Courtney Blissett sipped his cocktail of rum and Carnation milk apprehensively while he weighed up the alternatives put to him. It didn't take long.

'Why should I do this thing for you? What's in it for me?'

'Nothing,' Kent told him.

'Then fuck you, man!'

'OK.'

'Where you goin'?'

Kent stood up and raised his glass as if to down its contents. He took it only as far as his lips then stopped, lowered it, and looked down at the black man. 'I'm going to arrange a boat trip for you.'

Blissett's teeth disappeared behind his lips and his eyes hooded. 'What d'you mean?'

Kent told him.

The following evening, same pub, same time, Blissett smoothed out a crumpled piece of paper on the marble-topped table and narrowed his eyes over the hieroglyphics scrawled on it.

'It was booked out on a reading of 23,975 miles,' he murmured. 'There was no comeback figure – just a load of Chink writing.'

'Is that normal?' asked Kent.

'No.' Without raising his head from the scrap of paper Blissett fixed Kent with a flat, unhumorous stare. 'D'ya wanna make an official complaint?'

'Don't be funny. When was it next booked out?'

'Yesterday morning.'

'What was the entry?'

Blissett stuck a stubby finger on the five digits and said, 'That, plus a hundred and eighty-nine.'

'Who took it out?'

'Third Secretary and driver.'

'Where'd they go?'

'Dunno.'

'What time did they get back?'

'Dunno.'

'What d'you mean?'

'It didn't come back.'

'What?'

'It didn't come back.'

'You mean it's still out?'

'I dunno what I mean. It's not at Portland Place.'

'How about Lancaster Gate?'

'It's not there either.'

'How d'you know?'

'I asked.'

'Why?'

'Because the Third Secretary and driver are both back at the Embassy. I rang the garage. They know nothing about it.'

Kent stared into the black man's unconcerned eyes for several seconds as if looking for a hint of what was going on behind them. But nothing showed. Blissett put on his sincere look. 'Honest.' He flicked his empty glass with a dirty fingernail. 'You buying more of this?'

Kent came out of his trance. He slid a ten-pound note across the table. 'Help yourself. I'll have a whisky – Bell's – a large one. Don't go away. I'll be back in a minute.'

Fred Stone seemed to live with the telephone jammed in his ear. The bell had barely got into its stride before he answered. Kent didn't bother with preliminaries. 'Freddie, can you find out whether Granada, reg number 513 D 7932, has been impounded or blocked down some side street with its wheels stripped, or something?'

The pause was significant.

'Freddie?'

The phone came to life again. 'Chinese Embassy car,' intoned Stone. 'In a minute, young Kent, I'm going to ask how, why, where and when. But in the meantime – your car rolled down a hillside and burst into flames.'

'Anybody hurt?'

'Two bodies were recovered.'

Kent frowned across the room at Courtney Blissett. But Courtney Blissett was busy initiating a doubtful-looking barman into the intricacies of mixing black rum and Carnation milk. Kent moved his frown back to the phone. 'You sure about that, Freddie?'

'They said they were bodies. They were burnt beyond recognition. The guy who filled in the report reckoned they could have been spring rolls.'

'Chinese?'

'That's the assumption – Chinese Embassy car.'

'Identification?'

'Not yet. D'you want to tell me all about it?'

'Some other time Freddie. Cheers.'

'Just a bloody minute! How did you know about this car?'

'Educated guesswork. Will you let me know when they've put names to your spring rolls?'

'That's in the hands of the Embassy people. It'll have to come from them. They can say who the hell they like. They've claimed the bodies. They're in the Embassy now. They'll be shipped back to China in the diplomatic bag so I don't think we'll ever know the answer.'

'Thanks.'

Kent returned to his table and sipped his whisky thoughtfully. He had a good idea who'd got themselves cremated: a Chinese chauffeur and Mr Chin Xan Wah of the New Chinese News Agency and Chinese Central Intelligence. But where had they been for the best part of a week?

'When do I get me permit?' The black man's voice broke into his thoughts. Courtney Blissett had finished his second rum and was anxious to get back. His expression was flat. He wasn't optimistic.

Kent picked up his glass of whisky and frowned at it. The frown confirmed Blissett's fears. 'I'll see what I can do,' said Kent noncommittally. 'Can I reach you at your pub if I want you again?'

Blissett's eyes showed no enthusiasm. 'Use the bell, and I'll meet you. Don't show your face in my street. Once is enough – I don't want to get a bad name.' He wasn't joking.

Kent didn't laugh either.

3

David Kent awoke with a headache and a bad temper. It was still dark outside and the rain was bashing mercilessly against the bedroom window. It sounded as if it wanted to come in. It was a downpour, a good English downpour, but it wasn't loud enough to drown the timid burbling of the new-style telephone bell. Without raising his head from the pillow he lifted the receiver out of its bed and carried it to his ear. He didn't say anything.

It wasn't necessary.

It was Dick Mithers-Wayne.

MI5 and other British Security agencies have no powers within the civil law-enforcement organisation of the country; they have no formal powers of arrest and therefore tend to operate outside the normal police system. If, as in Kent's case, an investigation begins to rub against the official law-enforcement offices then a request for Special Branch assistance is made. Special Branch are always helpful. Kent made his request through Police Liaison at A Branch and was granted the temporary friendship of a Special Branch sergeant. He was lucky, he got Richard Mithers-Wayne, an expert on Chinese affairs.

'That Chinese car,' said Dick Mithers-Wayne, 'pipped across a red light at the junction of Barton and Headington on the A40 north of Oxford at half-past ten last Wednesday morning.' There was a satisfied smirk in his voice.

Kent was suddenly wide awake. 'How d'you know?' He kept the excitement under control and made it sound like disbelief.

'It's a major crossroads. They've installed a one-eyed police-man – a camera that takes a picture of anybody being bold on red traffic lights. You're in luck; it's only just been put there, an experiment to see if it'll pay for itself.'

'Stop waffling, Dick,' snapped Kent. He was sitting on the edge of the bed fumbling for a cigarette. 'Get to the point.'

Mithers-Wayne pulled a face down the phone and tapped the picture on the table in front of him with his finger, 'It's a fifty-fifty,' he said soberly. 'Probably an admonishment in court. But his number went through the strainer and came out "diplomatic". It goes into the N/A file.'

'How did you get hold of it?'

'A hunch.' Mithers-Wayne didn't elaborate. 'Ring me back when you've finished playing with your ruler and protractor – I'll be in Registry.'

Kent stuck a cigarette in his mouth, put on his dressing gown and clacked his way to the kitchen. It was a hangover from Hong Kong. He wore Chinese flip-flops with wooden soles. He hadn't asked his downstairs neighbour what he thought of them yet. He put the kettle on and stared out of the window at the wet, early-morning gloom. With a scowl, he draped his raincoat over his shoulders and went in search of the road map in his car. Ten yards up the road. It was enough to banish his headache, soak him through to the bone, and wonder what time it was. There was nobody else about, although one or two lights behind curtained windows showed that he wasn't the only person who'd been woken too early. The car clock said it was a quarter to six. Mithers-Wayne must be a bloody insomniac.

Back in the rapidly warming kitchen he threw the soaked raincoat over a chair and made himself a large mug of tea. He lit another cigarette. It was becoming quite cosy. He spread the map out on the table, put an ashtray on one corner and his mug of tea on the other and stared at Oxford. Ninety miles out, ninety miles back, give or take a yard or two. The Granada jumped the light – silly bastard! – there. He stuck his finger on the Headington crossroads. Forty-five miles; halfway there. But at least he'd found a direction. OK, from Headington north or east, forty-odd miles. He picked up a Biro and with his finger measured off forty miles against the scale chart. With Headington as the axis he moved the end of the pen in a narrow arc. Gloucester – Banbury – Chipping Norton. What the bloody hell would two Chinese spies want to bugger around there for? What was going on? Maybe somebody'd discovered the secret of making English terracotta soldiers. He threw the pen on to the map and picked up the mug of tea, staring blankly at the map while he sipped. After a moment he picked up the telephone and dialled Fred Stone's house.

Fred Stone was still in bed. But his wife was up. She sounded quite cheerful. It could have been put on. She was probably as miserable as sin and lonely; she wanted to chat. He asked for Fred to ring him when he got up.

She must have used it as an excuse to wake him. Kent had barely replaced the receiver when it rang. It was Stone.

'Freddie, can you tell me whether there's anything going up or going on in a triangle of Gloucester, Banbury and Chipping Norton?'

'Is that what you had me woken for?'

Kent didn't want to get her in trouble. 'It's important, Fred. Look at me, I'm up and about and worried about the nation's security!'

'Bollocks!'

'That doesn't help.'

'I'll ring you back when I've had a cup of tea.'

'Ta!'

It took the best part of an hour. It was an hour wasted. 'What exactly are you looking for?' asked Stone. His mood sounded smoother. It was probably the tea.

'Anything that you reckon would interest a couple of Peking Chinamen.'

Stone thought that one over for a second or two, then said, 'You're going to be disappointed. Apart from the American communications centre near Bloxham there's nothing to interest anyone, let alone Chinamen, and Bloxham's been there for about forty years. Maybe there's a new chop suey shop opened in Banbury.'

'You haven't been much help, Fred.'

'I did warn you.'

Kent went back to staring at the map. He drained his mug of lukewarm dregs and got up and changed the menu. Coffee, two paracetamols and another cigarette and then he sat down and rang Registry. The night porter answered. He sounded tired and resigned. He'd had to stay awake for some SB twit who'd had a row with his woman and got thrown out of bed – either that or he couldn't sleep, the inconsiderate bastard.

In comparison Mithers-Wayne sounded quite cheerful. Kent told him about the triangle and Stone's nil return on the security aspect. Mithers-Wayne's enthusiasm didn't falter. 'I'll go over to the Police National Computer at Hendon,' he said, 'and dig up anything unusual that's happened in that area during the past thirty days. It'll take a bit of time. Where can I reach you?'

'I'll buy you lunch. Meet me at the Soldier.'

'Fulham?'

'Half-past twelve.'

Kent was halfway through his second pint of Fuller's when Dick Mithers-Wayne slid into the seat beside him. Dark wavy hair, navy blue eyes with a young Tony Curtis's good looks, he didn't have to struggle for female company and the lack of frustration gave him a relaxed, easy-come, easy-go attitude. It belied a deep dedication to his job.

'I'll have the same as you,' he said as he sat down.

Kent slid his half-empty glass towards him and dropped the newspaper he was reading on to the seat. 'And I'll have another half-pint in there while you're getting it.' He didn't smile. 'Any joy?'

Mithers-Wayne stood up again. 'I'm not sure. But it'll wait.'

When he returned he sipped the top off his glass of beer, wiped the froth from his lips with the back of his hand and settled back in the seat.

'I rechecked the Security angle,' he began, and took another long pull from the glass. 'Your friend Stone's right – there's nothing doing. Routine point of view? Sickeningly normal. One murder, four rapes, eighteen burglaries, four robberies with violence.' Mithers-Wayne drank from his glass again and smiled into Kent's unresponsive face. 'We're going backwards. We could be living in the Wild West.'

'Anything else?'

'Eight major car crashes, on different days. Three killed – no foreigners.'

'Tell me about the murder,' said Kent.

'Not altogether straightforward.' Mithers-Wayne drank from his glass and put it down with a half-grimace, half-smile. It wasn't the taste of the beer that made him pull a face. 'It went with one of the burglaries, or rather a break-in – nothing stolen. A retired lieutenant colonel. Not short on guts. He must have disturbed them and took them on. Not surprising, really, he'd been a colonel in the SAS.'

Kent didn't seem impressed. 'Where?'

'Near Banbury.'

'How d'you know he took them on?'

'The report says so. Blood all over the place. Bullet holes in the woodwork – all that sort of thing.' Mithers-Wayne looked sideways at Kent. 'D'you think that's what the Chinks were after – a retired SAS colonel?'

Kent shook his head. 'I doubt it, unless there was something extra special about this one, something different from all the others. What about the other things, the car crashes, the other break-ins? And before you shake your head and say "bugger-all", did you check that there isn't somebody in that triangle who's been pinching things from China and selling them to Taiwan?'

Mithers-Wayne emptied his glass. He was one and a half pints behind Kent. He shook his head. 'Is that sort of thing going on?'

'All the time. They pay a million to a pilot who flies his airplane in. The bloody Taiwanese'll pay for anything they can pinch from the mainland Chinese. There could always be some smart bugger doing a bit of brokerage over here, along with the normal scavanging that goes on.'

It was Mithers-Wayne's turn to be unimpressed. But he hadn't lost touch with the original theme. 'Now you're getting into the realms of SAS colonels!'

'That might not be as funny as you meant it to be.' Kent stubbed out his cigarette and emptied his mug of beer. 'How long would it take to fix up a meeting with the guy running this murder enquiry?'

'I can do it now, it won't take a minute.' Mithers-Wayne looked up and scanned the pub menu scrawled on a large blackboard. 'But first, are you offering me a decent meal or am I expected to eat a plate of English curry?'

'Ugh!' Kent put his glass back on the table and stood up. 'Go and make your phone call. I'll meet you outside. You coming with me to Banbury?'

'Wild women wouldn't keep me away.'

Later that afternoon Mithers-Wayne pulled into the courtyard of Banbury Police Station and he and Kent were shown into a small, partitioned section of the main operations room. There was a small, dirty window overlooking the garage at the rear; the other three walls were hardboard.

Detective Sergeant Walgrave was a young man with a long way to go and a short time in which to do it. But he had patience. It made up for his abrupt and suspicious manner.

'Has Mr Kent come for the ride?' he asked Mithers-Wayne, 'or is there something I should know about the dead man that I haven't been told?'

'Mr Kent's interest runs along different lines to yours, Sergeant,' replied Mithers-Wayne, amiably. 'He's, er, trying to forge a link between a Government security leak and your dead colonel.'

Walgrave's expression didn't change. 'And what exactly is Special Branch's interest?'

'The same as MI5's'

'I think I'm going to have to ask you to be a bit more specific than that . . .' Walgrave smiled into Mithers-Wayne's eyes but there was no warmth in it. '. . . Sergeant,' he added after the hint of a pause.

Before Mithers-Wayne could respond Kent took over. 'Provided, Sergeant, you don't mind adding this to your report.'

Walgrave didn't give him time. 'It depends on what "this" is.'

Kent said the first thing that came into his mind. 'Your dead colonel is on the route we think was taken by two members of the Polish diplomatic establishment. It's only a possibility but like all possibilities it has to be covered. Ex-colonels of the SAS dying in strange circumstances are one of my hobbies. I'd like to connect the two things up but I wouldn't like my hobby made available for general consumption. Do you understand that, Sergeant?'

Walgrave was no longer smiling. 'I don't know about general consumption, Mr Kent, but what you've just told me seems to have an awful lot of relevance to my investigations, and, as such, goes into my report. I shall want to know the names of these Polish people you mentioned.'

'Out of the question!' snapped Kent, his urbanity slipping slightly. 'And I'll suppress any part of your report that mentions the Polish Embassy or MI5 interest.'

'You could try, sir,' said Walgrave respectfully. He kept his misgivings hidden. Poles, spies and MI5 were elements he could do without on a routine murder enquiry. There was a weight somewhere here that threatened to swing very hard; he felt vulnerable between the legs and had a vague sense of standing on slightly shifting sand. He responded to Kent's smile, but made sure it didn't show surrender.

'Good! So now that we've established a friendly relationship,' Kent rekindled the smile, 'perhaps you could tell us a bit about the good colonel's way of life – and death?'

Sergeant Walgrave shrugged his shoulders. 'Why don't we go over to the house and have a look around. I can point things out to you.' He looked Kent directly in the eye. 'The suggestion of Polish spies hobnailing around the place gives it a new dimension.'

'I didn't say anything about Polish spies,' said Kent warily but Walgrave ignored him. 'And I'll fill you in on the way over. Shall we go in my car? You can collect yours on the way back.'

Lieutenant Colonel Robert 'Dixie' Dean DSO, MC, MM leaned on his garden fork and watched the dark grey Granada drive slowly up the leafy lane and draw into the open gate leading to his cottage. The odd visitor from old times never failed to remark on the cottage's loneliness and its isolated position. Neither worried Dixie Dean. He'd chosen it for those reasons. The nearest neighbour was another three miles along the twisting lane from whence the Granada had appeared and on the outskirts of a typical, quiet Cotswolds village. In the other direction the lane turned into a gated road that cut across the grounds of a minor stately home, the lawn-like fields of which were patrolled by a sizeable herd of rare, shaggy, longhorn cattle. Dean enjoyed the company of the cattle; they made good neighbours, good companions – no bad habits. He was fed up with the human variety. And he didn't care very much for what was coming towards him.

A thin, well-dressed, taller than average Chinese had got out of the back of the car and was walking briskly across the well-kept lawn. Dean watched him come. There was no sign of welcome on his face.

It didn't trouble the Chinese. Twenty yards away he opened his jacket and put his hand inside. It came away with a stubby but long-barrelled bulbous-ended pistol. Without breaking his stride he stretched his arm out straight and squeezed the trigger. The bullet hit Dean in the left thigh. There was no noise, just a plop and the thud-like sound of a tenderising hammer hitting a rump steak. It was quick. The surprise hadn't got to Dean yet. Neither had the pain.

Plop!

The Chinese fired again. This time the bullet sliced into Dean's right leg and hit the bone, shattering it just above the knee. Dean crashed to the ground with his mouth wide open for the scream of pain that was working its way from his neck. But it never got there.

It had taken a few seconds and the Chinese hadn't even stopped walking. Arriving at Dean's side, and without pausing to survey his work, he stooped, picked up the garden fork with his free hand, and smashed the wooden haft just above its tines across the side of Dean's bowed head. The crunch was explosive. The Chinese slipped the automatic back inside his jacket and grasped the collar of Dean's open-necked shirt, then pulled him on to his back. Dean opened his eyes and tried to speak. Nothing coherent came out. It was a reflex action – curiosity, anger and pain, not necessarily in that order. The Chinese stared down at him, expressionless. His jet-black eyes, slitted, slightly hooded, showed nothing; he could have been looking at an exhausted fish as if making up his mind where to apply the gaff. And it was with that action that, without effort, he propped Dean on to his useless knees and, letting go of the collar of his shirt, hit him again across the back of the head with the fork. For the second time Dean collapsed into a heap. The whole operation had taken less than sixty seconds.

The Chinaman looked over his shoulder at the car. Two men got out. Both Chinese. One sauntered, without haste, to the back of the house while the other, the driver, strolled across the lawn to the hedge surrounding the garden and peered over. He stared first in one direction, then the other, and then took a long, searching look across the grazing fields at the unconcerned cattle. He turned away and joined the first man by Dean's body. He touched the body with his foot and opened his mouth to speak. But before he could say a word, from the back of the house came the sound of a cork being pulled from a bottle of good claret, then, after a short pause, another cork.

The chauffeur spun on his heel. A gun had appeared in his hand.

'Go and see,' said the first Chinese unhurriedly. There was no concern in his eyes. Before his companion could move, the third man came out of the front door, said 'dog' and went back in.

They picked Dean up and followed the other man into the low-beamed cottage. It was plainly furnished – no frilleries – a soldier's home. A woman's hand hadn't interfered with this room, but it had a careless, cosy feel about it. The three Chinese weren't interested in the décor.

'Strip him,' said the man who'd shot the dog. 'Remove everything. Put him there – ' he pointed to the heavy Chippendale-style carver at the head of the pine kitchen table ' – and cover his mouth.' He spoke in the harsh Hokkian dialect. The others understood. There was no question of his authority. His commands were obeyed without hesitation.

He watched the two men strip the unconscious Dean in silence, then came to life again.

'You,' he pointed with his chin at the chauffeur, 'look upstairs – everywhere. Xan Wah . . .' He addressed the other man; there was respect in his voice and he used his first names. '. . . close all the windows, lock the front door behind me.' He pointed to the phone. 'Don't touch that if it rings. While I'm outside check for a cellar, other rooms downstairs.' He got as far as the door and stopped. 'Is he going to able to feel?' He didn't finish the sentence but stared at Dean's unconscious form slumped in the chair. He wasn't disturbed by the Englishman's nakedness; it was the wide strip of surgical plaster that covered his mouth and chin and encircled his head like a badly treated casualty that prompted the note of concern.

'He won't miss anything,' said the man named Xan Wah, lifting Dean's head by its thinning hair and letting it drop on to the back of the chair. 'He'll awaken when he's called.'

'Don't choke him to death.'

The other man shrugged his shoulders and looked at the watch on his wrist. He frowned. 'What about. . . ?'

Goh Peng didn't reply. He turned his back and went out into the garden through the front door. He slid behind the wheel of the Granada and drove it to the rear of the cottage, where he tucked it out of sight of the road. When he climbed out he had a short-wave two-way radio in his hand. He pressed the button and said, 'Everything is done, Excellency. We await your arrival.' He didn't *wait for a reply but opened the car door and threw the handset on to the front seat. He turned to go back into the house.*

BOOM!

The roar of a shotgun blast almost knocked him off his feet. One shot. From inside the house. A long-drawn-out scream. Then silence. He dropped to one knee and dragged the long-barrelled automatic from his belt. It was already fully cocked. He half straightened and took one hesitant step towards the back door. He got no further. Two lighter, pistol shots banged out, but these had barely scratched the silence when they were drowned out by a second thunderous roar of a heavy-gauge shotgun cartridge. Again the windows rattled and the loosely latched back door crashed shatteringly on its hinges. Goh Peng didn't hesitate. Elbowing aside the swinging door, and at a half-crouch, he threw himself into the kitchen and began crawling along the passageway.

'He'd been dead three days before anybody found him,' said Walgrave as he turned the car onto the A361 and headed for Bloxham. 'He wasn't your cheerful, noisy, extrovert retired colonel, the TV's pride and joy, the idiotic monocled caricature of the senior British Army officer. Quite the opposite. Solitary type, unmarried, kept himself to himself. Did a bit of gardening, a lot of reading, liked a drop of Scotch – his own not the pub's, though he had been seen knocking back the odd pint in Barford. But as I said, kept well to himself.'

'Had he ever been married?' asked Mithers-Wayne from the back of the car. 'Or any current girlfriend?'

'Nope.'

'Queer?'

'His bum looked normal, according to the pathologist.'

'That doesn't prove anything.'

'There's no indication of his being queer,' insisted Walgrave. 'We looked at that angle – a gay argument, a little spat over who's going to be mum – but nothing doing. When they fall out they slap each other across the mouth; what they don't do is fill the naughty party with bullets.'

'Who found him?' asked Kent. He wasn't really interested in who'd tripped over the poor old sod's body – he had a feeling this was going to end up having nothing to do with his Chinese puzzle – but the policeman in him came, uninvited, to the foreground.

'The milkman.' Walgrave drove through Bloxham and took the narrow cross-country road that led to Barford. 'He missed the dog – a Labrador, friendly, not a bit like his master! On the third trip he got suspicious about two bottles of milk he'd left in the thing by the kitchen door. When he went round to the front door he noticed for the first time that all the curtains were drawn.'

'We need people like that in Special Branch!' interposed Mithers-Wayne. 'What did he do, break the door down?'

'No.' Walgrave seemed not to have a sense of humour. He didn't even smile. 'He waited until he got home that evening and his conscience pricked him. He rang the local nick and a patrol car popped in, routinely, the following afternoon.'

'Christ!' muttered Mithers-Wayne.

Walgrave made no comment, or excuse. 'They found the dog first. He'd been killed and bundled into a shed used for coal and wood at the back of the house. The Colonel they found in the cellar – stark-bollock – after they'd kicked the door in . . .' He broke off and slowed down to cross the cattle-grid, then turned right. After a few moments he said, 'Here we are.' He pulled the car into the drive and stopped where the Chinese had parked nearly a week earlier.

Walgrave had been here before, several times. There was no enthusiasm in his manner, only a sort of matter-of-fact attitude, one that said 'I've got a lot more on my plate than spending time buggering around this place at the whim of a couple of pinstripes from the multicultural capital of the world.' Kent felt the same. He was wasting his time – he knew it. He'd decided several miles back that a naked colonel with bullet holes had nothing to do with running Chinamen. He'd taken the wrong turning; he felt as if he was jogging up a street that had no end to it.

From the outside there was no evidence of what had happened the previous week. Dean's garden fork had gone – it was now propping up the wall in Oxford's pathology laboratory, even though the tea lady could have made a fair diagnosis of what had caused the dent in the shaft and the congealed blood on the stock. But the removal people had left the inside of the cottage intact. Mithers-Wayne's informant hadn't exaggerated; there was blood all over the place, much of it splattered against the timber framed walls.

'Shotgun,' said Walgrave, interpreting Kent's glance. 'SG – heavy load. One there,' he jerked his chin at the wall nearest Kent, 'and another one there.' He patted the wall beside a rough, oak-studded door and poked his head round the corner. 'This corridor leads to a downstairs bedroom with a door halfway along that goes to the cellar. That's where they found the body – in the cellar, curled up in a corner.'

'Riddled by a blast of SG?'

'No. He'd got a bullet in each leg, one in the shoulder, and one close range in the back of the head – no SG.'

'The one in the head killed him?' Kent made the question sound casual. But he couldn't hide his growing interest.

'No. It was fired into his head after he was dead.'

'You're kidding?' Kent searched the detective's face for signs of smugness but all it revealed was that kidding was not part of Walgrave's repertoire. Walgrave didn't bother to shake his head. He stared back and waited for Kent's next question.

'So what killed him?'

'A heart attack.'

'I don't believe it!'

'That's what I said. Pathology said there was no question about it. D'you want to come to the lab and look at the bullet holes?'

'Thanks.' Kent was still shaking his head. He didn't believe it. He stared again at the bloodstains on the walls. 'What about these?'

'It looked as if somebody's guts had been stippled into the plaster.' Walgrave joined Mithers-Wayne and Kent and peered closely at the wall. He'd already done it several times before. It still fascinated him. 'I'll bet the owner of that lot didn't die of a heart attack.' He didn't smile as he ran his hand over the pitted, discoloured surface. 'After being hit with something of that weight I doubt whether he'd have much left of anything to suffer an attack on. There was about three-quarters of an average fully grown man's gut plastered on there.'

Mithers-Wayne looked around at him. 'What happened to the rest of his body?' He met Kent's eyes briefly, then moved his glance to the other wall and the other stain. 'And that one?'

'We're still searching,' replied Walgrave. 'But come and have a look at this.' He led them out into the garden, crossed the lawn to Dean's daffodil-covered rose-bed and stepped gingerly across it to the hedge that surrounded the garden. 'There.' He went down on to his ankles and ruffled the grass with his fingers.

'What is it?' Mithers-Wayne didn't bother kneeling. His glance was perfunctory. He was more interested in the road on the other side of the hedge.

'Traces of blood,' replied Walgrave. 'There – and there. Two bodies were stashed here. And if you come along here . . .' He stood up, moved a few feet to his left and knelt again. '. . . you'll see where they were dragged through the hedge on to the road.'

'And carried away for a quiet burial somewhere in the bush,' grunted Mithers-Wayne.

'Or cremation?' Kent and Mithers-Wayne exchanged glances. It wasn't lost on Walgrave.

'Do I get the feeling that there's more to this than meets my eye?' He stared stonily at Kent. 'If this ties up in any way with your Polish travellers I think I ought to have a word with my superintendent about talking to their embassy, unless . . .' He left a space for Kent to step through. Kent accepted.

'They wouldn't waive immunity. But you can take my word, Sergeant Walgrave, this has nothing to do with Poles.' He looked frankly into the sergeant's disbelieving eyes. 'Nothing at all. And if you'd like my advice . . .' Walgrave shook his head – he wouldn't – but Kent went on regardless, '. . . you can file this one away. You're not going to get any further down the road than you've already got. You'll be wasting your time from now on.'

Walgrave stared blankly at the two men for a few moments, then shrugged his shoulders. Kent stared back and then smiled a friendly smile. He was happy. There was no doubt that the Chinese had passed this way and that two of them were Fred Stone's spring rolls in the burnt-out Granada. But his happiness was tinged – what the bloody hell had it all got to do with the late Lieutenant Colonel Robert Dean DSO, MC, MM?

There was no answering smile from Sergeant Walgrave.

They went back inside the cottage and while Walgrave gave Mithers-Wayne a conducted tour Kent sat down in the much-used carver and stared at the kitchen tabletop. At his end was the pink suggestion of washed blood. He stared intently for a second or two, then leaned forward and rubbed his finger lightly over the stripped pine surface. There were two screw holes, hardly noticeable after the scrubbing. They were four inches apart. Kent moved his head slightly and found another pair eighteen inches to the left. He sat back in the chair and awaited for the two men to come downstairs.

'What did your people make of that, Sergeant?' he asked Walgrave. 'If anything?'

Walgrave didn't have to inspect the tabletop; he knew what Kent was talking about. 'Nothing sinister,' he replied. 'Just screw holes.'

Mithers-Wayne peered at the table for a better view. 'Probably where the colonel screwed down his mincer,' he suggested.

'One here – and one there?' said Kent. 'What does he do with two mincers – play tunes on them?'

Dixie Dean had a much harder head than the Chinese had credited him with. And he knew how to look dead. He'd seen enough dead men in forty years to know how they looked. He almost knew how they felt. But he couldn't work this one out. His befuddled brain refused to reason. Why would a Chinese come all this way into the sticks, shoot him without warning in both legs, and bash him across the head with his garden fork? And not just one. There were others – he'd heard them. What the bloody hell was it all about? He kept his head bowed, his eyes shut and his teeth clamped tightly on the surging waves of pain, cursing himself for standing around like a banana, allowing a yellow face to stroll across his lawn and put him down like a diseased dog. That's what old age does for you! If he'd been a bloody Irishman, Dean, you'd have been up a tree before he'd stepped out of his car! He allowed one eyelid to flicker. Christ! he was stark-bollock-naked and covered in blood. What the bloody hell . . . He listened. There was nobody in the room. He tried to stop the thudding of his heart. How do you stop fear? He held his breath and listened again. The floorboards above his head creaked and complained as somebody moved around upstairs, and along the passageway the unlatched back door rattled metronomically against its catch. He moved his hands. They weren't tied. The silly bastards must have thought they'd done the job properly – bloody amateurs – fuckin' Chinamen! He wished he hadn't sworn. The rush of blood burst into his wounded legs, bringing another smothered scream of pain. He almost fainted. But fear got the better of him. He bit his lip, then gritted his teeth and slithered to the floor.

The Indian rug felt smooth against his naked skin but he didn't dwell on it. The creaks above his head had moved to the far corner – whoever it was was inspecting the spare room. What the bloody hell were they looking for? Downstairs, at his level, the cellar door opened and closed quietly and he heard light footsteps patter towards the kitchen. Maybe this one was going to close that bloody rattling back door. But Dean was in no mood for funny thoughts.

He dragged himself on his elbows across the floor to the narrow cupboard beside the open fireplace. It had once been a brick oven. He opened its door soundlessly and his hand found the battered stock of his old companion, his favourite, a much-used Remington Wingmaster with a shortened barrel and – *Christ!* – how many rounds? *You stupid, inefficient bastard, Dean!* One or two? Three? And how old? Cocked? *Naturally – we haven't gone that far over the bloody hill . . .*

With his two useless legs splayed out in front of him he pressed himself against the brick fireside and waited.

The creaking upstairs transferred to the short staircase that descended into the drawing room and moved down. Dean watched the two feet, in cheap, grey, imitation-leather pointed shoes, come into view. It was the Chinese chauffeur. His automatic was back in its hiding place somewhere under his arm and it took the flash of a second for the empty chair to register. His reflexes were quick. He threw himself to one side of the room and scrabbled madly for his weapon. But his reflexes weren't quick enough.

BOOM!

The half-dozen ball-bearing-sized shots hit him squarely in the chest. It stopped him in mid-flight, picked him up like a rag doll and splashed his chest and back against the timber-framed wall. Dean didn't stop to study the result. He jerked another round into the breech.

The thunder was still reverberating around the room when the other man came through the kitchen door. Without aiming, he wildly fired two rapid shots at the small cloud of blue smoke hovering above Dean's head before the next round of SG removed

his stomach and lower chest. Dean recocked. The empty cartridge
case shot over his shoulder, bounced against the brick fireplace and
trickled into the hearth.

But nothing took its place.

'Oh, fucking hell!'

He cocked the Remington again.

Nothing.

And then he saw the third Chinese lying on the floor by the door,
with a bulbous-ended pistol grasped steadily in his two hands aimed
directly at his face. He pointed the empty shotgun forlornly at the
Chinese, but he didn't flinch: he'd seen Dean's fruitless pumping.
He raised himself to his knees, lowered the pistol slightly and, with
all the time in the world, took careful aim and fired.

Dixie Dean didn't hear the shot – not even the silenced plop.
Neither did he feel the lead-nosed bullet plough into the upper part
of his chest. The deep, bottomless blackness surprised him as he
went down the tunnel – it somehow didn't feel like death.

It wasn't.

The man with a beard and John Lennon glasses, a long white coat
and a miserable expression looked up from Dixie Dean's naked
body lying in a zinc tray in the antiseptic, brightly shining
pathology lab inside the morgue, and studied Kent disdainfully.
He could have been one of the specimens on the shelf. 'Roger
Sandford,' introduced Walgrave. 'Assistant County Pathologist.'

Kent nodded and stared down at Dean, stark, cold and marble-
hard in death, white as if every ounce of blood had been drained
out of his system. It had. A cut from neck to pelvis had been
crudely stitched together but, notwithstanding, Dixie's body
betrayed his profession. The three recent bullet entry holes in his
legs and chest were still open, red, blue, and black, but clean; two
others were healed into tiny puckered scars; and a shrapnel wound
in his groin, now shaved and shyly pale, stood out as a badly
stitched battlefield operation – it was almost as crudely stitched as
the recent autopsy opening. Kent ran his finger down the length of
the raised join and pulled a face.

Sandford intercepted his disapproving frown. 'We don't call in a
seamstress for bodies.' His flat eyes showed no expression behind
the wire-rimmed glasses. He poked his finger into Dixie Dean's

stomach and nodded with satisfaction at the indentation it left. 'There's not much left inside.'

Kent did not raise his eyes from the corpse. In reply he pulled the polythene shroud up as far as Dean's stomach, as if sensing the soldier's modesty, and said, 'You put his death down to a heart attack.'

'That's right.'

'I find that hard to believe.' Kent stared down at Dean's scarred body. 'You're quite sure about that?'

Sandford made no reply.

Kent touched the bullet entry wound in Dean's chest. 'That wouldn't have killed him?'

'It didn't.'

Kent looked up from Dean's body.

'It couldn't have killed him,' said Sandford, 'but the shock gave his already battered system a nasty jolt. It could have brought on the heart attack that killed him – it would definitely have caused a state of unconsciousness so that he wasn't aware of the attack.'

Kent's eyes went back to Dean's body. 'What about the bullet in the back of the head Sergeant Walgrave mentioned?'

'It was fired at very close range from the top of the neck upwards after he was dead. The person who did it probably thought he was unconscious – that's the appearance he would have given.'

'Thanks.' Kent stared for a moment at the lower part of Dean's body, distorted by the transparent sheet. He then slipped the sheet below his stomach and, with difficulty, lifted one of the stiff icy hands. He studied the heavy bruising just above the wrist. Below the wristbone where the hand commenced was a ring of heavy crusted blood. Kent turned the wrist over. The scab went only half-way round.

Sandford said in a quiet voice, 'It's the same with the other wrist. They must have been vicious bastards to tie a man's hands with wire and pull it that tight.'

Kent didn't look up. 'Is that what you reckon, doctor? Sergeant, were his hands tied when you found him?'

Walgrave frowned until his eyes were almost closed, then they snapped open. 'No; they must have untied him before shoving him down the cellar.' The sergeant didn't look happy. He looked like a man who'd missed something, but he held his silence.

Kent picked an inch of scab from the cut and stared intently at the wound. Walgrave grimaced.

'Is that necessary, sir?'

Kent still didn't look up. 'I'm not doing this for pleasure, Sergeant. Did you look at these, Doctor?'

Sandford shook his head. 'I was asked to determine the cause of death, and I've done that. The coroner has the report and the sergeant has a copy of my findings. The man died of a heart attack – he didn't die of having his hands tied together.'

Kent said, 'He didn't have his hands tied. These wounds are clean. They're quarter-inch knife cuts. I suggest you re-examine them and make an addendum to your report. They may be significant to his death. And at the same time you can tell me what was injected into his hand.'

'I beg your pardon?'

'There are three syringe marks. Two here . . .' He put his finger on the middle of Dixie Dean's wrist. '. . . and one here, in line with his thumb.'

Walgrave came quickly to Kent's side and picked up Dean's left hand. He peered at it intently, then nodded his head. 'He's right,' he muttered, 'and he's right about the cuts. This one's quite deep – it wasn't done by wire.'

There was no smugness in Kent's expression. His question was gentle. 'How long will it take, Doctor?'

'Pardon?'

'How soon can you give me some answers? An hour. Hour and a half?'

Sandford touched the wire bridge of his glasses and pushed them up tight against his eye sockets, then bowed low over Dixie Dean's empty corpse. He shook his head as he peered intently at the cuts on the wrists. 'Call in on your way back to London; if I'm not here the report will be in my office.' He waved them away without looking up.

Dick Mithers-Wayne, propping up the door, shrugged his shoulders. 'Suits me,' he grinned. 'D'you know a pub with decent beer around here, Walgrave?'

Dixie Dean's second journey to consciousness was slow and painful.

He was back in the chair at the table and staring at his naked and bloody thighs. They must have been waiting.

No sooner had his eyes opened than he felt his hair grabbed and his head jerked up to slam against the headrest of the chair. He coughed, nearly choking over a mouthful of blood and phlegm, and forced his eyes to focus. The pain in his chest was a numb ache which rivalled the throbbing in his legs. He could feel the onset of shock and wished he could drift off into a warm unconsciousness again; he wished, in fact, he could die. The mist began to clear and through it, like a smeared window, he could see his hands resting on the table. He tried to move them. They wouldn't move – they were stuck. He blinked away the mist and his eyes clicked sharply into focus.

Just above each wrist was an iron clamp, like a manacle, screwed to the tabletop. He panicked as he tried to move – nothing happened. It was clamped tight. He could move his elbow – he wasn't tied to the chair – but, anchored by his wrists to the table, he was as helpless as a baby stuck in a high chair. Once he knew the form he calmed down and closed his eyes.

When he opened them again he stared into a pair of almond-shaped eyes at the far end of the table. They gave him no comfort. She was an attractive woman but her face had no laughter lines. It was a face that had spent a totally humourless life; a face that gave the impression it had never learnt to laugh – had never tried. He sensed somebody behind him.

'Colonel Dean.' It was a statement, not a question. He stared into the almost hypnotic eyes. 'How is your memory?'

It didn't make sense.

He managed a bubbly rasp. He wanted to say, 'Who are you? What d'you want?' but nothing came from behind the wide band of plaster that encircled his mouth and head. They didn't seem to expect a reply. The voice continued, 'Search your memory, Colonel Dean, and while you're doing it perhaps this will remind you.' The eyes left his face and went to a point just above his head.

'Take off his left hand.'

Dixie Dean didn't understand.

The person he'd sensed behind him came to his side. He stared at him from the corner of his eye. It was the Chinese who'd shot him in the chest. But it wasn't a gun he held this time. In his right hand he held a fifteen-inch kukri with ten inches of hard unpolished steel; the cutting edge gleamed with razor sharpness.

Without a word the Chinese laid it just below Dean's wrist bone and drew it towards him. The blood spurted. There was no pain. Dean's bottom came off the cushioned chair as if a spring had exploded under him. At the same time he tried to pull his arm away from the iron grip, but the manacle dug into his wrist, not giving a fraction. Dixie Dean didn't feel a thing. He screamed at the top of his voice, without sound, and without knowing or caring, his bladder emptied and he fainted.

'Give the injection,' said the unemotional voice in Chinese. 'Be quick!'

The tall Chinese placed the knife on the table and reached behind him for one of two prepared hypodermics. He wiped some of the blood away with a wodge of tissues and peered at Dean's wrist. He'd done his homework. He knew exactly where to put it. He inserted the needle first in the ulnar nerve, squeezed in half the contents and, like a man who knew exactly what he was doing, reinserted the needle in the median and emptied the balance of the phial. He picked up the other hypodermic, lying in sterile purity on a white cloth, found the radial nerve and lowered the plunger. It emptied with a tiny gurgle.

He released the hand from the manacle, pulled over it, as far as the bloodied cut, a small black plastic bag, and tightened it round the wrist with a thick elastic band. He studied the effect for a moment, then allowed the hand to drop to Dean's side. That done, he returned to his place behind the chair and commenced gently slapping the side of the unconscious man's face. There was no conversation between the two Chinese.

It was nearly ten minutes before Dixie Dean returned to the nightmare. He'd dreamt somebody had chopped off his hand and heaved a sigh of relief when he realised he'd dropped off to sleep in his dining chair – this bloody getting old again! Then he felt the wetness around his groin and opened his eyes. He began to scream again.

His left arm no longer rested on the table. The bracket was empty, he could no longer see his hand. He raised his head slightly. The eyes stared at him impassively from the other end of the table. The scream went on and on behind the plastic – it came out as a strangled gurgle, like a baby choking over the strength of its bottle. But

Dixie's eyes took up the scream and the Chinese eyes stared with just the faintest touch of satisfaction.

When he'd finished screaming, Dean looked, with bulging eyeballs, at his left shoulder. He felt no pain; not in his legs, not in his chest, not in his hand . . .

HIS HAND!

Christ Almighty!

The scream came back again. He looked down slowly. There was his elbow, there was his arm – and there was his wrist . . . Oh, Jesus Christ! Oh God! The bile rose over the scream and filled his mouth with vomit. His hand had gone. There was no feeling – just a dead sensation where it used to be and a plastic bag to catch the blood. There was feeling only down to the wrist, nothing beyond . . .

The hand behind his head was still gently slapping his cheek – not unkindly, not roughly, but like a troubled nurse massaging a stiff muscle to keep it alive. Dean wanted to faint again but it wouldn't happen, the gentle slapping wouldn't permit it. And then, at a nod from the other end of the table, the Chinese's other hand came from behind his head and the sharp, cutting, eye-watering ammonia of smelling salts burned into his nostrils and cleared the final vestige of mugginess from his brain. He turned his head away and rubbed the tears from his eyes with his bare shoulder. The sobbing inside had stopped. There was nothing more they could do. Now they'd say what they wanted – and he'd tell them . . . There was no mention in the anti-interrogation manual about having your hands sawn off. He choked back another sob. He'd tell them anything. He'd got nothing left to fight with.

But they hadn't finished.

The hand came round over his eyes and fingers felt for the end of the surgical tape. Without ceremony it was ripped off his face, unwound from his head and torn once again from his mouth. He didn't feel a thing. He took a deep breath through his mouth, once, twice, three times and then the two hands came on either side of his face and directed it towards the foot of the table.

'Have you remembered, Colonel Dean?' The voice was like silk; no emotion, no feeling.

Remembered what for Christ's sake? He said nothing. The hands were removed from his face. He continued to stare back. There was nothing else he wanted to look at.

51

'Remembered what?' he managed at length. But it didn't sound like that. He said it again. 'Remembered what?' That was better.

It was the voice from behind his head that replied. 'Take your mind back, Colonel Dean . . . Take it back thirty-five years. Malaya . . . Johor . . . You killed a man.'

'I killed many men.'

'You cut this one's hands off.'

Dean remembered. 'I don't know what you're talking about.'

'Then I'll remind you.' Goh Peng came from behind the chair and stood at Dean's side. He was quite unperturbed: his face betrayed nothing, his intentions he kept to himself.

'No!'

Dean turned at the interruption.

'I shall remind him,' said the voice from the end of the table.

The reminder wasn't necessary, but Dixie Dean sat, head bowed, staring at the thick sticky blood oozing from the wounds in his legs, listening to the Chinese voice relating, in detail, the events that had happened in the clearing in the jungle over half a lifetime ago. He didn't try to understand what it was all about. Memories were long – unquenchable things – ask Adolf Eichmann . . . But this was no Holocaust vendetta; this was about a single killing in a war of a thousand single killings. What made this one so special? The voice had stopped.

The man at his side tapped him on the shoulder. 'So what we want to know, Colonel Dean, is where does Mr Fylough live and under what name is he living?'

'I've no idea.' But you have, you stupid bastard! You know exactly where he is, what he is, and what he calls himself.

'Take off the other hand.'

They didn't give him a chance to change his mind. The plaster was slapped back in place. The knife again. The cut. The blood. The scream. The vomit. The bladder again and the merciful black fog that closed in and shut it all out. And this time it stayed. Dixie Dean was dead.

'Wake him up.'

The Chinese man lifted Dean's head and stared into his face. 'I think he's dead, Excellency.'

'Make sure.'

He let go of Dean's hair and allowed his head to fall on to his *chest. He held the bulbous end of the automatic an inch away from the back of the exposed neck, and lowering his wrist so that the barrel pointed slightly upwards, fired into Dixie Dean's head.*

The person at the foot of the table watched dispassionately.

'Take that stuff off his face and put him in the cellar.' No explanation, no change of expression. *'And what about those two?'* An arm languidly waved in the direction of the two dead Chinese. *'Can you get them away?'*

'Leave it to me. They can spend the night in the garden and tomorrow, or the day after, I'll arrange an accident for them; there'll be no repercussions.'

'If there are they'll be on your head.' The hand waved at Dixie Dean. *'He's the last but one. So, where now, Goh Peng?'*

The man she called Goh Peng lowered Dean's body to the ground and straightened up. *'We'll let them take up the last few yards.'*

'Them?'

'The kwai lo.'

'How are you going to get them – the English – to work for us?'

Goh Peng almost smiled. *'They've bribed one of the foreigners who do menial tasks in the Embassy garage to scavenge among the garbage for them. We know who's controlling this person so I'll give them a few more things to be curious about. We'll sit back and watch for a few days.'* He rolled Dixie Dean's body in a tablecloth and lifted him across his shoulders as effortlessly as if he were a bag of potatoes. *'You go now,'* he said. *'I'll attend to matters here.'*

'You'll take care of those two?'

'Leave it all to me, Excellency.'

4

Evelyn St John Woodhouse swung his leather-upholstered chair round so that he was looking out of his fourth-floor window and down on to a wet late-afternoon Mayfair street. The end of April, an English spring, and the orange streetlamps were on, making it look later than it was. The road was full of traffic, mostly taxis. Nobody was walking; it was too wet and miserable. It looked from up there like an Atkinson Grimshaw painting of a dismal Northern city street on a late November evening. Contemplating all of this from his office, Evelyn St John Woodhouse felt smug and cosy.

He loosely held the sheaf of papers he'd been reading in his hand at his side and kept his back to Kent as he spoke. He could see a ghost-like reflection of himself in the window, its background darkened by the artificial evening which had descended with the rain and heavy clouds permanently anchored above London, and he studied critically, but without displeasure, his new red-striped Harvie & Hudson shirt with its crisp white collar, and the small, immaculate knot of his dark red Hermès silk tie. The combination pleased him and he bared his teeth at his reflection in a satisfied grimace.

'This is a police matter, David,' he said to his reflection. He was a ready Christian-name user. He'd read somewhere that the use of Christian names by a superior to his subordinates carried weight when it came to inspiring loyalty. 'Nothing to do with us if an old soldier gets himself knocked over by a Chinese burning crew – let the Met deal with the Embassy angle and if it shows promise Special Branch can put their pads on and go in and bat. There's no need for you to waste any more of your time – or mine.' He gave himself a final once-over in the window and swung the chair to look Kent in the face. He missed Kent's eyes by a fraction and spoke to his forehead. 'Why have you gone over Arthur's head?'

It was like a gramophone record. Kent kept his feelings off his face. Arthur had said the same thing; 'It's a police matter, not MI5, so mind your own business!' Woodhouse must have had lunch-time gins with Arthur. Kent repeated his argument while Woodhouse went back to studying his reflection.

'Chinese Intelligence is involved, sir,' he said to the back of Woodhouse's head. 'They wouldn't have killed Dean because he found them rifling his house. There's something deeper – I've got a feeling about it.'

'K is not run on the feelings of junior executives, David. I can't go to the Director and say one of my young people has a feeling about Chinese involvement in an unsolved murder.' He swung back again and crossed one leg over the other, so that the chair tilted as if he were going to have his hair washed. He riffled the papers again. 'Feelings apart, David, can you make any connection between these Chinese burners and the American wireless station at Barford?'

Kent grasped the line he'd been thrown. 'The coincidence is too great for there not to be. Dean, being an ex-SAS man, might have stumbled on to something fishy. There could be a cell of some description.'

'A Chinese cell in deepest Oxfordshire? Be a bit obvious, wouldn't they?' Woodhouse allowed himself a gentle smiling rebuke. He was playing hard to get. 'Chinese running about the Cotswolds with their pinched-up toes and long moustaches and pigtails?'

Kent stared back politely. Woodhouse's idea of the Chinese dated back to Dr Fu Manchu. 'Not to mention the silk-embroidered dressing gowns.'

'What d'you mean?' Woodhouse's imitation smile vanished. 'What've dressing gowns got to do with it?'

'It was a joke, sir.' Kent had misjudged Woodhouse's sense of humour.

'This is not a joking matter, David.'

'Sorry, sir.'

Woodhouse primmed his lips and conceded. 'All right. Against my better judgement I'm prepared to give your feelings a light airing – we'll give it a few more overs with this ball. I'll tell Arthur you're full-time Chinese for the time being, and until I say otherwise.' He frowned as if he had second thoughts, and paused while he considered the possible repercussions on himself; it didn't take long. He lowered himself behind the sandbags. 'Don't take any direct action until you first discuss it with me. And, David – '

Kent lowered his bottom on to the hard chair again.

' – keep this Special Branch connection you've established. We'll make it a semi-permanent arrangement. You make the request and I'll initial it and support it.' He tapped Kent's report to show what he was going to support, adding, with another parting of the lips, 'And if anything looks as if it's taking a wrong turning, make sure the Special Branch man is well up to the front, pressing against the wire; they're better equipped than us for fielding balls-ups.'

Mithers-Wayne had some interesting news.

He'd spent several hours in the Police Computer Centre at Hendon and had left a message at Charles Street for Kent to meet him that evening.

'*Modus operandi*,' he said to Kent when he joined him at a table in the corner of the pub. 'I was struck by that poor bastard being shot in the legs and having his hands almost severed by wire binding.'

'It wasn't wire,' said Kent. 'And it was deliberate. The Chinese – if Chinese they were – started to saw his hands off. They wanted the poor bugger to think, for some reason, that they were amputating them.'

'Christ!' Mithers-Wayne looked horror-struck. 'Are you sure? How do you know?'

'I had a close look at those wounds. The cuts were made with a knife.'

'What the bloody hell for?'

'Christ knows. But go on with your *modus operandi*.'

Mithers-Wayne lit a cigarette to remove the look from his face. He took a deep lungful of smoke to purify his thoughts and as he blew it out, said, 'Two months ago – January, about the twelfth – an elderly guy was found dead in his flat in Manchester. I say about the twelfth because he'd been dead for three days. But here's the rub – he was stark-bollock-naked, like the Colonel. His wrists – deep cuts. Manchester forensic thought the same as Oxford – wire binding.'

'Bullet holes in each thigh?' queried Kent.

Dick Mithers-Wayne shook his head. 'No bullet holes. But he'd died of a heart attack. Fright, the pathologist suggested. I wonder how they can tell?'

Kent ignored the question. 'Ex-soldier? SAS?'

'Uhuh. A football pools collector.'

'That's supposed to be a connection?'

'Somebody said they'd seen an Asian peering from behind the curtains a few days before the body was discovered.'

'Chinese?'

'They said Asian.'

Kent pulled a face. 'Manchester's full of Asians – Pakistanis. Bangladeshis. Indians.'

Mithers-Wayne shrugged his shoulders. 'Why don't you ask your boy to have a look at the Embassy logbooks for those days?'

'That thought had just crossed my mind – a sort of last resort!'

'Make it a first. In the meantime I think I'll take a sandwich and a cup of cocoa to the Centre with me and spend the rest of the evening trying to make common ground between our colonel and a Manchester football pools collector.'

The Chinese Embassy logbooks meant nothing to Courtney Blissett and there had been too much coming and going during the period designated by Kent for him to make notes on. Kent's threats had had no effect. Blissett decided he didn't want to stay after all; he didn't like the weather, the rum was too expensive and the Social Security hand-out people were giving him funny looks. He'd said Kent's white face down his street would get him into trouble. The neighbours had started talking. Would Kent please arrange for him to be repatriated immediately – before somebody cut off his balls for narking. No problem – he'd done his stuff.

But not for Kent. For the Chinese. Unwittingly, Blissett had pointed his finger directly at Kent – just what the Chinese had wanted from him. The Chinese who'd killed Dixie Dean had promised that he would let the English carry them the last few yards. They'd found their Englishman: David Kent. They checked: possibly British MI. Perfect. He would have the resources to steer them to their goal – with a little guidance and help from the CELD.

Blissett went back to the sun and the crystal-blue waters of home without a second's regret. His replacement in the Embassy carwash business was a different kettle of fish, an undercover man on loan from the Metropolitan Police. He gave himself two days to settle in – he even cleaned cars better than Blissett – and on the third day he went to work with a wristwatch camera supplied from Gower Street's tricks cupboard. He photographed the pages covering the 9th to the 14th January of all the logbooks. He did it under the eye of one of CELD's agents, and the hand-over of the camera to Kent in a Baker Street pub was watched, logged and similarly photographed by the Intelligence people on the Embassy staff.

But the logbook photographs proved of little use to Kent. None of the recorded mileages agreed with the distance from London to Manchester – nothing like it on a single trip. Kent turned his interest to Lancaster Gate. The Commercial Section, in keeping with the Chinese security edict of not employing Englishmen, used a Sikh as dogsbody. Kent didn't bother approaching him – he'd had dealings with Sikhs in Hong Kong.

A few days later the Sikh was run down by a hit-and-run lorry in Southall. Both his legs were broken. He arranged for his brother-in-law to carry out his duties while he recovered. The brother-in-law fell off the towpath into the Grand Union canal and drowned. Chinese Intelligence kept the position open until another of Fred Stone's West Indians applied. The Commercial yielded a better harvest. The figures agreed. Kent was happy. The Chinese had killed the man in Manchester. But he already knew that; this was just confirmation. Kent kept his frustration under wraps. But *why*? Why the bloody hell why?

'David, come and have a drink with me this evening.' Woodhouse's velvet voice came round the wall of Kent's partitioned corner on the third floor. It wasn't a request, nor an invitation – it was an order. 'The Pig and Eye; half-past six. Don't be late.' And then he was gone.

It was two days since the confirmation of the Chinese Embassy involvement in the Manchester killing. Woodhouse had been informed. Dick Mithers-Wayne had gone under the blanket. Kent had heard nothing from the young Special Branch officer since he'd set the tapes rolling in Hendon Central in an attempt to join the two totally incompatible characters in marriage. It could go back a long time – and a long way. Kent had patience. He kept his hand away from the phone. Mithers-Wayne would ring when he was ready, and when he had something to say.

Evelyn St John Woodhouse felt more at home in the comfortable male chauvinist stronghold of the Pig and Eye Club in Leconfield House than he did in his own drawing room; if he cared to work it out, he probably spent more of his leisure time there than in his own house. It was all to do with status; at home he was only a husband. His companion looked equally at ease.

'So it's so far, so good, Woody. You've got this boy, whatsis-name – Kent – dangling in front of Goh Peng's nose, but how do we know, (a) that Goh Peng and his lot have taken him up, and (b) that he's going to behave like the worm and not want to clamber off the hook and handle the rod himself?'

Woodhouse smiled in spite of himself; he was a different man in the company of equals – or betters. This one could possibly fit into the latter category. 'I like that, Peter – the worm casting the rod. What a splendid description. D'you mind if I use it?'

The other man shrugged and looked pointedly at his watch. 'Help yourself, Woody. What time did you say he was going to be here?'

'Half-past six – plenty of time. Right. I chose Kent after some very serious reflection. I brought him out of the wilderness because he's not been around us long enough to develop that healthy mistrust of his superiors and because he's an expert in Chinese ways. He came to us from the Hong Kong Police, who are very good at things Chinese – '

'Woody, for Christ's sake!'

Woody sniggered and lifted his drink to his lips. 'Just a little joke. We mustn't get too serious about our work, Peter, we could all end up with the efficiency bug like the Americans. Christ! How bloody boring. Anyway, as I was saying, I had him moved into A4 – Watching – when that poor bugger Dean went the same way as Harry Kenning. You were right about the route the Chinese would take, but I really think we ought to have helped Dean out, warned him, dropped a hint – anything. It was a bloody poor show . . .'

'If we'd warned him we warn everybody, and then we might as well stop the bloody game here and now. Plausible – that's the whole fucking theme, Woody. You don't get plausibility by letting everybody know in advance what's going to happen. Besides, Dixie should have known how to look after himself. He was SAS. They're supposed to be tough and resourceful; that's what he should have been – tough and bloody resourceful. I'm surprised they haven't already smelled a rat over the ease with which they dragged the poor old bugger through the wire.'

Fylough's hard line did the trick. Woodhouse looked slightly relieved. He thought about the poor bugger being dragged through the wire for a moment, then frowned. 'Kenning, by all accounts, didn't put up much of a show either.'

Fylough shrugged. 'There was nothing more he could do. I underestimated them; I didn't think they'd go as far as killing him. Harry, poor bugger, like Dixie Dean, didn't know a bloody thing, but it looks as if they didn't believe him. Very sad, Woody, but you can't have wars without casualties.' He shrugged aside the casualty list with a large pull on his glass of whisky and water, replaced the glass on the table and ran a slim finger over each side of his carefully trimmed grey military moustache. 'The fact that Harry went down screaming must have impressed the butchers – you can't play make-believe with an act like that.'

'For Christ's sake, Peter, you're a cruel bastard!' Woodhouse sought refuge in his glass. It was getting too near trench warfare for his liking.

'This is nothing to do with Christ, Woody! We're playing for very high stakes here. The Chinese are not simple – they've got their task and they won't thank anybody if things are made easy for them. When we set this thing on the road we did it with our eyes open; now we just have to sit back, watch the buggers at work and grit our teeth when things we don't like very much happen. They've got to be led, but at the same time they've got to think that they're making the running.

'This is why your man Kent has got to have a good look at me – no name, mind you, he's got to do that for himself, the hard way – so that when he takes the Chinese with him on the paper chase and ends up with four of the bastards pinning him down on the operating table and Goh Peng grasping his balls in one hand and a potato peeler in the other, he'll be able to look at the photograph they'll be holding under his nose and say with conviction, "I recognise him, I met him at the Pig and Eye Club – his name's Peter Fylough, and I know where the bastard can be found". That's doing it the hard way, and that's the only way Goh Peng'll swallow it. We've been through this all before, Woody. Goh Peng's voice is a small one, but it's an essential one to the game. He's the boy who's going to put his hand on his breast and tell the people at home that everything had to be clawed up by its roots. We've got him going – let's not make a balls-up at this point.'

Woodhouse had his reservations. He looked across the room at the door, in case Kent was waiting there, then leaned across the table and said, 'Why don't we tell Kent exactly what the form is? It'll save time and a lot of blood in the long run. Let's tell him, without the major end factor that we want the Chinese led to your front door but they're not to know they're on the end of a string. I'm sure even ex-Hong Kong policemen have some idea of the devious game, and he's been with us long enough to know that that's the bedrock of our club . . .' He wasn't joking. And Fylough didn't laugh. He didn't even smile. He just shook his head. It didn't stop Woodhouse. 'It would be quicker if he was in on it; quicker and cleaner. What if he wants to go hawking off to Malaya to find out what Harry, Dixie and Bentley had in common? Christ, Peter, the more I think about it, the more bloody complicated it becomes.'

Fylough didn't move from his comfortable position in the armchair, but his voice didn't go beyond Woodhouse. 'Forget it, Woody. You can't act the bloody dummy if you know what's going on. Even Larry Oliver couldn't act his way through a Chinese interrogation team. They'd know immediately, after the first bloody scream, that it was a set-up and then you might just as well set fire to the whole bloody file. Nothing doing, Woody! The bugger goes in blind and ignorant. He's not to be given the slightest hint what the Chinese really want – even when he's tied me in, pointed me out, and brought them round for tea . . . By the way, have you briefed Wang Peng Soon to expect a visit to Malaysia from this fellow?'

'Not yet. It's only really just started happening, hasn't it?'

'Wang's got to be kept in touch – all the way. Ring him tonight, bring him up to date . . .' Fylough stopped and glanced over Woodhouse's shoulder. 'Is this your boy at the door?'

Woodhouse turned slowly and glanced to his right. Kent was standing at the door. He'd seen Woodhouse but made no attempt to join him. 'Yes. But before he sits down, what if he homes in on Jimmy Morgan?'

'Pray like fuck that he doesn't! Jimmy's my end card. I don't want him turned face upwards until the final shout. If Kent mentions the name, kill him!'

Woodhouse paled slightly. 'Is that a joke, Peter?'

'I'm not sure. Call the bugger over, Woody, and let's have a closer look at him. I don't want the name "Fylough" mentioned, by the way.'

'Of course!'

'David, I want you to meet Mr . . . er . . . erm . . . Smith,' said Evelyn Woodhouse when Kent joined him in the far corner of the club. Neither of the two men stood up to greet him but Smith produced a slim, well-manicured hand and held it across the table. Kent was surprised at the firm grasp. Smith gave him a brief, friendly smile, took his hand back and replaced it round a stubby dimpled tumbler half full of whisky and water.

He was a tall man; it showed even when he was sitting down. In his late fifties, early sixties, slim, well dressed, he had a frank, honest face – it showed he was in the 'business'. He looked like a man who'd been around places that mattered; his pale blue eyes appeared to be no longer capable of surprise. He studied Kent with interest.

'I understand from Evelyn,' he said casually, as if Woodhouse and Kent belonged on the same park bench, 'that you've got a Chinese puzzle on your hands?' He didn't elaborate. Without taking his eyes off Kent he sipped his drink and waited. Kent stared back blankly, watching Smith deal with his glass and its contents, and then deliberately turned his face towards Woodhouse. He showed him the question in his eyes.

Woodhouse was good at unspoken questions. He nodded briefly. 'Tell Mr . . . er . . . Smith everything, David – and what you think about it all.'

'I think I'd like a whisky and soda, please sir,' replied Kent, breaking his self-imposed silence, and smiled carefully at Woodhouse.

Woodhouse frowned back, as if sensing insubordination, then cleared his face quickly. 'Of course, David. I'm sorry.' But Smith was already there.

'Allow me.'

The clubby atmosphere was restored. Kent sipped his drink, nodded his satisfaction and told Smith exactly what had happened. Smith didn't interrupt. He'd heard it before from Woodhouse and he'd read the report. But it didn't show. He listened attentively as if it were all new to him.

'So?' Smith raised his new, untouched drink to his lips and drank a mouthful. He kept the glass in his hand near his mouth, ready for the next swig. 'What do you make of it?' he asked Kent. 'And where are you going next?'

'I don't know what to make of it, Mr Smith,' said Kent, frankly. The name was coming quite naturally now; there was no instinctive pause between the Mr and the Smith. 'What I'd like to do is have a quiet chat with Mr Goh Peng – Third Secretary at the Embassy . . .' he explained with a raised eyebrow. It was a wasted gesture; both Woodhouse and Mr er-Smith knew what third secretaries' extra-curricular activities involved. Their expressions didn't change. Kent waited for a second, drank a mouthful of whisky and soda, then picked up where he'd left off. '. . . without immunity, to ask him what the bloody hell's going on!' He forestalled Woodhouse's rebuke. 'Which, of course, is out of the question. But . . .'

Smith smiled gently, encouragingly. He seemed to understand the gutter end of the profession more than Evelyn St John Woodhouse – it showed he hadn't spent all his life worrying about what shirt to wear with what tie. 'Of course. But. . . ?' he insisted. There was nothing wrong with his perception either.

'But I'd like to place a permanent watch on him. Twenty-four hours – in and out.'

'OK,' nodded Woodhouse. 'I'll put in the indent. You talk direct with A4 and tell them what you're looking for and what you want out of it. Talk to me about any exception, otherwise carry on until you reach the buffers.' He raised his eyebrows as if he could read Kent's mind. 'No break-ins, mind you. Nothing like that, or you'll carry the can yourself – all the way into your own little cell in

Wandsworth. Is that clear, David? No law-breaking. Definitely no law-breaking.'

Kent finished his drink and rose. 'One thing, sir.'
   'What's that?'
   'What's Mr Smith's interest, or involvement, in this business?'
   Smith, over Woodhouse's frown and shaking head, answered the question himself. 'Government,' he said. 'Statistics Department.' He didn't elaborate; he didn't smile. He looked Kent square in the eyes and allowed him to see that any searching for verification in that direction would end up in a ball of wool. Kent got the message but tried another throw of the dice.
   'The Chinese tried to hack off Dean's hands – or at least they went through the motions. They did the same to some poor old bugger in the North and another in Suffolk. Totally unconnected – or so it seems. I've never heard of this form of Chinese amusement, and up till now I thought I'd either seen or heard of most things that went through their devious minds . . .' Kent allowed himself a half-smile, mainly in reaction to the expression on Woodhouse's face. '. . . but this is a totally new one. They either wanted to know something or they were dishing out punishment for services rendered – a sort of Chinese version of Irish kneecapping.' Kent looked down for a second at Smith's thinning hair. Smith didn't look up: he'd found something of great interest floating in his whisky and water. Kent disturbed his concentration. 'Could you make a guess, Mr Smith, as to what these two had done – jointly – to earn their punishment?'
   Smith looked up at Kent. He allowed a few seconds before shaking his head. It looked almost as though he'd given some thought to the question. But that was all – just a shake of the head. Woodhouse took over again.
   'Ring me in the morning, David, and I'll let you know how many Watchers they've allowed you.' He didn't stand up. Nobody offered to shake hands or say goodbye. Smith almost managed a slight nod but, like the smile, it didn't develop.
   Kent took his glass with him and when he deposited it on the bar he glanced carefully back at the two men he'd just left. They were sitting exactly as he'd left them, staring, unspeaking, at each other. He suddenly had an urgent desire for a pint of bitter in an ordinary London pub. Something to wash the taste out of his mouth.

64

5

Dick Mithers-Wayne sagged back into his chair and stared at the screen of the large IBM monitor. He lit a cigarette slowly and blew the smoke into the air-conditioned atmosphere with a whoosh of satisfaction. His eyes were tired – as well they should be. He'd been staring at this screen, on and off, for three days. He grinned to himself. It seemed that MI5's Evelyn St John Woodhouse had influence in SB's longhouse. Either that or a good friend near the top of the ladder, or he was blackmailing the Head of Operations, or sleeping with him. Mithers-Wayne allowed his tired brain a moment's fantasy. According to David Kent, E. St J. Woodhouse was capable of all three. Mithers-Wayne been given free rein, or rather a long leash, to co-operate with MI5. Co-operation was a treasured aspect of life between the two organisations. It contrasted with the non-relationship between MI5 and its jet-setting sister across the city in Westminster Bridge Road, MI6. MI6 was closer to the KGB than to MI5.

Mithers-Wayne brought himself back to reality. He'd made his impossible marriage. Colonel Dean and Mr Gilbert Bentley, football pools coupon collector of Manchester, were related by isolation. The only place and time their fingers interwined was in Malaya, way back in the bandit war that reached its peak of horribleness in 1953.

'Dixie' Dean. Sergeant, Coldstream Guards. 1950, remustered corporal in the recently resurrected 22nd Special Air Service Regiment. He'd never gone back to shiny boots – if he had he'd have retired as a colour-sergeant. Instead, he'd stayed with the real soldiers and gone to the top. Lieutenant Colonel Richard Dean DSO, MC, MM, retired colonel of the SAS Regiment: died of fright in Oxfordshire.

Mithers-Wayne stubbed his half-smoked cigarette out and absently lit another one.

The screen was still blinking its success at him.

Mr Gilbert Bentley. Area football pools coupon collector. 1948–54 Malayan Police Service.

Bingo! Bingo! Bingo!

Mithers-Wayne rubbed the tiredness out of his eyes and leaned forward for another look at Gilbert Bentley's black-on-green dossier: Malayan Police Service. Joined 1948. Assistant OCPD, Chabis, Johor. 1950, transferred Special Branch. Deputy Superintendent Gilbert Bentley, Malayan Police Service: died of fright in Lancashire.

Mithers-Wayne blew smoke at the screen. Special Branch? Area of operation 1953: North Johor. Dixie Dean? Area of operation 1953: North Johor. What a small world!

There followed a brief table of the downward chart of Bentley's life. He'd lost his nerve in Malaya; he was never made for violence, he'd said so, often – too often. Transferred to the Uganda Police Service. Sacked. Shifty – something to do with black women, the keys to the safe and missing funds. They didn't want him in Rhodesia, North or South; even South Africa resisted employing him. England wasn't too welcoming either. No returning hero this; his last proper job had been traffic warden, London. There didn't appear to be anything lower. But he'd found something – a part-time pools collector. A marriage, but it didn't last; no issue. What a way to die – nobody to give a damn. Except David Kent, and yours truly. Mithers-Wayne dropped back into the chair again as the machine hummed out a paper copy of the details.

North Johor, Malaya. 1953 . . .

But it wasn't enough.

He accepted a cup of lukewarm coffee from the pretty girl assigned to guide him through the mysteries of the floppy disc and sipped reflectively as he studied the printout. His mind was numb. 'Why don't you look at all ex-members of the Malayan Police living in this country?' she suggested. The crumbs of her mid-morning digestive biscuit lingered tantalisingly at the corners of her well-shaped mouth. Mithers-Wayne stared, fascinated. With her wide innocent eyes she looked like an unconcerned schoolgirl peeking at her friend's prep. Mithers-Wayne crossed his legs and sipped more coffee; the biscuit crumbs tempted him.

'It wouldn't work, love,' he said. 'They'd only be on record if they'd been naughty, and their past would only figure if they'd taken on an official job.' He reached forward and pointed with his pen at Bentley's name on the screen. 'Like him. He put down Mal/Pol Special Branch in order to sound interesting. And it is. Wouldn't sound half as fascinating if he'd put down bin man or part-time lavatory wallah! He didn't realise that as a traffic warden he was going downstream from those two honourable professions!'

She laughed. 'Have you looked at dead men with sore wrists?'

The smile vanished slowly from Dick Mithers-Wayne's lips and he put the cup down carefully on the table. He leaned from the side of his chair, resisted the temptation to kiss the side of her mouth, and stared at her. He could almost taste the biscuit crumbs. His stare worried her. Her eyes widened, but she didn't pull away. 'Thank you, darling,' he said gruffly. 'They say these bloody machines destroy your mind. Why didn't I think of that?'

'I'm glad you didn't,' she murmured. She'd read his mind. She would like to have been kissed by Mithers-Wayne, but the moment passed and she knew she wasn't going to be. Mithers-Wayne became business-like. 'Killings over the last ten years, solved and unsolved. Unusual deaths, male only. Bodies with limbs tied, or marks of having been so.' He patted her bare knee. It was a friendly pat – nothing in it for her. '. . . And British white males murdered abroad. Tap the Interpol computer for that.'

'Why white?'

'Nineteen fifty-three Malaya, darling. No blacks from this country in the Colonial Police – or Army. They hadn't arrived here yet.'

'I think you British bobbies are ever so clever!'

Mithers-Wayne shook his head and stood up. 'I'm going out for a walk – clear my head.' He looked at his watch. 'Why not meet me for a beer and a sandwich?'

'Sorry. I promised my boyfriend.'

'See you at two, then.' Mithers-Wayne wasn't disappointed. The sea was full of all sorts of fish.

He gave her plenty of time. A leisurely pint of bitter, a cold beef sandwich and an unenthusiastic glance at the sports pages of the *Standard* took him past two o'clock. She smiled happily when he sauntered across the shiny floor. He looked for more traces of biscuit but her lips were clean and moist; the boyfriend must have had the crumbs this time. 'I've got three possibles for you,' she said.

'Out of how many?'

'The machine went berserk.' She worked the corners of her mouth with the tip of her tongue – biscuit crumbs or memory? It didn't show. 'The times we live in,' she smiled.

But Mithers-Wayne wasn't interested in the times she was living in. 'Tell me about the three,' he said.

The smile vanished. 'An Englishman taken out of Kowloon harbour six weeks ago, mouth taped. He'd been knocked about, tortured. His hands were tied behind his back with wire.'

'Deep, even cuts in the wrists?'

She shook her head. 'Conforms with light wire. Uneven, jagged. Appropriate to a struggle to get free.'

'Died of fright? Heart attack?'

'Drowned.'

'Scrub him. Next?'

She dropped the sheet of perforated paper into a tray bearing the legend 'For shredding' and picked up another sheet.

'A hanging case in Southampton. Gouges in the wrists; not regular cuts, rough gouges. Unexplained.'

'Why murder?'

'No chair, no stool, just hanging from a beam in a barn. No way he could have got up there on his own, it says here.'

She offered Mithers-Wayne the sheet of paper, but he didn't reach for it. Instead he said, 'How old was he?'

'Thirty-two,' she replied.

'Scrub him.'

The sheet of paper followed the first one. 'I've been saving this for last,' she said archly. She wished he'd smile or touch her leg again. Perhaps she should have had lunch with him. He was morose, unenthusiastic – maybe drinking alone didn't suit him. She frowned and dropped her eyes to the paper in her hand. 'A pig farmer in Norfolk. Early November. Well off, wife, two grown-up daughters. Found dead on a mountain of pig muck – ugh!'

'Never mind about that. Go on.'

'Deep razor cuts around both wrists.'

'Razor – is that what it says?'

'Yes, or very sharp knife. He was naked – no clothes – not a stitch.' She seemed fascinated. Mithers-Wayne hurried her along.

68

'Did he die of a heart attack?'

She'd memorised the rest of it. She looked up into his face. 'He died of a bullet in the back of the head.'

'Where was his wife?'

'Tenerife, on holiday. They have a flat out there. She goes fairly often – probably to escape the smell of pig muck!'

'Age?'

'Who, the wife?'

'No, him.'

'Fifty-nine. Ex-Colonial Police.'

Mithers-Wayne reached out and took the sheet of paper from her hand. 'Malaya?'

She nodded.

6

Goh Peng blew discreetly across the rim of his tiny bowl of scalding hot tea before sipping delicately. One sip at a time and after each he pursed his lips and savoured the flavour of the tender Chinese leaf. When he'd finished the bowl he replaced it on the tray and took a sheet of paper from his pocket.

'There are two men involved at the moment,' he said. 'One is Special Branch, the other is a shadow, not possible to define. Our watcher is borrowed from the Yugoslav Embassy.'

'You didn't. . . ?'

'No, Excellency,' Goh hurried, not allowing his companion's frowning rebuke to take root. 'A return favour, nothing specific. It is he who states Special Branch – the man is open, pure police work. The other man, the shadow, he suspects intelligence – MI5. Probably K5 or K6.'

'And have these two men moved us in any direction?'

Goh Peng refilled the two bowls on the tray from a wicker-covered teapot, passed one across the table and brought his own up to his pursed lips. But he didn't drink. His narrow eyes hooded for a moment, virtually disappearing into a thin line, then he shook his head.

'If he is MI5 he'll have to be brought into the open. We have no way of supervising his actions here and the only way we can confirm his movements or progress is by getting him out of the country.'

'Won't the Special Branch man tell you what you want to know?'

Goh sipped more tea and said patiently, 'He's only a policeman. He's digging, not pointing. He's spent a lot of time in the National Police Computer Centre; he's looking for the base of a triangle. We pointed him towards Bentley, but we couldn't be too obvious over Kenning – he had to work for that.'

'And?'

'He's made his triangle.'

'How do you know? Are you inside the Computer Centre?'

'The Yugoslavs have a link to a female analysist. She talks freely, given the right circumstances.' Goh Peng didn't leer or elaborate on the 'right circumstances'; he didn't even smile. It wasn't funny. Incompetence never was. It would never happen in the CELD's own computer centre in Bow Street Alley in Peking. He emptied his bowl of tea in one swallow, but kept the empty vessel in his hand, resting it against his bottom lip. He changed the subject abruptly. 'I think I should take a trip to Malaysia, and take Mr whateverhisnameis with me on a long lead.'

'Will he follow?'

'He must once his Special Branch colleague has passed on his findings. It all started in Malaya. He'll want to find out about the beginning, and when he starts he'll need to dig into Fylough's past – and his present. It's a long way round, but we can't wait another thirty years.'

'It won't matter then. How will you let these people know where you've gone?'

'They'll know.'

7

Dick Mithers-Wayne settled deeper into the old imitation-leather armchair and stuck his feet out as far as they would go. They just reached the glass-topped coffee table. Kent stretched out full length on Mithers-Wayne's settee.

'Kenning fought the war out to the end,' said Mithers-Wayne, 'or, rather, until Malayan independence in '57 when white policemen were no longer needed. He was given the chance to go to Africa, one of the colonies there, but turned it down. Instead, he became a rubber planter, starting at the foot of the ladder.'

'That must have been a bit of a comedown.'

'Doesn't seem to have upset him. He established himself very quickly and on his first leave to the UK got married – nice girl, attractive, good family, money too, I believe. He retired in the mid-seventies, moved around a bit and finally settled in East Anglia. Pigs were a hobby. He didn't really need the cash – '

'He won't now,' said Kent.

'Try not to interrupt or we'll never get to the end of this saga!' growled Mithers-Wayne. But they had all the time in the world, or so it seemed.

'He passed the Chinese on to one Bentley, similarly ex-Malayan Police, but his later career wasn't quite as cosy and rewarding. He gets the same treatment and, in turn, nods his head in Dean's direction – ' Mithers-Wayne stopped in mid-flow. 'You've got a question?'

Kent didn't answer immediately. He raised his head from the settee's armrest and gazed around Mithers-Wayne's rented flat. Basic; just two rooms, one for everything and one for sleeping. None of his girlfriends had stayed long enough to tidy the place up. 'D'you have anything to drink in this doghouse?'

Mithers-Wayne wasn't insulted. He pointed to the small, noisy refrigerator in the corner. 'There's a couple of tins of lager in there. No whisky, no soda. My father always said never drink hard stuff on your own.'

'You're not on your own.'

Mithers-Wayne dropped his feet to the floor and dragged himself out of the armchair. 'I've always admired people with powers of observation.'

'And fish and chips,' said Kent, without moving his head. 'They're usually next door to the off-licence . . .'

Fifteen minutes later Mithers-Wayne returned with a bottle of Bells and two newspaper-wrapped bundles. They ate off their knees.

Kent spoke first. 'To hurry you along a bit, Dickie, three men, all of whom served in some capacity or other in Malaya in the early fifties, are killed by Chinese agents in England in 1987–88, two of them frightened to death, one executed KGB-style – head pushed forward, bullet aimed upwards into the back of the neck – and all three bearing preliminary amputation cuts around the wrists.' He popped another chip into his mouth and picked up his glass of whisky and soda from the floor. 'It's almost ritualistic – as if the killers wanted the victims to be reminded of something before the light went out.'

'Have you noticed the dates?' Mithers-Wayne crumpled his chip paper up into a ball and aimed it at the basket by the fireplace. It missed, bounced off the wall and came to rest untidily on the floor. It didn't look out of place. He left it there and concentrated on his drink. He cheered up considerably when Kent shook his head.

'The dates,' he repeated. 'There's two months between each killing – two months almost to the day.'

'Interesting,' said Kent. He had more luck with his chip paper. 'What does it mean?'

'I think they're warning somebody that they're coming for him. I reckon that two months from the date of the old Colonel's killing there'll be another – same pattern, same type of person. Somebody involved with the three who've already gone down the chute; somebody who must have upset the Chinese in Malaya.'

Kent replenished his glass with whisky and topped it up with warmish soda. Instead of sitting down again he opened the curtains and watched the rain clattering against the window. It looked thoroughly miserable. Without turning round he said, 'I wonder if Woodhouse would allow a trip to Malaysia?'

73

Mithers-Wayne tilted his head back and drained his glass, then stared at the back of Kent's head.

'Nothing to do with warm sunshine, dusky maidens and golden beaches, I suppose?'

Kent's head didn't move. 'A sudden sense of urgency. I think I'll get him to suggest it tomorrow!'

8

'I don't mind telling you, David, but I'm buggered if I can see how a jaunt to Malaysia is going to do anything except give you Singapore foot and a bloody good suntan.' Evelyn St John Woodhouse snapped in two a new Bic he'd been twirling around in his fingers and tossed the two pieces on to the desk to emphasise his point. 'As far as I can read into this sitrep of yours, it's developed into a local police matter with Special Branch undertones where the Chinese Embassy is involved. It's fuck-all to do with Five – it never was! I don't know why the bloody hell I allowed myself to be influenced in the first place.'

'Mr Smith said – ' began Kent, but was cut out by Woodhouse.

'I know what Mr Smith said – but what concerns you is what I say, not what he says.'

'Who is he?' Kent had chosen his moment.

'Actually,' replied Woodhouse in a fit of rare confidential exchange, 'he's head of FO's private intelligence-gathering and collating organisation.' He lowered the bushes of his eyebrows and glanced across the desk. 'Very whisperish, shadowy – they don't admit its existence. As far as you're concerned he's very important. Don't upset him.'

'What's his real name, so I'll know who not to upset?'

Woodhouse grimaced. It started off as a smile to show he was about to say something funny, then lost heart and faded. 'Haven't you been trained not to ask your superiors direct questions? Be devious, David.' He still didn't allow the smile to develop but shrugged his shoulders and sent his eyes upwards to inspect the inside of their lids. 'I'm buggered if I know, David,' he said finally, ' – or care. But I do know what you're going to do.'

'What's that, sir?'

'You're going to mind your own bloody business.' He picked up the two jagged pieces of Biro and tried to join them together. His mind wasn't on it. He studied them for a second, then threw them into the metal basket at the side of the desk. He frowned at length into Kent's face, as if trying to remember where he'd seen him before, then raised his eyebrows.

'Don't get the wrong idea, David, I'm not changing my mind, but what were you going to say about this Chinese business? And if I did change my mind, what would you want to do about it?'

'There's nothing more to say, sir,' said Kent patiently. 'My conclusions and what action I feel should be taken are on the final page of the report.'

'Tell me in as few words as possible.'

Kent wanted to raise his eyes to the ceiling in exasperation but fought the urge to a standstill. 'Every two months,' he began, 'a murder squad of the Chinese Embassy Intelligence staff is going to kill somebody in England who had connections with the guerilla war in Malaya. That means – '

'That means,' interrupted Woodhouse, 'about a hundred and fifty thousand sixty-year-old Englishmen are going to get the chop! Cut out the bloody crap, David. Open up the nut and show me what's inside – without the storybook fantasy!'

Kent wasn't disturbed. He almost smiled. Open up the nut and show me what's inside! He managed not to laugh out loud. 'These three men were involved in something together – something special. There are probably others involved as well; other Englishmen and certainly locals.'

'Why locals!'

'Two of the dead men were policemen. They would have commanded Malays and local Chinese. The third was a soldier – SAS. He'd have been with them on special operations. In my conclusion I suggested I go to Malaysia and ask a few questions, dig a few holes, walk around the jungle a bit and try to make sense of what's upsetting the Chinese here. At least I should be able to stop any more of these poor old buggers from having their hands interfered with.'

Woodhouse had closed his eyes. Whether the easier to listen or whether it allowed his thoughts freer rein was not at first obvious. He might well have been tired and gone to sleep; there was no way of knowing. Kent stopped speaking until the eyes opened. He didn't fancy talking to a sleeping man.

'Go on,' said Woodhouse. His eyelids fluttered but didn't open.

'There's nothing more to go on with. Do I have permission to follow this up in Malaysia?'

'You'll be treading on SIFE's toes, not to mention our own E Branch . . .'

Kent said nothing.

'Security Intelligence Far East,' recited Woodhouse. 'We have a Defence Security Officer in Singapore – couldn't he do this for you?'

Kent shook his head. 'His interest would be lukewarm – at best. It would take too long to get him sufficiently enthusiastic to go digging for something he probably couldn't care less about.'

'You speak the language, of course.' Woodhouse seemed to have forgotten his earlier misgivings and was now embracing the project with an unusual enthusiasm. Kent didn't notice the change of colour, nor did he disillusion him; he knew one phrase in Malay: '*bunyak terimah kasi*' – thank you very much. He let Woodhouse have his head.

'It can't do any harm – probably quite a lot of good. We can't have a bunch of slit-eyes using Embassy privileges wandering around England settling old scores.' Woodhouse stopped speculating and sat forward in his chair. 'OK. Go to Malaysia. Make it three weeks – unofficial, so we don't upset E2. Buy your ticket and put it through emergency expenses to me. I'll sign it over Accounts authority. Er . . . Kuala Lumpur . . .' He stood up and walked across the room to the solid government-issue safe that doubled as a bookcase base, and, making sure his body obscured the dial, spun it around and creaked it open. Kent had had a good look at it – he could have opened it with a cotton bud – but said nothing to spoil Woodhouse's confidence in the impregnability of his safe. Woodhouse removed a hardbacked exercise book from the safe and flipped it open at the index. He riffled through the pages and when he'd found what he wanted he scribbled on a scrap of paper and passed it to Kent.

'Wang Peng Soon,' he pronounced. 'Runs an anti-terrorist room in Kuala Lumpur. He's Malaysian Police but you wouldn't notice it. Has his own organisation – official. He's extreme right of Special Branch. Over here they'd pin on him the name *Geheime Staatspolizei*.' He waited for the laugh that didn't come, then shrugged his shoulders. 'Well they would, wouldn't they – the

Commie bastards!' He clanged the safe door shut and turned round. He was almost smiling. 'A bit like us, really, eh?' He still didn't get the expected smile from Kent. 'Never mind. I'll send a courier note to Wang so that he'll expect you. Trust him.'

'Why?'

'Why what?'

'Why should I trust Wang Peng Soon?'

'You trust Wang Peng Soon because he's also a member of MI5. A long-term sitting tenant. He was a police inspector when we issued the truncheons in colonial days. He went from policing to spying, via us. He liked our ways of doing things and decided to stay with the Raj. Now he draws wages from both us and them.'

'Nice if you can get it,' suggested Kent.

'Don't get ideas.' Woodhouse wasn't smiling.

'Shall you tell your friend Smith about this trip?'

Woodhouse didn't give it a thought. 'I think he's got enough on his plate without concerning himself about a junior officer's holiday, don't you?' He didn't allow Kent a chance to reply. He stood up again and walked round the table. 'Goodbye, David,' he said. The abruptness of the dismissal took Kent by surprise. He stood up so quickly that the blood rushed to his head and he nearly sat down again. For a moment he feared that Evelyn St John Woodhouse was going to shake his hand, but his fears were groundless. Woodhouse had come to the door to order himself a cup of tea.

'Bring me back a stick of whatever they use for rock out there!' This time Woodhouse did laugh. It sounded totally out of character.

9

Kent eased the back of his seat into a more relaxed position and stared out of the small oval window to inspect the huge engine just below him. The sun had gone down on somebody's horizon, but on his it reflected off the aircraft's wing, turning it into a white-hot silver dance floor. He stared for longer than he'd intended, then turned his head and blinked the sun's impression from his eyes.

He was still blinking when the stewardess invited him for a drink. At least that's what he thought she'd done. In fact she'd invited him to have a drink – about £2 difference.

He drank a whisky as an aperitif and ordered another one to help him through the meal. Dinner was edible – in fact it was very good – the whisky had done its duty. He declined the coffee afterwards and when the debris had been cleared away he rammed two lumps of gun wax in his ears, took two Mogadons, washed down with the dregs of his whisky and water, and wrapped himself in the soft pink blanket given to him by an unsympathetic stewardess.

'Wake me up when we get to Kuala Lumpur,' he told her, and went fast asleep.

The next aircraft on the route was Malaysian Airways flying direct to Kuala Lumpur. It was twenty minutes behind the BA 747 London to Sydney and the slumbering Kent.

Goh Peng in a rear corner seat ate his meal without enthusiasm and stared at the same setting sun that had fascinated Kent. He was doing it the long way round – the hard way. He'd given himself no choice. 'I shall follow him and watch. There'll be no conversation, no persuasion, no pain . . . Just a simple follow-and-watch programme.' He'd easily lost the MI5 Watchers team – all Chinese look alike. Big horn-rimmed glasses and buck teeth with lumps of gold flashing in a perpetual humble grin. With forty of them in the Embassy – take your pick, Englishmen! The Special Branch man was a nuisance. As had been expected. But it wasn't important.

Goh Peng dismissed Richard Mithers-Wayne from his thoughts and stared blankly at the slice of fresh pineapple on the tray in front of him.

He was a Malaysian citizen now. His passport confirmed it – genuine, made in Malaysia, and issued to one Lim Tan Thong, a hotel employee resident in Ipoh. Lim Tan Thong was dead and buried – with a different name – courtesy of the Central External Liaison Department. It was easy to chop and change families with part of the family eating its daily rice quota under the walls of the dreaded Tsao Lan-Tze, Peking's prison for political pawns. The Chinese put great value on the strength of the family. Goh had no doubts about the security of his new identity.

He waited until the uneaten pineapple and the rest of his barely touched meal had been removed by the pretty Malay stewardess, then closed his eyes. Unlike Kent, he needed nothing to help him sleep. Goh had no conscience. His mind was clear. Within seconds he'd drifted into a deep, dreamless slumber.

10

The young Malay woman sat in the cocktail lounge overlooking the tarmac of Kuala Lumpur's International Airport at Subang.

She sipped her fresh iced mango juice through full sensuous lips and ignored the mass of humanity chattering around her. She'd been at the table long enough to see off two of the occupants of the other three chairs, one of which she'd tilted forward to show that she wasn't alone.

She was tall for a Malay, about five feet five, and her short haircut made her look like a twelve-year-old schoolboy, but her body was neither boyish or that of a twelve year old. The traditional Malay sarong and kebaya that she wore with an unaffected elegance failed to conceal that she had a beautiful figure, but this wasn't the place to flaunt it.

She appeared to be in no hurry and continued to sip from her glass as she watched the British Airways 747 taxi to a bay just below her. She put her empty glass on the table but didn't stand up until all the arrivals had been separated from the transit passengers and shepherded into the Immigration and Customs lounge. She waited a few minutes longer, then picked up her shoulder-bag from beside her sandalled feet and moved away from the crowd and down the stairs towards the exit hall.

With the rest of the disembarking passengers, who were mainly Chinese in stiff, starched shirts, rolled-up sleeves and ties, and Indians, most of them in baggy creased trousers and dirty leather shoes, the heels crushed down and worn flip-flop fashion in time with their slovenly gait, Kent moved patiently through the Immigration and Customs controls.

In the main hall he was casually aware of a lantern-jawed, squat Malay, wearing a worn, black-velvet *songkok* on his head and a white shirt, the tails of which dangled unselfconsciously outside his unpressed khaki trousers, joining the small exodus behind him. He didn't see the exchange of glances between him and the girl standing near the exit door, nor the man's slight, almost imperceptible nod of recognition.

She moved like a dancer alongside him as he went through the door towards the taxi rank. 'Mr Kent,' she said in a soft voice. 'Your car's over there, in the car park.' She spoke in English, slightly husky and with the faintest of accents, yet pure, as if it had been her first language and was now slightly diluted with lack of use. She smiled to take the look of cautiousness from his face. 'Inspector Bedah binte Ariffin,' she added softly, and continued in spite of his blank expression: 'Saleh will take your bag.' Saleh was the man with the black velvet headwear. He moved up behind Kent as if on cue, deftly removed the single bag from his hand and went into the lead.

Kent followed obediently with a smiling but unspeaking Inspector Bedah at his side as the Malay crossed the road and wiggled his way through the car park to stop beside a white Volvo. Kent smiled to himself. He made sure it didn't touch his lips, or his eyes. It was the same in Hong Kong – Volvos made up 80 per cent of the crowded car park, and they were all white.

While the Malay opened the doors and switched on the engine and the air-conditioning, Kent stared around him briefly before inspecting the taxi rank outside the airport's main entrance. It looked like any other airport main entrance. He studied the queue of new arrivals waiting to share transport into town and noticed that Inspector Bedah was doing the same. He saw a thin Chinese standing on his own staring back at her. It was a short confrontation. The Chinese shook his head slowly at Bedah.

The Malay driver thumped his foot on the Volvo's accelerator – he was feeling the heat too – and the air-conditioning responded with a whoosh and a blast of chilled air. He slammed the front door shut to keep the cold in as Bedah opened the rear door.

'After you, Mr Kent.'

Kent didn't move.

She knew what he was waiting for.

'I'll show you when we get inside,' she said.

Kent smiled down at her but still made no move.

'I'd hate to make a scene by screaming,' he said softly, and nodded at a white-helmeted motorcycle policeman who'd joined the tall Chinese on the far pavement. 'Let's have a little flash of something before we tumble about on the back seat.'

She wasn't amused. Her generous lips tightened into a thin line of exasperation and the good humour vanished from her dark eyes as she flipped the catch on her shoulder-bag and brought out a small wallet which, under the protection of the bag's flap, she allowed him to study. The photograph didn't do her justice. She was much prettier in the flesh. But Kent barely glanced at it; he'd smelt policewoman the instant she'd approached him in the airport concourse. He was more interested in the stubby, girl-sized .25 Spanish Astra tucked into its little holster inside the bag. She saw the movement of his eyes and dropped the flap back into place.

'Satisfied? Can we go now?' Little beads of sweat had collected just above her lip and she ran her tongue lightly over it as she stared at him for a brief second before turning away to step into the rapidly cooling car.

She didn't quite make it.

'More,' said Kent lightly.

'What do you mean?' Her eyes had become quite cold and unfriendly.

'Who sent you?'

Another flight had cleared Customs and people were filtering across the road towards the car park. The white-helmeted policeman and the Chinese still stood together in the entrance, out of the sun. The Chinese had a frown on his face. It could be seen quite clearly. It looked as though he was tossing a mental coin whether to come across and find out what the delay was in getting out of the car park. But he didn't have to move.

'Wang Peng Soon,' hissed Inspector Bedah quickly. 'Can we go now, please?'

She'd woken up in a good mood that morning; it wasn't often, not this time of the month. She had liked him on sight: tall, clear-cut features that she could go quite silly over, and a strong chin with a suggestion of fair stubble that should have been taken off earlier that day. That didn't worry her – quite the opposite. Her immediate feeling had been of anticipation. Meeting good-looking, thirty-year-old Englishmen wasn't an everyday chore for one of Wang Peng Soon's women, and she liked playing with tall men as much as she liked working with them. But this one had done it all wrong. He looked nice but his manner wasn't. She sat in her corner of the car and began to build up an interesting hatred of this suddenly supercilious-looking Englishman, and she made no effort at conversation on the long drive into Kuala Lumpur. Kent glanced sideways several times at her very attractive profile but if she felt his eyes on her she made no acknowledgement. His questions she either ignored or answered monosyllabically. He'd upset her – and she showed it.

Chief Superintendent Wang Peng Soon had been allowed to make his own domestic arrangements. The people who decided on the iron fist didn't want to know from whence it came. Wang Peng Soon was an individual – Special Branch handled the finances, but Department F2 was nobody's. If anything went wrong there would be only one head to roll – the one where the buck stopped – the one that sat on Wang Peng Soon's shoulders. And the men who'd given him the power would be the first to pay for it – but only when things went wrong.

The large colonial bungalow that housed F2 was tucked away in a quiet backwater off the Ampang Road – Kuala Lumpur's upper-class suburbia. Total anonymity. Nobody sat around watching Wang's house. Further down the tree-lined avenue was another, smaller version of the bungalow. This housed the Watcher service. Its main job was to ensure the security of Wang's department with twenty-four-hour cover, which was why nobody stayed long enough to find out what was going on behind the walls. Wang's people had a healthy axiom: better six innocent people end up dead in the cellar than one guilty man escape. They'd selected the best of British legal principles and turned them around so that they made sense.

Inspector Bedah showed Kent into Wang's large but almost windowless office and vanished, as if in relief. She didn't say goodbye to Kent.

'Woody's told me all about your problem,' said Wang as he came round the table at a slow waddle, his hand outstretched.

Kent took it. 'Woody?' he asked. It seemed as good a way as any to open the conversation.

'Woodhouse,' said Wang. 'Evelyn St John Woodhouse.' He stopped and thought about it for a moment. 'Funny – I always thought Evelyn was a girl's name.'

'So did I,' said Kent.

Wang laughed. It suited his round, flat face, whose narrow-slitted eyes completely disappeared into mere suggestions of eyes to join the laugh lines that seemed to have had plenty of exercise. His teeth were perfect, white and even, with the exception of one large incisor which was covered with high-grade certified gold. It reinforced the theory that all Chinese carry their funeral expenses around in their mouths.

Short and fat, Wang sat down with a bump and touched a button on the underside of his desk. A face appeared instantly round the corner of the door. 'Coffee or tea?' Wang asked Kent.

'Coffee, please – black, iced, sweet,' replied Kent.

'Ah!' Wang held two fingers up to the face. '*Kopi o peng* – two . . . Now, Mr Kent – '

'David, please,' insisted Kent.

'David. About these dead men. Two of the names Woody mentioned ring little bells up here.' Wang touched his smooth forehead with his thumb. 'Bentley was Special Branch in the 1950s and 60s and then left on a colonial roundabout. I knew him. He's documented, so we can probably tie him in somewhere with the other one – Kenning.'

'The rubber planter?'

'And ex-policeman. All post-war documents, reports on emergency operations, as well as lists of personnel, have been computerised. One of our trained monkeys at Central Police Records should be able to cross-check these names and see where they coincide. God knows what we would have done ten years ago!' Wang sipped his iced coffee and smacked his lips with satisfaction. 'The third name – what was it?'

'Dean.'

'Yup. I doubt the records will show anything. There were tens of thousands of British soldiers wandering about the jungle here in those days and their names wouldn't have been documented – not in our records. Probably not even in the list of those who didn't make the boat home . . .' Wang paused and stared at Kent over the rim of his cup. 'Unless – ' He stopped again and drank from his glass cup. His eyes once more vanished into his face. 'Unless,' he repeated, 'his name featured in an operational report – a sitrep – something like that; something registering a successful police

85

operation with, say, a kill or two . . .' His eyes reappeared, serious, dark brown, almost black. 'But I don't think individual British soldiers took to the field with police units.'

'He was SAS,' Kent reminded him.

Wang showed his gold tooth. 'A point in favour.' He held his cup carefully over his saucer, as if it were a chess piece and he wasn't sure the move was a good one. He kept it hovering a fraction of an inch above its pad before making up his mind and allowing it to settle. He and Kent studied the move critically before Wang removed his hand and said, 'I've arranged for you to spend tomorrow at the computer centre. Everything else has been taken care of. You're booked into the Equatorial. I thought about the Hilton but decided it might be a bit too flash. I don't think, at this stage, you want curious eyes taking an interest in your bedroom.' He looked sideways at Kent. 'I have an arrangement with the Equatorial.' It could have meant anything. He didn't elaborate. 'There's a car for you – Bedah'll give you the keys when you see her on the way out.' His eyes twinkled. 'Pretty girl, Bedah . . . ?'

Kent didn't respond.

It didn't stop Wang. 'Her bite's just as bad as her bark! But don't let it put you off, she's a very good agent.'

Kent grinned. 'That's the build-up – what's the let-down?'

Wang's eyes vanished again. 'She's going to stay with you until you've settled your little bit of business – she's going to help you.' He ignored Kent's sceptical expression. 'It's necessary.'

Kent knew what he meant and spared him the embarrassment of explaining that the Federal Police would be very quick to stamp their feet and click their tongues and fingers at the antics of an SB-sponsored European wandering unchaperoned through Central Records and hallowed places. The Malays in Bukit Aman had become very haughty, and touchy, since the last Englishman had vacated his swivel chair in Police Headquarters. Bedah would make all the difference to their feelings.

'She doesn't know yet,' added Wang as an afterthought. 'Oh, and I think you'd better have this too . . .' He opened a side drawer in his desk and peered into it as if it were a box of soft-centred chocolates. When he'd made up his mind he reached in, brought out a well-used .32 Sauer P-220 automatic and slid it heavily across the desk. Two empty magazines followed it. 'It's nothing special,' he said, 'but it'll keep any unpleasantness at arm's length. Don't worry about using it; it hasn't got any marks on it. Bedah'll give you a box of caps for it, and I'll send you over a temporary attachment warrant in the morning. Get me a photograph sometime this afternoon – Bedah'll arrange it for you.' Bedah's perks were mounting by the minute. She was going to be delighted with her new responsibilities.

11

The 'Do not disturb' sign hanging from the doorknob of Kent's room didn't apply to the telephone. It ground noisily in his ear and brought him out of a deep, contented sleep. Bedah carried on where she'd left off – unfriendly.

'I've brought your car and arranged a room at the Records Centre,' she said briskly. 'For half-past ten.' She didn't wait for his groan. 'It's ten o'clock now.'

Kent felt as if he'd got a hedgehog in his mouth. He couldn't find his tongue – the hedgehog had made a nest on it. He knew when he'd flopped into bed last night that he was going to regret it. He wasn't disappointed. He'd made a night of it. Solitary but fun. A six-course Cantonese in Chinatown's Jalan Sultan – far too much . . . Drinks in the Federal with a drunken Irish Australian that got out of control and a rapid retreat to the Merlin. More bloody Australians, and a boring disco in the basement of the Hilton with the best part of a bottle of Remy Martin. He blamed his poor state of health on jet lag. His tongue detached itself from the roof of his mouth.

'Give me ten minutes. I'll meet you in the coffee room. Have something while I'm getting ready.'

'I've had everything, thank you.'

He didn't quite know what to make of that. 'Coffee? Breakfast?'

'Don't be long.'

Bedah put down the telephone and walked through the foyer to the hotel's verandah and ordered coffee and papaya.

Kent arrived before she'd finished.

His eyes betrayed the interesting night out, but a crisp white short-sleeved shirt, a Royal Hong Kong Police tie and light tropical-weight cotton slacks belied the state of his head. He studied her as he sat down.

She was in her working clothes of pale faded jeans and flat-heeled leather sandals with gold-coloured straps on her tiny, child-size feet. The jeans were skin-tight, and there was no tell-tale impression of underwear – she'd had to have lay down flat on her back and throw her legs into the air to get them on. It tortured the imagination . . . And the yellow T-shirt that held two firm, out-thrust breasts, modestly supported, emphasised her light coffee-coloured, velvet-textured skin. It all looked very promising.

Bedah returned his scrutiny without pity. 'You enjoyed your first night in Kuala Lumpur?'

'I'd have enjoyed it more had you done your duty and come with me.'

Kent had asked her. She'd refused – curtly, against her natural feelings. Bedah felt that after his unpleasant manner at the airport her refusal had made them all square.

She gazed directly into his eyes and her look softened slightly. She held his eyes for a second longer than was good for him, then looked at her wrist. 'You've got time for coffee, and the papaya'll do some good. You've no time for anything else.'

Kent stared back at her. For a girl of twenty-three, or thereabouts, he reflected, she had a very domineering nature. She'd been allowed to get away with too much – men were suckers for a woman in a schoolgirl's body. She'd be a dragon when she grew up if somebody didn't tame her soon . . .

But not him. She wasn't his problem. He sat down. 'Whatever you say, Inspector!'

She ordered briskly. Even the waitress kow-towed to her.

Police Central Records was housed in the massive, modern Police HQ in what under British management used, appropriately, to be called Bluff Road. It was now named Bukit Aman – the hill of peace. Bedah and Kent weren't allowed in, even with Bedah's personality and authorisation, until they were both cleared, documented and handed over to another female inspector, a much more amicable Chinese named Chan Moi – 'Please call me Nancy.' She liked Europeans; she liked the look of this one.

'Can we get on, please, Inspector?' Bedah wasn't going to call her Nancy. 'We haven't got much time – we're in a hurry.'

The Chinese woman's smile vanished and she shrugged her shoulders apologetically at Kent. 'Come this way please.' It was Kent she invited, but it was Bedah who fell in behind her.

Nancy was good at her job.

She listened without interrupting to Kent's outline, taking her eyes off his face only occasionally to jot down the names and other single-word notes, then went to work.

'Shall we start with 1953?'

'Whatever you suggest, Nancy,' smiled Kent. Bedah sat apart, away from the computer, and stared at the back of Nancy's head. Her expression didn't change when she met Kent's eyes. He didn't try to include her in the friendly atmosphere.

'Johor?' asked Nancy.

'We could start there.'

Her hands flew across the keys like a piano virtuoso. Her long expressive fingers were everywhere. She'd have made a good masseuse – and lover. 'Right . . . Establishment, Johor, 1953. Kenning first,' she whispered. The silicon chips scratched their heads and within seconds the screen cleared and produced the legend: *Kenning H. A. – P/Lieut. 10th Federal Jungle Company, Cha'ah*. Nancy's eyes swung away from the screen and searched Kent's face.

'Bentley?' prompted Kent.

Bentley G. L. – ASP Special Branch. Segamat. Transferred 14.11.53 – code FL (see BUKIT MERTAJAM. KEDAH).

'D'you want to see Bukit Mertajam Kedah?' asked Nancy.

'No. Try Dean.'

The machine took off again, longer this time, and finally apologetically reported: *Not on record*.

'Not to worry!' said Nancy cheerfully. 'That's just establishment. The name might appear in a situation report.' She went to work on the keys again and as she tapped out the codes she said, without looking up, 'I'm asking for all police sitreps where the name Kenning appears; also for those with Bentley and Dean. Let's see what happens.'

The computer went to work as if it had found something to get its teeth into. It made a meal of it. There were thirty-odd instances where Kenning had featured in reportable action of some description or other: ambush; bandit camp attacked; patrol ambushed; brief encounter, undercover elimination of Communist agent . . . Kent raised his eyebrows at that entry but kept his own discreet counsel. It seemed Lieutenant Kenning had had quite a war! Of Bentley there was only one entry. Kent stared at it. Nothing unusual. Bentley was Special Branch – he'd be behind in the shadows, peering over the wall. He'd set things up, he wouldn't normally be expected to do the biting as well as the barking.

And then came the plum.

Dean R. P. – Cpl. SAS. Just the one entry.

'Can we join those three together?' Kent managed to keep his voice flat, even, but underneath the excitement bubbled – it was like reading off the numbers of the first-prize lottery ticket. Nancy caught the undertone. She moved her slim buttocks and slid her chair forward slightly on its smooth casters. Bedah, behind them and against the wall, felt a whiff of the adrenalin that was hovering over their heads. She left her chair and her expression of boredom and joined Kent and Nancy at the machine.

Nancy depressed a key and relaxed back into the upholstered swing chair. She didn't take her eyes off the screen. Neither did Kent. It went on – and on, and on – and then, with a suddenness that startled them, the screen stopped moving and was full of words. Nancy moved slightly to one side so that Kent could get a head-on view and pointed with the nib end of her pen.

'There you are, Mr Kent: ASP Bentley, Corporal Dean, Lieutenant Kenning . . .' She rested her finger on a key, making everything move upwards and allowing the bottom portion of the report to come into view. *Officer commanding patrol: P. Fylough, P/Lieut. Countersigned: F. Miller, Commanding Officer 10th Federal Jungle Company, Chaah.*

'Pop it back to the beginning, please Nancy.' Kent leaned forward, rested his elbows on the computer table and began reading: . . . *A patrol of 10th FJC commanded by Lieut. Fylough with Lieut. Kenning, accompanied by ASP Bentley observing operation, and Cpl. Dean SAS attached for special duties* . . .

Kent read it again. It was an unembellished report of a single action in a long-forgotten war; it gave him a slightly queasy feeling at the back of his neck, as if some of the nastiness was rubbing off the report. It had been a nasty little affair, a grim and unpleasant war, fought in a dark, never-ending nightmare of ambush and merciless killing – an eye-to-eye, face-to-face war where prisoner was a doubtful word. The laconic wording of the sitrep made no glamour out of the occasion; the originator was used to what he was doing – there was no feeling in his words.

'This is obviously what it was all about,' said Kent, more to himself than to his two companions. 'Something happened on this patrol.' He looked, unseeing, at Nancy. 'But what?'

'There's a continuation sheet,' said Nancy. She'd been studying the heading. 'This is numbered 10FJC/11/17A. Eleven's the month – November. Then comes the number of sitreps so far that month – 17A.'

'And the "A"?' Kent watched Nancy's lip purse. Something wasn't as it should be.

'I don't understand,' she said plaintively. She was pressing one of the keys, sending the text on the screen whirling upwards and then back again.

'What is it?'

'Seventeen A means this particular sitrep comes in two parts; the second part is not a new sitrep but becomes 17B. Normally the message is headed with just a number.'

'So what's the problem? Let's have a look at 17B – it'll probably tell us everything we've been sitting here looking for.'

'The problem is, Mr Kent . . .' whispered Nancy. She'd gone slightly cross-eyed as she stared into his face – it gave her a look of added sexuality. But Kent wasn't interested in sexuality; he was interested in the 1953 jungle war. 'The problem is there's no 17B on the file – the next number's 10FJC/11/18.'

'Has it been rubbed out?'

Nancy shook her head.

'How do you know?'

She flicked her fingers over the keyboard and completely changed the format. She touched the screen with her Biro. 'If there had been any erasures it would show there. There's a memory bank that would hold it even if it had been erased, but it would show there. See? No limbo.'

'So what do you reckon happened to it?'

Nancy shook her head and gave a little giggle. 'I only operate the machine, Mr Kent. They don't pay me to solve puzzles. Sorry.' Without waiting for Kent's permission she cleared the screen and flipped the sitrep they'd been studying back into place.

Kent stared at the brick wall. It seemed to go on for ever. The two women sat quietly, unseen and unheard, neither prepared to interrupt. They didn't look at each other. Kent finally sat back in his chair. 'Can we look up this fellow Miller?' he said to Nancy, and after another glance at the screen, 'And Fylough?' He pointed to two other names. 'I presume these two are Malays?' Nobody answered.

'Are they?' he insisted.

Bedah leaned forward. Her tight jean-clad thigh pressed against Kent's. It was unintentional. She felt the pressure but didn't move away. 'Johari,' she pronounced. 'And Togom. Both Malays, probably Japanese originally. There was a Johari in charge of graduate selection at the Police College when I joined. He was Assistant Commissioner (P) – Personnel,' she added unnecessarily. 'I wonder if it's the same person?'

'Hardly likely,' said Kent. He put his finger on Johari's name. 'Sergeant, it says there. That's a hell of a long way from Assistant Commissioner.'

'Just because he's a Malay doesn't exclude him from having brains – or ability.'

'I didn't mean – '

She didn't allow Kent to apologise. 'My father was a corporal in the 4th Field Force during the Emergency.'

Kent turned his head. 'And he retired as an assistant commissioner?'

'Not quite.' She stared into his eyes for a second, then laughed. It suited her. But it didn't last. 'He retired as a corporal.' Kent laughed. Nancy didn't. She and Bedah were never going to be friends.

Nancy tapped the screen with the chewing end of her Biro and brought the meeting to order. 'Can I return that?' she asked Kent. 'Have you finished with it?'

'Can I have a print?'

'Of course. Shall I go for these other names?'

'Please.'

An hour later they'd advanced only to the stage of discovering that Assistant Commissioner (P) Johari was now dead and had, indeed, risen from the rank of Sergeant. Kent's earlier excitement took a nosedive. Johari's death closed what had initially looked a highly promising and interesting avenue. To David Kent's raised eyebrows Nancy checked and discovered that the Assistant Commissioner and ex-jungle-fighting Sergeant had died of natural causes. Kent's cup of disappointment overflowed. But there was better news. Corporal Togom was still alive and was still drawing a police pension. He was living in a kampong north of Pontian Ketchil in Johore.

Kent had had enough. He decided it was lunch-time. Bedah made sure the invitation wasn't extended to Nancy. It didn't bother Kent; his headache had returned and his hangover cried out for cold beer, aspirin and a cool quiet room – women weren't included.

Nevertheless Bedah persuaded him into a small Malay café at the busy end of Jalan Bukit Bintang.

She read the menu as, with a coloured plastic straw, she sucked from a glassful of cracked ice and 7Up. Kent attempted to drink ice-cold Carlsberg Special. The condensation almost stuck the glass to his lips and he recoiled when his sinuses were cauterised by the freezing temperature of the beer. But it didn't worry him. With beer it was either one or the other – too cold to taste or as warm as local tea. In Malay cafés there was nothing in between.

With his head propped in his hand Kent studied the wodge of computer print-outs Nancy had given him. The gurgle of Bedah's straw emptying her glass of 7Up reminded him that he wasn't alone. He raised his eyes and looked across the table. She didn't seem to mind being ignored.

'What would you like to eat?' she asked.

'Nothing – how far is it to Pontian?'

'Corporal Togom?'

He didn't answer.

She shrugged her shoulders. 'About a hundred and fifty miles. D'you want to go this afternoon?'

He frowned, hesitated, then shook his head. There was something not quite definite about it. She accepted the challenge.

'It'll only take about two and a half hours. Plenty of time to find him, talk about his war, and still get back here in good time for you to make another appointment to see Nancy.'

He looked at her sharply and searched her eyes. They mocked

him, but there was nothing of what was going on behind them. She looked like a cheeky boy scout.

'Why would I want another appointment to see Nancy?'

'She left some unfinished sentences. I think she'd like to see you again – without me around.'

Kent wasn't in the mood. He sat and drank another freezing Carlsberg while he watched Bedah pick her way through a Malay salad and a bowl swimming with fresh lychees. He was intrigued by her attitude to Nancy. Jealousy? He toyed briefly with the idea of asking her back for an afternoon drink in the hotel, until his hangover made him think the better of it. But it was as if she had read his mind.

'Would you like to have some satay with me tonight?' she asked.

He felt his headache slipping away. 'Your place?'

She smiled kindly. 'I thought Kampong Bahru – you can watch us natives at play!'

'Shall I pick you up?'

Another little smile; she was getting the habit. It made her look quite beautiful – if only she'd do it more often. But there were no promises. 'I'll call for you at the Equatorial – about eight.'

Kent stripped off his sweat-soaked clothes and threw them into the wicker laundry basket. After a brisk warm shower he took a cold Tiger beer from the fridge, poured it into a glass, then, with the air-conditioning unit turned full on, stretched naked on to the crisp white sheets and stared at the ceiling.

Nancy had left him more problems than he'd started with. To begin with, who the bloody hell was Fylough, and where had he gone to? And wherever he was, why hadn't he had *his* hands operated on? He checked the computer print-out for the umpteenth time: *Lieut. P. Fylough transferred to MI 1/4/53* – ten days after the incident on the report. What was MI? Malayan Intelligence? Military Intelligence? Nothing more had been heard of him since. The computer didn't lie. Lieutenant P. Fylough, 2i/c 10th Federal Jungle Company, Malayan Police Force, had transferred out of the service without a dot against his name. He'd gone to MI – whatever that was – and disappeared for ever, never to be mentioned again!

Miller? Who the bloody hell has he become? Discharged, the

records said, in 1955, on medical grounds. What medical grounds?
No hands? Don't be bloody silly. He took a long pull from his glass
of Tiger and put it back on the side table. What fun – staring at the
ceiling, while the sweat poured off and chilled in the frosty room.
Where was I? Miller's medical grounds . . . Nothing mentioned,
just discharged on medical grounds. Bedah said she'd look into it.
If he had been discharged on medical grounds he'd have a medical
pension, and if he had been discharged to the UK, Wang could
invoke the help of his old friend Woody – though he wouldn't get a
lot of sense from that quarter! But what if Woody's name in a
previous life had been Miller . . . Goodbye hands, Woody!

Kent smiled to himself and filled his mouth again with Tiger. It
was not as sinus-jolting as the café's Carlsberg. At least he could
taste it. He drank some more and went back to his thoughts.

Sergeant Johari and Corporal Togom – only two un-English
names out of what must have been a fairly sizeable patrol. Why
only these two mentioned? He balanced the half-empty glass
carefully on his chest and thrilled at the chilling sensation. He
cursed himself for wriggling his mind into added complications –
as if there weren't enough already. These two Malays were
mentioned because one was the senior NCO and the other had
killed himself a bandit – simple as that. But was it?

According to Nancy's machine, soon after Fylough's disappearing act Togom had been transferred to the 4th Field Force in Kulai,
where he had continued to distinguish himself, soldiering out his
time until he was retired on pension. The pension was paid at
Pontian Ketchil sub post office – monthly. Thank God for lady
police inspectors who knew how to work computers! But first
things first. Kent finished up his beer. They would go and see
Togom bin Yussof tomorrow morning.

Bedah's image frowned down from the ceiling.
Why not this afternoon? There's still time.
Because I want to try and get you into bed tonight!
Wishful thinking – a smile without promise.
It cost Togom his life.

12

Malaysia was not friendly with the People's Republic of China, who had no embassy in Kuala Lumpur. But it didn't hinder CELD's extensive Malaysian operations.

The Chinese Intelligence organisation was housed in Race Course Road, in an imposing old relic of British colonial days and under the cover of a satellite corporation of an (authentic) Hong Kong-based conglomerate. The building had been done over, cleansed of any ideas it might have had about hanging on to its nostalgic past and electrically disinfected against any twentieth-century device that might have been introduced into its nineteenth-century structure. It had several annexes, each studiously watched by Malaysian Special Branch and Wang Peng Soon's F2. The Chinese were not unaware of the interest and for this reason it remained clean and antiseptic and any covert activity by the large CELD presence in Malaysia was carried out from under the even more innocent auspices of the Chan Toh Wen Banking Corporation building in Leboh Belandar.

In Singapore CELD handled its problems differently. Its communications centre was located in a lead-lined room in the basement of a tailor's shop in Dhoby Gaut, from which there was a direct link to the Chan Toh Wen building in Kuala Lumpur. It was a treated line that persistently defied all Singapore Intelligence Service attempts to penetrate it – or to locate its source.

Goh Peng was put through to the Resident Director immediately.

As provisional head of the London bureau of CELD Goh Peng carried weight – but not as much as he would have liked with his opposite number in the equally important section in Singapore. Explanations were required; windbreaks needed to be erected against failure and its repercussions; nothing was given freely. Goh Peng spoke and Singapore listened to London's requirements.

'The Malay, Togom, bought his life with his tongue,' said the tailor after listening to Goh Peng's request. 'Why do you now want me to risk a team, and my security, for an insignificant old man who has served his purpose. He guided you to the people you wanted. You could have killed him then and there.'

Goh Peng didn't raise his voice. 'It was my intention to keep the Malay active until the mission was fulfilled. I anticipated difficulties that might require further discussion with him, but that need no longer exists. An English Intelligence officer has picked up the Malay's trail. I do not wish the two to meet – the Malay must, therefore, be despatched. I want that done now – this evening.'

'And if the Malay has documents, or other things connected with your mission?'

'There are certain things the Malay has that I would like the Englishman to find. Kill the Malay, and leave everything else exactly as it is.' Goh Peng allowed a trace of urgency into his voice. 'We are running out of time . . .'

Singapore was still not convinced. 'I need Peking's authority.'

'No you don't. I already have that authority.'

'I need confirmation.'

'There's no time for that. I want it done now, this afternoon. Tomorrow will be too late – even this evening may be too late. I take full responsibility. Do it now. Seek your umbrella after you have put it in motion.'

'A name? For the record . . .'

Goh mentioned the name of the head of Chinese military and civil Intelligence, Tang Shi, Co-ordinator of the Social Affairs Department and controller of the largest Intelligence network in the world – the man who was, it was whispered, one of two highly fancied successors to fill the tiny shoes of the Chairman of the People's Republic. Goh Peng carried very serious credentials. They were strong enough for the head of the Singapore agency.

Just over an hour after Goh Peng had put down his telephone in Kuala Lumpur an innocent-looking fishing boat with four Chinese on board pulled slowly out of the harbour village of Choa Chu Kang. The men smoked and chatted noisily, chugging along the Singapore side of the Johor Strait until they reached the open sea. They sailed openly past the village of Tuas and headed south, but once out of sight of land the chugging diesel was switched off and the powerful twin screws of a petrol engine dug into the flat, calm water of the Malacca Strait and they turned west. Keeping well to the south of Tanjong Piai they skirted Pulau Kukup and with the engine at full revs headed northwards.

Two hours later they turned towards land. The sun had dropped into the sea behind them in a flaming red ball and the dusk visibility was barely sufficient for them to find the narrow channel through the mangrove roots to the north of Pontian.

They'd been there before. They knew exactly where to go. Two of the men stayed with the moored and partially concealed boat while the other two, one with a sack of fish over his shoulder and the other, just behind him, with a rolled net draped round his neck, headed inland. In the sack under the fish, snugly wrapped in an oiled cloth, lay an Indonesian-copied Ingram 11 silenced machine-pistol, magazine fully loaded, weapon cocked.

The man bringing up the rear made no pretence of concealing his weapon. In his hand he carried an unnumbered, unmarked 7.62 Tokarev TT, its barrel modified to take a three-inch noise suppressor. He walked lightly, testing the ground, until he joined his companion on the firm track that led to the kampong at the end of the creek.

Corporal Togom's house was at the far end of the village, with the narrow front verandah overlooking the fishing bay. When the two Chinese arrived the light in the house had just been turned on. They squatted among the mangrove roots and viewed the village with suspicion. They were ill at ease. They'd been here before, a year ago, with the big-head from Peking's Central Intelligence. They'd watched the surrounding area from the other direction while the old Malay was quietly persuaded to talk about things and people of long ago. They'd been uneasy even then. Myth took a long time to fade, longer still to die. The myth surrounding this village was still fresh and green, even after nearly forty years. This was the village of the inoffensive, unarmed Malays who had wanted no part of the 'running dog' argument, had wanted to be left alone. But it wasn't to be. The village had been taken over by a roving gang of Yap Ah Lee's bandits in the early months of the 'Liberation War'.

To begin with, the Malays – mainly old men, a few boys and the women and children – had been subservient, pliant, even cooperative when the Chinese demanded food and shelter. There were a lot of them, fifteen, twenty, maybe more, and they could have rested and fed with impunity while regaining their strength. But they were stupid. Their heads turned by the cowed Malays, they abused them, accusing them of running with the British; of being dogs – running dogs, cowards . . . As they warmed to their power, one or two of the younger bandits – peasants, with peasant mentalities – entered the small mosque and in front of the old men gleefully defecated and urinated in the holy shrine.

Then, in another part of the mosque, they settled down for the night. Bellies full, their two women, now desirable after a meal and a bath and clean clothing, did their duty acquiescently and grunted and squealed their satisfaction as the men took their turns in the darkest corners of the mosque – all comrades in the great struggle . . .

When they'd all finished they slept. There were only two guards – it was a holiday camp and the Malay villagers were spineless. The Chinese slept like exhausted babies.

But the Malays didn't sleep. Then men exchanged glances, and at a nod from their leaders the women took the children and silently drifted to the outer perimeter houses. Then, no words necessary, the men and the boys picked up their *parang-panjangs* – three-foot-long, one-and-a-half-inch-razor-sharp, curved machetes with handles of hardened latex normally used for slashing undergrowth – and moved in the dark to where the jungle encroached on the village. The discussion was whispered, short, and without passion.

At 1 a.m. the two half-asleep Chinese guards were despatched with single blows of the *parangs*. The mosque was quietly surrounded and at a given signal the men moved in among the sleeping bandits. No mercy was shown. The Malays hacked and cut. A few shots were fired by bemused bandits and a burst of Sten from an instinctive grasping hand killed two of the villagers. But the slaughter continued unabated. Screams of terror and pain rent the cold, silent night air, only to be drowned out by the triumphantly shouted holy words of the Malays as, by the dim, ghostly light of two pressure lamps, they hacked and cut their way through the building.

When it was finished, of the Chinese only the two women

remained alive. They were dragged outside, stripped, and beaten mercilessly with rattan canes, then left to shiver where they lay until morning.

At first light the two young women, bruised, bloody and frightened and covered only by thin cotton sarongs, were pushed and shoved back into the mosque, where the smell of death and blood was already beginning to taint the crisp morning air. Watched by the silent inhabitants the two girls were made to drag their dead, mutilated comrades, one by one, out into the centre of the village.

Retching, crying and petrified they made the journey back into the bloodied, defiled mosque eighteen times, until the last body, a youth of seventeen, his head almost severed from his neck, was laid out in a long, straggled line.

But it wasn't finished.

Boiling water was produced in galvanised latex collecting buckets and huge lumps of misshapen yellow soap were thrust into the two girl's hands. The men and boys stood silently around the walls inside the building while outside, squatting in groups on the small grassless padang, women gossiped quietly among themselves. One or two of the younger women, out of curiosity, approached the main entrance and peered timidly round the corner. No one shooed them away. The men stood watching, saying nothing.

They watched the two Chinese girls scrub first the defiled walls then the floor. The mihrab – the holy niche of Mecca – where the girls had lain for their friends was the last to be thoroughly disinfected. But it would never be fully cleansed. When it was finished the two exhausted girls were taken outside to be spat upon and abused and pushed about by the Malay women. Then they were killed, quickly and neatly, by blows from the *parang-panjangs*.

The massacre of the Communist terrorists was widely reported at the time. It was a turning point that placed the uncommitted Malay people 100 per cent against the Communists. The word jihad was mentioned. Jihad showed what simple, peace-loving villagers could do when roused to anger. It was a salutary lesson to the Chinese – after that they avoided Malay villages like the plague.

The two Singapore Chinese exchanged white-eyed glances as they settled down amongst the mangrove roots and waited for Togom's evening to finish. When the light was finally switched off in his bedroom the two men straightened up from their cramped, damp positions and moved on the balls of their feet towards the raised, *atap*-roofed house. They stood underneath the bedroom and listened. The only sound was Togom's laboured breathing, and, every so often, irregular grunt-like snores. Somewhere in the village a baby awoke and cried its fright but was rapidly quietened with a large brown nipple thrust into its gaping mouth. On the perimeter a scavenging dog barked. Otherwise, everything was quiet.

The Chinese with the pistol moved cautiously on his bare feet towards the ladder-like steps that led into the house. He mounted them slowly, careful to keep his weight on one side to avoid them squeaking, and when he reached the narrow verandah he stopped to listen at the door. A gentle, regular breathing came from the left-hand side of the room, partitioned from Togom's bed by a rush-matting curtain, where his juvenile fourth wife slept contentedly. He crossed the matted floor on his belly. The regular breathing continued uninterrupted: she was young, fit, and very tired. He paused and listened again – she'd have been hard-pressed to hear an elephant bumbling around the house. He slid alongside Togom. The tiny flashlight clutched tightly in his fist gave just enough light to confirm that Togom was fast asleep, curled into a ball, with his sarong pulled up to his chin like a blanket. His mouth was wide open.

An ugly man at his best, the years had done Togom no favours. Two protruding teeth were all that remained in his mouth and these were part blackened, and stained yellow from the nicotine of forty-odd cigarettes a day.

He snorted in his sleep, coughed, and stopped breathing, holding his breath as if something primeval had jogged him. The Chinese hesitated, but only for a second, then moved his hand and placed the bulbous end of the Tokarev a fraction of an inch below the white-whiskered underside of Togom's chin. It didn't touch but Togom's eyes opened. The whites gleamed momentarily in the dark. He might well have been smiling with gratitude, but the Chinese didn't give it a thought.

102

The pistol juddered in his hand as he stroked the trigger. The muted explosion sounded louder in the confines of the dark room but it didn't travel. The girl continued sleeping behind the partition; her breathing remained as regular as a life-support system. The gunman listened for a second longer, then flashed his light again, briefly, on Togom's face. Togom looked undisturbed, but the Chinese man knew better. The bullet had torn into Togom's chin, through the roof of his mouth, and ripped into his brain. The old corporal had died instantly.

The cold-eyed Chinese closed Togom's eyelids and gently eased up the sarong so that it covered the lower part of his face. Nobody would try to wake Togom. He'd lie there, as if asleep, until the midday meal.

The two Chinese crept out of the kampong and made their way back to the boat. Once aboard they headed west until out of sight of the Malaysian coast, they turned south. They dropped the weapons overboard off Pulau Kukup and began fishing. They returned to Choa Chu Chang at first light with the rest of the night fishers. Their catch was average. Nobody gave them a second glance.

Goh Peng was in the middle of his breakfast when the phone rang. He put down his sugar-coated pancake, wiped the corner of his mouth of sugar grains and picked up the buzzing instrument.

'It's done,' said the voice in his ear.

'Complications?' he asked.

'None. Nothing will be known for some hours.'

'Good.' Goh Peng replaced the receiver, finished eating his breakfast pancake and swallowed the last of his cup of sweet milky tea. He wiped his lips again with a crisp napkin, brushed his fingers and picked up the phone.

'You said the Englishman, Kent, showed interest in Togom,' he stated. 'Did he say he was going to Johor to talk with him?'

'That was the impression I got.' The voice was female, sleepy, as if she'd been dragged out of a nice comfortable bed. Nancy was very fond of her bed. But it had no effect on Goh Peng.

'Did he indicate what he expected to learn from Togom?'

'No.'

103

'Did he take his address?'

'No – and he or the Malay girl will have to come to me if he wants it.'

'I'm to be informed when it happens.' Goh Peng thought for a few seconds. Then, 'This Malay woman, what part is she playing?'

'She's one of F2's people. She's holding the Englishman's hand while he digs.'

'Does she know anything?'

'She doesn't give that impression.'

'What impression does she give?'

'Reluctant nursemaid.'

'She shall be watched.'

'I think you'd be wise to do that.'

13

Kent dined Bedah in style in the magnificent Hilton basement restaurant. He was quite proud of her. She didn't look the least bit like a policeman. Her hair was swept up, emphasising her slim, swan-like neck and slightly rounded jawbone. She wore a jet-black sarong and kebaya – the latter supported, seemingly, only by the out-thrust of her breasts, which appeared to object to the confinement. Kent wondered where she kept the little Spanish automatic. The only embellishment to the plain black outfit was a thin string of cultured pearls that glistened like her tiny teeth. Kent had difficulty in dragging his eyes away from her.

'Shall we dance?' she suggested.

The walked through to the dimly lit, noisy, coloured-light-flashing disco in the insulated part of the hotel. The disco was Bedah's wish. Kent was indifferent, but as they walked through the concrete channel he took her hand automatically. She seemed to like the intimate touch; at least she didn't pull away.

It took two hours to get it out of her system. She discoed like a teenager – no holds barred – and it was he who had to suggest they call it a day. It seemed the obvious thing to do. She was becoming friendlier by the minute. After the last strenuous session she collapsed beside him in the darkened booth and with childlike innocence rested her head on his shoulder as she recovered her breath. It was very heady stuff. He was home and dry, and he stared optimistically at the soft, round, unsupported breasts revealed as the loose kebaya fell forward from her bare shoulders. Perfection. He fought the urge to lower his head and take the firm little nipples between his teeth; instead he lifted his glass and drained it like a man dying of thirst. Finally, she turned her head on his shoulder and looked into his face.

'David?'

'Hmm?'

'Can we go home now?'

He uncrossed his legs. Your place or mine . . . But he kept it to himself and let her make the decision.

She did. Again it wasn't going to be Kent's night. She spoke to the driver in Malay and the taxi moved in the opposite direction to the Equatorial and stopped quietly on the corner of an unlit leafy street on the outskirts of the town. She leaned over and kissed the side of his face. 'Thank you, David,' she whispered. That was all – 'Thank you, David.' She said nothing more but didn't resist when he turned his head and found her mouth. There was enough passion in her reply to rekindle his hopes as he searched for her tongue with his and she responded – deliciously – but only briefly. His hand moved to a soft, warm, smooth, slightly damp armpit and rested on the yielding mound of her breast. It felt like silk. His fingers moved for the nipple. Hard. Then her hand came up, stroked his face and gently came between their mouths. She searched his eyes for a moment, as if looking for something she knew she wouldn't find, then said firmly, 'No.' There was no basis for argument in her voice.

'Jesus!'

Kent passed a fitful night.

He was up early, shaved and dressed in a lightweight bush jacket and trousers, a yellow light cotton cravat, and suede boots. Sitting in the foyer restaurant with coffee, boiled eggs, toast and fruit he looked fresh and crisp and ready for whatever the day had to offer; he looked like the man who'd gone to bed with a good book and a cup of cocoa and thoughts as pure as water. It was illusory. He felt like death. After leaving Bedah he'd had two overweight brandies – for the frustration – followed by a pint of freezing Tiger. It hadn't helped. The taste of her had lingered and was still there when he woke up.

She spotted him as she came through the main door. She hadn't got his problems. She'd had her exercise and a good, untroubled night's sleep. She looked like a freshly peeled apple – delicious – and eatable.

Kent looked up with a forced smile. She was back to looking like a policewoman. No provocative off-the-shoulder kebaya; a severe polka-dotted shirt with long sleeves rolled halfway up her arms. The faintest suggestion of a bra strap showed that she perhaps had some heavy running in mind – she must have interpreted the look she'd seen in Kent's eyes when she left the taxi last night. But the jeans were just as tight, and they stretched tighter as she lowered her firm buttocks onto a chair and took a few male minds off the quality of their papayas.

'Coffee?' asked Kent. 'Eggs? Toast?'

'Just coffee, please. I like the outfit.' She smiled brightly.

Kent didn't smile back. He stuck a piece of toast in his egg and carried it to his mouth; it dribbled, just missing his nice crisp jacket.

She laughed openly; it was just what the morning needed. A couple of young Malay businessmen looked enviously over their coffee cups. It was that sort of laugh – there was intimacy somewhere in the air. Kent stared at her. After just a sterile kiss and a handful of expectation? What would she be like after. . . ? *Forget it, Kent. She's one of those – she's a bloody prick-teaser*. She stopped laughing when her coffee arrived and allowed the young Malays to concentrate on their breakfast. She waited until the waitress had gone, then said, 'We'll go to Pontian by the quickest route. We can come back on the coast road. I rang your friend Nancy this morning and got Togom's address.'

'Did you tell her we were going to see him?'

'Of course.' Bedah looked sharply at Kent. The laughter had gone from her eyes. 'Should I not have done?'

Kent frowned at her. 'You're a very aggressive young lady at times – you ought to try and control it.'

It didn't worry her. 'Would you rather I simpered a bit?'

Kent didn't reply. He finished his coffee with a swig and stood up. 'Are you ready to go?'

She pointed to her untouched cup. 'Can I finish this?'

'Don't hurry.' He went back upstairs to his room and removed from behind the water cistern in the bathroom the automatic Wang had given him. It nestled in a plastic bag, clean and dry. He checked the magazine, just in case. Full. He replaced it and slipped the spare magazine in a small holdall. On top of this he threw two shirts, a spare pair of trousers and a change of underwear. He smiled wryly as he wrapped the automatic in a large handkerchief and tucked it into his trousers. It was uncomfortable, just like old times. He hadn't carried a sweaty automatic since Hong Kong; it brought back memories. He looked in the wardrobe mirror. Nothing showed; no bulge, none of the discomfort of a heavy lump of iron pressed into bare flesh. He frowned at his reflection. So why? There was no sense of danger, no signs of needing comfort – nothing, just a light buzzing in the inner ear. Not to be confused with the heavy pounding behind the eyes from the consolation brandies after the Bedah sex lesson. He picked up a spare jacket, slung the bag over his shoulder and joined Bedah in the foyer.

She'd finished her coffee. He noticed she carried only a handbag. She obviously didn't intend to spend the night on the road. It was going to be down to Johor, back to KL and goodnight David, thanks for the trip – again. He hadn't had this sort of trouble with a woman before. Not recently. He was beginning to have doubts about himself. He took another long hard look in the mirror – maybe it was the aftershave?

14

Togom's kampong was at the end of one of those tracks off the coast road that looked like an unmade-up road to someone's back garden. But once you got there it was worth it. A postcard picture of the idyllic Malay village, it could have been taken from a glossy tourist board brochure, and nobody would have believed it: waving coconut palms, houses on stilts, almond-eyed, coffee-coloured children and bare-armed Malay women in gaily coloured sarongs with the appraising look that only bare-armed Malay women can offer tall, fair-haired strangers.

But a discordant note removed the charm and the curiosity; it was only the women and children who were studying Kent. The men were all standing around staring at the police Land Rover, the ambulance, and the unmarked car shimmering on the open ground in front of the mosque. From the shade of an *atap*-roofed coffee shop three armed policemen in blue shirts and tight khaki trousers looked up from their thick cups of milky tea and watched the approach of Bedah and Kent. One of them, a sergeant, with a reluctance apparent on his dark features, stood up, frowned at Bedah, stared with curiosity at Kent and disappeared into the darkness at the back of the wooden hut. Just as Bedah and Kent entered the shop, he returned with a young Malay police inspector, hatless, a cigarette in one hand and a mug of iced black coffee in the other.

Bedah's appearance quickly removed the frown of disapproval from the inspector's face and after a brisk conversation in Malay she introduced him to Kent. They didn't shake hands.

'Togom was killed sometime in the night,' Bedah said to Kent. She made it sound as if it was the young inspector's fault, but he wasn't unduly disturbed by this. 'Apparently,' she went on with a sideways glance at the inspector, 'Togom's wife didn't discover he was dead until two hours ago.' She glanced down at her wrist. 'About half-past ten. Inspector Abidin says –'

'He was shot in the head,' Abidin took over the conversation.

He hadn't met Bedah before, otherwise he might have thought twice about interrupting. But she conceded gracefully – he was a startlingly good-looking young man. He also spoke impeccable English. 'Close range, about an inch and a half away.' He allowed Kent to digest this while he studied, openly, Bedah's thigh-tight jeans – they didn't have anything like Bedah to play with in Johor Bahru, let alone Pontian. After he'd worked out what Bedah had under her jeans he turned once again to Kent: 'There were two of them, both men, probably Chinese –'

'How d'you know that?' asked Kent.

'We found the spot where they waited. They were there a long time – hours by the look of the disturbed undergrowth.'

'And Chinese?'

'They wore shoes.' Abidin looked at Kent as if it were all so terribly obvious. 'They took them off to come into the village and Togom's house. They probably came by sea. We tracked their path back through the swamp.'

'Where's the body now?' asked Bedah.

'I've sent it to JB – autopsy, forensic, looking at the bullet and all that sort of thing.' He was talking to Kent but looking at Bedah out of the corner of his eye to see whether she was impressed. She wasn't.

'How long ago?'

'Just before you got here.'

She mouthed a crude Malay swearword at Kent and then said, 'Does it matter? We can go on to Johor Bahru if you like.'

Kent shook his head. 'It's not important.' He turned back to Inspector Abidin. 'Can we talk to Mrs Togom?' He didn't know what good that would do. He couldn't imagine what a Malaysian kampong wife could have to contribute towards making the death of three Englishmen ten thousand miles away any clearer, but you never knew.

'Of course. Follow me.' Abidin waved his two constables and the sergeant to stay where they were – they hadn't moved an inch – and moved off through the ring of curious but silently waiting village men who'd stopped gazing blankly at Togom's house, and had bored of the Pontian police, but who stared with rekindled interest at the tall European and the Malay girl in trousers with the authoritarian air. Abidin stopped in his tracks. 'Of course, she doesn't speak English, you know,' he apologised to Kent.

'But I do,' interposed Bedah quickly, before Abidin volunteered for interpreter duties. 'And Malay,' she added unnecessarily, and followed it up with her first smile of the day. Abidin got the message. He almost smiled back but it would have been wasted; Bedah was already on her way up the steps to the Togom house.

Togom's wife didn't move when they arrived. She remained squatted, huddled in the corner of the room, out of sight of the curious villagers. Her head was covered with a brightly coloured batik shawl and only the top part of her face was visible. Yet she was not as upset as she should have been and her curiosity at seeing a fair-haired European in the most private corner of her house pushed the reason for his being there into the background.

'Tell her we're sorry to hear about her husband's death,' Kent whispered to Bedah, 'and then ask her if he'd been afraid of anything over the past few weeks.'

'I wouldn't bother offering condolences,' suggested Abidin, unfeelingly. 'I don't think she's got any reason to mourn. He was an ugly old buffer and I gather from them,' he jerked his thumb over his shoulder at the villagers below, 'he was as bad-tempered as he was ugly –'

That was as far as he got with his verdict on the late Corporal Togom. Bedah snapped, 'Which is neither here nor there, so if you don't mind . . .' She gave Abidin a witheringly icy look and asked Kent's question sympathetically of the huddled woman.

After a brief, softly spoken exchange Bedah turned to Kent and said, 'She said no. He'd got over it.'

'Got over what?' asked Kent.

Bedah shook her head. 'Go and sit down over there. This might take a minute or two and you're making the room look crowded.' She didn't smile. She meant it. The room wasn't made for people of Kent's size; with four people in it, it was beginning to look like a communal telephone box. Kent did as he was told. Abidin included himself in Bedah's admonishment and squatted in the far corner with his back against the flimsy wall, where he listened to the conversation between Bedah and the woman. It seemed to go on for ever.

After a final flurry of exchanges, Bedah raised her eyebrows at Abidin and said to Kent, 'About eight or nine months ago three

111

Chinese came to see Togom. Two spoke Malay – not well, but understandable – Chinese Malay. The third spoke only Chinese. She listened from round there.' Bedah pointed with her chin to the other room behind the rush curtain. 'They wanted to know about something that had happened many years ago in the bandit war – something that had happened in the jungle. They talked about a place called Labis, and another one called Chaah –'

'Villages further north,' explained Abidin. 'Just before you get to Segamat. Not very nice places during the Emergency.'

Bedah frowned at the interruption but let him finish before she took up Togom's widow's story. 'She said they threatened to kill him and when she peered through the screen she saw that one of the Chinese was holding a pistol against Togom's eye –'

It wasn't going quick enough for Kent. 'What did they want from him?'

'She doesn't know. She said she screamed when she saw what they were doing and one of the Chinese barged round the screen and aimed a kick at her. Togom ignored the gun in his face and shouted for him to leave her alone; then he ordered her to go downstairs and boil some tea. She heard nothing more, except . . .' Bedah paused.

Kent raised his eyebrows. 'Except?'

'Except some *orang-puteh* names.'

'English names,' clarified Abidin, then shut up at a glare from Bedah.

'What English names?' Kent frowned at the woman's bowed head. 'Ask her if she remembers any of the names.'

Bedah spoke softly and urgently to the woman.

The woman shook her head.

'What were they talking about when they mentioned these English names?'

'*Barang-barang* . . .' Bedah tried not to smile at Kent's expression. 'Things . . .'

'We're not getting anywhere.' Kent's exasperation was beginning to show. The bloody language, or lack of it, was grating on his nerves. Bedah's interrogation technique was about as effective as a chocolate thumbscrew.

Bedah and Abidin looked at each other for mutual support and waited for Kent's next question. He managed to keep the impatience out of his voice. 'Ask her if there was anything among Togom's things that had any bearing on the Chinese people's visit.'

Before Bedah could react Abidin came to life again. 'He had nothing – nothing except a tin box containing his medals and some old photographs.'

Kent perked up. 'Photographs? Photographs of what?'

'I'll get them for you.'

Abidin knew his way around the house. He pushed himself up from the floor and ambled into what had been Togom's bedroom. He was back within seconds with a battered tin box that had seen much better times and bore an almost obliterated logo advertising a dry rye biscuit that had long vanished from Malaysian supermarket shelves. He handed it to Kent, sat down again and, disregarding Bedah's disapproving frown, brought out a packet of cigarettes and lit one. He didn't offer them around. Kent didn't notice; he was engrossed in the box's contents. He lifted out a chain of half a dozen or so tarnished British Army campaign medals, each with Togom's name engraved on the rim and attached to a strip of ribbons, frayed and moth-eaten through lack of display. It was obvious Togom hadn't worn them since his Jungle Force and Field Force days. Whether they'd given him any pride of possession was another matter.

Kent placed them carefully on the floor beside him. He lifted out a small, navy blue, leather-covered box, opened it, and stared at a near mint-condition, if somewhat tarnished, George Medal. Kent gave a silent whistle to himself; George Medals were not issued in the jungle war for collecting coconuts. He wrinkled his nose and allowed the lid to drop with a click. Bedah and Abidin watched without interest. He picked out a wodge of dog-eared photographs and riffled them into a small pack. Unlike the medals these had been well used; old Togom must have had fond memories of his finest hours. Kent flicked through them. They were all black and white prints, little groups of men in jungle green, some neat – just going out? Some with muddy, torn uniforms, tired-looking, with haunted eyes and the tension of action still showing on their young brown faces. Others were smiling little men in crisp khaki drill with wide-bottomed, laughable shorts, snow-white gaiters and old-fashioned pillbox hats balanced to the side above grinning faces. It was like looking at a history book of an age and a people already long forgotten.

Kent stared closely at a group of eight men in torn, sweat-stained jungle green kneeling in a semi-circle, their eyes slitted against the sun as they peered at the camera. Four bullet-ridden Chinese lay in a straight line within the confines of the half-circle. They were stripped to the waist, still wearing the bandit army Chinese-style puttees criss-crossed up to their knees and rubber-soled canvas boots. But it wasn't the dead Chinese that Kent was staring at so intently. Togom, his mouth open in his interpretation of a grin and his large protruding teeth splitting his face like a row of stalactites hanging from a dank cavern, he recognised from the other photographs. No, it wasn't Togom that made him narrow his eyes in concentration but the two unsmiling European faces among the happy Malays. He turned the photograph over. A faint pencil mark, just legible, read *10 FJC '53*. He passed it to Bedah.

She glanced at it, grimaced at the casual spectacle of death, and held it at an angle so that Abidin could get a better view. He was fascinated. Thirty years ago one of the Malays could well have been him.

'What do you want me to say about this?' asked Bedah.

'Nothing,' replied Kent, curtly. 'I want you to impound it.' He didn't look up from the other pictures in his hand. 'I don't suppose Mrs Togom would know the names of those two Europeans?'

'I won't even bother asking her,' replied Bedah tartly. 'How would she know? She's not much older than me.' She looked to the young inspector for his endorsement on the age question and he managed a shy smile and a nod, then chanced his arm and murmured in Malay, 'But not half as pretty.' Bedah pulled a face; she wasn't flattered. Kent didn't look up. He passed her another of the photographs.

'And that one too, please.'

This one featured no dead Chinese. It was a formal pose of a quarter-guard at the base of a flagpole. Togom was at one end, his carbine at the present arms, and just in front of him an officer, European, stood at the salute. The latter wore crisp KD and a Sam Browne. He was not either of the two in the other picture. Kent glanced quickly through the rest of the old photos, then dropped them into the tin box and closed the lid. He'd got photographs of three white men from a jungle war. What they had to do with three white men dead in civilised England, and one dead Malay who'd won a George Medal for killing Chinamen and got his face blown in thirty years later for his trouble, was anybody's guess . . .

Kent stood up and nodded to Togom's wife. He didn't even know how to say sorry, so he smiled gently and hoped she understood. She didn't respond. She probably didn't understand – or care.

Bedah made herself comfortable in the car and glanced sideways at Kent. He didn't drive off immediately but sat staring out of the window. She had a good idea what was going through his mind.

'David, you can't blame yourself for that old man's death.' She herself felt no remorse over the sudden and violent end to Togom's life. Togom had been only a name to her; if she had any feelings at all over his going it was for the young widow he'd left behind. In a male-oriented society like this one her future was bleak. Togom had taken the bloom off her and she wasn't pretty or young enough to find a local to take her on. Everyone wanted a young virgin – there was no queue for widows. But Bedah dismissed Togom and his widow from her mind. It was finished, and there was nothing that could be done about it now. She glanced surreptitiously at Kent again as he started the car. His jaw was set, his eyes cold.

She was pleased with the way she'd handled him last night. He was exactly what she'd expected – and he was very nice to kiss. Gentle? Well, perhaps a little question mark on the gentle, but that was not entirely undesirable. Attractive men like Kent – she knew the type well – who were used to women flinging off their sarongs at the first probing kiss would improve with the odd rejection – it was only a question of how long and of how many rejections. Bedah had worked it all out, and the knowledge of her power was to her a very strong aphrodisiac; she almost regretted last night's abrupt ending now. There was a row of tiny pinpricks of sweat on Kent's upper lip. She longed to lean across and kiss them away, and in return she wanted to be kissed back hard and deep – like last night. She shuddered in recollection – and why not? Last night she'd won, hadn't she?

Her mood was broken by Kent grating the gears of the car as he

115

pulled slowly out of the kampong track and onto the main road. 'Of course it's my bloody fault,' he snapped. 'I should have come yesterday afternoon – I was a bloody fool!'

'Why didn't you?'

He didn't reply.

She left him in peace for a few miles to flog himself with self-recrimination but when a major turn-off appeared she sat up, touched his knee, and said, 'Why don't we take the coast road back to KL?'

He grunted. Not very promising. 'Whatever you want.' The flogging had obviously not finished.

It didn't worry Bedah. 'Take the Bandar Penggaram road, then join the road to Bandar Maharani – after that I'll direct you to Melaka. Enjoy the scenery! She snuggled back into her seat and brought her knees up, clasping them in a loose embrace. She looked relaxed and contented. Kent glanced sideways, briefly – she looked very desirable. It hurried the process of absolution for his late arrival at Corporal Togom's farewell party.

Behind them, an air-conditioned Toyota with smoked-glass windows hovered just out of sight in a shady lay-by, waiting for Kent and Bedah to make up their minds which road they were going to take.

The car had followed them from KL at a leisurely pace. It had waited just south of the track that led to Togom's village and had rejoined them a few minutes earlier when they left. The air-conditioning unit was grinding at maximum – it wasn't going to make a good second-hand buy. But Goh Peng and his two companions didn't mind the wait; they knew what they were doing and they weren't going to be rushed. Goh Peng sat in the back – the coolest part of the limousine – and relaxed into the soft upholstery as they tracked Kent and Bedah through Johor to Melaka. It was all very straightforward. He smoked a cigarette. He wasn't concerned about polluting the atmosphere inside the vehicle; he had other things on his mind.

An impatient man, the game was not moving fast enough for Goh Peng. He would have liked the Englishman shivering with pain in a white room – that was where the questions would be

116

answered. But that was not the game; the game was Ah Lian's: '. . . let Englishman turn the stones; let us guide him if he falters – this is how the game is played, and this is how we'll win it . . .' Goh Peng shrugged aside a woman's theories and concentrated on his own. They were much simpler – there was too much running on the Englishman, and too many questions. Today's questions; had he discovered the picture? Had he found the fourth man's face? Had he got enough now to move on to the next square? Goh Peng stared moodily out of the window. The Englishman wouldn't tell without pain. But the Malay girl – lucky the Englishman had brought her. Now he'll take her home, and that was where they would talk to her; perhaps they could inject a few ideas into her head. Goh Peng closed his eyes and filled the car up with tobacco smoke. The scenery bored him; it wasn't his home.

But it nearly went wrong in Melaka.

They trickled behind Kent's car into Melaka City and Goh Peng decided his quarry would take the coast road out and then turn for Seremban and Kuala Lumpur. They signalled a left turn from Jalan Laksamana preparatory to crossing the bridge over the Sungai Melaka and then, committed, watched Kent drive straight on. It was a tight moment.

'Follow him!'

'Too late!'

'Do as I say!' Goh Peng sat forward and thumped the driver in the back of the neck. The driver broke four rules, but squeezed past two lanes of startled drivers. They were lucky. The police were all at home having tea. Goh Peng was just in time to see Kent's car squeal to a stop outside the main post office in lower Jalan Laksamana.

It was Bedah's fault.

During the flat featureless drive to the Bandar Maharani ferry she had been quiet and pensive, studying the sea on her left and the horizon whenever it came into view. On board the ferry they leaned, side by side, on the iron bulwark and stared into the thick, muddy-brown Sungai Muar. After a few minutes she nudged Kent's arm and said, 'D'you fancy a swim?'

'In that?' Kent flicked a half-smoked cigarette into the swirling brown liquid and watched it settle on the thick coat of scum that accompanied the ferry. It floated for a good ten seconds before being sucked out of sight. Kent didn't smile. He didn't look into her face – it had to be a joke. 'I wouldn't go into that stuff in a submarine!'

She took no notice. 'I was thinking of Port Dickson – it's on our way.'

He still had the road map in his hand. 'No it's not.'

'Yes it is!'

He looked at the map again. 'That's cheating.' Then looked down into her eyes. She was like a child about to be refused a treat. He remembered last night. His groin softened his resolve. 'It'll be time for dinner – can we eat in Port Dickson?'

'Leave it up to me.'

She directed him through the busy Melaka city centre and just before the turn for the bridge and the road to Port Dickson she sat up suddenly and without warning snapped, 'Get in the other lane – quick! Good – that was close.' She giggled like an excited schoolgirl. It was out of character but Kent had no time to enjoy it. 'Go straight on. OK! This'll do.'

'What?'

'Post office.'

She leapt out of the car and disappeared into the red-brick building. It didn't take very long. When she slid back in beside him she said, mysteriously, 'I told you to leave it up to me.'

'Why, what've you done?'

She didn't reply immediately. Conscientiously, she directed him through the centre of Melaka, back to the bridge and on to the Port Dickson road with its emerald-green floating *padi* fields, then said: 'I rang my brother. He's a rubber planter. He works for a company that owns a bungalow on a cliff just outside Port Dickson. It's private – and at the moment unoccupied. It has its own beach. He has the use of it . . .' She still didn't look at him. 'He's ringing the housekeeper now and having dinner and two rooms prepared. Nice?'

Two rooms?

Kent grunted noncommittally. 'Lovely.'

Bedah wasn't deterred by his lack of enthusiasm but left it with him and changed the subject. 'What are those photographs going to tell you?'

He didn't reply for several miles. The countryside after Melaka was startling; spectacular and breathtaking in its beauty. It gave him time to ponder on how much Wang might have told her about what he was doing in Malaysia. It wasn't difficult to work out. From what he'd seen of Wang's thinking there would be very little background music played when it wasn't needed. According to Wang, Bedah was going to look after him. He knew what Wang meant by that; so did Bedah. And it didn't mean the sort of looking after he didn't get last night, or, by the sound of it, that he wasn't going to get tonight.

'I'm looking for a connection between a killing in England and a happening some time ago here in Malaysia,' he said at length.

She looked at him closely again. 'How does that concern us?'

'Us?'

'Wang Peng Soon and F2.'

'A long story, Bedah. It's deeper than just killing.'

'So what are Togom's photographs going to do for you?' she persisted.

He glanced at her quickly, out of the corner of his eye. She'd slipped her shoes off and was sitting back with her feet on the edge of the seat and with her chin resting on her knees. She looked fourteen.

'The two Europeans in that picture with the dead bandits may already have been killed,' he said slowly. He was thinking aloud. 'But if they're not and I can find them they will probably be able to tell me exactly what I'm looking for – or what I'm supposed to be looking for! At the moment I haven't got a bloody clue what it's all about.'

'I thought your Nancy had made things a bit clearer for you?'

'My Nancy made nothing clear at all. She gave us Togom's name – he was going to paint the little pictures for us. Now all we've got is a couple of photographs of two guys who will have altered out of almost all recognition. Thirty-five years on? Think about it.' He glanced sideways again. 'Would you recognise me in thirty-five years?'

If he wanted a compliment he'd come to the wrong girl. 'I don't think I'll recognise you this time next year. David.' She wasn't smiling. She meant it. The romance had finished before it had started.

'Thanks! Does that answer your question?'

'About the photographs? Yes. And I'm sorry I asked!'

Kent smiled to himself and shook his head. She had turned in her seat and was studying his profile with a quizzical expression. He didn't notice; he was concentrating on the road.

'Didn't Togom's wife say three Chinese visited him nine months ago?'

She nodded. He caught her eye in a quick glance; she was sizing him up for something. He didn't let it prey on his mind. 'That fits in with when the killings started in the UK. Togom gave these Chinese the names of the people involved in one specific operation – the "Special" – then they went off and tracked them down.'

'How?'

'Good question.'

'Chinese . . .' she said enigmatically, and allowed her tiny white teeth to chew on her bottom lip while she concentrated her thoughts. The pause caused him to glance at her again. She was no longer looking at him. Her forehead was creased in a frown. '*They* can find addresses of ex-policemen in England, but we can't because it doesn't come up on our national computer system . . .' She paused again, but it was a fractional pause, and nothing to do with not hurting his feelings. '. . . which is operated, in our particular case, by a Chinese named Nancy – Help! Stop! Quick! Turn left here!' She came out of her reverie in a panic. She'd nearly missed the turning.

Not difficult – it was a tarmacadamed drive that vanished between a lane of overhanging shade trees. Beyond the trees Kent could see the orange-coloured tiles of a large sprawling colonial-type bungalow, and to the side, as he drove up, the shimmering, late-afternoon heat mist rising off the placid sea which stretched uncluttered into infinity. It looked idyllic. He wondered who Bedah had last come here with and whether that time it had been two bedrooms she'd arranged with her brother to have prepared – or one. He didn't thank his thoughts for the suggestion.

The grey Toyota, some distance behind them, pulled into the side of the road and drifted slowly to a halt while Goh Peng studied the drive along which Kent's car had vanished. After a moment he nodded to the eyes watching him in the rear mirror and the car pulled away. But it didn't go far. A quarter of a mile on, where the road bent away from the sea, a hotel jutted into prominence. The Toyota crept quietly into its large car park and slid alongside another, similar, dark car. The engine was switched off and the three Chinese waited and sweated as the huge red ball of the sun drifted slowly down behind the oil palms covering the gentle slope in the middle distance, and the night, less hot but heavy with sticky moisture, arrived dead on time. Half-past eight. The darkness was total. Shortly the thin segment of white moon would come and bathe the sandy beach in a improbable ghostly silver hue, but for the moment the blanket had descended and the three Chinese prepared to move.

They left the car and removed their trousers and shirts. Then they took off their shoes, put their socks with the rest of their clothes and donned rubber plimsoles. On the main road they walked in single file, picking their feet straight up and down in the manner of Chinese coolies, and headed for the turning into the bungalow. They attracted no attention. Three Chinese in singlets and baggy underpants – three coolies on their way to their beached fishing boat.

The bungalow, perched on a rocky promontory two hundred feet above the sea, was in the luxury class. It showed that the modern Malaysian rubber planter looked after his welfare in no less a grand manner than his European predecessor. It comprised two wings, each with two large bedrooms, bathrooms, a lounge and separate dining room for the unsociable, and a large patio that overlooked the exotic Melaka Straits. It was a demi-paradise.

Kent studied his pale blue boxer shorts in the full-length mirror and wondered how Miss Hard-to-get was going to overcome her apparent prudishness.

They met on the patio.

Bedah wore a bright orange towel wrapped just below her armpits. It stopped three inches above her knees. Kent stared in admiration. He wondered what she had on underneath. Nothing? An evening swim in the tea-warm water in the nude? *Oh, Father Christmas – I promise I'll never ask for anything else!* His groin joined his mind in speculation and he turned quickly towards the rough steps leading down to the gentle white breakers that crept up over the white sand before filtering with an apologetic whoosh back to Sumatra.

'Stop staring at me!' Bedah glared across the sand, now a silver carpet under the soft glow of the thin evening moon. 'Go and swim – and stop showing off your fancy underwear!'

'Talking about fancy underwear . . .' he began. *Oh Christ! She's not going to swim with that bloody towel round her?*

'Go away!'

He swam out a hundred yards and turned round. She was still standing on the edge of the water. No towel. She wore a brassière, white and crisp against her body, and the briefest of tiny briefs. The soft light confirmed what he already knew; she was beautiful. Five feet nothing of cream and coffee, she was perfection in velvet.

She plunged into the sea head first, regardless of what it was going to do to her hair, and swam in a strong overarm crawl towards Sumatra. Kent followed her until they were both out of their depth. Then she turned, shook the water from her face, laughed, and clung to him for support. Their bodies slithered together. 'Aren't you glad you came, David Kent?' It had to be deliberate. Treading water he took her in his arms and lay back, bringing her almost out of the water so that she lay on top of him. He kissed her. She didn't object, not at first, then she tried to break away and her head went under. She gasped and choked but he held her close to him. No words, and then his mouth found hers again – wet, salty, gasping, breathless, open . . . She stopped struggling, became limp and her tongue darted into his mouth and stayed there. It was half an inch further than they'd got last night, so it couldn't have been the after-shave. A prick-teaser?

No!

She wriggled as if in agony and they both went under. Their mouths separated as they surfaced and gasped for air, then locked together again and Kent put his hand inside her tiny pants and began to remove them. She didn't help him. It was awkward. He searched for the seabed – something solid – with his foot, but found only water. He kicked hard to keep himself afloat. She didn't help. She took her mouth away for a second and laughed – little bells tinkling; a little girl amused – but it stopped when he turned her around, still on top of him, and slipped the briefs over her thighs until he could reach no lower . . .

'Bedah!'

She wriggled half-heartedly but her thighs remained glued together. This was no bloody good! He straightened up, grabbed the briefs, held on to them and tipped her upside down, slipping them down her legs and over her feet as she disappeared under the water. She came to the surface with a scream – not angry, a laughing scream as he grabbed her again – and then a high-pitched giggle.

'Don't lose them!' She snatched the tiny panties off him and clutched them in one hand. Her back was to him, her bottom grinding into his front, and his penis – rock hard – thrust itself between her struggling thighs as she tried to keep afloat. She reached down and behind her, took the whole length in her hand and pushed it away. She was no longer giggling. She turned round to face him and put her hands on his shoulders. 'No, David, please!' She choked again as her mouth filled with sea water and she spat it out, looking into his face. 'David – not here . . . Not in the water!' She gasped as if in agony. 'Wait . . . Upstairs . . .' But it was too late. He was inside her.

The water was velvet; it wrapped itself around them like a warm blanket. Kent swam on his back, every so often kissing Bedah's wet lips until he found his depth. With a grunt of relief he placed both feet gratefully on the soft sand. It was still more than a foot too deep for Bedah.

She hung on to him. 'I didn't enjoy that,' she murmured into his neck. 'I swallowed too much water . . .'

'It won't happen next time.'

'Huh!'

But next time she kept her head above the water and her lips covered Kent's face and neck, drinking the salty moisture and depositing it in his open, gasping mouth as she cried louder and louder. Refusing to stay still, and with her voice echoing over the flat deserted sea, she fought him every inch of the way.

'More!'

'Can't!'

But she wasn't embarrassed. She squirmed against him merci-lessly until finally, with a gurgled laugh, she gently pushed his spent penis out of her and swam away until she could stand up. Kent didn't try to stop her.

After a few moments he floated on his back alongside her and ran his hands over her body. She had adjusted her brassière and replaced the brief panties. Her two hands rested between her legs, one on top of the other as if protecting herself from further assault. He stroked her hand and left it there. 'What was wrong with last night?'

'Nothing. Last night I didn't feel like it.'

'And now?'

'I do.'

Simple. Logical. The female mind. Kent smiled to himself in the silver light.

'Besides, I didn't know you well enough. I do now!'

Goh Peng surveyed the bungalow from the cover of a bank of huge hibiscus bushes. After a moment the other two Chinese joined him. They came from different directions.

'The Englishman and the girl are in the water.'

The speaker was a squat, powerfully built pig of a man, his heavy muscular body, flat and toneless under the shadowless light, on the point of turning to fat. 'They're in two rooms on that side.' He jerked his oversized head at the right wing of the bungalow. 'Both – '

'Two rooms?' interrupted Goh Peng. He almost showed surprise.

The heavy Chinese grunted. He'd watched Kent and Bedah in the water, but all he'd seen were two heads close together; he'd heard nothing except Bedah's final exultant screams and they were too far away to mean anything to him. He had no imagination. 'Two rooms,' he repeated.

'Servants?' Goh Peng searched the face of the third man, a wiry, pointed-face Chinese with a cruel squint in his right eye. He was the driver. A Malaysian Chinese it said on his identity card. A fifteen-year member of Chinese Intelligence's Central External Liaison Department, it said on his record sheet in Peking's Central Records office, on permanent residential duty in West Malaysia. He wasn't the only one.

'Malay cook, wife, four children. Gardener, also Malay, lives alone in a hut at the far end.'

Goh Peng thought for a moment. 'OK. Put them all away.'

The driver made a sound in his throat; it sounded like a dry stick snapping.

Another pause. 'No. Lock them away. No noise. Meet me back here.'

The two men drifted away silently and Goh Peng squatted on his heels, staring blankly at the moon-soaked bungalow.

It didn't take very long. He heard nothing, but he knew his two companions were back. They were like shadows. There was no need to ask them how they'd got on. He crooked his finger and led them across the blind side of the bungalow, round the corner and through the open french windows of the patio into Kent's bedroom. He sent the squint-eyed man to the top of the steps that led down to the beach and stationed the other one in the shadows by the patio window. Kent had left his light on. Goh Peng went straight to the bed, lifted the pillow and picked up Kent's automatic. Without expression he removed the magazine, replaced the pistol and dropped the pillow back in place.

'Tay says the girl's coming up the steps,' the man at the window leaned round and whispered to Goh Peng.

'And the Englishman?'

'Only the girl.'

'Tell him to stay there and watch the man.' He moved across the patio and stepped into Bedah's room. 'You come with me. Stand there . . .'

The heavily built Chinese pressed himself against the curtained window and waited, his ear cocked towards the verandah and the top of the steps. It took only a few seconds. A frog croak came across the strip of open ground, then another.

'She comes,' he whispered.

Bedah and Kent swam for another half-hour. Again the tiny briefs were taken off and again they made love, this time slowly, with awareness, a deliberate gentleness by Kent. As they clung together and allowed the warm water to quieten their bodies, Bedah took her mouth from the side of his nose, bit him gently, and said, 'I'm hungry.'

'So am I – shall we go?'

'No.' She unwound from his body, doubled into the water to replace her briefs and straightened up with a gasping whoosh. 'I shall go – you wait here.'

'Why?'

'Surprise.'

'Tell me.'

'Then it won't be a surprise.' She draped the towel over her shoulders and took the steps up to the bungalow at a run. She stopped halfway, turned, and waved. Kent wasn't looking. He was lying on his back with his eyes closed. He was conserving his energy – it was going to be a long, heady night.

She walked the last few steps breathlessly but had recovered by the time she reached the patio. She unhooked the wet brassière and went through the open French window swinging it in her hand. She broke into a tuneless whistle; she felt slightly light-headed.

Goh Peng made no effort to hide. He sat on the edge of the bed, studying the contents of her bag spread out before him. He looked up casually as she came into the room. Her reactions were quick. A stifled gasp, she covered her breasts instinctively and made a darting turn for the window.

Then she saw pig-face.

He didn't give her a chance.

Without moving his position he wrapped his huge arms around her, crushed her to his chest and lifted her easily off the floor. She was as helpless as a baby. He'd left her no breath to scream with, but, again instinctively, she swung her foot up and backwards, aiming for his groin. She was being grasped and had her back to him. It was a forlorn attempt – desperate – instinctive. She missed but caught him on the knee. He felt it. He grunted an obscenity and loosened his grip, but before she could gain an advantage he grabbed both arms, picked her up again, and with a mighty swing threw her on to the thick-piled white carpet. The carpet took some of the force from the fall. She bounced and cried out then curled up on to her knees and shook her head to clear the mist. The respite was brief. The heavy Chinese allowed himself a fraction of a second to aim, then threw himself bodily on to her crouching figure.

Bedah's second scream was choked into the carpet as she flattened

126

under the enormous weight of the pig-faced Chinese. She couldn't breathe. She couldn't move a muscle. It was like lying under a dead elephant, her head smothered by his heaving chest. She panicked and tried to scream again but when she opened her mouth it filled with carpet. The black stodge thundered like a waterfall in her ears and she felt herself dying. Her body went limp and for a second the roaring water stilled and she heard, vaguely, a word in Chinese coming from across the room.

The word meant salvation. She felt the huge body, without any lessening of its weight, slither downwards away from her head. The Chinese grasped her wet hair, raised her face from the depths of the carpet and slid his other arm under her neck. His hand grasped the muscle of the arm holding the back of her head and tightened. She knew the grip. It was a death grip. She allowed her body to go limp. She was a fraction of an inch away from a broken neck.

Goh Peng watched from his position on the side of the bed without expression.

'Lift her head up,' he said in Mandarin. Then in English, 'You speak English, Inspector . . .' He glanced at the warrant card he'd taken from her bag. '. . . Bedah binte Ariffin?'

Her head was pulled back so that she could look the speaker in the face. But the heavy Chinese's arm remained lightly across her neck, making speech impossible. She closed her eyes and opened her mouth. Nothing came out.

'Allow her to speak,' said Goh Peng.

The arm relaxed, but only slightly. She couldn't think of anything intelligent to say – other than Who are you and what do you want? And, For God's sake get this gorilla off my back so that I can breathe . . . But she said nothing. She prayed that David would come – only not like a wild bull! Why had she told him to wait down there in the water for his surprise. . . ? There was a much bigger surprise up here. But, she blinked furiously, where was Sadan? Where were the others who were supposed to be looking after the bungalow? She stopped thinking and concentrated on trying to breathe with the dead weight on her back. The man on the bed was speaking again.

'It says police here. What branch are you?'

She said nothing.

Goh Peng nodded to the man on her back.

She felt his knee grind upwards between her thighs and her face was thrust into the carpet to muffle the scream that clawed out of her throat. She heard him say in Mandarin, 'She's one of that dog Wang's bitches – Special Operations Group. Chan Moi has marked her – and others. She should be killed.'

'Shut up!' snapped Goh Peng. But he was too late. Bedah managed to bite her lip. Chan Moi. Long legs, bedroom eyes and call me Nancy. It gave her a tiny moment of gratitude. That slip of the tongue signed Inspector Nancy's death warrant.

'What did you discover at Togom's village?' Goh Peng went back into English.

'Nothing,' she managed.

'Hurt her!'

She screamed in outrage into the carpet again and when pig-face pulled her head up she told Goh Peng exactly what had been said in the village. When she got to the photographs his expression changed.

'Where are they?'

'He has them.'

'The Englishman?' Goh Peng didn't wait for her reply. He went through the door into the other room, picked up Kent's bush shirt and went rapidly through the pockets. He found the pictures tucked into his wallet. Bedah was still spread-eagled under the Chinese when he returned. He knelt beside her head.

'Open your eyes.'

'She did, reluctantly.

He placed the pictures on the carpet in front of her. 'Who are the white men?' he asked.

'I don't know – neither does Kent.'

'Again,' he hissed to the man on her back.

She fainted.

When she came round Goh Peng asked her again. Again she said, 'I don't know.' It seemed to satisfy him. He didn't look at pig-face. There was nearly a look of satisfaction on his face when he picked up the pictures and replaced them in Kent's wallet. When he came back from Kent's bedroom Bedah's warder said, 'Tay reports the Englishman is on his way up.'

Goh Peng didn't panic. He stared into the ugly Chinese's flat face. 'You know what to do. He mustn't be killed.'

Pig-face got up but kept his knee in the small of Bedah's back. 'And this one?'

'Worry about the man. I'll look after her.' Goh Peng picked up Bedah's small automatic from among the debris on the bed and cocked it. He pointed it at her face. 'Stay where you are,' he hissed. 'Lie still and don't make a sound.'

Bedah did as she was told. Once the weight had been removed from her body she became conscious of being almost nude. But she didn't blush; she was beyond blushing. She brought her arms up to cover her naked breasts. She needn't have troubled on Goh Peng's behalf. He couldn't have given a damn. Goh Peng wasn't into half-naked Malay girls – not even pretty ones.

Kent was fed up swimming around in the sea, alone under a wishy-washy moon. He trod water for the umpteenth time and stared up at the bungalow on the hill. The lights of the two bedrooms glowed like the film set of a tropical romance and he zeroed in on them like a horny moth spotting its first candle of the season. He put his head down and, doing a fast crawl, headed for the deserted beach. He towelled himself dry and at a leisurely plod – in case the surprise was on its way down – mounted the steep steps. Near the top he paused briefly and listened. The only sound was the croaking of a bull-frog. Nothing else. He shook his head and then made his way across the grass strip to the patio. Absolute silence. *Strange!*

'Bedah!'

There was no response.

Louder. 'BEDAH!'

He opened the glass door to Bedah's bedroom.

'David!' Bedah was lying on the floor. He just had time to absorb her warning before the Chinese behind him exploded his doubled fists onto the back of his neck. It was a potentially lethal blow, but the Chinaman knew exactly what he was doing. Kent lurched forward and, not quite conscious, his eyes met those of Goh Peng, who was standing beside the dressing table. He blinked. He should have left it at that but he managed to drag his eyelids up again – and met the flat, disinterested look of the Third

Secretary at the London Embassy of the People's Republic of China. He heard, faintly, another cry from Bedah but then, behind his ear, came the second explosion, and he zoomed into a whirlpool, going faster and faster, until the speed threw him off into unbroken darkness.

Bedah's next scream was cut off by the fat Chinese's bare foot slamming into the back of her neck and grinding her face once more on the carpet. It wasn't for long. The battering she had been subjected to was having its effect. She began to cry. She couldn't help it; there was no way of preventing it. It was her turn again.

'Stand her up,' said Goh Peng, tonelessly.

Pig-face reached down, grabbed the back of her hair and straightened up. It was no effort. She came off the carpet like a rag doll and hung limply in his hand, her feet barely touching the ground.

Goh Peng turned his eyes away from Bedah and indicated to the third Chinese. 'Take that stool over there,' he pointed to the middle of the room, 'and kneel her.'

Bedah tried to comprehend. Her eyes were filled with tears and, interspersed with the sobs of pain, were the whimpers of a frightened child. She had no way of knowing why the two Chinese were forcing her to kneel. She complied meekly when they pressed her shoulders down on to the stool and offered no resistance when they eased her forward so that her head hung over the edge. She continued to sob – it made no difference. Fright had turned to terror and she didn't see Goh Peng walk across and stand behind her.

At a nod from him the man pressing down on her shoulders removed his hands and stood to one side. Bedah made no movement. It was as if she were paralysed. But she came to life again when she felt the small automatic touch the back of her neck. She knew what it was. She began to scream at the top of her voice as Goh Peng moved the automatic away by an inch. He straightened his arm and squeezed the trigger – just the one shot – then, without taking his eyes off the back of Bedah's head, he handed the gun to the man at his side. He continued staring, his eyes fractionally narrowing as Bedah began her dance of death, but otherwise his face was devoid of expression.

*

130

Kent awoke shivering. The place was in darkness, with only the moon's insubstantial light playing tricks with his imagination. How long had he been here? Where was he?

It all rushed back with a neck-jarring cascade of coloured flashes when he moved his head.

Christ!

Bedah. . . ?

His last recollection was of her lying on the floor . . . 'David!' He remembered her cry before the roof caved in on his head. What was she doing on the floor? The Chinese. . . ? He clenched his eyes tightly and the sparks cleared for a fraction of a blink, bringing back the vision that had etched on his retina before he'd died. The Chinese – last seen in a chauffeur's hat driving past the iron gates in Portland Place, London. *London?* But this was Malaysia – bloody Malaysia – Port Dickson . . . He decided to chance the flashes again and opened his eyes. Nothing had changed. The moon had moved a few inches and a sliver of brighter light now glanced across the floor.

Level with his eyes was a pair of legs.

He reached out and touched them. Smooth and hairless. He stroked upwards. A shapely little bottom – he knew that bottom – its flimsy nylon covering still damp with sea water. He raised his head and ignored the shaft of pain. *Bedah!* She was still there.

'Wake up, Bedah! Let's get out of here . . .'

There was no response.

He put his hand on her waist and shook her. 'Come on, Bedah, wake up . . .'

She didn't move.

He pulled himself on to his knees and elbows and flopped forward so that his face was level with her head. 'Bedah . . .' He put his hand on her wet head and turned her face towards him.

Her eyes were open.

'Bedah? Oh, Jesus!'

He took his hand away. It was wet, but not sea wet. He held it up to the light. It was black. It was sticky.

He crawled to the bedside, switched on the lamp and crawled back again. He didn't trust himself yet on his feet. He remained on his knees beside Bedah. She looked peaceful, but then didn't everybody when they were dead?

Kent felt slightly hysterical as he crawled round her and stared at the back of her head. They wouldn't have needed to warn her – she must have known what they were going to do. *Oh, Christ! The bastards!* The killer must have done a tour with the KGB's First Chief Directorate – Department V, the Assassination Bureau – it had all the hallmarks. They'd come up behind the helpless Bedah, and shot her at close range in the base of the head. A neat entry hole winked back at him and a small pool of thick blood had collected in the ridge of her neck. He could almost hear her whispering, 'Please don't hurt me . . .' Well they hadn't. She wouldn't have felt a thing.

He reached up to pull the cover off the bed and dropped it lightly over her. He hadn't even started to think why – that would come in a minute. First, though . . . He dragged himself wearily to his feet and shakily made his way to the room next door. He pushed the light switch. His room was undisturbed. He reached under the pillow and withdrew the automatic Wang had given him. It was too light. He turned it over and stared at the hollow grip.

'Fuck it!'

Swearing helped a bit. He changed his sopping underwear, pulled on his trousers and dug a clean shirt out of the holdall. Dressed, and dry, he felt less vulnerable, but it didn't matter now. Where the hell was everybody? It was too quiet everywhere. The bungalow was like a bloody morgue! He staggered into the bathroom and dunked his head in a bowl of cold water. It helped. He felt the back of his head – nothing broken. Whoever had hit him knew how to hit. He sat on the edge of the bed, clenching some life into his eyes, then picked up the telephone – and dropped it without dialling. He wasn't thinking. He went back to Bedah's room and rummaged among the things that had been emptied from her bag.

They'd taken her toy of an automatic – they'd probably used it to kill her – and all that was left was the usual rubbish that lived in the bottom of a woman's handbag; lipstick, make-up, keys, tissues, a card of pills with spaces indicating the days of the month, a bottle of paracetamol – everything for headaches and unwanted pregnancies, but nothing marked 'Chief Superintendent Wang Peng Soon's telephone number'. He looked up and scowled at the wall. And where the bloody hell were the staff who were supposed to be running this place? He looked down at the mound on the carpet and after a moment shook his head, partly in sorrow, partly in exasperation. Leave them where they were – dead or alive. No point in having half a dozen hysterical Malays jumping up and down and pointing accusing fingers at the *orang-puteh*, and screaming murder at anybody who'd listen.

His brain started working again. He looked up the telephone number of Police HQ, Bukit Aman, KL.

'Can you tell me how I can get hold of Chief Superintendent Wang Peng Soon, please?'

The pause was just long enough for the operator to glance at the list of restricted names. 'I'm sorry, there's no one of that name in the establishment. Who's calling please?'

Kent put the phone down.

He dialled the number again and spoke in Cantonese. 'May I be put through to Central Records, please?' The operator didn't recognise the voice. But he wasn't going to make it easy.

'Please speak *bahasa Malayu*.'

'No speak . . .'

'*Chakap* English?'

'Little.'

'Who do you want?'

'Want to talk to cousin – Inspector Chan Moi, Records Department.'

'She not there. Records closed. She gone home.'

'Home number, please?'

The operator was bored with the conversation too. 'Just a minute . . .' The minute lasted nearly three. 'Six-four-six-one-two.'

'KL?'

'*Yeh-la!*'

Jesus! Kent put his finger on the cradle, wiped the sweat from his ear and started all over again.

He recognised Nancy's voice immediately.

'Nancy?'

'Who's that?' Nancy's voice dripped with apprehension.

'David Kent – we met yesterday morning in your computer room. I came with Inspector Bedah . . .'

'I remember.' The apprehension was replaced by suspicion; her voice was dry and harsh. But she said nothing more.

Kent didn't give her time to settle down. 'Can you find Mr Wang Peng Soon's phone number for me, please?'

'It's not listed,' she said quickly. There was none of yesterday's cheeky fraternisation. She was being distinctly unhelpful.

'How do I get in touch with him?'

'You can't – not direct.' She paused, and seemed to relent. 'Take down this number. Leave your message. Mr Wang'll ring you back if he feels it's necessary. Where are you? Are you in trouble?'

Of course I'm in bloody trouble, you silly bitch! What d'you think I'm ringing you for?

'No, nothing serious, thank you Nancy – just routine. Goodbye.' He didn't wait for her response. His finger dropped across the cradle again but he didn't dial immediately. Why hadn't Nancy suggested he ask Bedah for Wang's telephone number? He stared at his reflection in the dressing-table mirror as if there, perhaps, was the answer. But all he saw was a face that looked like death. He could see his head resting on his shoulders, but it didn't feel as though it belonged there. It was thumping like a pneumatic hammer and threatened to pressure his eyeballs, already feeling as though they were working independently of each other, out of their sockets altogether. He stopped admiring himself to rummage among Bedah's things and found the little plastic barrel of paracetamol. He prised the lid off, worked three tablets into his hand and swallowed them dry. One stuck halfway down his throat so he helped dislodge it with a long swig from the decanter on Bedah's bedside table, then wiped the phone's earpiece again.

The voice that answered him was educated Malay. Female. Kent pulled a face at the death's-head. Wang must have a monopoly of sexy-voiced Malay policewomen. There was no small talk. She advised him to stay where he was, by the phone, and she'd get his message to Mr Wang who'd ring straight back – hopefully.

He did. Kent barely had time to pour himself a glass of water and fetch his cigarettes from the other room. He'd just lit one when the phone buzzed. He grabbed it. He felt like a man anxious not to wake his sleeping partner, only it didn't bother Bedah.

'What's the trouble, David?' Why did everybody automatically think he had trouble? He tried a sick smile at the death's-head but it came out as a grimace, a baring of teeth, and he gave it up,

134

allowing his features to drop back into a scowl as he concentrated on what Wang was saying. It wasn't difficult. Wang's voice was unhurried, unworried, and the fact that he was standing in a pool of warm water with nothing on but soap to show for his interrupted shower had no effect on his unflappable demeanour. He clicked his fingers and smiled at number-three wife, a slip of a nineteen-year-old doe-eyed beauty hovering by the door, to bring him a whisky, and told Kent to tell him about his problems.

As he listened his face lost some of its cherubic cheerfulness and when his drink appeared he took it like the survivor of a desert trek. He carried it from the silver tray to his lips in one motion and half the contents of the glass vanished down his throat before he answered Kent.

'Get out of there now, David. Don't hang around and don't leave anything of yours there. Come to KL – direct. Don't go to your hotel until I've had it disinfected. Leave Bedah as she is – I'll have a removal team down there in a couple of hours . . .' He glanced at the ornate clock on the wall to make sure he hadn't been over-optimistic, and, satisfied, emptied the rest of the glass of whisky down his throat.

Kent listened enviously to the gurgle. He was thirsty, but he didn't fancy any more water. 'What about the servants?'

'Don't worry about them. My people'll look into it. If they're dead they won't be bothered,' said Wang cynically – or it may have been philosophically; his voice carried the same even tone – 'and if they're alive they'll be so pleased to see my people that they'll do exactly as they're instructed.' He waggled his fingers for another drink. There was no delay; it was there waiting for him on the tray. 'But that's neither here nor there. Do you know the Campbell shopping centre?'

'I'll find it. Is it in KL?'

'Near the Odeon cinema. Put your car in the shopping-centre basement and walk through to the eating stalls. If I'm not there waiting, look for the stall named Yew Ah Tong.' Wang waited. Kent said nothing. 'Have you got that name?'

'Yew Ah Tong,' repeated Kent.

'Good. His fried *bee-hoon* is quite famous!'

Fried *bee-hoon* was the last thing on Kent's mind.

15

Kent had no appetite to test whether Wang was right about Yew Ah Tong's *bee-hoon* but he ordered a bowl for the sake of appearances.

The night was heavier and more humid than normal; it felt as though a storm was on its way, but nobody was particularly worried. There were a lot of people about, but no Wang Peng Soon – number-three wife must have kept him longer than he'd anticipated. Perhaps the whisky had slowed everything down; she was a quick learner.

Kent chose a table on the fringe of Yew Ah Tong's small area and stuck his cane chopsticks into his untouched *bee-hoon*. Still he didn't eat. He sat uncomfortably at the picnic-type wooden slatted table with his long legs tucked awkwardly underneath the seat. Ah Tong didn't apologise for the discomfort – there was no concession to being a European in this shop – but the noise and the lights and the mingled smells of outdoor Chinese cooking gave Kent a misplaced sense of security, and as nobody wanted to share his out-of-the-limelight table, he sat alone. It seemed as though the local Chinese were still reluctant to perform in the presence of the always unhealthy-looking white face.

He was three-quarters of the way down his second long glass of barely chilled Anchor beer when Wang slipped on to the wooden bench beside him. For a man of his affluent build he moved like a back-row ballet dancer. It wasn't fitness, more an attitude of self-preservation – Wang believed that the 'quick' in the 'quick and the dead' meant the fastest man stayed alive. Like most of the other Chinese around him, he wore a multi-coloured batik open-necked shirt, its tails hanging over black linen trousers. Wang hadn't come alone. His friends, inconspicuous young men without the half-asleep attitude of most of the other eaters, sat warily at tables within shooting distance of any threat to their master's peace of mind.

'Ah Tong used to work for me,' Wang said as he made himself

comfortable, 'so you can relax.' He didn't specify what sort of work Ah Tong had done, but, judging by the man's fifty-five-odd years and the far-away look in his eye as he stirred the spitting, steaming contents of the huge cast-iron wok, 'butcher' might not have been too far off the mark. Wang stared for a moment at Kent's untouched plate then nodded and smiled sadly. He understood. 'The *bee-hoon* not to your liking?' He didn't wait for a reply – he didn't want one – and he didn't join him, tucking in instead into a bowl of boiling-hot thin chicken soup. He wasn't hungry, he was simply being sociable; but no beer. With Wang beer sat in the wrong place and excited an easily excitable hiatus hernia. But Ah Tong had the cure. Unasked he set a small tumbler of dark gold liquid beside Wang's bowl. Mr Hennessy would have had no trouble in recognising it. Neither did Wang, and as he sipped from the glass he listened attentively to Kent's story.

He had his priorities right. He held his hand out for the photographs and, settling a pair of half-rimmed British NHS spectacles on the middle of his nose, tilted the pictures towards the light to study them from different angles. After a few moments he handed the pictures back to Kent.

'They didn't kill Bedah for those.'

Kent shrugged his shoulders. He agreed – otherwise what were they still doing in his pocket? He'd had plenty of time to think about it on his way from Port Dickson to KL. He stared at the images again, only looking up when Wang pointed his soup spoon at the print with the dead bandits and the group of killers, and said casually, 'The one on the extreme right's Fylough. I think you can take it that the other one is Kenning.'

Kent looked back at the pictures with renewed interest. The face was slightly fuzzy – poor film, too much sunlight, cheap camera – but it was all there.

'Who was he? I've heard his name, but he hasn't been a major player so far.'

Wang continued to slurp Ah Tong's soup. He didn't look up from his bowl. 'He and Kenning were a sort of unfunny comedy act. They built up an interesting reputation in the Chaah and Labis area of Johor during the "argument". Ran their own circus – undercover people, urban knock-off-units – a sort of close-circuit SAS-type organisation before the SAS had any organisation.

137

They did that sort of thing in addition to scouring the jungle for the shy comrades, the less adventurous Commies.'

At the mention of the SAS Kent's eyes narrowed. It might have been nothing, a Wang-type analogy, but it made a slightly elastic connection. 'Did you ever hear mention of a guy named Dean – an SAS corporal – running with these two at any time?' he asked cautiously.

Wang took another medicinal sip of Hennessy, compressed his lips over it, and thought for a few moments. 'Dean?' he repeated, then shook his head. 'Not at that time. No corporal – but I did know a Major Dean at Hereford when I did a refresher some years ago.'

It was no help. Coincidence. Kent dropped the Dean connection. 'Who's this?' He placed the picture of the man in the Sam Browne in front of Wang who lowered his eyes again and glanced briefly at it before coming back to admire the dregs in his glass.

'That's a very interesting bloke,' he pronounced. 'Jimmy Morgan. He was OSPC Segament. That meant, in those days, he commanded what was called a "Police Circle" – in his case an area about as big as Surrey. Very good at his job. He was tipped for high office – a future Commissioner no less.'

'So what happened to him? Obviously he didn't make it.'

'Right. He left the police.' Wang almost touched the side of his nose, but thought better of it. 'Went into MI6.'

Kent raised his eyebrows. 'A bit sudden? Would this have been about 1953?'

Wang smiled. His funeral fund caught the light and glistened like a jeweller's shop window on a wet winter's evening. But he didn't reply. The silence didn't last very long.

'Morgan suddenly appeared in Hong Kong – I heard.' Wang added the last two words in response to Kent's sceptical stare. 'And before you ask, I've no idea what it was that sent him rushing off to pastures new, as you say in England!'

If Wang thought his knowledge of English sayings was going to deter Kent he was wrong. But he already knew that. 'And you're going to ask me if I know where he is now?'

Kent managed a smile.

'Like I said,' Wang answered the question without waiting for it to be asked, 'MI6 – still.'

'Surprise me,' invited Kent.

The gold in Wang's mouth flashed again, the good white ones remaining coyly unobtrusive. 'C,' he responded.

'Beg your pardon?'

'Head of Service – C – Chief of SIS.'

Kent stared back at Wang's tooth for several seconds then picked up his glass from the table and drained the last quarter of an inch from it. 'Can I change the subject?'

'Be my guest.'

'What about Bedah?'

Wang's blank expression didn't change. 'It'll have to be a whisper job. We'll fill up the holes and make it a quiet accident . . . You just can't trust a female to clean a weapon without blowing her nose off!'

'Is that it?'

Wang didn't make excuses. 'I can't afford to have Europeans or Chinese involved in the publicity of a Special Branch officer getting herself killed. Accidents happen all the time.'

Kent continued staring into the Chinese man's face. There was nothing he could add. Wang had closed Bedah's file. But there were still the odds and ends. Wang's eyes, hardly visible in the narrowed slits in his face, studied Kent closely. 'You tell me. Why would they kill the child, unless she heard something she shouldn't have heard? Or saw something . . .' He paused for Kent to say something. He was no fool was Wang.

'Jesus!' hissed Kent. 'Saw something . . .' He had a mental flash like the flicker of an image on a TV screen. 'Goh Peng.' He grimaced as this association brought Bedah's warning cry back again, and the blinding crack on the back of his neck. He unconsciously touched the spot with his fingers. It was still spongy – and very sore.

'Who's he?' asked Wang patiently.

'Third Secretary, Chinese Embassy, London. I thought I caught a glimpse of him just before the light went out.'

'But you're not sure?'

'It was a flash – an image.'

'And at that speed we all look alike!' The voice was smiling but Wang's face was flat and expressionless. 'It can be checked with London to see if your Goh Peng is on attachment to KL, or on

139

holiday. I'll have a word with Immigration. I wonder what he's doing here? Following you, obviously, but . . .' Wang's slits parted and his eyes peeped out admonishingly. '. . . you would have noticed, wouldn't you? You'd have noticed any activity behind you in London before you came here?'

Kent stared back at Wang's unsmiling features. He couldn't keep the look of guilt from his eyes. He hadn't got the foggiest bloody idea! He hadn't looked; he hadn't once turned round . . . *Christ Almighty! Complacency? You stupid bastard, Kent! We were watching them – why the bloody hell did we assume they hadn't turned the queue? We? Me! You stupid, irresponsible bastard!*

Wang helped him off the grating. 'It's not serious – it doesn't matter, now that we know.'

Doesn't matter? Kent wasn't finished with himself yet. *Of course it isn't serious! Just a nasty bullet hole in the back of the head for a lovely, happy nymph who didn't like doing it in the sea because she swallowed too much water, who wanted to do it properly in a darkened bedroom with the bed soft and springy and the sheets nicely rumpled. No, Mr Wang, not serious at all . . .*

'You got to me through Inspector Chan Moi at Police Registry?' Wang carried on without worrying about Kent's conscience. He didn't wait for the Englishman to reply. 'Didn't Bedah give you my contact number?'

'No.'

'Did you mention to Chan Moi that Bedah had been killed?'

'No. Are you thinking the same thing that I'm thinking?'

Wang waggled his fingers at Ah Tong and showed him his empty glass. 'D'you want one of these, David? You look as though it would do you a lot more good than that.' He jerked his chin at the empty beer flute and, without waiting for Kent's acknowledgement, stuck out two fingers like a snake's fangs at Ah Tong.

'What are you thinking?'

Kent was waiting for him. 'That it was a bit peculiar for Inspector Chan Moi not to ask why Bedah couldn't contact you for me.'

Wang lowered his head almost level with the tabletop and studied the two glasses Ah Tong had brought. He looked as though he were making sure that one hadn't got a little bit more in it than the other. Satisfied, he sent a glass sliding across the slatted top to Kent, then picked up the other and carried it to his lips. But he didn't drink from it.

'Somebody had to direct your Chinese friends to Port Dickson. They obviously followed you from KL, but they knew where you were going – they knew you were going to pay a visit to *inche* Togom, so they didn't have to follow you in the true sense of the word. If they had, Bedah would have spotted them, she's good at that, she knows – knew . . .' He corrected himself and took the overdue sip from his glass. '. . . that game too well. But she wouldn't have expected a follower from Johor – that's why she allowed herself to relax.' He sipped again, delicately. 'I'm going to have to have a little chat with Inspector Chan Moi.' It sounded as if Nancy Chan was in for an early bath, but that was all Wang was prepared to commit himself to. He changed the subject: 'Your stuff has been moved out of the Equatorial. They probably had already made you there, but it's no big deal. I've put you in the Hilton – flashy, as I said the other day, but secure – a bit more like a beehive, with all the bees wearing different strips!' Wang laughed mirthlessly. 'I can look after you there. We can spot a watcher a mile away. But,' Wang looked intently into Kent's face, 'there's not an awful lot for you to do here now, is there? I think you're going to have to go back and talk to Mr C, Jimmy Morgan, and see if he can help you with your missing links. And, of course, the interesting Mr Fylough. He must be around somewhere, waiting to enlighten you on our strange Chinese amputation customs!'

Kent studied Wang's broad smile with a blank expression. Wang didn't mind. He smothered the glow from his tooth with a mouthful of brandy and added, 'At least you haven't wasted your time with us. Togom, it seems, earlier pointed the Chinese in the right direction and now he's done the same for you. Fylough'll tell you what they got up to on that operation – you'll probably find all your new friends gathered in his front room discussing it over glasses of sweet sherry.'

Kent didn't share Wang's humour. He still didn't smile, but instead shrugged his shoulders noncommittally. It was all catching up, and he was feeling desperately tired. It showed. Wang studied him sympathetically.

'Go and get a good night's sleep, David,' he said at length. 'Your stuff's all in the Hilton, room 382. Give me the keys to the car – I'll have it put away. It's probably logged and distributed by now so it'll have to change colour and number. Not to worry. We'll get you a taxi. But, one thing, David . . .'

Kent emptied his glass of brandy with a swig. It did him no end of good. He stared at Wang. 'What's that?'

'What did you say the name of that policeman in Pontian was?'

'Abidin. Inspector.'

'Abidin?'

'That's right – why?'

Wang finished his drink and stood up. 'Nothing for you to worry about.' He waggled his finger at one of the young men. 'Get Mr Kent a taxi. And David – have a good night's sleep. I'll leave a message for you if anything crops up. Good night.'

Kent stopped the taxi, paid him off at the foot of the slope leading to the hotel entrance and walked the rest of the way. In the distance he could hear, vaguely, the muffled racket of the canned music from the disco. Somebody must have opened the door and stepped out to clear the disturbed wax from his ears. He carried on walking and blanked out the vision of Bedah, excited, eager and cheeky, throwing herself into the action like a coffee-coloured Olga Korbut. It was a difficult vision to erase.

He collected his key and took the lift to the top floor. He'd been there before. Then it had been clinical: now it was therapeutic. He stopped at the bar, drank a large brandy and soda and carried another with him into the dimly lit massage chamber. Nothing worked. The girl's skimpy undress left him unmoved; her hands and fingers did nothing for him. He allowed her to bathe him and tipped her handsomely. The brandy and soda went into the bath water, untouched. He went to his room, undressed and lay on the bed in the dark, watching the pictures flash across his brain. It wasn't, somehow, how the night was supposed to have ended.

Wang dropped into his 'shop' on the way home. He picked up the phone. In London it was 5 p.m.

'Hello, Woody,' he said.

'How's it going?' asked Evelyn Woodhouse.

142

'Like clockwork,' answered Wang. 'I think he knows who he's looking for now; I think you'd better ask him to come home.'

'Fair enough. What about Fylough's person? Can you drop her in his lap?'

'Leave it up to me.'

'OK. Thanks.'

'It's a pleasure, Woody.'

16

Kent woke up at half-past ten the next morning with another splitting headache.

He breakfasted in his room on half a pint of fresh, slightly chilled mango juice, a pint of coffee and two servings of paracetamol.

The headache survived but he felt a lot better. He finished off the coffee, lit his first cigarette of the day, then dragged the telephone to the edge of the table and asked for an outside line.

He dialled, blew a stream of smoke at the ceiling and waited.

It rang for ages.

'Mithers-Wayne,' said a sleepy voice at length.

'Dickie? It's David Kent.'

'Where are you?'

'Kuala Lumpur.'

'Do you know what bloody time it is?'

Kent glanced at his wrist. 'Quarter-past eleven.'

'It's three-a-bloody-clock – in the bloody morning! It's pissing down with rain and I was fast asleep. It'd better be bloody vital.' Mithers-Wayne was now wide awake. 'What the bloody hell d'you want that can't wait until morning?'

Kent emptied the last of the coffee into his cup, crushed out his cigarette and lit another one. The line was crisp and clear; apart from the time lag, Mithers-Wayne could have been in the room next door. 'Listen. When you wake up ring Portland Place and ask to speak to Goh Peng. Don't take no for an answer. Make them say if he's not there – tell them it's an official request. If he's not in residence get them to – '

Mithers-Wayne's interruption was well under way when it arrived in Kent's ear. '. . . need to go through all that. He's not here. He's gone on his holidays. Didn't you get the message?'

'What message?'

'He followed you out of the country. Went to Malaysia. False passport, false nose – the lot! But they rumbled him. Immigration spotted him and gave him an "S" – you know, a hard look and a nod to the resident SB. It came up on a routine clip. The duty officer knew I was interested in Chinks and slipped a note under my saucer.'

'You mentioned a message?'

'I rang your head clown and told him to let you know you had company, and who the company was . . .' There was a pause – about three pounds' worth – and then: 'He didn't tell you?'

'No. But thanks, Dickie. You can go back to sleep now – goodnight!' He dropped the phone back on to its rest without waiting for Mithers-Wayne's response.

That Woodhouse hadn't passed on Mithers-Wayne's warning came as no real surprise. Maybe he hadn't thought it important. Bedah might have taken a different view. Kent lit his third cigarette and blew a stream of smoke across the table. There was a bitter taste in his mouth. He studied the end of the cigarette. It wasn't that.

The decision was made. It wasn't a difficult one. There was no point in staying any longer in Malaysia. The visit to Corporal Togom had moved the curtain, but only slightly – not enough to explain the three deaths in the UK. But he had a couple of names, Fylough for one – he'd know what it was all about if he still had a tongue that moved and a couple of hands on the end of his arms to wave in the air as he described what had drawn them all together – and what had split them up so suddenly thirty years earlier . . . And not to forget the big tick against Morgan's name – Mr MI6 himself! How did one get to sit in his lap and start tweaking the memory glands? What was it that had sent him rushing away from the top job in the Malayan Police to an indeterminate future with the Secret Service, and in Hong Kong, of all places? Kent rocked the chair back on two legs and stared at the ceiling; it was clean and pure – no stains, and no help. The crackling of the telephone saved him from forcing any sort of conclusion.

'David?' It was Wang. 'Didn't think I'd catch you in – lovely sunny day like this! I'm sending a car to pick you up, it should be there in, say, fifteen minutes. I've got something interesting to show you.' He put down the receiver without waiting for Kent's agreement. Kent hadn't said a word from start to finish – not even 'Hello'.

*

Wang met him with what, to Kent, was his usual flat-faced smile. The burial fund glistened under its earlier buffing with Colgate fluoride but the eyes were barely visible behind their slits.

'Bring Mr Kent a cup of coffee,' he said to the messenger. 'And another one for me.'

'No thanks,' declined Kent quickly. He was awash with Hilton coffee. Wang's warm, shop-made liquid treacle would have made hard work finding a resting place anywhere in Kent's system.

'Just one for me, then.' Wang wasn't put out. 'Come and see what arrived in the small hours.'

He allowed his hand to rest on Kent's back as he guided him through the door on the other side of the room and along a narrow, windowless corridor. A young Chinese with his shirt-sleeves rolled up and wearing a striped tie stood to one side of another solid-looking door. He wore a lightweight shoulder harness and from under his arm a 9 mm Browning peeped coyly out of its leather pouch when he moved to let them through.

The room was in darkness and completely bare – no furniture, no windows, no sharp edges, nothing. The single light buried somewhere in the ceiling was only switched on when Wang and Kent entered.

But the room wasn't empty.

In one of its corners crouched a man, a heavy man, muscular but turning to fat. Bedah would have recognised him.

He squatted on his haunches with his body jammed hard into the wall, as if somehow there was security in having his back protected. He was completely naked. His head was bowed and, by the way he clutched his knees to his chest he seemed at first glance to be suffering from a severe stomach disorder. A thin dribble of pink-mottled liquid had collected in a small puddle just behind his feet, where it had trickled, uncontrollably, to settle in a shallow depression in the concrete floor. He seemed to be studying it. He didn't look up.

'His name used to be Lau Boon,' said Wang, looking at the crouched figure as if it were a garden gnome. 'At least that's what he introduced himself as.'

'Why "used to be"?' asked Kent naïvely. 'What's his name now?'

'He hasn't got one,' replied Wang. 'He's only a number in the ledger. He's dead.' There was no expression on Wang's face. It was a fact; he wasn't offering anything to Kent, or to the Chinese clutching his stomach. 'He came from China to live with us – so he says. Stand up, dead man!' he snapped in Mandarin, and watched Kent's face as the man slowly uncurled and pulled himself painfully to his feet. He couldn't quite make the upright position and stopped halfway, pressing his bottom into the wall to hold himself steady. He looked into Wang's face, a look of intense pain, while his arms still encircled his stomach as if he were holding it all in place.

A gentle scraping on the door distracted them for a moment and Wang opened it to accept a thick cup of sweet coffee. He sipped it critically as he stared at his prisoner. He seemed more interested in the sweetness of the liquid than in the health of the dying man.

'What's he done?' asked Kent. He kept his features set, unconcerned, disinterested. His voice sounded hollow. The only other sound in the tiny room was the contented slurping of coffee as Wang worked his way down the cup.

'I'm surprised you don't recognise him,' answered Wang without the slightest suggestion of sarcasm. 'Look at me, shit-head!' he snapped at the man, and then looked askance at Kent. Kent raised his eyebrows but didn't take his eyes off the man in the corner.

The Chinese man's face was untouched, but the yellowy-grey complexion was not natural. It came from deep down somewhere, from some death-like, knife-cutting agony, as if his insides had been dragged out through his belly button and threaded back in through his anus. He kept his eyes closed. But he could hear what was being said, and understood.

'He was following you all day yesterday. He went down to Johor and then followed you to Port Dickson. He was one of the team that killed Bedah.'

Kent studied the man with interest. It was all going to come out in a minute but for the moment he couldn't for the life of him work out how Wang, in the passage of a few hours – sleeping hours – had uncovered a trail, found the team, and heard the man's confession. With difficulty he kept everything on Wang's placid, unexcited level.

'What's the matter with him now?' he asked.

'Something he ate.' Wang finished his coffee, opened the door behind him and passed the empty cup through. 'We're going to put a stomach pump on him in a minute. He got only so far with his autobiography before he ran out of words.'

'How did he find his way here?'

The question pleased Wang. 'The policeman you met in Pontian, Abidin, followed you out of Togom's kampong in his Land Rover. When you turned left for Muar he went in the other direction for Pontian. Just up the road from the turn-off he saw a car parked in a lay-by – it was his . . .' Wang jerked his chin at the man propped against the wall. 'Abidin couldn't see the occupants – smoked-glass windows and all that sort of thing – but as he looked over his shoulder out of curiosity, he saw the car pull out and cruise along in your direction. He took its number as a matter of course. I spoke to him on the telephone after I left you last night to see if he had anything to offer on why Bedah should have been killed. He'd no idea but he mentioned this car . . .' Wang stopped talking and watched the sick Chinese who, unable to hold his position against the wall any longer, slid slowly down to the floor in an uncomfortable crouch. He squatted in the stream of pink water which increased in volume as he struggled to maintain his balance. Wang shook his head regretfully. 'Let's go to my office. If you've anything to ask this person we'll write it down and leave it for the surgeon to deal with.'

'Surgeon?' queried Kent. He allowed himself to be led through the door and out into the corridor. He noticed the light go out, leaving the room in pitch-darkness as the door hissed shut behind them. The Chinaman probably welcomed the black solitude.

Wang took up Kent's question as they moved along the corridor. 'A doctor,' he said, 'bona fide – awarded his stethoscope in London, in one of those excellent teaching hospitals you specialise in over there. Much more efficient than us old-fashioned boxers. They've got the art of asking questions down to a razor-blade. You can't use force on the modern terrorist . . .' There was a touch of sadness in his voice. '. . . it's the urban variety who're the dangerous buggers, always have been. I put it down to too much education. They can stand being screwed because they think it'll all come right in the end – they've read their history books. Nowadays it all has to be done delicately – the pain has to be

148

inserted without any of the pleasure. The guy we've just left could probably tell you more about that than I could. Still it won't make any difference. He'll die, of course, but he'll tell us everything before he goes.' Wang opened the door to his office and stared at the sunshine that burned its way through the narrow window only to lose the battle against the silently efficient air-conditioning system.

'But going back again to your question. The car was in his name. He's quite a useful contact really. Chinese Intelligence, you know.'

Wang knew Kent didn't know, and didn't enlighten him any further. He didn't tell Kent that he owed him a favour for leading him to a major Chinese cell operating fairly efficiently within the Malaysian capital. It was already being unravelled and watched with great interest. Wang was more than content with the harvest. He was almost content with the attrition rate; one dead female Malay inspector, Bedah binte Ariffin = a complete foreign Intelligence network.

'What about Goh Peng?' asked Kent.

'He didn't seem to know very much about him,' replied Wang. 'He was following orders.'

'Whose?'

'The head market manager's – the guy with the gut ache's leader. Who, incidentally, is the manager of the Chan Toh Wen Bank. Your man Goh Peng has gone to ground. He'll be out of KL when he tries for the man in the cupboard and discovers he's gone up in flames! No bad deal. It wouldn't do for a Chinese diplomat on holiday, even one pretending to be someone else, to be roped in on an espionage deal. We'll have to tread very carefully with him.' He gave Kent the impression that if Goh Peng wanted to ride out to Subang on the back of a Chinese dragon he, Wang, wouldn't be all that put out. Wang worked on the assumption that London had broader shoulders than KL for an espionage scandal. 'There were three of them,' said Wang on a change of tack. 'The one that we're looking after at the moment was the muscleman, the guy responsible for the bruises on Bedah's neck, her back and her thighs. We had another one here this morning – a different kettle of fish. Nasty little squint-eyed bugger. We offered him breakfast but he had no stomach for it.' Wang didn't smile.

'Unfortunately he couldn't stay. Pity – we'd almost cured his squint by the time he decided to leave.'

Kent raised his eyebrows; nothing seemed to be the best thing to say.

'He slipped away while we weren't looking! One minute we were chatting about what they'd done to Bedah and the next minute he developed a nasty cough and keeled over. But I think at that stage he quite welcomed the trip.'

Wang spoke without emotion; he could have been talking about the stuffing coming out of his daughter's broken teddy bear. Kent knew the sort. People like Wang Peng Soon bore grudges – and bore them for ever. Wang would want a fair return for a wrong; he wouldn't lose any sleep about the method of repayment. He'd been in the game far too long to give too much thought to a death here and there.

'But going back to what I was saying about the nearly late Lau Boon,' continued Wang. 'When he's been sick and had his tummy emptied of evil thoughts he'll be able to talk to us again. Is there anything you'd like to ask of him?'

Kent nodded. He had a good idea what the answer was going to be before he posed the question. 'In the Port Dickson bungalow Goh Peng went through my pockets. He found the gun you gave me and lifted the magazine from it. Will you ask why he didn't find the photographs while he was poking around – he had plenty of time.'

Wang didn't look smug – or thoughtful. 'He's already been asked. And he obliged. Goh Peng did find them. He showed them to Bedah and asked if she knew who the Englishmen were. When she said she didn't know he put them back in your wallet.' Wang pursed his lips. It was the first time Kent had seen him show anything other than cold analysis. 'After, of course, he'd made sure she was telling the truth.'

Kent stared back at him. 'Why did they kill her?'

'The fat one said Goh Peng put the bullet in. He did it, he said, to preserve Chan Moi – your Nancy. They let slip her name in front of Bedah – among other things.'

'Bedah spoke Mandarin?'

'Our Bedah was a clever little girl. I've had a word with Nancy. I felt it necessary to find out why she wasn't curious about Bedah when you rang her. And I was right about her – even before pig-face signed her going-away chit!'

Kent was in no mood to smile. 'A local girl working for Chinese illegals. What did they have on her?'

'You had this problem in Hong Kong?' Wang's interest was genuine.

Kent nodded. 'Relatives?'

Wang understood. 'It's amazing how the Chinese family ties the Orient together. Uncle twice removed, aunt's cousin's brother, they're all blood, they all sit at the top table at the wedding, but that wasn't Chan Moi's problem. I think she was ready for turning. She was getting herself looked after by the one with the squint; they'd picked her out, it was arranged – stupid bitch!' Wang hawked in his throat but nothing appeared. If he'd been outside he might have found something to spit, it was his way of showing contempt for stupidity.

'And I hope, David, you're not going to give me any of that biscuits and tea stuff about how long will she be locked up!'

Kent didn't smile. He'd been among the Chinese long enough to know what Wang was saying. Nancy wasn't going to be locked up anyway. She was gone. She didn't exist any more. He didn't ask. But out of curiosity he said casually, 'Your friend in the monk's cell . . . Wouldn't you consider him for exchange?'

'Exchange for what?' Wang flopped into his chair and pulled a packet of Rothmans out of a drawer. He took one out but didn't light it. He slid the packet across the table at Kent. 'They haven't got anybody to exchange. They don't take prisoners. Any of our people who make the big mistake get the chop. We never hear of them again. Their pips are squeezed and then they're put through the mincer.'

'You mean like you're doing to that poor bugger in there?' Kent leaned across the table and held a match under Wang's cigarette.

Wang didn't reply, but instead drew heavily on the cigarette and then said, 'Have dinner with me tonight?' He blew smoke at the ceiling and didn't look at Kent. 'A sort of farewell party – just you and me.'

'Who said I'm leaving?'

'Woody phoned me. He doesn't think there's anything more you can do here.'

'Funny – he hasn't told me yet.'

'He will. I'll pick you up tonight. You can buy me a drink in the Hilton and I'll pay for dinner.'

Kent lit his own cigarette. 'I'll look forward to it,' he said. But there was no enthusiasm in his voice.

17

The Coq d'Or restaurant in Jalan Ampang was a magnificent old heap of a building. A leftover from colonial days, it was a nineteenth-century Chinese towkay's town house that had been turned into a restaurant in the early sixties for the then large European – mainly rubber planters – community. It was popular then; it was even more popular now with prosperous Malaysians. But they were mainly Chinese – very rich ones. The Coq d'Or hadn't changed with the times. The food was exceptional, the service impeccable – it was that sort of restaurant and you paid for what you got.

Wang sat Kent on the open verandah. Here one could feel the Orient – the slightly sticky, scent-laden air that hung, breathless, on a cloudless night sky. But it wasn't for the feel of the Orient that Wang had chosen this spot to drink his second and third whiskies. From here he could survey the expanse of car park, the massive concrete pillars surmounted by Chinese lions stonily guarding the entrance, and the busy, never-ending stream of traffic on the Ampang Road. He could see, without difficulty, his modest, unobtrusive car, its driver curled up on the back seat, overlooked by another modest, unobtrusive car with three young Chinese taking turns to leave their well-used H & K machine-pistols on the seat and make for the nearest *mah-mee* stall. Wang had a thing about survival. The thing worked.

He could also view everybody who mounted the steps to the restaurant.

But Kent saw her first.

Lighting a cigarette he leaned across the table and dropped the spent match into the large decorated Chinese porcelain ashtray. He turned his head to study her as she stood at the top of the stone stairs and waited for someone to come and claim her.

She was tall, with dark hair that even from a distance, and by the dim light of the candle-lit restaurant, emphasised her startlingly lovely pale features. She was not a sun worshipper. She wore a cascading, bright orange chiffon dress, and she was smiling. She looked, to Kent, like an advertisement for something very nice.

'Hilary West,' said Wang, staring over the top of his half-moon glasses. He didn't miss much. 'Junior partner in a firm of KL solicitors; has a red ID card . . .'

'What does that mean?'

'She's a permanent resident but not a citizen – she can be thrown out on her ear if she misbehaves or upsets the establishment. She's been here for about six years, apart from a year's sabbatical, so she's not likely to do anything silly now . . .'

Kent couldn't take his eyes off her. 'Do you keep hooks on every stranger in the country?'

'Only the pretty ones. Let's go and eat.'

Kent had no appetite. Usually resilient, he'd taken Bedah's death in his stride; regret and sadness were shallow emotions of the moment that could be sandbagged out of existence. It took an effort, but yesterday was gone – this was today. His lack of appetite was nothing to do with sadness. It was something else, and she was sitting on the other side of the room enjoying her dinner. There was nothing wrong with Hilary West's appetite.

Nor with Wang's. After a huge helping of cherry gateau he sat back in his chair and took the glasses off his nose. He looked like a contented, overfed Buddha. He was waiting for David Kent to reopen the negotiations. He knew what was coming; he was only surprised Kent had held off for so long.

'How does one get to meet her?'

'Who?'

Kent swivelled his eyes across the room again and nodded.

Wang didn't need to look. His eyes vanished into a smile. 'You could commit a crime, get locked up, and ask for her to come and sort things out for you – an expensive way of getting to shake a girl's hand, which is probably about all you would get. Hilary West is not an easy girl to make friends with. She's too attractive – she's spoilt for choice. A lot have tried their luck with her, but I don't think many have listened to the tok-tok bird from her bedroom window!'

Kent didn't want to hear about nocturnal birds and bedroom windows; his interest went much deeper. He shrugged noncommittally. How do you tell a middle-aged Chinese cynic that you think you've fallen in love with a vision? Talking about her seemed to be the next best thing.

'Does she have any family living here?'

'Her husband . . .'

Husband? Oh, Jesus – no!

'. . . was in the British High Commission. He was transferred about four years ago – South America somewhere. She didn't go with him. It was probably all over then – they don't last very long, marriages nowadays, do they? I think this one lasted a couple of years at the most. They're divorced now.'

'Is West her maiden name?'

'No, his. I'm not sure what name she was born with.' Wang's eyes vanished again. 'You sure you want to meet her?'

Kent said nothing.

'You see those two people at her table?'

Kent didn't need to look. Without taking his eyes off Wang he tipped his brandy glass up and emptied most of its contents down his throat.

'They're old friends of mine. When you were washing your hands I asked them all to come and have coffee with us on the verandah. Is that all right with you?'

She gave Kent a small firm hand and a similar sort of smile. She was even lovelier close up. But there was no excitement or pleasure in her manner. Perhaps that would come later.

First, however, Wang Peng Soon's Noël Coward dialogue. 'Would you like to dance, Hilary?' He didn't move from his seat or put his glass down. Hilary smiled her acceptance. Wang still didn't move. He smiled back. 'Would you mind if I delegate my young friend from England? He's got much more energy than I and he's a very good dancer. Knows all the new steps from London . . .' Kent winced. It could have been 1928. 'I envy him . . .' Kent caught his eye but didn't smile. What could she do?

The dance floor was about the size of a large dinner plate and the dance band a quartet of small Filipinos. The music was very good; soft, sexual, slow, and quiet; even the tropical fish in their tank beside the podium slumbered and seemed to enjoy the gentle sound.

155

So did Hilary. She snuggled up against him as if they were in a cold bed. It wasn't sexual, not for her, it was simply the way she danced the fox trot – standing still and moving her weight from one hip to the other. Kent wondered if she could feel the hard lump in his groin. If she did she didn't show it.

'Well,' she said softly without raising her face from his chest, 'am I to understand that you're here to give us all dancing lessons?'

So she had a sense of humour. Kent's mouth was almost in her ear; the Chanel she'd dabbed behind it was doing its job and made him feel like a gauche schoolboy with his first grown-up girl. But he kept the conversation as light and as silly as she seemed to want it and by the time the Filipinos had run out of breath he and she had sorted out the rest of the evening.

It was unnecessary.

Wang had done it for them.

'It's getting near my bedtime,' he said when they joined him on the verandah.

'And ours,' parroted the other two. It sounded as if they'd been primed from the same canister. 'Do you have transport, Hilary?'

'Oh, she'll be all right.' Wang took over again. 'David'll look after her, won't you David? You'll take Hilary home?'

Kent joined the game as the ball was being thumped around the court. 'If Hilary wants to be taken home. Do you want to be taken home, Hilary?' It was the first time he'd used her name. It fitted his tongue perfectly. She smiled and sat down. It seemed to answer the question. Kent said goodbye to Wang and his two friends and joined her. She stared at him across the table.

'What is your friend Wang playing at?' she said.

Kent had no time to tell her what his friend Wang was playing at. Who knew what Wang was playing at? Wang didn't even know himself – or did he? He was saved from having to shake his head by the appearance of the head waiter carrying an ice bucket covered with a white towel. He placed it on the table and whipped the towel away. A gold foil top peeped out of the bed of ice and water and he twirled it like a croupier spinning a roulette wheel. He didn't stop beaming as he withdrew the cork expertly, allowing only the most modest of gentle plops.

'Krug,' he announced proudly. 'The '75. Compliments of Mr Wang.' He poured a quantity in each glass, placed the bottle reverently back in its bucket and, still smiling, returned to his place at the corner of the bar.

Hilary's eyes hadn't moved from his face. Kent winced. She was going to spoil the champagne! But she didn't persist with the question – it seemed that the Krug '75 had removed thoughts of Wang from her mind and given her thoughts of a different kind. Kent picked up the wavelength as she sipped and enjoyed the classic champagne. She seemed to like the stuff; it said a lot for the company she kept. Kent bought another bottle. And another one.

She wasn't tight. Just very happy. And who wouldn't be after sharing £180 worth of champagne.

But Hilary's happiness was an illusion – it was make-believe, a game, and a dirty game at that, not for the queasy. They'd put David Kent into the water and dropped the pretty fly on to his nose – they were unprincipled bastards. What did that make her?

They were all in it: Wang, Peter, Jimmy Morgan, that oily bugger Woodhouse, and, of course, Hilary West. She smiled at Kent over the top of her champagne glass; under different circumstances she could have let herself go and it showed. She liked David Kent. It was a phenomenon that took her by surprise. He was not her ideal; he was too self-assured for her taste and he had that arrogance that came from too many conquests with too little effort on his part. That had been the first impression. But he had a kind face and his eyes were soft; there was a troubled mind behind them and under the veneer of arrogance was a man who, whilst trying to hide it, desperately wanted her to like him. She suspected that, like her, he too was experiencing a surprising sensation. But there was a difference – she was not in it for pleasure.

She'd gone into it with her eyes open. Every girl should have a father who knows the answer to a cruel marital mismatch. He'd warned her about West, and if anybody could detect a bastard it was another bastard. It wouldn't have surprised her if he'd been behind Paddy West's sudden departure to the plug-hole of ambition, the diplomatic arsehole named Guatemala. That's the sort of bastard Daddy was, and he had that sort of connection. But then he made things work – usually to his advantage. 'Let's drive this out of your system, darling. I know just the sort of thing to make you forget. Take a year off. Go and see this friend of mine who'll give you something interesting to do; something to take your mind off Irish boys . . .'

Something interesting . . . Another Daddy clone: 'Your father thinks you could hold down a little sinecure for us in Malaysia. You're law, aren't you? In a partnership? Couldn't be better. How's your Chinese?'

'Pardon?'

'Never mind, we'll sort it all out for you. First of all, how about going to school for four months? We've got a non-competitive place on the Army's 14th Int. course at Hereford. You'll meet some nice people there. Tough, but nice. Then we'd like you to go to China – the Ningbo Wuhan University – ostensibly to learn the language, but mainly to get yourself noticed, join the groups, read the little red book . . .'

'The *Little Red Book*'s out. They don't read that one any more.'

'Well, read whatever colour book they're reading. We'd like you to be recruited by the Chinese Central External Liaison Department. We want you to become a Chinese spy before you go back to Malaysia. We call it the double game.'

'Was this all the suggestion of my father?'

'Didn't he explain it to you?'

Of course he bloody didn't!

'No.'

'That was naughty of him.'

Naughty? But I'll do it – that'll show the bastard!

'When do you want me to start?'

Wang was like a kind elderly uncle, but it was only skin-deep. His involvement in dirty bastardy was second nature; he'd been at it all his life; he did it by instinct. ' . . . Any contact, Hilary?'

'Nothing. I'm going to be the spy world's longest sleeper!'

'Don't be complacent; they'll be waking you up any minute now. But I've got something for you to do . . .'

'You have?'

'Peter's edict. He spoke to you about a David Kent, he says. You know the involvement. He wants you to meet him. You play hard to get, but not too hard – hard to get-ish. Peter says he's not your type, so you shouldn't have any trouble there – '

'Peter's talking out of his backside! He knows nothing about "my type". What does he want me to do with this lamb?'

'Your friends from Peking are watching him, you'll be instructed to get to know him so they'll be quite pleased when they see you sidle up against him as if by chance. Don't worry about that part of it; I'll arrange for the two of you to meet tomorrow evening. When you do, play it natural, the way you would with any other strange male. When you've softened him up try to find out if . . . erm . . . he's come to any conclusions during his visit to Malaysia. Tell him how fascinated you are about the old jungle war; try to get him to chat about it. Show mild interest, be curious, but don't probe. Say you once knew somebody in the old Malayan Police and see what reaction it brings – no names, mind you, he's not silly. If you start chatting personalities he's likely to put that dark frown on his forehead and start acting like a policeman again. Don't give him cause to doubt that you're anything more than a pretty face and let him do the running.'

'I've got the picture, Peng Soon. Is that it?'

'Not quite. Once you're in, stay with him all the way, until he fetches up on Peter's doorstep. Goh Peng's people will be going with you and if Kent falters it'll be you who has to do the final lap for them. Peter said he'd explained all that to you – '

'He did.'

'OK, so when you get to London expect them to contact you. They'll assume that by then Kent will have opened up his heart and mind to you.' Wang smiled sadly. 'The Chinese think English men and women have no secrets from each other – even after such a short acquaintance . . . Funny people, aren't we?'

'How do you know Peking wants me with this man?'

Wang studied her for a moment, then smiled again and shook his head. He didn't answer her question, but instead said, 'Ring your office right away and tell them you're taking a spot of leave. Kent's going back to London tomorrow. I'll confirm the time and flight. You'll be with him. Don't tell him you're going; we'll make that a pleasant surprise. I'll tell Mohammed Salleh at Subang to have your ticket and to be ready to join your seats together. Don't worry, he's good at that sort of thing – Kent won't suspect a thing. By the way, let your CELD contact know that you have a provisional booking to London that you made some weeks ago –

nothing to do with this. Ask if they want you to travel on the same plane as Kent. They'll say yes; they like coincidence, they'll treat it as a clever bonus. They'll be happy about that.'

'Whom do I contact in London?'

'Peter. Don't try to be clever. Be natural, and take your lead from him.'

Hilary suddenly felt the energy drain out of her. Kent looked tired, too, but he didn't want to let go. Neither did she. She said it without thinking; it seemed a most natural thing to suggest.

'Let's go and have breakfast at my place.'

The taxi took them along Jalan Ampang to Ukay Heights. Hilary's flat was on the third floor. The view all round was spectacular and after they'd eaten the eggs and bacon she'd cooked they sat on the iron railing of the balcony, drinking black coffee and iced Kahlua. The segment of moon in a star-filled sky bathed the distant city in liquid silver. From behind the flat, in a small patch of undevelopable jungle, the frogs and the insects chattered in time with the metronomic tocks of the insomniac bird. It was idyllic. It should have been kissing time, but he didn't want to risk spoiling it.

'And now you're going to tell me exactly what you're doing here.' Hilary had slipped off her tiny sandals and, sitting low in a recliner, propped her feet on the iron guard-railing that ran the length of the balcony. The back light from the room made a halo round her hair and highlighted the soft curve of her chin. She was a beautiful woman. However, at that moment it wasn't her beauty but her direct approach which disturbed Kent. Maybe it was only skin deep – not the beauty, the direct approach. She was waiting.

'I'm looking for information on a couple of old jungle fighters who were knocking around Malaya in the fifties,' he said. He didn't look at her directly but he knew she'd turned her head. He didn't give her time to interrupt. 'I'm writing a book on guerilla warfare – it seemed a good idea to combine holiday and research. Wang's helping me. He's the friend of a friend . . .'

He turned and looked her in the face; she seemed very pale – it was the moonlight. But her voice had gone pale, too.

'Have you had any success?'

He sipped his Kahlua and thought about it. There had to be

more interesting things to talk about with a beautiful woman on the balcony of her flat at half-past four in the morning – but anything was better than a pointed yawn.

'Not much. It was a long time ago, people don't seem to know an awful lot about it here. I'll have to wait until I go home and dig around a bit more there. But still, it's not a very interesting subject, not to you, anyway.'

'I wouldn't say that. I think one of my father's friends spent some time in the jungle here.'

'There were thousands of them, Hilary. Almost the whole of the British Army joined in at some time or other. You father's friend wouldn't be exceptional.'

'He wasn't in the army. He was a policeman.'

'Malayan Police?' The small hairs at the back of Kent's head began to twitch. He lit a cigarette and tried to be casual – too casual. 'There were a lot of those too. What was his name?'

'I can't remember. He was my father's friend, not mine.'

Kent moved off the balcony and went to his jacket hanging on the back of one of the dining chairs. He came back with his wallet. The occasion had dulled his senses; he saw nothing suspicious, nothing unusual in the final reel of an evening's coincidences. He'd got his two favourite subjects wrapped up in one packet. He took out Togom's picture of the dead terrorists and debated whether the subject might be too meaty for this delicate beauty, but he was galloping too fast now to think of Hilary's sensibilities. He held it out to her.

'Yuk!'

'Is he in that?'

She glanced down at it. 'I don't think so. He'd be over sixty now . . .' She handed the picture back.

He didn't take it. 'Have a good look at that European on the right – could that be your father's friend?'

She looked again. She'd put her thumb across the bottom of the print, blotting out the row of dead Chinese and brought it closer to her face. After a moment she handed it back again and pulled a face. 'I wouldn't swear to it.' She made it sound definite. 'Now put it away please – it's very ugly.'

He studied it himself for a second then shook his head. 'Where can I find this chap?'

'I've no idea. London somewhere, I think.'

'Perhaps your father. . . ?'

He saw her stiffen. He knew he'd pushed too far too quickly. She didn't reply immediately but stood up, stared at the lights of the distant but encroaching KL, and stretched, with her hands on the back of her neck. It was a provocative gesture; she could almost have been standing there with no clothes on. But Kent knew the provocation was not for him. It was goodnight, David . . .

'Shall I ring for a taxi for you?'

'Thanks. Can I see you again?'

'I'm not sure, I might be going away for a few weeks. Why don't you ring me?'

Kent tried not to show his disappointment. 'I'm going back to England, today or tomorrow . . . Where will you be going?'

She didn't reply. She picked up the phone. It was definitely goodnight, David – and, by the sound of it, goodbye.

The massage parlour in the Hilton was still open for business. There must have been a special night shift. The girl he got was pretty in a porcelain sort of way, minute Chinese and fragile, but she had fingers like six-inch nails; she probably squeezed tennis balls all day when she wasn't probing muscles. Bright, cheerful and talkative. Too talkative – she talked herself out of an extracurricular suggestion. Maybe that was her intention. She'd probably learned what AIDS spelled. Kent tipped her generously and she gave him her real name and suggested she'd be available any time – massage, nothing else. She didn't say 'nothing else', but her high-pitched non-stop chatter ensured it. He made a note of her name – to make sure he didn't get her next time.

But there wasn't going to be a next time. He poured himself a miniature Bell's, doubled it with a splash of Perrier and lay down on the bed. Sleep would have to wait for a few minutes. The wait wasn't very long. It took him by surprise – it came at about the same time as the decision.

18

Wang waited until 5 p.m. the next evening before ringing London.
Even then, Evelyn St John Woodhouse wasn't too pleased to have to
scramble his phone at 9 a.m., before he'd had time to relax in his new
swivel armchair and swallow his first cup of coffee. It wasn't civilised.

'Our young friend, David Kent, has gone to Hong Kong . . .'
Wang imagined the agitation at the other end of the line. He
thought he could hear the rain beating against the windows in
Mayfair but shut the noise out of his mind and concentrated on
enjoying the heat of an airless tropical afternoon.

'What the bloody hell's going on, Wang? He's not supposed to
go to bloody Hong Kong. Did he clear it with you?' came
Woodhouse's disjointed voice.

Wang shook his head. 'No. Why should he? I'm not his mother.'

'The inconsiderate young bastard!' Woodhouse kept his
annoyance under control. 'Did he mention he was going?'

'No.'

'Not a word? What the bloody hell's he gone to Hong Kong
for?'

Wang's eyes widened into slits. He almost smiled. 'Maybe he
wants to get a new suit and couple of silk shirts. He wasn't looking
too fresh the last time I saw him.'

Woodhouse ignored the first part of the sentence. 'What do you
mean?'

'He's been galloping about all over the country. Led one of my
best female agents astray.'

'The horny young bastard! These bloody people ought to be
castrated before we turn them loose on foreigners – they all think
they're bloody James Bond!'

Wang didn't laugh. He didn't even smile. 'He didn't lead her
astray that way – he got her killed.'

Woodhouse went silent for a moment. It was relief. Then he got
worried again. 'Wang, this bugger rushing off to Hong Kong – give
me some thoughts about it?'

Wang had already done that for himself. 'I think it might have been something I said, Woody; something that slipped into his mind, and then popped up when he felt a little niggle of frustration coming over him . . .'

'Wangy, can you get to the bloody point, please?'

'He showed me a picture of Jimmy Morgan in his old working clothes and I mentioned that he'd slipped off to Hong Kong just after the Chaah incident. He's trying to tie it all in.'

'He's acting like a fucking policeman, you mean!'

Wang shrugged to himself. 'I think he's got Fylough and Morgan as a twosome. He'll go for Fylough in the UK but he wants to see if there's anything to join them up in Hong Kong. He knows the ropes there and he probably has friends – he can look where others fear to tread. The big worry if he does turn over the right stones, Woody, is that having discovered who he's looking for he might then get ambitious and start wondering why. I think he's already realised he's on to something a bit more involved than the killing of a handful of old jungle warriors. He could become a bloody nuisance.'

'Then let's hope for his sake he doesn't,' said Woodhouse, ominously. 'Have you got anybody in Hong Kong to keep an eye on him?'

'I sent somebody with him. They'll look after him.'

'Not a woman, I hope?'

'Relax, Woody. We don't send egg noodles to Peking.'

'What?'

'Coals to Newcastle!'

Woodhouse wasn't in the mood. 'What about the Chinaman?'

'What Chinaman, Woody? We're all Chinamen here!'

'Stop fucking around, Wang! You know what bloody Chinaman I'm talking about.'

Wang's eyes vanished from sight as his face creased into a smile. 'Ah, Mr Goh Peng . . . What about him? Well, he's made a bolt for it. When we unravelled his little cell he made a beeline for the airport. Got as far as Petaling Jaya and then his instincts turned him round and he headed north.'

'You gave him a clear run, I hope?'

'More or less. I tickled his tail occasionally so that he wouldn't get suspicious. He'd expect opposition. He got it – gently. He slipped round the Thai border and caught UTA from Bangkok. He'll come home to you via Paris. He'll be a diplomat again by the time he boards the London flight from Charles de Gaulle.'

'Thanks.' Woodhouse didn't go over the top. 'What about Hilary?'

'Went like clockwork. They make a very striking couple. He likes her – '

'Wang, I'm not bloody interested in what he likes and doesn't like – did he tell her anything?'

'Oh yes. Told her what he was doing; showed her pictures of dead bandits and a little snap of the bloke he thinks he's looking for – '

'We've already been over this. Did he put a name to him?'

'No, but she recognised Fylough. That's the one he was interested in. He didn't show her the snap of Jimmy Morgan. But Woody, I think we'd better make contingencies if he flies direct from Hong Kong to London. I assumed he was leaving from here; I'd got Hilary lined up in a seat next to him. Looks like we'll have to send her on her own and arrange another meeting in London – that'll be your baby.'

'Maybe he'll come back to KL?' Woodhouse didn't sound too hopeful.

Neither did Wang.

19

Hong Kong hadn't changed at all.

Kent finished his whisky and soda, propped his elbows on the wooden bar and put on his sincere look. His friend got there first.

'I'm surprised they let you through Immigration! We don't like renegades, particularly those who come back asking favours. We circulated your name – "not welcome"!'

'What makes you think I want a favour?'

'I'm a policeman – I can tell.'

Kent bought another two whiskies, took a Dunhill International from the packet lying between them on the bar and said, 'I'd like to spend a couple of hours in Records – a bit longer if they still write them with a chisel. Can you arrange it?'

'What for?'

'Old times' sake?'

'Bollocks! Why don't you do it through your own people? You've got a Defence Security Officer here, highly paid, doing fuck-all! He comes under your E Section – as if you didn't know.' There was no response from Kent. His friend took a long pull from his new whisky and looked at him out of the corner of his eye. 'You *did* know, didn't you?'

Kent smiled. 'I prefer to use my friends.'

'You're up to something fishy, Kent. What're you looking for? Plans of the mass exodus in '97?'

'Nothing fishy. Ginger. I want to see if one of the nosy bastards who worked in Records in the fifties made a case out of an MI6 briefing. Simple as that.'

'The fifties! You're bloody joking?'

'Dead serious.'

'Ginger' Whittle's look of disbelief vanished. He turned on his bar stool and studied Kent's blank expression. He looked for the catch, the kick, but found nothing. Then curiosity won. 'OK. On two conditions.'

Kent nodded his agreement and prepared to reel off the story he'd put together. But it wasn't necessary.

Whittle allowed a crafty smile to touch his lips briefly. 'If I let you into our holy of holies you'll tell me what you're looking for – when you find it. I can't be bothered knowing beforehand, you might want me to help you look!'

'I hadn't thought of that,' grinned Kent. 'OK, you're on. And the next?'

'You buy me a bloody good dinner in Hugo's and send me home with a serious, thumping hangover.'

'Done!'

The Police Registry, housed in the massive headquarters building of the Royal Hong Kong Police in Arsenal Street contained a totally computerised records centre with everything available at the touch of a button.

Kent found the atmosphere crisp, bright, and healthy. He also found that 1960 was the cut-off date. The button-pushing ended there; beyond 1960 was the impenetrable swamp – the paper filing system. He stared at the rack of bulging files for 1950. He wasn't surprised, only grateful that somebody had thought they were worth keeping and hadn't heaved them on to the New Year bonfire.

He expected no favours. The files were stored in dark, crisp, dry and temperature-controlled cellars. One day, hopefully, before the People's Republic Gestapo moved in to sort out names for thinning out the population of Hong Kong, they'd join the sixties in computer banks with instantaneous destruct mechanisms. But, Kent shook his head, not this century. He removed his jacket and hung it on the back of a chair. Nobody was particularly worried about leaving him on his own; thirty-year-old files had a low priority in anybody's currency. Anybody in Hong Kong who wanted to look at what was happening thirty years ago had to be 'funny'. Hong Kong was concerned with today and tomorrow – thirty years ago was the Bronze Age. 'Please don't smoke,' was the only condition. 'Not in here. Out in the corridor? Sure, no problem. Give us a shout if you want a cup of coffee.' A heavy fire door clanged shut and he was left on his own.

He continued to stare at the long bank of files. The fifties

167

seemed to vanish into a black hole about half a mile away. He blinked. *Where the bloody hell do I start? 1953, September, Jim Morgan was in Malaya as OSPC, Officer Superintending Police Circle, Segamat. OK, forget September; try October, November, December* . . . He walked slowly along the shelves, flicking on the lights as he went. *1953.* He stopped. *What heading?* He looked closely. *Jesus! There's a thousand different bloody headings* . . . *What's this?* At the end of each month was a thin, in many cases insignificant, file, the legacy of a long-retired, conscientious filing clerk. *Sleep in peace, brother!* He pulled out September's file. 'Unclassified' it said on the shiny sticker, and in small neat handwriting, 'inc. British Military Co-op./MI5-E/MI6 etc . . .' *Bless you!*

He opened it.

September 1953: nothing.

Then October 1953: nothing.

And November 1953: nothing.

But December 1953 . . . His eyes glazed over. *Bingo! Bingo! Bingo!*

3.12.53. STN 10/B/LOMACH.
EXTRA PATROL 1CG DEPLOYED BORDER LOKMACHAU XXXXX NO EXPLAN. ENDIT.

3.12.53. SUNFLOWER. KWANTUNG PROVINCE.
ONE BRITCIV PLUS ONE CHINCIV MET TWO UNIDENTIFIED REP/CHIN OFFICIALS N-M-L
AREA YUNONGCUN (PRCO2940498) ONE HOUR BORDER REGION XXXXX.

3.12.53. SB CLASSIFIED T/S ASSESSMENT. BRITCIV IDENTIFIED MI6 J. MORGAN. AUTHORITY: DSO E (A). RET ALONE UNIDENTIFIED CHINESE OFFICIALS EX-KWANTUNG REGION. CHINCIV UNIDENTIFIED. NO REPORT LODGED. SUNFLOWER CONFIRMS.

Kent put the file to one side and went through the first three months of 1954. There was no other mention of the incident. He cross-checked the main files for December 1953 under the heading: 'Border incidents/Special Branch action'. For the 3rd of December he found only the legend: 'See unclass 3/12'. Kent gave a wry smile. It was known as the ping-pong ball – you went backwards and forwards for ever and ever, getting nowhere, finding nothing. He closed the file. So that was it.

He tucked it under his arm and took it into the corridor. There was a table and chair conveniently placed just outside the door. Kent sat down and lit a cigarette. He opened the file again and cupped his chin in his hands as he studied the photocopied sheets. There was nothing else in the file except a small white card on which was written in Biro: 'Original claimed 15/12/53 by DSO Hong Kong for London File. Refer FO: F/S TS H3936. Group: F0148. File No. 23142. (INDICATION NOT AUTHORISED)'.

Kent puffed reflectively on his cigarette and stared at the white card. 'Refer FO' – Foreign Office Registry. Not MI5 Registry, or Cheltenham Registry, but London FO . . . *Very interesting!* And what did it all boil down to? The police observation post – LOMACH – at Lok Ma Chau reports a patrol of the 1st Battalion Coldstream Guards taking up a defensive position on the border. They have a European civilian with them and one Chinese civilian. SUN-FLOWER, a Special Branch undercover agent bedded down in Kwantung Province, reports the two civilians hold a meeting in the middle of no man's land with Chinese officials from the heavy red part of the countryside. Whatever next . . .

A top-secret Special Branch assessment names the European as J. Morgan. Kent almost smiled as he blew smoke into the insulated pipework above his head. They didn't manage to identify the Chinese from our side whose hand he held – a clever bugger who probably took his teeth out and wore a Lone Ranger mask! But he didn't come back. Tough. So what?

Neither the Army, nor MI5's Defence Security Officer reports to Special Branch. Special Branch keep quiet. They don't want to compromise their agent. It's known as close interdepartmental co-operation between all participating agencies. And now for the dirty bit! MI5 have an informant within Special Branch, Hong Hong Police; he whistles down the wind and the ears prick up like a eunuch's imagination at a honeymoon. MI5 demand, under Foreign Office authority, that all documents of the incident be handed over. But some bright bastard photocopies them – probably at the same time his friends are castrating MI5's informant – and takes the trouble to explain where the originals have gone to, with a warning to anybody wanting to make anything out of it, hence the 'Indication not authorised . . .'

But why?

Kent crushed his cigarette into the ashtray and lit another one. It was like a paper chase. The bits and pieces were lying all around, waiting to be picked up. So he picked up another piece. What was Morgan rubbing noses with the real Chinese about? And how did it match up with the return of a patrol from a jungle operation in Malaya, the murder of most of the performers of that operation, and the elevation to the highest perch in the British Military Intelligence network of one James Morgan, clandestine fraterniser of Chinese officials? And it was 'officials' Sunflower had described. What had he meant by that? Kent stared at the pipes again. This time he'd had enough. He stood up, put the file together and went back into the shelf-filled room. Morgan was showing himself to be a shifty bugger. But why the surprise? Morgan? He had to be Welsh, didn't he? *Evans-the-post, Jones-the-fish – Morgan-the-spy! Just like Philby . . . Was Philby a bloody Welshman? No, you silly bugger – Philby was working for the other side . . . Morgan working for the Chinese? Jesus Christ!*

He put the file back in its place, switched the lights off and closed the door behind him. The cigarette was still glowing between his lips. He gave another wry smile, then grinned as he spat it out and trod on it. What would they have said if he'd set the bloody place on fire? They'd probably be delighted – some poor bugger was going to have to put all this old rubbish on to film at some point. What a bloody waste of time.

Kent spent another thirty-six hours in Hong Kong, most of them recovering from a monumental hangover, then caught the 1640 Cathay Pacific London flight and got off at KL. Wang's two agents did the same. They'd quite enjoyed their little trip to Hong Kong. They had gone everywhere he'd gone except into the bowels of Police HQ. They'd marked his Chinese Watcher right up to his return to the back door of the People's Embassy, but they'd taken no action. Neither had the Watcher. Everybody was Watching; nobody was doing anything. They reported everything by phone to Wang Peng Soon. He wasn't excited. He repeated his instructions; follow, note, protect, but don't interfere. They did as they were told – they were sticklers for following instructions, especially Wang Peng Soon's. At KL they handed him over to two others – just in case . . .

Next morning Kent rang Wang to say goodbye. Wang sounded surprised. Neither man mentioned Kent's trip to the Colony. Wang asked him to give his regards to his old friend Woody. That was all – he could have been just finishing a short holiday.

Kent then rang Hilary's flat. There was no reply. He looked up her office number and rang that. They said she was away. Where? They couldn't say. When would she be back? They didn't know. *Bloody efficient office!* Today? Tomorrow? Next week? Sorry!

He put the phone down. Too bad. But he'd known she was never going to be an easy one; he hadn't even managed to get his finger on the starting button. Perhaps he'd come to KL for Christmas and try again!

For the outward journey Subang Airport was typically Eastern, noisy and slightly scruffy, with untidy, sloppy policemen and the new music of the Orient – the slapping of a thousand rubber flip-flops on imitation marble floors.

On the first floor was the oasis for the new easy money, the bar, monopolised by loud-mouthed Chinese yuppies waiting to go somewhere – God only knew where – their once starched, short-sleeved white shirts now crinkled and damp with the exertions of living up to the image with whisky and ginger ale, cognac and F&N orange squash . . .

Kent forced his way to the counter and managed to prise out of the barman an almost chilled bottle of Tiger. The glass was extra. He fought his way out again and headed for the verandah and the warm, almost breatheable, air. The MSA London flight was starting here. It was only going to be forty minutes late and nobody gave a bugger – including Kent. He drank his beer slowly and parched his throat with another cigarette. He recognised the perfume before she spoke; it was Shalimar.

'You weren't thinking of leaving without saying goodbye?' She seemed to have appeared from nowhere. She was wearing a yellow dress; it suited her. She looked fresh, unflustered and very beautiful; he felt hot, scruffy, sweaty, and had a compulsive urge to take her in his arms and kiss her. But she didn't encourage it. 'I tried to get in touch with you yesterday,' she said. She made it sound like an admission of guilt or total breakdown. 'I don't make a habit, as a rule, of chasing men.'

He didn't apologise for making her break her habit. 'Would you like a drink?'

'Gin and tonic, please. Lots of ice, and insist on lemon, not lime.' She sounded like James Bond.

He left her standing, guarding his Tiger beer, and re-entered the scrum. The Chinese had looked her over – they were interested in what she was drinking. There was going to be a big demand for lemon, not lime, in their brandy orange squashes from now on. He handed her the gin and tonic and waited until her lip lightly kissed the top layer of ice cubes.

'How did you know I was leaving today?' he said.

The glass was lowered and the tip of her tongue carefully wet the chilled lip. 'I didn't,' she replied and sipped again, gently. 'I'm not here to see you off . . .' She didn't lower the glass but allowed it to bounce gently against her bottom lip as she spoke. 'I'm here to catch an aeroplane . . .'

He liked the way she said aeroplane and not airplane. Old-fashioned pronunciation – old-fashioned values. Maybe she was the type that relaxed the rules on the second outing. *Maybe!*

'Where to?'

'London.'

Thank you, Father Christmas!

20

The room in London in which Goh Peng sat had all the cosy warmth and charm of a blockhouse on one of the snow-covered peaks overlooking Lhasa.

He shifted uncomfortably in his chair. He would have liked a cigarette, a sociable bowl of tea – he reckoned his status demanded it. But there was nothing from the two people sitting upright, like two book-ends, one male, one female, at each end of the overlarge table that took up most of the room. He kept his feelings to himself as he came to the end of his report and folded his arms.

The woman fixed him with her blank, fish-like stare, but said nothing. She was an attractive Chinese of indefinable age – she could have been fifty or thirty. Her name was Ah Lian. She had wide eyes, wider than the usual Chinese eyes, and an oval, more European than Chinese, face. Hers was a classical beauty, with full lips, make-up, and complexion that benefited from expensive London treatment. This was her one indulgence; when she returned to Peking there would be no trace of make-up, her eyes would narrow and her newly acquired London clothes would join the others in the Cultural Attaché's wardrobes. She continued to study Goh Peng for several moments, absorbing what he'd told them, then, as if satisfied, pursed her lips and nodded. It was an almost imperceptible nod. Goh Peng relaxed.

But the man at the table wasn't satisfied. Taking his time, he removed a cigarette from the packet on the table in front of him, put it between his lips and waited for the woman to rise from her chair and light it for him. He studied the glowing end of the cigarette for a moment, then puffed a little more life into it and looked up into Goh Peng's face. 'Are you quite certain you can now locate and arrange a meeting with Fylough?' His voice was casual; too casual – deceptive.

'Yes, Comrade Kim Cheong.'

'Where and when?'

'Ah . . .' Goh Peng avoided eye contact with the man. Grey stubbly hair, thin as a rake, he could have been anything in age from sixty to eighty. He looked as though he'd had a rough passage in life and the pinched look around his mouth which pulled it into a thin straight line showed that he knew what pain was all about. He had no hands. In their place were two functional hooks which every so often opened fractionally and shut with a tiny click as if they had a mind of their own. As if to hear better Goh Peng's excuse, he hunched forward, his elbows on the table, the two hooks just touching each other, and his eyes narrowed into fine slits as protection against the thin thread of smoke drifting upwards from the cigarette held loosely between his lips. Goh Peng was aware of the thickness of the ice he was standing on. This was Kim Cheong, whose position in the hierarchy of the TEWA, the Department for Special Affairs – the sanitised title for the supreme organisation of the Chinese Intelligence Service – guaranteed a special sort of fear. And here he was, in London, waiting for Goh Peng to tell him how clever he'd been in not quite tracking down the target he'd been set.

It had started in 1986 when he'd been invited to a select – just him and Kim Cheong – viewing of film shot by Kim Cheong's Special Intelligence group during the British Queen's visit to China. Goh Peng neither asked nor questioned the motive behind his selection to this privilege. He did as he was told and watched assiduously the concentration of footage on one man.

'Find him,' had been Kim Cheong's edict. 'My sister will provide your authority both here and abroad and you will report to her at every stage.' Kim Cheong's sister was Ah Lian, who now sat staring, impassively, across the table in the stark room.

Goh Peng's first report to Ah Lian had been brief and unambiguous:

. . . The man's name is Fylough and he was accompanying his queen as a member of the Cultural Mission of Central China. No such mission exists. The name is a cover for members of the British Intelligence Organisation in the Far East. This is normal practice. There was nothing unusual in the presence of this man on the visit . . .

His second report, made in London:

. . . My enquiries in China came to nothing. The man did not exist; he was a shadow, a face without substance. Nobody knew the name Fylough. I reported thus to Comrade Kim Cheong, who ordered me to take my enquiries to Malaysia. 'Start,' he advised me, 'in 1953. Johor. Try Segament, Labis, Chaah, Yong Peng . . . Look for the name in police files . . .' He gave me another name: Togom, a Malay who had served with Fylough during the running dog war. Fylough was not known or remembered in any of the towns mentioned by Comrade Kim Cheong but the Malay was and we traced him to a village on the west coast of Malaysia. He was difficult and uncooperative at first but eventually became helpful. He remembered Fylough but lost track of him in 1954. Togom knew of a man named Kenning, who had served in the same fascist terror organisation with Fylough. Kenning had become a rubber planter; it was no difficult task to find his address in England.

Before I moved on I checked that there were no other associates of this man Fylough. We had access to Malaysian Police records via their computer room. There was nothing on record of significance, except names. I then left for England after arranging to be included on the list of diplomatic staff of the People's Embassy in London. I accepted full control of Central External Liaison Department affairs in the UK, using the position of Third Secretary. We found the man Kenning in England without difficulty, but he too proved uncooperative. We spent some considerable time with him but it was only upon your advice to go through the motions of removing his hands that his memory suddenly came to life and he remembered not only Fylough but another individual who might offer assistance. However, he knew nothing of Fylough's whereabouts or activities; he stated he hadn't seen him since the early days in Malaya. I accepted this statement – under the stress we placed him he had no alternative but to tell the truth. He said he knew nothing of the recent Fylough and I believed him. We disposed of him and, two months later, moved on to the other name he gave us – one Gilbert Bentley.

175

This one was not easy to find. It was as if he had got wind of events and covered his tracks, but we eventually found him in the North of England.

It was a waste of time.

This wasn't a man, and with every gentle tap he screamed another name – names of no consequence, some going back to his childhood – anything to please. But through his pleadings we gleaned another name from the jungle war – Dean.

Dean was a different creature altogether. A real soldier, not too difficult to find and, having done so, we waited for some reaction from him to the deaths of the other two. Nothing happened. He probably hadn't connected the two with events in Malaya thirty years previously and when we finally paid him a visit our arrival was as much a surprise to him as the ease with which we neutralised him was to us. Unfortunately, our methods – similar to those used on the other two – resulted in his death before he was able to further our mission. He was also allowed to eliminate two of our agents; one the senior CELD resident in the UK.

The Dean affair was an unsatisfactory one from all points of view. It was handled inefficiently and I accept full responsibility for the deaths and mishandling. Dean could have told us more. I am sure he was well acquainted with Fylough, but, although we were left without a lead, someone was taking notice. An agent of British MI blackmailed a menial at our embassy to supply details of Embassy vehicle movements. We decided that Fylough, following the interrogation and elimination of Kenning, had picked up the deaths of these other men, had seen where the arrow pointed and had taken action through British MI. When the British agent exposed himself we decided to use him to further our advances. We gave him the information he required and placed a surveillance team to monitor his progress . . .

Goh Peng thus ended his second report to Ah Lian.

It was to Kim Cheong himself, however, sitting beside his sister at the long table in a semi-bare room in an anonymous house in London, that Goh Peng concluded his reports:

'. . . The British agent, a low-grade officer named Kent, brought together the deaths of the three ex-officers and traced the origin of their association to Malaya during the liberation war in the 1950s. He decided to carry his investigations to that country. This suited us. We gave him all the assistance at our disposal, even to the extent of pointing him in the right direction in Malaysia. We sent him to the Malay Togom so that he would learn who his quarry was – '

'But you killed the Malay,' interjected Kim Cheong.

'We wanted the British agent to know who his quarry was,' stated Goh Peng, 'But not why he was seeking him. In amongst the Malay's belongings were photographs of Fylough and other people who might help him to locate Fylough in this country. We checked later that he had collected these items. It was necessary at that stage to remove the helper Malaysia's F2 had assigned to him.'

'And that was a mistake.'

'Not a critical one,' Goh Peng sidestepped the accusation. 'It made room to insert the West woman.'

Kim Cheong removed another cigarette from the packet in front of him and tapped one of his shiny steel hooks on the tabletop. Ah Lian scraped her chair back, stood up, and held a match to the cigarette.

'Tell me about her,' he said after he'd drawn in a deep lungful of smoke.

Goh Peng looked longingly at the smouldering cigarette pinched in the twin sprung elements of Kim Cheong's right hook but immediately banished the thought. It was a puzzling question. The order for Hilary West's recruitment had come from Central Office, Kim Cheong's own. However, he kept his expression blank.

'During a break from her law practice in Kuala Lumpur, she spent a year in Ningbo Wuhan University to learn Mandarin and *putonghua*. It was there that she was recruited on the instructions of – '

'Never mind whose instructions,' snapped Kim Cheong. 'She was recruited. And. . . ?'

'And the usual steps taken to ensure loyalty.' Goh Peng neither smiled nor smirked. 'Steps taken to ensure loyalty' was not a trite phrase in the TEWA recruitment of foreign nationals manual; it was a method. 'In her case, photos, talk, and, with models and technical experts, the faking of a highly compromising video featuring one of Mugabe's big black bulls. It was a very convincing video. She was most surprised when she watched it. Finally she was inveigled to join one of the more radical student societies in Peking. The Malaysian authorities don't like members of radical Communist student societies among their permanent residents in Kuala Lumpur – or lawyers who star in pornographic videos. We'd marked her and showed her how deeply it had been done. We told her to go to Kuala Lumpur and forget all about it. When the call came she did as she was told. She had no choice.'

'Why did you pick on her?' asked Ah Lian, after a sideways glance at Kim Cheong. He frowned but allowed the interruption.

'No specific reason,' stated Goh Peng. 'She was there and one of many. Who knows whether broadly scattered seed will one day germinate and flower. We were lucky with this one. Europeans are not usually available in the People's Republic for induction; Europeans established in prominent positions in sensitive areas in our local sphere are almost non-existent. It was only when Comrade Kim Cheong revealed a TEWA interest in the man Fylough and the Malaysian connection to his activities that we realised we had here a seed of enormous consequence. It was luck.'

Ah Lian's expression was sceptical. 'How did you arrange for her to meet Kent?'

Goh Peng frowned. 'I didn't. Again, we had luck. I used one of our people in KL to remind her of her obligations, but apparently the meeting had already been made. Pure chance, Excellency.'

Ah Lian shook her head. She wasn't happy. She told Goh Peng so.

'I don't like your use of the word luck, Goh Pong – there's too much of it. And now we have "chance". This is not a game of mahjong; there are serious repercussions for you, me, the Department, and, consequently, China if this particular event is left in the hands of luck and chance . . .' She paused, without taking her eyes off Goh Peng's face, but before she could continue Kim Cheong rapped on the table with one of his hooks.

'Enough,' he growled, and resumed control. 'So this woman,

Hilary West, will find Fylough for us through a relationship with Kent?'

'That is the idea. Kent is on course to take us to him.'

'But you don't know where Fylough is at this moment?'

Goh Peng kept his head still and his eyes focused on Kim Cheong's grey head. He was treading lightly; the danger was in the old man's voice. 'We have given the impression to Kent's team that Kent is of only secondary importance. He will shrug aside this inept Watch and lower his vigilance. The real watcher will not be dislodged. Kent's next move will be to arrange a confrontation with Fylough to clarify his findings. We must not lose sight of the fact that Kent's original mission was to discover the reason for Colonel Dean's strange death, and Fylough is the man who can enlighten him. That, simply, is the sole objective of his investigation. The Chaah file means nothing to him – '

'Or shouldn't,' interjected Ah Lian.

Goh Peng didn't offer a comment, neither did he take his eyes from Kim Cheong. 'But if he discovers beforehand the real reason why he is doing this he will stop all his activities in the interest of British national security and report to his superiors accordingly. If this happens he will have to be eliminated before he makes this report. Thus, we have two prongs for the end run: Kent, who knows where to take us, and Hilary West, who knows how to loosen his tongue.'

Kim Cheong finished smoking his cigarette, then shook his head. Ah Lian and Goh Peng both stiffened as he dropped the half-smoked cigarette into a tray and clipped the life from it with one click of the hook. He studied the beheaded stub for a moment, then looked up.

'Your motives are correct, Goh Peng, but your thinking is flawed. The woman must not be relied upon to help – she must be used. You had her brought to London to make herself agreeable to the British agent. If she has achieved this she becomes more than a forced helper – she becomes a lever . . .'

'I don't follow – ' began Goh Peng. But he got no further.

'Then listen. You have stopped thinking beyond the identification and location of Peter Fylough. True?'

Goh Peng merely stared at Kim Cheong. The worm was wriggling in his brain. The man at the table was a long way ahead.

Kim Cheong didn't wait for affirmation. He didn't need it. He continued: 'Englishmen are easily persuaded to see another's point of view when a woman is spread across the table in front of them. You believe that Kent has served his purpose. I believe there is more for him yet. Fylough has certain obligations to me which he won't fulfil voluntarily. I don't even think that pain will bring forth his co-operation. But, bring Fylough to me and we shall perform on Hilary West to encourage his co-operation. You're nodding your head, Goh Peng. Good! Don't go to sleep! If Fylough shrugs her screams aside then Kent will be brought back into the game to listen to them. In that way we will persuade him to help us in delving into Fylough's memory ducts. Between the two of them and the woman's screaming we should achieve at least one objective.'

21

Hilary West didn't sleep off her jet lag. She waited until Kent's taxi vanished round the corner at the end of the road, then picked up the telephone and dialled a London number. Peter Fylough was expecting the call.

'Lunch,' he told her. 'The Grenadier, Whitehall Court. Don't tell your friends – let them find out.'

'I'm not sure – '

'Do as you're told. Half-past one. And, Hilary . . .'

'Yes?'

'Dodge and weave a bit. Don't make it too easy for them.'

'Stop playing spies, Daddy . . .'

'Don't be late.'

The foreign-looking man in the phone booth surveyed the dining room as he waited for someone to answer his call. Definitely foreign, probably East European, with jet-black hair sleeked flat with sickly smelling brilliantine – all the rage in Dubrovnik, but in London it made him look as if he was wearing a shiny wet seal on his head. However, he didn't look all that much out of place in the Grenadier. He turned his back on the room when the ringing stopped and murmured, 'The West woman has joined a man in a restaurant in Whitehall. Grey hair, tall, about sixty. Very friendly, familiar, almost intimate . . .'

Goh Peng stared thoughtfully at the huge mass-produced head and shoulders of Mao Tse-tung that hung on the wall of his office before speaking. Just when his Yugoslav friend thought he'd gone to sleep, he said, 'Are they still there?'

'They're having lunch. They've only just started. It's also a hotel – they may have a room, I haven't checked. But it has a bar and they spent some time there talking and drinking. As I said, they are not strangers; they kissed on meeting.'

'Sexual?'

'It's a public place . . .'

Goh Peng paused again and frowned at Chairman Mao. The thoughts came quicker. 'Are you obvious? Can you stay and watch?'

'I'm a drinker at the bar. I'm not the only one.'

'Where are you calling from?'

'The foyer.' The Yugoslav foiled Goh Peng's next question. 'There's no other way out of the restaurant.'

'Stay with them until they finish. I'll send other Watchers for the woman and help for you. Make the man your business. Find out who he is, what he is, where he goes when he leaves the woman, and where he lives. Forget her. Leave her to the others, and deal with any followers yourself.'

'Your girlfriend,' said Dick Mithers-Wayne, 'was followed by the Yugoslav to the Grenadier in Whitehall Court and is now sitting with her legs crossed, staring dewy-eyed across a table into the eyes of a good-looking, well-dressed old gent . . .' He sniffed unappreciatively at the after-smell of heavy musk-laced male perfume left by the previous occupant of the foyer telephone cabinet and jammed the door partly open with the toe of his suede boot; the smell refused to go. 'They're friendly – very friendly. I wouldn't be too pleased if she was my bird. You know what effect these silver-haired old buggers have on impressionable girls!'

Kent didn't share Mithers-Wayne's humour. His voice grated in the damp earpiece. 'Any idea who he is?'

Mithers-Wayne pulled a face and opened the door wider. 'There'll be pictures when he leaves, provided my boy's not towed away for overstaying his welcome, and I'll stroll along with Romeo to see where he hangs his hat once he leaves your girl. I'll be in touch.' He wiped his damp ear with the back of his hand and returned to the bar to wash the sickly taste of Yves St Laurent's scent for men from his throat with a long swig of iced lager. He glanced casually into the dining room and studied Hilary West.

He would like to have taken longer over it – preferably in a little candle-lit basement restaurant, just the two of them . . . He had to admit Kent was right. She was beautiful. It was all in the right places – and she was in the right place, too. The elegant restaurant surroundings suited her. So did her companion. And he was attentive. Mithers-Wayne would have given a lot to know what they were talking about.

Hilary slid her fork into the tender sole *bonne femme* and extracted a tiny sliver of white fish. Before raising it to her mouth she made a pretence of studying its composition. She continued to stare at it as she spoke.

'Before this goes any further, Daddy, I think I have a right to know what's behind it all. When you asked me to make an idiot of myself in Ningbo you said it was "long-term". I visualised something like twenty or thirty years, not eighteen months before they, or you, invited me to jump in and splash around in the Jacuzzi!'

Fylough smiled wryly. There was nothing sympathetic in his manner. He pondered for a moment, watching the tip of the fork and the sole disappear between two perfect lips, then, after a long swallow from his glass, said, 'It's all about a man named Kim Cheong – '

'Goh Peng's lord and master?' she interrupted.

Fylough nodded. 'Thirty-five years or more ago he was a special courier employed by K'ang Sheng's TEWA. In 1953 he was sent to Singapore with funds and words of encouragement for the Malayan Communist Party, which was fighting the British for control of Malaya. Before leaving Singapore to return to Peking he was handed a sealed packet. He was told broadly of its contents, but not the details. It was sufficient for him to realise that this packet was worth more than his life.' Fylough paused while he sipped from his glass again.

'What would be worth that?' Hilary stopped eating.

'Documents about a number of American-trained Chinese who'd been infiltrated through Hong Kong into the Chinese mainland and had established themselves in the central body of the Chinese Communist Party.'

'How on earth. . . ?'

'You might well ask! The documents were taken off an American agent who was ambushed and murdered on his way to the States. He was taking the documents to be lodged deep inside the Washington bunker depository. These documents, all originals, contained photographs, aliases, histories, cover stories,

183

originations – everything. Total death warrants for the agents concerned.'

'Wasn't that rather stupid of them, compiling detailed records of people settled nicely into their new homes?' Hilary moved the fish around on its plate with her fork, but she didn't eat. 'Somehow I'd have expected better of the Americans.'

'Not at all,' said Fylough, 'it's done all the time with relocated foreign nationals, particularly those who are returned to their home country. We call it insurance, in case the agent changes his mind, and his allegiance, and forgets, as his hair gets greyer, who's been paying his wages all these years!'

'I'd be inclined to call that blackmail, myself.'

'Heaven forbid! May I continue?'

'Please.'

'When the enormity of the loss was realised, the Americans – with us, their British friends, standing at the club bar with our hands up in horror saying "nothing to do with us, old boy! But if we can help . . ." – flooded the island with everything they had available. They covered every loophole and put their people on every street corner – they were going to get these things back if it meant stripping Singapore down to its bones. It worked, partially. It blocked Kim Cheong's route home. But to the Americans, and to us, Kim Cheong was an unknown quantity. They hadn't marked *his* card. They didn't know him – and that was the loophole they hadn't covered. It was only when they broke the central Communist cell in Singapore that people started whispering. Kim Cheong was blown – but it was too late for the Yanks. He'd decided to take the long way home, through the Malaya courier route, and was already across the Causeway and into the Johor jungle. He was on his own, but through the Min Yuen, the Communist underground organisation in Malaya, he made contact with elements of the Communist 5th Regiment who led him deep into the north of Johor and out of reach of the pursuing Americans. The head of the Min Yuen cell that made the contact for him sent his daughter as a guide. For propriety's sake, and they're like that in certain Chinese communities, she was given to him as a sister and it was as brother and sister that they joined up with the 7th Platoon operating near a place called Chaah.'

'How did you know about all these goings-on from your side of the fence?' asked Hilary. She had stopped eating. Her father's story had taken over her appetite.

Fylough refilled her glass and topped up his own. The man with the shiny hair remained standing at the bar nursing the same glass of brandy he'd ordered when he arrived. Dick Mithers-Wayne lit another cigarette, called for another Warsteiner and wished he'd taken the trouble to go on a lip-reading course.

She was staring at him, waiting expectantly.

He didn't answer her question. Instead he pulled a face and lifted his glass to his lips. 'Kim Cheong was dedicated to his mission. He had the documents, they were in English, and sealed, but he had a bloody good idea what they were all about and it didn't need impressing on him the urgency with which they should be got to Peking. The Americans realised they were on a hiding to nothing in sending agents into the jungle to look for him, so, in their magnanimous, and as usual too late, way they informed their British counterparts of this new development to their problem. They didn't mention the details – nothing about inserting political agents into Peking – just the fact that a Chinaman they particularly wanted had gone walkies in the jungle and they didn't know how they could find him! It wasn't exactly a flea in the ear they got, but the next best thing. They were told to forget it. Their man was never going to be seen again. "Why do you want him?" "No particular reason. He has something we want – strictly American – no interest to you, cousins . . . Maybe we can do the same for you one day! Sure, guys. Thanks a lot!" ' Fylough smiled wryly. Things hadn't changed, not even a lifetime later. 'But deviousness is not the prerogative of the gum-chewers. From an undercover agent in the Communists' Johor Regional Committee we got word of an interesting stranger in one of the Labis-Yong Peng units. A real Chinaman, was the word, waiting to move on with interesting papers for the people in Bow Street Alley – '

'What's that?'

'Fifteen Bow Street Alley, Peking – Chinese Central Intelligence – the People's CIA and SIS rolled into one. If they were excited about some papers stuck in a young Chinaman's inside pocket in our jungle, then so were we. The information trickled in second- and third-hand – sometimes fourth. Christ knows how it varied from the original but the interesting bit cost the informant his head. That's another story. "They say," whispered the informant, "that the stranger stays with the 7th Platoon until the chase for the documents dies down, when he will be taken north, cross to the east coast to join with the army there, wait for the next arms shipment to arrive by sampan, and then return with it".' Fylough touched his moustache with the crisp napkin and when he lowered it, pursed his lips as if he was throwing Hilary a kiss. Except that he wasn't. 'Then he ran into a bit of bad luck.'

'Do I want to hear about this?' Hilary recognised the signs of something unpleasant about to be murmured across the table. At the moment she didn't think she could digest anything stronger than the half-eaten sole.

Fylough smiled into her eyes but didn't falter. 'He ran into me, Harry Kenning, and a few friends. It was speculative. Nothing planned. An on-the-spot ambush. Tough luck for him, really. There was an awful lot of jungle about at that time. He didn't have to stroll into our little bit of it.'

'So you killed him?'

'That was the object of the game. Anyway, strapped around his waist was a waterproof wallet. At that time I hadn't been privy to the CIA/MI5 saga and Kim Cheong's Causeway dash, but I knew what sort of bomb I held in my hand when I opened it . . .' Fylough stopped talking when the waiter arrived and moved away the remnants of the first course. Hilary had lost her appetite but she settled for another glass of wine while Fylough sorted out with the waiter what sauce he wanted on his roast duckling. The trip back into the 1950s jungle fun and games hadn't harmed his appetite. He changed wines – the heady '83 *La Chapelle* from Hermitage – and while he wandered in and out of the crispy-coated carcase, continued his story.

They stayed in the jungle for several days, he told her, chasing the remnants of the people Kim Cheong had attached himself to, but without luck. On return to civilisation he, Fylough, went direct to Jim Morgan, OSPC Segamat, a man of great charm and ability, with a reputation for knowing what to do in any circumstances – a man who was going to the top whether he liked it or not. Morgan told him, much later, that he didn't inform the CIA that he had the documents, or anybody else come to that. He didn't even tell his own people in Kuala Lumpur. Instead, he flew to Singapore, went into a private huddle with the head of SIFE, which in those days was the joint MI5/MI6 establishment for the Far East, and between them they arranged for an immediate disposal of the ambush party – a sound move, because Morgan knew that eventually the news of the killing of Kim Cheong would filter out of the jungle and he didn't want anybody involved in that particular jaunt available for conversation, either to the Yanks or, in the future, the People's investigation teams. He, Fylough, found himself assigned to MI5; Kenning, one of the party, moved to the Northern Border Field Force and then opted out and became a rubber planter; and two attached Europeans, one a soldier, the other a police Special Branch officer, were returned without explanation to their respective parent organisations. The Malays in the party were routinely moved around within the Malayan Police structure.

In fact none of this had really been necessary, Fylough told Hilary, as only he and one or two of the Malays knew that something had been taken off the dead bandit, and only he knew exactly what the contents of the wallet were. He hadn't even informed Kenning. 'Just goes to show what trusting buggers we were in those days!' Fylough filled his glass again. Hilary remained with the Meursault. She wasn't quite sure where her father was taking her. But the story was interesting. She wondered where she and Kent came into the act.

Fylough continued to attack the duckling and talk at the same time.

It wasn't until later, he told her, that he learned Morgan had left the Malayan Police Force literally overnight, and had become Joint Defence Security Officer SIFE – Security Intelligence Far East. But the Americans were sniffing – very suspicious they were . . . Funny how they could put their noses unwaveringly on to something smelly. They asked Morgan how life was up in the firing line. He told them. They asked him whether he'd come across a running Chinaman – a real Chinaman – with a sackful of funny mail. That's strange, Morgan told them, a special Chinese courier had been killed in the Segamat area by a routine patrol, but his bag had been destroyed during the action. Nothing was salvageable, just bits and pieces, and those were fairly ordinary – there was nothing special, nothing with an American slant . . . They didn't believe him but accepted that from their point of view the situation had been made safe. Still, only time would tell. They'd just have to sit on their butts and see whether heads rolled in Peking over the next two or three years. Morgan, however, had his own ideas. What was good for the Americans could only be the same for their cousins the British, so he arranged . . .

Hilary's eyebrows shot up.

Fylough chewed a mouthful of young duckling. '. . . blackmailed . . .' He swallowed and wiped his lips; no sign of reproach. '. . . the American/Chinese agents in position in Peking to allow a high-ranking British agent to be placed in amongst them. They had no choice. Our man was of somewhat higher calibre than the Yanks; it was reckoned that given time he'd do quite well. Morgan went to Hong Kong and made all the arrangements himself, right down to taking his man to the border and handing him into the care of his new associates, and . . .' Fylough placed his knife and fork carefully on top of the debris on his plate and looked up, without smiling, into Hilary's eyes. '. . . and everybody lived happily ever after.'

She stared back. 'Is that it?'

'That's it.'

'What has all that got to do with your friend Kenning and those other men being killed and David Kent dashing around the world looking for God knows what?'

Fylough wiped his moustache again and picked up the menu. But he didn't read from it. 'That's part one,' he said. 'Part two is a different kettle of trout altogether.'

'Is it going to take long?'

'I got the feeling you'd lost interest.'

Hilary smiled and shook her head. 'Quite the opposite. I was wondering whether I had time to take a closer look at that dessert trolley.'

Fylough steeled himself and settled for a wedge of Stilton with which to finish off his wine, staring with envy at the mound of chocolate-orange gateau on Hilary's plate whilst he waited. When the waiter left he stuck a lump of cheese on to the bread crust, carried it up to his mouth, kept it there for a second, then lowered it, holding it in his fingers and studying it with a frown as he continued.

'When the Queen visited China in 1986 Jim Morgan and I decided it was a good opportunity to say hello to our chap and give a *coup d'Œil* at the American implants. Even as recently as 1986 the Chinese were still being unsociable about private visits. Anybody, let alone a couple of shifty-looking English, would have been given very short shrift in the visa office, so we tacked ourselves on to the crew of nodding heads and went out as minor officials of the Foreign Office's cultural team. It was easy to hide amongst that lot – there were enough of them!'

'You weren't afraid of loosening your agent's cover?'

'Hilary, we're not bloody idiots!'

Hilary raised her eyebrows. Fylough stared at her for a moment, gave her the benefit of the doubt, then continued. 'Everybody had done well. It was sleeping at its very best. And why not? They were highly trained operators, head and shoulders above the working-class rabble that had taken over China. The survivors were all in positions, if not of influence, certainly of some degree of importance. Of the four Americans, one had been killed accidently; one had died of oversmoking; and the other two were in Peking University shaping young minds – a very dangerous occupation!

'But our man had actually made it right to the top: Party Secretary-General, deputy to the Chairman of the People's Republic himself . . .' He stared into Hilary's eyes, then smiled thinly and began to eat his cheese.

Hilary didn't want to know. She let the pause lengthen, then nudged him back to her earlier question. 'You were going to tell me what today has got to do with thirty years ago.'

He continued to stare as he debated, mentally, whether he'd sown enough seed, then drank some more Hermitage, swirled it around his mouth and carried on.

'While everybody was oohing and aahing over the flowerpot soldiers at Xi'an I secretly met our man, who told me that shortly, next year or the year after, a great upheaval would be taking place in Chinese politics. He and his American colleagues were stirring the pot so that it was bubbling like warm toffee. They were working on the most receptive minds – the students, the young intelligentsia, the gullible – and leading them sideways to the American way of thinking. When they reckoned the time was right, he and his friends would have them out on the street screaming for the little man's head and the rest of the Politburo to be tossed into the pit. When they'd got everything moving nicely they'd ring the school bell, drag the little buggers off the streets and back into the classrooms, and glue their little revolutionary arses to their desks. They'd then take over the major role and start reshuffling. But . . .'

There was always a but.

'. . . our man suddenly felt the sand under his feet start to shift. Not for the first time in his thirty-five years' bedtime he sensed a sharp knife edging near the back of his neck. And the reason? A good one. A new broom had arrived at TEWA. The TEWA's a very nasty branch of Chinese internal Intelligence, at that time under the benign guidance of one Hu Bang. Hu Bang was a Long Marcher, and Long Marchers were getting thin on the ground – he could do no wrong. A very unpleasant piece of work is Hu Bang. He's retired now, but he still pops along to the office for a bit of pistol practice on the back of some poor bugger's neck! But it wasn't Hu Bang who worried our friend, it was this other fellow – the new broom. Our man pointed him out at a reception and Morgan and I had a good look at him. We came away with an uncomfortable feeling.'

Fylough paused for a second and picked up his glass.

'The new broom had no bloody hands – just a pair of shiny, highly polished steel hooks.'

He raised the glass to his lips and drained it.

'His name was Kim Cheong. The man we'd killed and buried in the jungle, whose hands we had brought back in a shopping bag, was named Kim Cheong.'

'How did you know the jungle Chinese was named Kim Cheong?' asked Hilary.

'Good question,' replied Fylough. 'His fingers had told us nothing other than that he was not a regular Malayan Communist. But then we'd suspected that at the time of the killing. He was filed as "unknown", but some months later a courier carrying a bagful of reports from the 5th Regiment was killed. Among the documents was a record of the death of a transient named Kim Cheong and the disappearance of his guide, a girl named Ah Lian. These details came to Morgan's new department as a matter of course. He checked the dates. They matched.'

'The girl. . . ?'

'Nothing to do with us. We didn't make war on women and children.' Fylough stared blandly into Hilary's eyes. 'She must have got sick of the war and gone off on her own to get her hair permed.'

'So how did a dead bandit with no hands get himself out of a grave from deep in the Malayan jungle and into a top job in the Chinese Gestapo in Peking nearly forty years later?'

'And be in Peking knowing that somewhere out there is a file with stuff in it that could give the next führer of the People's Republic a very sore bottom on his way to the pit in the Shaanxi Street gulag.'

'So how did your Kim Cheong do it?'

Fylough's tongue found a tiny morsel of Stilton jammed in his moustache at the corner of his mouth. He worried it for a moment with the tip of his tongue then brought his napkin up to finish the job. He shook his head. He'd asked himself that question, and the answer had always been the same.

'I'm buggered if I know, Hilary. Maybe Paul Daniels could tell us how it's done.'

'Who's Paul Daniels?'

'A TV magician – does vanishing Chinaman tricks.' Fylough's smile vanished before it took hold. 'But this wasn't a joke. Six months after the Queen's China jaunt, when everything had quietened down and the warlike Chinese were beginning to look to the world like a sort of Far Eastern Sweden, things started to happen over here. Kenning for one, a fellow in Manchester for two, and a former SAS colonel for three. They were all killed in the same manner, a manner that would be very obvious to the fourth man after he'd put one or two things together.'

'What sort of things?'

'The sort of things don't matter. But to answer your earlier questions, I'm the man who's supposed to know where this file is lodged, and I'm supposed to know how to lay my hands on it.'

'Where is it now?'

Fylough hesitated, but only for a second. 'It's buried in the tunnels under Whitehall. It'd take a thousand years to find it if you didn't have the right numbers. Morgan knows how to raise them – I don't. But Morgan's not known as a player in the game to this travelling troupe of Chinese surgeons – that's how I won the bleating goat job. However, you were asking about the first to go – Kenning . . .'

She was about to say it didn't matter any longer, but he got in first.

'Harry Kenning was killed because he refused to point TEWA's people in my direction; the others because they didn't know. David Kent was slipped into the action at the third go to find out what it was all about.'

'And did he?'

'I don't know, he hasn't talked to anybody yet. But he was used, you know. He was only a stalking horse to take the Chinese the long way round. Now he's brought them back to where we started and he still hasn't twigged that that's what we wanted.'

'And what was that?'

Fylough hadn't noticed the tightening of his daughter's lips. He was too busy congratulating himself on the outcome. 'To give them the run-around. They think they've been manipulating him but in fact everybody's been manipulating the poor bugger!'

'What's going to happen to him now?'

Fylough didn't have to think about it. He'd got it all worked out. 'Well, the best thing he can do is duck out of sight, go back to licking envelope flaps or whatever he normally does in Gordon Street – anything so long as he stays out of the way. If he pokes his head round the corner at this point he's likely to get it blown off his shoulders.'

'By whom?'

'That's a bloody silly question, Hilary. The Chinese don't want him any more. If he gets in their way they'll screw him to the floorboards. And we don't want him any more, either. He's an embarrassment. If they don't tidy him up we may have to. The business is now back in the hands of the people who know what they're doing.'

'You didn't say what his objective was supposed to have been, apart from, as you put it, giving them the run-around.'

'Point Goh Peng at me.'

'And he's done that?'

Fylough smiled round the rim of his glass. 'No – you've done it for him. That's why I said he's redundant. The other thing we

192

wanted was to have you in London for the final phase, and he did that too; he brought you over without causing the Chinese to wonder why you should suddenly pick up your skirts and come tripping home. So, by scuffing his feet all over the place he's gathered everybody round the fountain.'

'You really are a bunch of bastards, aren't you?'

'I suppose we are. I think it depends from which angle you're judging . . .' He paused and studied her closely from under his eyebrows. 'Does Kent mean something to you?'

She didn't reply.

'How friendly have you two become?' he insisted.

'I don't consider that any of your business, Dad!' She didn't colour but her eyes gave it away. Fylough wasn't too happy with the effect of his question. She changed the subject. 'Why have you told me all this, I'm not sure I should know about those people in Peking.'

Fylough hesitated for a second, then said, 'You're one of their people; they put you in David Kent's lap as a double pointer to me. You've done it for him – you've pointed. Goh Peng's people will probably want your help later on when the conversation round the dinner table lapses. I've just given you something you can talk about if they become insistent.'

'And how do I explain this – if they become insistent?'

'You tell them David Kent sent you to check me out.'

'You don't expect them to believe that, do you?'

'They will – trust me.'

Hilary stared into her father's eyes for several seconds. He didn't blink. He had on his sincere look. She wished she knew him better. 'I don't think I like the sound of that,' she said at length and tightened her lips. 'When will they move then?'

Fylough glanced casually over her shoulder at the people in the bar. He didn't linger on the man with the wet seal on his head, or on Mithers-Wayne staring at the warm dregs of his German lager.

'They've started,' he said.

Kim Cheong was sitting on his own staring at the ceiling when, after a hesitant knock on the door, Goh Peng entered the room. His normal, impassive expression was replaced by one of apprehension. Kim Cheong lowered his eyes and studied him with interest.

'There is something not right, Comrade Kim Cheong,' said Goh Peng. 'Kent has reported to Curzon Street to seek agreement to interview Fylough – '

'What's wrong with that?' asked Kim Cheong calmly.

'But the woman, West, has made contact with someone identified as a senior executive in the British Intelligence network.'

'Who identified him?'

'Seles, the Yugoslav watching West, followed her to a restaurant in Whitehall. She met this man. She knew him well, according to Seles. Seles met by chance in the bar of the restaurant a female contact, a secretary in the MOD. She made the identification.'

'I don't understand why you are surprised.'

'The contact said that West was the man's daughter – '

'So?'

'She identified the man as Peter Fylough.'

Kim Cheong touched the tips of his hooks together. The sound echoed in the bare room. Nothing was said for several long seconds, then, his gaze centred on the two hooks, Kim Cheong said, 'You have reason, Goh Peng, to be confused. Have you taken care of things?'

'Of course. I believe we must now consider the woman, Hilary West, as an enemy.

'Then treat her accordingly.'

22

Mithers-Wayne was first out of the Grenadier.

When he saw Fylough call for his bill he drained his glass of lager and left. He spotted his cameraman's car tucked in a parking space, strolled across the road and slid into the back seat. The Yugoslav did it the other way round. He waited until Fylough and Hilary had left the restaurant, then came out behind them, nodded briefly to his contact on the other side of the road and moved off, turning left towards Horseguards. He had a knack for getting things right. The taxi Fylough had ordered came from the other end of Whitehall Court and moved in the same direction. The Yugoslav hadn't gone far before a well-dressed Chinese man came up to him, shook his hand openly as if it were an arranged rendezvous and invited him into a dark grey Granada with diplomatic plates and a chauffeur, which was waiting, double-parked, at the beginning of Horseguards. Nobody took the slightest notice. Not even Mithers-Wayne who, having pointed out Fylough to the photographer, got into his own car and followed the taxi. Another car waiting at the Whitehall end of Horseguards with four Chinese occupants, tagged on behind to cover the Granada. The Chinese knew what they were doing. Mithers-Wayne, intent on Fylough's taxi, failed to spot the lengthening tail behind him.

Fylough dropped Hilary off at her Chelsea house. She took the phone off the hook, undressed, showered, and naked, flopped into bed. She blamed the jet lag. The Chinese dropped off a man to look after her. He took up the Yugoslav's old position outside the pub at the end of her cul-de-sac and sat, staring across the road with an untouched half-pint of lager on the table in front of him.

Fylough's taxi turned back along the King's Road and headed west, skirting Hammersmith Broadway and joining Shepherd's Bush Road turning off into a row of tall Victorian houses, most of which were either converted into flats or in the process of being so. Only the odd few remained intact. One of these was number 20, but it didn't say so – it was a MI5 safe house, as was the one that overlooked it from the opposite side of the road.

Fylough paid off the taxi and without looking round walked briskly up the steps as if he'd lived there for the past ten years.

In the second-floor flat opposite two men sat and watched from behind the lace curtains. One of them lowered his head over a Nikon F3 camera, sitting rock solid on a heavy tripod, and turned the bevelled ring of the 600mm F4 Nikon telephoto until Fylough's front door zoomed up against his eyeball; he could see quite clearly the grain of wood wearing through the thin paint-work. He looked up from the camera, stared through the gap in the curtains for a moment, then picked up a headphone set, held one of the earpieces to his ear and listened for several minutes. He was listening to the sounds in Fylough's drawing room through one of the listening devices built into the room's fabric. Satisfied with the quality, he withdrew the headphone plug from its home in the amplifier and plugged it into another socket. This connected to a slim metal lance aimed at a tiny, almost invisible hole in the upper corner of the window opposite. He put the set on his head and listened. Across the road, Fylough coughed and accidentally touched the whisky decanter against his glass. The sound of kissing crystal echoed in the listener's ear like the peal of finely tuned bells. He was satisfied. But it didn't show on his face. He replaced the plug in its earlier socket, sat back in his chair and winked at his companion. The other man didn't respond. He was busy stripping the wrapper off a roll of high-speed infra-red film and it took all his attention as he threaded the leader into the Haselblad he held open on his knees. Neither of them spoke. It looked like being a long evening.

Mithers-Wayne waited at the end of Fylough's road until the taxi had disgorged its passenger and continued on its way before parking his car and strolling casually towards the house. There wasn't a Chinese in sight. Nor a Yugoslav. As he walked past he glanced casually at the door; he couldn't see a number. He didn't slow down. There was nothing, not even *Chez nous* or *Dunroaming*, just a blank, neutral front door. The one on its right said number 18.

At the far end of the road stood one of London's old-fashioned red urinal telephone boxes. It stank. But it didn't put off Mithers-Wayne. He stuck his foot in the door to jam it open and lit a cigarette as he dialled Central Records.

He identified himself and asked, 'Who owns number twenty Bellamy Avenue, W12, and who's occupying it at the moment?'

There was a longish pause while buttons were tapped and then the voice came back, accusingly, as if Mithers-Wayne was wasting the computer's time.

'DOE,' it said.

Mithers-Wayne blew out the mouthful of cigarette smoke he'd been holding in lieu of breathing stale urine fumes and frowned at his reflection in the small mirror. 'Department of the Environment? What are they doing with one house in a Shepherd's Bush backstreet? What about the other houses – those on either side. . . ?'

'Nothing specific, but one has an agreement to access.'

'What does that mean?'

'Christ knows. Number twenty sounds like one of your funny houses and the one next door probably has a bolt-hole.'

'Anything else?'

'There's another one opposite with the same designation.'

Mithers-Wayne replaced the receiver and waited to see if there was any money to come back. There wasn't. But he didn't leave the box for the clean air outside; he remained where he was, deep in thought, with the door half open, and finished his cigarette. A safe house? MI5? SIS? So who the hell was this guy who'd been sitting through a fancy lunch with his hand up Kent's girlfriend's skirt, and how come Kent didn't know who he was?

Mithers-Wayne scowled at himself and ground his cigarette into the debris on the floor of the kiosk. He didn't bloody well know because nobody had put a name to the face. And talking about faces, what about a picture? He dialled another number.

'Has Taffy Lloyd come back yet?' he asked. He had, they said. 'Go and get him then . . .'

'Taffy? Did you get any pictures and have you done anything about it yet?'

The Welsh voice was a mixture of coal dust and male voice choirs. 'Give us a bloody chance, man, I've only just walked through the bloody door.'

'I haven't got a lot of time, Taff.'

'Then you're lucky to have friends who are also efficient, Richard. The girl's a cracker. I'd like to do an artistic session on her – '

'Cut out the crap, Taffy. Tell me about the efficiency.'

' – without a stitch on!'

'Taffy!'

'Calm down, laddo! I did an instant of your bridegroom and when all the fuss had died down I went into the Grenadier, had a quick beer and asked the barman if he could put a name to my picture. He didn't have to ask the waiter; the guy was a regular – '

'I don't want a blow-by-blow account, Taffy, just the bloody name please?'

'Fylough.'

'Christian name?'

'They weren't on those terms.'

'What's he do?'

'No idea. I haven't started on him yet. Try me in half an hour.'

'Thanks, Taff. See you . . .'

It was time to talk to David Kent. Mithers-Wayne opened his diary at the address section and found Kent's home number. He propped the diary open and began to dial. He had only got to the fourth digit when the phone-box door was dragged open.

'I haven't finished – ' he snarled and half turned. He got no further.

In front of him stood a squat, heavily built Chinese and just behind him, a tall, greasy-black-haired, sallow-looking man. He recognised him but barely had time to register that he'd last seen him propping up the bar in The Grenadier, when the Chinese, perfectly balanced, jabbed three fingers, as hard as metal rods, into his stomach, just below the ribcage.

The wind rushed out of his lungs with a whoosh and the phone flew out of his hand as he doubled forward.

The Chinese leaned forward to rest his hands casually on Dick Mithers-Wayne's shoulders and then, without apparent effort, pushed downwards so that, still gasping, he ended up crouched on the floor in the corner of the box. A hand came over the Chinese man's shoulder to replace the phone on its hook and then the Chinese stepped back out of the way and his place was taken by the tall, dark-haired man. Mithers-Wayne recognised the smell and opened his eyes.

'Get up,' the man said in little more than a whisper, and touched Mithers-Wayne's chin with the bulbous end of a short-barrelled revolver. Mithers-Wayne stood with difficulty. His head was clearing and his breath, although having difficulty getting past his throat, was actually filtering into his lungs. He pulled himself up the side of the telephone box and wondered where these two had come from. But he had no time to make conclusions. The man with the gun picked up the diary from the ledge and with his free hand guided him out of the kiosk. The squat Chinese took up a position on his other side and the three of them stood on the pavement as the grey Granada appeared from the right, driven by another Chinese.

Mithers-Wayne didn't struggle. What was the point? If nothing else, he was a pragmatist. What the bloody hell did you do with your knees feeling like jelly, your gut almost bursting with the agony of a bunch of six-inch rivets having been rammed into it, and a foreign-looking guy holding against your ear a nasty piece of what looked like Czechoslovakian ironwork, silenced down to an almost noiseless plop?

They sat him in the back, one on either side of him, and once someone had closed the door, one of the Chinese grabbed him by the hair and pressed his head down between his knees. The pistol held by the other man ground into the soft part of the back of his head, just above his neck. Nobody said a word, but a hand went into his jacket pocket and brought out his car key.

The car stopped at the top of Bellamy Avenue and the Yugoslav with the greasy hair and smelly aftershave slipped out of the Granada and walked briskly towards Dick Mithers-Wayne's car. Sliding behind the steering wheel he followed the Granada along Holland Road into Kensington High Street and then to Hyde Park. The Chinese seemed to know exactly what they were doing and where they were going. The Yugoslav closed up on them as they descended the slope into the underground car park and kept on their tail. Dick Mithers-Wayne tried to raise his head to see what was going on but the Chinese man's pistol gouging into the back of his neck kept it jammed between his knees.

He'd worked out where they were, but he couldn't make out why – the underground car park didn't make sense.

The Granada pulled into a space on the third level; the Yugoslav slid in neatly beside them.

'Get out,' said one of the Chinese. It was the first time any of them had spoken. He did as he was told. The second Chinese held open the front door of his car and pushed him into the driver's seat. He looked around. Just two Chinese. The Yugoslav had vanished.

The first misgivings began like a little worm wriggling its way around his stomach. He sat in the driving seat and the door was closed gently, not noisily, just closed and the latch caught by the weight of the Chinaman's body leaning on it. The other Chinese slid into the back seat. *So we're going for more ta-tas? Must be a new Chinese game* . . . He grasped the familiar steering wheel and saw that the key was still in the lock. Mistake? He reached for it at the same time as he felt the metal on the back of his neck and a hand grasp the collar of his coat.

He didn't hear the shot.

The bullet carved upwards into his brain. He didn't feel a thing. The Chinese hung on to his collar until he stopped shaking, then leaned over and carefully lowered Mithers-Wayne's body so that he was spread across the two front seats.

The Chinese man got out, took the key from the ignition and locked the doors. He peered into the side windows. It was dark and gloomy in the subterranean car park; it was darker inside the car. They'd gone to an awful lot of trouble. Dickie Mithers-Wayne was going to be there, curled up, invisible, until somebody got fed up with seeing the same car parked in the same spot and decided to do something about it.

23

Four Chinese, concealed in two cars, hung around Bellamy Avenue until dusk.

Fylough made it easy for them.

At a quarter-past seven the front door opened and he stepped out into the street. He'd changed from city gent to country squire. Dressed in a pale blue turtleneck sweater over a checked shirt, a scarf knotted around his neck, white corduroys, and dark brown suede boots, he turned right and headed up the street towards the pub on the other side of the crossroads, just opposite Mithers-Wayne's telephone box. One of the Chinese took off his dark blue jacket, removed his tie and followed him in.

In the second car Goh Peng watched the house until dusk. It remained in darkness. It was what he was waiting for; there was nobody else in there. He left the car and with the other passenger, nipped across the road and descended the basement steps. His companion carried a small black suitcase which he placed carefully at his feet as he and Goh Peng studied the basement door. After a moment he nodded, stepped back and motioned the other man forward. Placing his finger to his lips Goh Peng turned to the steps, raised himself on his toes and with just the top of his head level with the pavement surveyed both ends of the avenue. Nothing moved.

He hissed to the waiting man, who at once opened his case. Within seconds he had neutralised the alarm system on the door. He turned the lock and cautiously slid through the gap. He took his time screening the corridor and then quickly deactivated the basement security system. He did the same with the first floor. The top floor was unused; he could see it was not covered by the alarm system.

'Check the phone and clean it,' Goh Peng told the other man when they'd entered the main part of the house. 'Then go back to the car and send the others, one at a time. You stay there and forward the message when the Englishman leaves the pub.'

The housebreaker did more than clean the phone. He totally disinfected the room of all built-in surveillance equipment, and in case there was something he'd overlooked, and his flat peasant Chinese face almost smiled at the unthinkable, he filled the room with an ultrasonic electronic blanket.

Across the road the man listening at the decoding amplifier merely shrugged his shoulders at the sudden cotton-wool-like silence and winked at his companion as he disconnected and plugged into the laser socket. The Chinese had blocked the window vibrations, but he hadn't blocked the hole.

Fylough kept them waiting. It wasn't until half-past ten that the message came through to Goh Peng that he'd left the pub and was on his way home. Goh Peng put down the phone and the only change in his manner was a slight stiffness in his back as he sat upright in the armchair by the window. He'd left the curtains open and had a clear view of the front steps.

Fylough walked straight into the ambush.

An automatic was held against the side of his head as he came through the door. It was pitch-dark. He stood still. No sudden movement. No movement at all. Another man pushed him against the wall and steadied him there whilst a third ran his hands over him. Nothing was said. They found nothing. Just money, handkerchief, keys. The automatic moved to the back of his head and settled in the hollow of his neck. When one of the other men took his arm lightly and guided him along the dark corridor the pistol remained in place. The searcher stayed by the door. There'd been no words, no faces seen, no violence, but Fylough knew they were Chinese. It was the smell, a dry stomachy smell that hung around them; they were born with it; it was unforgettable. The Chinese said the same about the smell of the Englishman.

Goh Peng didn't move.

'Curtains . . .' he hissed and switched on the table lamp beside him. 'Sit there,' he instructed Fylough and pointed to a chair that had been placed on its own against the wall. The man with the gun went with him, sat him down, moved away and stood with his arms crossed, the gun resting in the crook of his arm.

Goh Peng studied Fylough for several long seconds. 'Is your name Fylough?' he asked at length.

Fylough stared back. His wallet and pocketbook were on the

dining-room table. He looked at them pointedly, then back at Goh Peng, and shrugged his shoulders.

'You know who I am,' he said. 'And I know who you are. Your name is Goh Peng and you're CELD – probably TEWA. You're at the Embassy. You're legal. But now you're busted. You've nothing to do here now you've broken out. And you're not going home without at least a charge of housebreaking.'

Goh Peng wasn't impressed. It was exactly what he expected. But, he almost smiled to himself, it was exactly what he would have said if it had been the other way round! He uncurled himself from the chair and walked to the telephone on the sideboard. He tapped out seven digits. Fylough counted them as matter of habit; the Chinese would be ringing the Embassy, or the Trade Commission. He looked at Goh Peng's crew. They were all staring back at him – no expression – just watching, unblinking, like three Chinamen staring at a dead man. He turned his attention back to the man with the phone.

'Fylough is here, waiting for you,' Goh Peng said softly into the mouthpiece. 'The car will fetch you. Come to the front door . . .' He paused, stared into Fylough's eyes and this time almost smiled; it was nearly, but not quite, the real thing. '. . . like welcome guests.' He put down the phone and went back to his chair.

'OK,' said Fylough, forcing a yawn into Goh Peng's face, 'what's this all about? You're keeping me out of bed.'

'Don't talk!' Goh Peng sat back in his chair, crossed his legs and stared at the wall above Fylough's head. He seemed to have gone into a trance.

'Perhaps you'd ask one of these gentlemen to make me a cup of coffee,' said Fylough.

There was no reply. Goh Peng's eyes remained on the wall. They never flickered. The three Chinese remained staring, unrelaxed, vigilant as if their lives depended on their not taking their eyes off Fylough – which they did. Fylough decided he was wasting his time. He loosened his body in the high-backed chair and joined Goh Peng in his trance.

24

David Kent knocked on the door of Evelyn St John Woodhouse's office and opened it without waiting for a response. Woodhouse looked up from under his eyebrows and said sarcastically, 'Come in.' There was no smile, but he nodded a welcome and waved his hand at the chair on the other side of his desk. '*Kong hee fatt choy!*'

'I beg your pardon?'

'I thought you spoke Chinese.'

'You've just wished me a happy New Year.'

'Just testing. Have you made a report on this Far East jaunt you've just done?'

'I'm making it now.'

'Don't bother. Jot something down on paper to justify the trip and cost and then forget about it.'

Kent's expression didn't change. He reached into his inside pocket, brought out an envelope and extracted from it one of the photographs he'd taken from Corporal Togom's tin box. It was the one of the two Europeans with the Malay head-hunting team in front of four samples of their work. He slid it across the desk so that it rested just in front of Woodhouse's fingers.

'What's the name of the guy on the right?' he asked tersely.

Woodhouse lowered his eyes and looked at the small grubby print. He didn't pick it up. He seemed quite interested in the composition of violent death and studied it for some time. On the other hand he might have been thinking up a snappy answer to Kent's question. After a few more moments, and without taking his eyes off the tableau, he said, 'Who? The one lying on his back with his guts on his stomach?'

'You know which one I mean.' Kent leaned forward across the desk and jabbed his finger on Fylough's face. 'That one there.'

'What makes you think – ?'

'Cut it out!' snapped Kent. 'When that picture was taken his name was Fylough. What does he call himself now?'

'I don't think I like the tone of your voice, David.'

Kent didn't change it. 'Have a closer look. It's "er"-Smith, isn't it? The FO's personal and private Dick Tracy. And this one . . .' He took from the envelope the picture of the OSPC, Segamat. 'Who's he, and what does he call himself nowadays, apart from Jim Morgan?'

Woodhouse looked up slowly. He didn't push the photograph away. 'I said you can forget it, David. We've lost interest in the Chinese. The Chink season's over. We've closed the file and moved on to other things.' He settled back in his chair and washed his hands with invisible soap. 'Take a couple of days off. Get rid of the jet lag, go and sit in the park and feed the ducks, and forget all about Chinamen . . .' He paused and studied Kent's blank face. 'And when you feel bright and frisky there's some stuff on your desk I'd like you to take an interest in. It's about all these Kurds who want to come and live with us. That should be up your street; you can talk Chinese to them.' The corners of his mouth moved in an imitation smile. But the smile didn't develop into a real one; it vanished with an almost audible click when Kent stood up.

'I'd like to see the Director-General.'

'I beg your pardon?'

'I'd like to see the D-G.'

'I thought that's what you said. What's the matter, David – you want to resign?'

'I didn't say anything about resigning.'

Woodhouse didn't exactly smirk. 'The only opportunity that boys of your status get to see the D-G is for a farewell handshake after tending your resignation and having it accepted – and you do that through me. Now, be a good chap, David, and go away and think about it while you're counting Turds coming through the gate at Heathrow. And, David, I'll be very cross if you don't put this Chinese business to bed. I might even be cross enough to send you back to Watching. Think about it – a permanent Watching job from an attic overlooking Ken Livingstone's council flat?' This time Woodhouse did smile. But it was wasted on Kent.

He shook his head, picked up the photograph of Jim Morgan and held it under Woodhouse's nose. 'In case you've missed the likeness,' he said calmly, 'this is Sir James Morgan when he was a boy scout. Now, as you know, he's Head of MI6. He drinks his coffee out of Royal Worcester on the top floor of Century House and allows the flies to call him "Cee". I want to talk to him. It's urgent. And after I've had my little chat I'll accept your invitation to go and shake hands with our own Mighty Mouse upstairs.'

'Out of the question, David.'

'I'd like permission to visit the Foreign Office Registry.'

'Also out of the question.'

'Then fuck you too!'

Kent ignored Woodhouse's startled look and reached across the desk to remove the photograph of the dead bandits from between his fingers. He didn't smile, he didn't grimace, he didn't say anything. He just took the pictures, turned on his heel and walked out of the office.

Woodhouse kept his startled look in place for a few seconds after the door closed in case Kent chose to come back and stick his fingers up his nose. Then he relaxed and smiled to himself, swinging his chair round so that he could view his image in the window. He studied himself for several minutes. He looked smug and content. The boat was slipping through the water without a ripple, his hand on the tiller steady as he manoeuvred to his captain's orders. He waited a few moments more, then picked up the telephone and asked the operator to ring Century House. After negotiating his protective screen he was put through to Sir James Morgan, the Head of MI6. The two men spoke at length before Woodhouse replaced the receiver and returned to his reflection in the window.

Kent didn't bother looking at his desk. He didn't want to know about Kurds; he had other matters on his mind, and Woodhouse, instead of allaying his curiosity about Fylough and Foreign Office files, had sharpened it. He wasn't worried. They were still advertising for bright young men for the Royal Hong Kong Police Force.

He carried on out of the building, caught a bus at the top end of Piccadilly and got off outside the National Gallery. He didn't look round or over his shoulder; if anybody was following him they were welcome to go all the way. But, just in case, he cut across Trafalgar Square, down Northumberland Avenue into Whitehall Place, and joined the queue outside the telephone boxes on the corner. When it was his turn he walked past the box and retraced his steps up Northumberland Avenue. There was nobody following him. He turned into Whitehall, crossed the road and presented himself at the desk in the entrance to the Foreign Office building. The MOD policeman studied him without curiosity; he was looking for Irishmen with bulging shopping bags. Kent smiled at the lady at the desk and showed her his authority. She raised her eyebrows but didn't smile or say good morning.

'I'd like to see Mr Fylough, please,' he said politely.

She studied the list of names pinned to the back of the desk just out of sight of the visitor, looked back into Kent's face and shook her head. Then, in a moment of weakness, she looked at the list again and pursed her lips in disapproval. 'Ministry of Defence,' she said and pointed her ballpoint at the door. 'Across the road and –'

'I know where it is,' said Kent. 'What room number?'

She shook her head again. 'Ask over there.' She lowered her head over the sheet of blank paper in front of her to indicate that that was the end of the interview. The MOD policeman nodded approvingly. Kent said 'Thanks for your help' and went back out into the sun and the ordinary people.

At the Ministry of Defence he showed his card again and was given a form to fill in. It was taken away and then brought back and handed to one of the MOD policemen standing in apparent idleness in the large busy vestibule. They were chosen for their smooth manner. ' 'E's not in.'

Kent stared back into the Neanderthal eyes. 'Where will I find him?'

The eyes stared back. Nothing came out of the mouth.

'Can I see his secretary?'

'You know 'er name?'

'No. What is it?'

'If yer don't know you can't see 'er.'

'Thanks.'

Kent went back into the sun again.

He debated whether to tell his story to Sir James Morgan and ask his advice, but dropped the idea in the same breath. If it was impossible to sit down and crook his little finger over a teacup with Fylough's secretary, what were the chances of gazing into the Head of MI6's pale blue eyes? He decided on a pint of bitter instead.

The King's Head was almost opposite the Horse Guards Building. Nothing pretentious, an ordinary Central London pub, unexceptional, except that it was full of civil servants complaining about their working conditions and discussing the next 60 per cent pay rise they were going to go on strike for. He picked up his pint of Watneys and sat down in a corner beside the only two non-suited, non-stripy-tied people in the bar. They took no notice of him. They didn't look up. They didn't stop talking, except to raise the tall glasses of lager to their mouths.

'Fuckin' 'Ammers, useless bastards!' said one.

'You've already gone over that,' said the other, an older man with traces of pink clay-like substance on the back of his hands and deep under his fingernails. 'If it's football you want – real football – you've gotta forget bleedin' Upton Park for the next five years and go and watch the Gunners.'

'Fuckin' nancy boys! They're all bleedin' black . . .'

The older man looked at his watch and emptied his glass. 'Drink your beer, sonny,' he said, 'and let's get back to those bloody pipes. We'll bugger off early this afternoon and you can go tonight an' be the only one watching West Ham getting their arses kicked around the park by Accrington Stanley or something.'

His mate didn't know what Accrington Stanley was so he let it go. 'But wha' abaht the Foreign Office boiler? Fred said – '

Kent pricked his ears up at the mention of the Foreign Office but continued to drink his beer and read the paper that had been left on the table. It was the *Sun*. But that didn't matter.

'I know what Fred said, but 'e ain't 'ere, is 'e. We'll go along the tunnel from the War Office, take some measurements, leave some of our gear there and start first thing in the morning. You can tell me all about what it's like watching third-division football.'

'Second division.'

'Come on.'

The two men left. So did Kent.

He followed them down Scotland Yard and under the arch into Whitehall Place. They stopped briefly at a battered transit and fed the parking meter without opening the door or taking anything out. The logo on the van read 'Dixon Insulation and Maintenance Ltd'. He watched the two men cross the road and go into the main entrance of the War Office. He didn't linger. He walked briskly up

Whitehall Place and darted into one of the phone boxes just as it was being vacated.

He rang Gower Street, where a specialised section of MI5's A Branch was housed, and asked to speak to John Mainwaring. John Mainwaring was a desk man in the Administration section. His speciality was 'resources', which meant he could supply anything from a burglar's kit to a false nose; if he didn't have it he'd find it, and if he didn't know about it he'd find out and ring you back within minutes. He was indispensable and he harboured no ill will. He was everybody's friend. 'John, it's David Kent. Can you give me a bit of advice – no entry in the book?'

'Depends, David. What's your plea?'

'What sort of pass does a workman need to get into the War Office?'

Mainwaring didn't have to think about it. 'That building, like most others in Whitehall, comes under the Department of the Environment. Contracts for work are handled by the Public Services Agency.'They issue passes for workmen to come and go as they please.'

'Individual passes, photographs, that sort of thing?'

'No – just the name. Minimum vetting. The onus if someone blows up the building rests with the contractor; it's up to him to have the right people. If anybody strays he goes up the Swanee with them. Anything else?'

'How do I get one?'

'You don't need it. Show your pass. The security people on the desk'll run it through the computer and then it'll be automatically entered into the records against the reason for your wanting to go in. Simple as that.'

Kent pulled a face. 'Thanks, John.'

'Any time.'

He walked back to the transit van, tried the door – openly. It was locked. He banged the side of it in exasperation, just in case anybody was looking, and walked across the road to the front entrance of the War Office. He went up the steps two at a time, pushed open the door and said to the group of people at the desk in the corner, 'Have my two men gone down yet, please? The silly so-and-so's have locked the van and taken the keys with them.'

'Dixon's people?' said the MOD policeman leaning against the sign that said 'Maximum Security area – no admittance without proper authority'. 'They've gone downstairs, about fifteen minutes ago. Who are you?'

'Dixon,' said Kent, 'Danny Dixon,' and hoped that Danny Dixon hadn't died ten years ago.

He obviously hadn't. 'You know where they're working?'

'On the pipes in the tunnel – I started them off myself . . .'

'You'll probably catch them before they've gone the distance,' grinned the policeman and pointed to a pair of old-fashioned swing doors. 'Those bloody tunnels go for miles.'

'Cheers, mate,' said Kent and went through the doors and found himself in a corridor. Easy as that. He didn't smile or gloat. It was bloody criminal.

He made his way downwards until he could go no further.

He met a West Indian wearing a brown overall, a jelly-bag hat and carrying a mop. The mop was dry and he had no bucket but he seemed to know what he was doing – whatever that was. Kent asked him if he'd seen two men working on some pipes. Sure he had. Laggers. Down there, about half a mile, metal door on the right, take the right fork and follow the newly lagged overhead pipes heading towards the top end of Whitehall. You a lagger too, mate? But Kent was gone at a brisk walk.

He slowed down when he heard voices echoing along the deserted, badly lit and unused passage. The conversation was still football; still effing 'Ammers. He turned the corner. The older man was up the ladder and the other one, the West Ham supporter, was standing on the bottom rung passing up lengths of half-round insulation sections. They stopped what they were doing and stared suspiciously when he approached them.

'I've lost my way,' he said cheerfully.

A posh voice. Supervision. They glanced a warning at each other and continued to stare. The man at the top of the ladder removed the two sections he was holding in place round the pipe and rested them on the little platform. 'Where you looking for, mate?'

'Foreign Office.' He took the card from his top pocket and showed it to the man at the foot of the ladder. The youth didn't look at it. 'Security check,' said Kent. 'I'm looking at all these tunnels – I think they ought to be signposted. Don't you?'

The man on the ladder laughed. No bother here, a worker – well, almost a worker – like us. He squatted on his haunches and took out a packet of Senior Service, no tips. He didn't offer them. They were a connoisseur's fags. He lit one, blew the smoke out with a gentle whoosh and pointed the cigarette in the direction Kent had come. 'You've gotta go back there for about four hundred yards and take a right-hand at the junction; you stay on that for about half a mile then take the door with a green half-light above it. That's the basement of the Foreign Office. D'you know where you are then?'

Kent nodded. 'I think so. I came through Records; that's on the same landing, isn't it?'

'No, mate. You've got yourself upside down. I'm not surprised; it's like being a bloody worm down 'ere. No, you want to go through that door, take the concrete stairs to the next landing and then the second door on the right.'

Kent nodded. 'Thanks.'

'If you'd like to wait half an hour or so we're going that way to look at the boiler.'

'No thanks. I'll struggle along. See you in a year's time if I haven't found my way out!'

He could still hear their condescending laughter as he vanished into the gloom and turned the corner. He passed the door where he'd entered the tunnel and peered into the stack of large cardboard boxes that he'd noticed on either side of the door. They were full of insulation sections and binding ready to cover the bare water pipes. One of the boxes was the rubbish bin. Bits of different-sized broken sections, pink plaster and dust, and, thrown carelessly in amongst the rubbish, a pair of grubby, torn white overalls. He listened for a moment to the voices of the two workmen: they were indistinct; they hadn't moved; they were working diligently. Mr Dixon would be very pleased with them. He picked up the overalls and an armful of lagging sections and moved off in the direction he'd been given.

He turned right and stopped by a fire point. He took off his jacket, rolled it up and shoved it behind the sand bucket. He left his tie on but loosened it and opened the top button of his shirt; that was how laggers dressed for Whitehall work. He slipped on the overalls, tucked the sections under his arm, then scuffed his shoes in the grey dust that had collected around the hydrant and moved on. He looked the part. All he needed now was a real security check!

The tunnel seemed to go on for ever. Claustrophobic – he began to understand how the old lagger felt – but then, just as it started to bite, he turned a shallow curve and saw the green light glowing dimly in the distance.

He went through the door and up the stairs. It was more civilised, carpet on the floor and plenty of lights, all burning brightly. There was a gentle, apologetic hum – the air-conditioning, cool and pleasant in the summer, boiling hot and pleasant in the winter, expense no object.

The sign on the door said 'Registry and Records'. He hesitated, then stepped back as two women, young and pretty but serious-looking – it was an important business working in the bowels of the old empire – appeared from the civilised direction. One of them gave him an interested look then rapidly corrected herself – the face was all right but the clothes all wrong. They pushed past him and went through the door.

He gave them a few seconds to settle themselves down then followed them in. It was like any other non-computerised registry, strip lighting burned the eyeballs and flattened out the shadows, making the place look like the inside of a specimen jar. The two girls were being helped by a man with the wrong face but the right clothes. He had on a smart, neatly knotted tie with light blue diagonal stripes on a black background; it showed he was from the right quarter and was going in the right direction. He looked at Kent with a disapproving frown.

'Can I help you?'

'Dixon's Insulation, replied Kent, 'we're lagging this part of the building. I've been told to come and look at the pipes for the PSA estimate.'

'I know nothing about this.'

'Sorry, sir . . .' The striped tie smirked with pleasure. The working classes were getting the message again. 'Sir' indeed. What a nice worker! '. . . my guvnor's back there in the tunnel; he's got the schedule. He told me to come on, check the piping in Records and wait for him – this is Records?'

'Of course. You're not going to make a mess?'

'Just looking, sir.'

'All right. But be a good fellow and don't touch anything. Don't move or open anything, and don't make a noise – and don't get in anybody's way.'

'Thank you, sir.'

Kent walked along the end of the first bank of shelves and stopped to stare at the ceiling. There were no pipes, just a white ceiling. The air-conditioning was gushing happily from narrow grilles in the wall at ground level, but striped tie didn't know, or care, by what method he was being spoiled. And he'd already forgotten the working classes. He was showing off his importance to the two secretaries.

Kent slipped his diary out of his back pocket and studied the notes he'd made in the Hong Kong Police Registry: N – for top secret. 3936.

He looked around him and stared at the blank ends of the banks of shelves. No A; no B; no C . . . no bloody nothing! How the bloody hell did you find your way around here? Security? Or just plain idiotic civil servant stupidity! That was something you could count on. He lowered his eyes slightly and glanced at the group round striped tie's desk. Where the bloody hell was N for top secret?

'I'll get yours at the same time, dear. Er, you didn't say what it was . . .' The man's voice raised itself slightly and Kent turned his attention to the other end of the room.

'It's an N file,' she shrieked. She could have gone to the same school as the tie; the accent was identical and slightly high-pitched, edging on the hysterical, as if she was about to reach orgasm. 'Sir Robert said you'd know – it's secret or something . . .'

Kent stopped in his tracks and turned slowly. He was covered by the length of the shelves, but by moving along the other side and staring at the blank ceiling he could see what was going on.

'Of course! Leave it up to me, both of you. What's the reference? Have you got a group number? Do sit down. Cup of tea?' It was a lonely job, Registry, particularly this one, where everything was dead and out of date. But he had all the social graces. He must be very popular on the Pimms and Buck's Fizz circuit.

213

'No thanks, really. We really must be getting back. Some other time?'

'The reference?'

'Oh, silly me! Here, it's all written down.'

Kent watched the tie. It moved out of sight. Kent moved rapidly down the other side of the shelf that was shielding him. He stopped just in time. He was in front of the N section – as was the tie, who was standing in front of a bank of pale blue files, studying the piece of paper in his hand. He frowned his annoyance at Kent, who moved apologetically past him and touched the blank ceiling with one of the rolls of lagging, making a clicking noise with his tongue. He watched out of the corner of his eye. The man knew his job. It took him only a second to deal with Sir Robert's business and then he moved off in search of the other girl's problem.

Kent stared at N at the same time as he studied another minute section of the ceiling. The Ns started at 1001; he wanted 3936. There it was – about there. The rest was easy. Group: WO . . . F & C . . . FE . . . FO – *Got it! Christ* There were acres of Group FO . . . He moved a few feet, still staring upwards and still watching the desk out of the corner of his eye. The young man had found what the second woman wanted and all three had moved towards the door. Kent watched them. Maybe they would all go for a pee together.

His luck was in.

'Will you be all right on your own for a few minutes, Mr Lagger? Where are you? I say, where are you?'

'I'm here, sir. Don't worry about me – there's not much more to do.'

'Good man. If anybody comes in tell them I shall be back in five. I've gone for a cuppa!'

'Leave it up to me, sir.' But sir had already gone. He'd gone to take tea with crumpet. Kent couldn't believe his luck.

Quick! FO 148 . . . Got it! A quick look at the diary. File number 23142. There it was: grubby, dusty, pale blue, and not very thick. He slid it out and flicked it open.

It was the swish of the door swinging back on its hinges that startled him. There was no time to put it back; no time to look at its contents.

'Simon?' The voice sounded senior.

Kent bent the file, rolled it, and stuck it between two of the

214

half-round sections of lagging. His eyes were just about halfway back up the shelving system on their way to the ceiling again when the face appeared round the corner.

'Who the devil are you?'

'Lagger, sir. Dixon's Insulation. Checking the hot water pipes and – '

'Where's Simon?'

'Beg pardon, sir?'

'Where is the officer in charge of this section?'

'He's just gone out, sir.'

'Gone out? Gone out? What the bloody hell are you doing in here, then? This is a restricted area. You're not allowed here unless supervised. Now, get outside and wait in the corridor until Mr Beauchamp comes back. I don't know what the bloody hell things are coming to!'

'Sorry, sir.' Kent bolted for the door and waited outside until Simon appeared along the corridor. 'I'm off now, sir,' he told him. 'I've finished in there.'

'Good man!'

Kent didn't wait to hear Simon get his bollocking. He went down the stairs and made his way back along the tunnel. He collected his jacket from behind the sand bucket and moved at a brisk silent trot back to his starting position. He cautiously approached the boxes of spare lagging by the door. Nothing had changed. He shoved the file down the back of his trousers and dropped everything else in the rubbish box. He straightened up and listened. There was no sound from the real laggers. Maybe they were waiting for him in the hallway – with half a dozen Stone Age MOD policemen. He was due for a spell of bad luck! He tiptoed along to the bend in the tunnel and peered round. The two laggers were sitting comfortably with their backs to the wall, smoking and drinking tea from a flask. They'd worked a full hour since lunch-time – they must have reckoned they'd earned their three-quarters of an hour pre-tea break.

Kent mounted the stairs and came out into the War Office entrance. There was a different policeman on duty. He looked keen. He'd only been there five minutes. Kent's heart sank.

'See yer pass, please?' He straightened up as Kent walked across the black and white tiled floor.

'E's orl right, Sandy.' The earlier policeman appeared from a cupboard. He'd removed his tunic and hat and now had on a Harris tweed jacket. He was in mufti. But he still looked like an over-age policeman going off duty. 'That's Mr Dixon – the laggers. 'is lads are down in the tunnels. Find 'em orl right, Mr Dixon?'

'Thanks very much.' Kent waved and went through the front door.

'Just a minute!'

It sounded like a Grenadier Guards sergeant-major calling the colour-guard to attention. Kent stopped dead. His back felt vulnerable. The last time he'd had a similar sensation was when he'd been caught in the open with a hopped-up crazy Chinaman banging away at him with an old Sten gun. Before he'd got under cover the whole magazine had thumped into the wall he was trying to get behind. Here it came! He turned slowly.

'You didn't forget what you went down for?'

'Pardon?'

'The keys, Mr Dixon – the van keys. You went down for the keys.'

Kent's hand shook as he brought out from his coat pocket a bunch of keys. He didn't have to waggle them. He just held them up and they waggled themselves.

25

The Chinese Watcher was very good; Kent hadn't once spotted him.

He waited until Kent had gone into his flat, then lit a cigarette and wandered along to the telephone kiosk halfway down the road, but at no time did his eyes leave the entrance to Kent's flat. He rang the Chinese Embassy, left his message and went back to his car at the other end of the street. He made himself comfortable on the front seat, lit another cigarette and waited.

The officer on duty in China's Portland Place branch of CELD logged the message, consulted the pad in front of him and dialled Fylough's flat number. Fylough passed the phone to Goh Peng, who listened without interrupting.

One of the men in the flat opposite also listened and when he put the phone down rechecked that the Sony tape recorder on the table beside the phone had come on automatically and recorded the conversation. He appeared satisfied. He picked up another phone, dialled, and after a brief conversation played the rewound section of tape into the telephone. Then he listened again. The man by the window blew across the scalding tea in the plastic top of a thermos.

'Anything?' he asked. He didn't turn round.

'Charlie Chan!' replied his companion. 'I didn't understand a bloody word he was saying. They ran it through the gizmo in the shop. It was the Chinese laundry telling a guy named Goh Peng that somebody named Kent spent three-quarters of an hour in the War Office and has now gone home.'

The man at the window grunted and sipped his tea. It was still too hot. He swore but otherwise offered no comment.

Goh Peng put down the phone and nodded to the man standing by the door. He ignored Fylough. 'Go and fetch the West woman.' He parted the curtains with his finger and studied the road. 'And you . . .' He allowed the curtains to fall together and glanced at one of the men standing beside Fylough. ' . . . go to the front door. When Comrade Kim Cheong arrives escort him here.' The two men left together and after a brief inspection of Fylough's apparent lack of agitation Goh Peng sat down and returned to his trance.

26

Kent threw the blue file on the kitchen table and poured himself a large whisky. He held it under the tap and filled the glass almost to the brim with water, then opened the fridge, broke out a handful of small round ice cubes and dropped them in one at a time until the glass nearly overflowed. He knew he was wasting time; he was delaying the moment; not savouring – delaying. He drank a large mouthful of whisky and water, swilled it round his mouth and put the glass on the table; then he lit a cigarette and sat down and opened the file. If Peter Fylough didn't want to tell him why Dixie Dean and his mates had been killed maybe this would. He spread the contents on the table and stared.

It was in three parts; three separate covers. He recognised the first – he'd studied it in Hong Kong. He read the introduction; '. . . contents associated with additional files – Classification; (Top Secret) N3936. Group: F0148 . . .' But he already knew this . . . Kent stared at it as he smoked his cigarette; he shook his head absently to dispense the smoke curling past his slitted eyes, and continued to read. '. . . HK file reallocated: Original 23141 attached to 23142 and one copy reserved under Group 149 (classified ULTRA. Chinese affairs)'. He turned the cover of the blue file to remind himself. It wasn't really necessary. 23142! Kent lifted the third envelope. It was sealed. He studied the inscription: '*For issue only by the designated authority* . . .' It was in red and underlined. He blew the ash off the end of his cigarette and then blew again to clear it off the papers on the table. '. . . *PM/FS/ through CM16.*'

'Jesus!' He almost had second thoughts. The designated authorities were the Prime Minister and the Foreign Secretary – under the advice of C of MI6. It was probably a hanging job just looking at the inscription; possible transportation to Australia for opening it. The hanging might be less painful. Kent didn't smile; there was nothing funny in losing your job the hard way, with a possible eighteen years in Parkhurst. He turned the envelope over and stared at the seal. Plain wax, no indentation. Easy. He went into the kitchen and boiled the kettle. He heated a knife in the water and inserted the blade under the seal. It came up like chewing gum. He steamed open the flap and shook the contents on to the table. Six thin sheets that looked like application forms for new passports spread out in front of him.

Kent allowed the breath he was holding to escape through his pursed lips and arranged the papers in a line. They were all originals; some had had a rough passage, crinkled, cracked and in places faded, with damp marks encroaching like bloodstains along the tattered edges. Was this what it was all about? Was this what men had been frightened to death for with razor cuts round their wrists? Kent lit another cigarette and stared at the documents. It was all there: photographs; details (all Chinese males aged twenty-five to thirty-five); names, cover names, double cover names; places of birth; and – wait for it, the chop behind the ear, the execution block! – *inducted USA; trained and equipped CIA/USA.*' Except one. British sphere of influence. Introduced mainland XX53 . . .

Kent heaved on the cigarette, then picked up one of the other documents and held the two up side by side. The British one was nice and clean and bright and shiny; the other one looked as though it had survived the Crimean War. And the dates. He looked closer. The British implant had been nearly a year after the CIA operation. Two different projects but both snuggled up together in an envelope in a file in the British Foreign Office Registry in the bowels of Whitehall. And then he looked again.

MI6's Chinese agent stared blankly back at him. He hadn't changed all that much; just thirty-odd years older. Kent felt a familiar chill at the base of his spine; the sort of chilly feeling a vertigo sufferer gets when standing on the edge of a sheer drop. He knew this face. It was going to be the one on the Chinese postage stamp when the current Chairman of the People's Republic finally coughed over his last cigarette. This was number-one boy, Lee Yuan, the next ruler of the largest power in the world.

27

On the other side of Bellamy Avenue the man sitting at the window looked up from the camera's viewfinder and said over his shoulder, 'It's getting like a bloody Chinese takeaway over there. Another two have gone in – a man and a woman – and another car with two more of the buggers is parked below us here.'

'Shall I inform Woodhouse?' asked his companion.

The man at the window continued to stare across the road. He was ticking off his fingers as he counted the number of Chinese who'd moved into the area. 'Six in the house,' he said aloud to himself; 'two down below here and another two at the top of the road. Ten of the buggers – enough for a human wave on Porkchop Hill! Ring him,' he said over his shoulder. 'I'll talk to him when you get through.'

The lights in the building had all gone out but Woodhouse was still at his desk. Nobody in the surveillance team seemed excited. 'Are you plugged in?' he asked. 'Can you hear what they're talking about?'

'We could be sitting in the room with them. We've got a laser join. They wiped off everything in the room and covered it with a blanket but they didn't consider outside interference.'

'What about the phone?'

'We lost the buzby when they flushed the phone but we've got an in and out on calls with an external join.'

'Good. You checked all the visitors? Was there anything unusual about one of the Chinese?'

'Yes. She was a woman.'

'I don't mean that.'

'What do you mean?'

'Anything unusual about one of the men.'

'Like what?'

'No hands.'

'Jesus! Is this a joke?'

'Forget it. I'm putting in an ident for a full orchestra plus a Special Branch front man to assist you. I think you'd better have a walk around and put them where you want them. You're equipped for conversation?'

'Yeh. Better have someone come here and take over the camera. Back door, tell him to bring a dog on a lead. At what point d'you want me to move in and collect the bodies?'

'It won't come to that. Tell your man to keep the line open so that I can monitor. I'll come back to you after I've sorted out the team. In the meantime – '

'Call you back – something's happening!'

The MI5 Watcher dropped the phone on the table and, at his partner's urgent beckoning, joined him at the window. A car had appeared, cruising slowly down Bellamy Avenue from the upper end. It stopped outside the house opposite, halfway up on the pavement. The driver got out, studied the empty street he'd just come down, then looked carefully in the opposite direction. Nothing moved. He walked round to the back door nearest the house, opened it and leaned inside. Another figure moved about inside the car. As the Watchers stared down through the narrow crack in the curtains they saw the two figures haul out between them a long bundle wrapped in shiny black polythene – a heavy-duty dustbin bag – and stagger, one at each end, towards Fylough's front door, which opened as they approached, then closed behind them.

'What did you make of that?'

'A body – female.'

'Female? You bloody psychic?'

'I saw a bare leg as they dragged her out of the car. Of course, it might have been a Scotsman – we've had every other fucking nationality so far!'

'Get Woodhouse on the blower again.'

28

David Kent slid the pictures and documents back in the envelope but didn't replace the seal or stick down the flap. There was no point. He closed the file and sat back in his chair, sipping slowly from his glass of whisky and water and staring blankly at the calendar on the wall. This month's picture was a fish's-eye view of Tower Bridge with the two sections wide open to allow nothing in sight to come through. But he wasn't reviewing it. He couldn't even see it. David Kent had other things on his mind. He'd committed a crime. One of the worst. And as well as this, he'd exposed a weakness in the network. The Old Boys would be after his neck – after they'd removed his balls – and there was nothing he could do to show them that it had all been part of his interpretation of the club rules, just a little bit of boyish fun and curiosity. It was more than that. He'd poked his nose into a little bit of very smelly cheese and now he knew something that only a selected three should know. After the squeaky-voice treatment they'd have to drag his tongue out by its roots to stop him from screaming that they had a top mole in the land of the spring roll if the Chinese ever got their hands on him. He stopped sipping whisky and took a large mouthful; he didn't drink it, not immediately, but puffed his cheeks out and swilled it around his mouth while he went on another unlikely tack.

He could reseal the envelope, put the file back into its dust-gathering niche and forget he'd ever seen it. *How?* He swallowed and allowed his cheeks to deflate. *You don't think those idiotic bastards are going to let you get away with it a second time?* How many Mr Dixons could he count on being on the payroll, and Christ knew what Simon would do if he turned up again to look at a ceiling without pipes . . .

What about Mr Evelyn St John Woodhouse?

What about him?

Nothing, except he'd have a black baby, burst into tears and call out the firing squad – in that order. Forget Woodhouse. Give Dickie

*Mithers-Wayne a ring and ask him to slip the file back. Good idea,
but it would put one more name on the not-for-your-eyes list . . .
Forget Mithers-Wayne for the time being . . . Anyway, why hasn't
the bugger phoned me? What's he doing about those bloody
pictures? I'll come back to Master Mithers-Wayne when I've sorted
this bloody mess out. Fylough? I'm not altogether sure I know Mr
Fylough and by this morning's song-and-dance routine in the
Foreign Office and Ministry of Defence it's highly unlikely that he'd
want to know me. In any case, I can scrub him for the time being. I
don't know where he hangs his spare shirt and keeps his shoe-
cleaning kit, not until – here we go again – until bloody Mithers-
Wayne gets his finger out of his arse and sticks it in a telephone box.
Forget Fylough, too. The list didn't say PM, FS and Mr-bloody-
Fylough – it just said PM and FS . . .*

No it didn't!

Kent brought his eyes back from space and stared at the file.
The bloody list said PM and FS – and C of MI6 . . . *So I'm back to
Mr James Morgan – beg his bloody pardon – Sir James Morgan,
who's about as accessible as Mrs Thatcher's handbag.* Kent's eyes
swivelled across the room to the telephone. *But he's all I've got so
I'd better give it a try – I can tell him what a naughty boy I've been
and fill in the details on the ferry to Parkhurst!*

There was never a delay on the Century House switchboard.

'This is Evelyn St John Woodhouse,' Kent told the Chief of
SIS's PA. 'Is Sir James free? Urgent, please.' He was free. 'I'm
sorry, Sir James,' said Kent quickly when Morgan answered. 'My
name is Kent – I'm with Mr Woodhouse, K Branch, at – '

'I know where it is,' broke in Morgan. His voice was gruff,
slightly Scottish, but not unkind or irritable, and with perhaps a
trace of curiosity. 'And now you've busted my system, what d'you
want?'

Kent told him about the file.

'Don't go away,' ordered Morgan and the phone went dead.
Kent pulled a face. Morgan was going to check whether the file
had indeed been pinched. It wouldn't take long. It looked as if
Simon was in for another bollocking, this time probably terminal.
Kent managed to reach his glass without letting go of the dead
phone. The wait was getting on his nerves. It was like standing
alone in the rain at night, waiting for the last bus – it never seemed

to come. He downed the remains of the whisky and water in one and reached for the bottle. He'd just slopped a good measure in when the phone came to life again. The water would have to wait. He took a solid pull, fought against the cough and jammed the phone against his ear.

Confirmation that the Foreign Office Registry had been penetrated – and plundered – hadn't affected Morgan's voice; it was the same cool, steady burr. 'Have you opened it?' he asked.

'Yes, sir.'

Pause.

Kent swallowed more whisky.

'And it meant something to you?'

'Yes. Can I tell you the whole story, sir?'

'Not over the telephone. Where are you now?'

Kent told him.

'Stay there. Make sure the file's secure and don't do anything or go anywhere until I get in touch again.'

Morgan put the phone back on its rest and stared with narrowed eyes at the blank wall opposite. He didn't look upset, nor did he look as if he were about to burst into tears. His quiet contemplation lasted for several minutes and then he nodded to himself and sat back in the large leather padded swing chair; the board looked much clearer now. His expression was that of an Anatoly Karpov who'd spotted the next four moves to checkmate. 'Get me Woodhouse at Five,' he told his PA on the intercom.

Again there was no delay. 'Have you got anybody watching Kent?' he asked Woodhouse when the connection was made.

'No,' replied Woodhouse. 'I've been concentrating on Peter Fylough. I reckoned that sooner or later everything was going to end up in his front room so I've covered it all round. Anything developing elsewhere?'

'I'm glad you asked.' Morgan gave a satisfied grunt. 'Kent wriggled his way into the Foreign Office Registry and pinched the file. He's sitting on it now. He's opened it, studied it, and I've got a bloody good idea that he knows what it's all about.'

'Then he'll have to go,' said Woodhouse. 'I'll get someone round to him right away.' He reached for his intercom switch. 'D'you think he's blown us?'

'No, I don't. But don't change anything, except have someone

225

near his doorstep to make sure the Chinaman watching him is not impeded by the local bobby. I'll leave it up to you . . .'

Woodhouse brought his hand back and continued with the pattern of doodles he'd interrupted. Morgan continued. '. . . but I think we'd better get a path beaten to Fylough's door now that all the actors have found their way on to the stage. Can you get someone into the house to sit up in the rafters, just in case?'

Woodhouse nodded to himself. 'It's a Company house; it's got a rat hole for getting out – we can use it for getting in. I'll slip a couple of men into the cellar . . .' He paused and added two more concentric circles to fill in a space on the pad. '. . . but I wasn't sure you wanted the risk?'

'Woody, I said just in case. I don't want anybody charging in with blazing Kalashnikovs until the principal players have left the house, hopefully with everything they came for.'

'What if there's a crunch?'

'Everybody on our side except Fylough's expendable.' Morgan paused briefly to underline the word expendable, then went on. 'I'll give Fylough another half-hour. If they haven't chopped his hands off by then to get something moving I'll have to throw the dice myself. You said Hilary West had joined the party?'

'My leader said he thought a lady had arrived. He didn't know who she was but as the West girl is no longer at home I presume it must be her.'

'That wasn't on the menu – but it may not be all bad,' acknowledged Morgan. 'When they start rapping her on the knees to get his attention Fylough'll have to sing for guidance. I'll handle that bit – just make sure that your people don't jump into the water with their nets before the fly's been taken. It's becoming complicated, Woody – are you totally happy running this show from the front room? Wouldn't you rather be in the kitchen with all the other cooks?'

Woodhouse knew what he meant. 'I didn't want to put them off their stride,' he said without a blush. 'But you're right, of course. I'll go down right away. I'll arrange a line for you.'

'Thanks. By the way, Wang's popped over from Malaysia to pay us a visit.'

Woodhouse's expression didn't change. 'Where's he staying?'

'With me. He's on his way round to see you now. Would you

mind taking him with you to Bellamy Avenue so that he can get a good look at the principal actors and confirm that they're the right players? I wouldn't know one from the other – would you?'

Woodhouse didn't commit himself. 'I'll be in touch, James.'

29

Fylough uncrossed his legs and slowly stood up, stretching himself like an old man whose bones have lost their spring. The two Chinese gunmen reacted instantly. Their right arms came up and two cocked automatics were aimed at his head.

'Sit down, Mr Fylough.' Goh Peng didn't raise his voice. He didn't move. He was in total control.

Fylough ignored him. He reached into his side pocket, slowly, without looking at the rock-steady pistols pointing at him, and brought out a packet of cigarettes. They didn't relax. One glanced quickly out of the corner of an eye at Goh Peng. There was no reaction from him. The eye swivelled back to Fylough, who reached into his other pocket and showed the Chinese a box of matches. He lit his cigarette and sat down, tensing his arms and back muscles as if pulling weights from the wall behind him. Goh Peng nodded to the two men, who relaxed their posture and lowered the automatics to their sides. Fylough resumed his cross-leg position and calmly smoked as if he were the only man in the room. He hadn't paid the slightest attention to the three Chinese.

But his sang-froid was about to be tested.

He'd barely finished his cigarette and crushed it out when the door opened and Kim Cheong strolled in.

He regarded the room, its occupants, and calmly sat down in an armchair opposite Fylough and stared expressionlessly into his face. Fylough stared back without recognition and after a short pause while the room readjusted itself the door opened again and Fylough instinctively stood up.

The woman who came into the room was extremely beautiful. But her eyes, almond-shaped and doe-like, gave him only the briefest of inspections. There was no cordiality, no hate or dislike; it was worse – there was nothing at all in those eyes as they flitted past his and settled on a now standing Goh Peng. He arranged a chair for her. Nothing had been said, no word spoken. And then she raised her head and inclined it, almost imperceptibly, for Goh

Peng to approach. It was like an imperial invitation. She spoke softly in *Putonghua*, the Chinese national language that is rarely used outside China.

'Does Fylough understand any Chinese dialect?' she asked.

Goh Peng said to Fylough in Cantonese, 'Did you understand what Madame Ah Lian said?'

Fylough sat down again. 'I don't speak Chinese,' he said casually. His composure was fully restored. 'Only Russian and Malay – plus a bit of English, of course.'

The joke fell flat.

'You know who I am?' Kim Cheong tapped his claws together to make sure he had his full attention. He had. Fylough's eyes locked on to his. There was no animosity in the Chinese man's face; no anger; no cruelty; if anything, Kim Cheong's expression was one of amiability, of the curiosity of a man studying the changes that time has wrought on an old friend. 'But of course you're going to say no, and so would I, Mr Peter Fylough, if I was suddenly confronted by the man whose hands I'd removed . . .' He almost smiled; it was as if Fylough had done him a favour and he preferred the shiny hooks to the ungainly things Fylough had at the end of *his* arms. '. . . so, let's do away with the formalities of lying and remind ourselves of our last meeting.'

'Do you mind if I smoke?'

'I'll join you.'

Ah Lian stared from one to the other. She looked intent, as if recording in her mind the words and the attitudes of the two men, but if she thought anything at all she kept it to herself and stared at Fylough's face.

Fylough ignored her. He waited for one of the guards to light Kim Cheong's cigarette, then he put a match to the end of his own, allowing the smoke to trickle luxuriously from his nose. He hadn't realised how much he'd needed the palliative. He took his eyes from Kim Cheong's expressionless face and nodded at the hooks. 'I remember,' he said evenly. 'At the time I thought you were dead. How, erm. . . ?'

Kim Cheong narrowed his eyes out of the way of the smoke from the cigarette in his mouth and stared for a moment at the shiny claws in his lap. 'I was dead to your way of thinking.'

'You were dead to everybody's way of thinking,' said Fylough lightly. 'Perhaps you'd like to reveal the secret?'

Kim Cheong didn't share Fylough's humour. He replied, seriously, 'Willingly. What do you know about *Jnana-Marga*?'

'Nothing.'

'Yoga,' clarified Kim Cheong.

Fylough didn't answer immediately. What he knew about yoga could be written on a fly's toenail – bearded weirdos in tucked-up dhotis standing on their head in the corner of a room pumping blood into non-existent brains. But he didn't say that.

'Enough to know that it doesn't stop bullets,' he replied.

'Quite right,' agreed Kim Cheong, 'but, properly applied, it can prevent the final one – and we all know about final bullets in our business, don't we?' He didn't wait for Fylough's agreement, continuing without pause. He was pleased to see an interested frown appear on Fylough's otherwise smooth forehead. 'When I walked into your ambush I heard and felt nothing – no pain, no explosions, just one second's intuitive terror, then blackness. I was fortunate. Your marksmanship was good – all body shots. None of them touched a vital organ, but I was dying, have no doubt of that. I don't know how long I lay in the steaming mud; I've presumed since that it could only have been a matter of minutes. Still no pain, just a heavy cloying numbness and a realisation of what had happened. I didn't open my eyes. The silence was complete; no voices, no movement around me. I lay exactly where I'd dropped. I felt for my Sten without moving my hands. They were empty . . .' Kim Cheong studied the ends of his arms as if recalling the sensation of having hands there, then looked back into Fylough's eyes.

'Your Western ideas of yoga are infantile; you haven't yet scratched the surface of its most elementary discipline. I was even then an advanced master of the most important elements. Raja yoga, hatha yoga were, and still are, basics of my being; I have achieved samadhi . . .' He stopped and shook his head, realising he was in the presence of a spiritual philistine. '. . . the highest limb a yogi can achieve. *Pratyahara* – total withdrawal of the senses; *samyama* – control of the mind and body . . . These things mean nothing to you. I can stop my heart beating to the point of death; I can reduce my body temperature to that of a dead being; I can banish pain and I can dull every sense in my body. That is my command of yoga. To you and anyone else I am dead and that is the state I willed myself into on that muddy track. There was no point that you should waste your bullets on a dead man. I knew nothing else until I was brought out of what you would call my trance, and then the pain was there. That had to be fought in the conscious state. And, of course, it wasn't just the bullet wounds that you had inflicted on me . . .' Kim Cheong's eyes gouged deeply into Fylough's. There was no rancour there, simply an examination of another man's soul. He wasn't critical. Kim Cheong had his own brand of cruelty, and in a way he seemed to understand Fylough's motives, even though the motives for amputating a young man's hands had not been cruelty. He probably viewed it a worse crime that it had been done out of expediency, without the pleasure gained from the inflicting of pain on an enemy. Fylough didn't drop his eyes.

'You bear part of the blame for that yourself,' he nodded to the ugly hooks. 'Had I known you were not dead you would have been carried out of the jungle and your wounds healed. There would have been no need for that . . .'

He looked again at the hooks, but before he could continue Kim Cheong broke in with a mirthless smile. 'After which I'd have been taken along to Pudu and hanged.'

Fylough didn't return the smile. He shrugged his shoulders and stubbed out his cigarette. 'Those were the rules of the game. You killed without mercy. We patched you up, made you healthy, then killed you. We could go on for ever bouncing this one backwards and forwards and still get nowhere. But there's still the big question . . .'

Kim Cheong raised his eyebrows and passed his half-smoked cigarette to Goh Peng to stub out.

'What's that?'

'You were buried in the jungle at least three days' march from the nearest kampong. It must have taken more than a knowledge of yoga to get yourself out of a grave and into the hands of someone who knew medicine – even elementary medicine. And it needed more than that to cure you of your problems.'

Kim Cheong didn't take umbrage at the flippant end to Fylough's question. There was nothing wrong with his sense of

231

humour; he even smiled when Fylough leaned forward and offered him another cigarette. 'I think my sister . . .' He paused and looked over his shoulder. 'Have you met my sister?'

Fylough looked into her eyes and shook his head. There was none of the Kim Cheong amiability there. He stared into two unforgiving black diamonds.

'I think I'll let her tell you what happened, Mr Fylough. She too was there, in the jungle, wet and hungry and lonely – and afraid. We all owe Ah Lian a great deal.' He turned in his chair and looked into Ah Lian's face; there was more than love in his eyes. 'Tell Fylough your story, Ah Lian.'

Ah Lian stared into Fylough's face for several seconds. Fylough ﹏ in't wilt under the scrutiny. He returned her inspection but didn't allow his findings to show on his face. There was no doubt about it, she was a beautiful woman in any language – everything except the eyes. They'd probably be beautiful too, in the subdued lighting of a pink bedroom, but at that moment all they showed was that she didn't like him and she never would; she didn't try to disguise it. I think you can forget all about pink bedrooms and limpid eyes with this one, Fylough told himself, but it didn't stop him wondering about something of that quality being lonely, hungry and afraid in his part of the forest . . . *I wonder what old Togom would have made of it if he'd known she was shivering in her rags just down the track?*

Fylough brought himself back to the present. She was talking – and to him.

'. . . I was working in the garden. We had a secret pit in the jungle fringe to save the person working on the far permimeter in case of sudden attack, and, on the spur of the moment, I threw myself in it. I was worried about Kim Cheong; I wanted to see him come back and was ready to help with the other plan. An ambushed party – if they escaped the killing zone – would entice the soldiers back to the camp, where a small counter-ambush would be laid . . .' She stopped and curled her lip at Fylough. 'But you know all this.'

'I didn't know about your hole.'

'Otherwise you would have given me the same treatment you gave Lam Lee?'

Fylough stared back into her dark eyes but said nothing. He

232

remembered the bandit being blasted by Togom. She was right; Togom didn't look between their legs until he'd killed them.

She didn't demand a reply, but instead, in the same toneless voice, continued. 'I covered up the hole and heard more shooting above me, and after a spell of silence I heard talking. I couldn't make out whether it was Malay or Chinese. I forced myself to raise the lid of the hole just enough to see out. I saw the Malay with the machine-gun, and you, standing over Lam Lee, who was on the ground. I thought it was Kim Cheong and wanted to scream when the Malay fired into the body. I pushed my face into the muddy sides of the hole and filled my mouth with dirt. When I plucked up courage to look again you and the Malay were dragging the body across the vegetable garden. I watched you drop it into the pit and disappear into the jungle. I crawled out of my hole, scrambled across the garden and looked into the pit. I nearly fainted. Lam Lee looked so small and frail, huddled in a heap on a pile of bamboo at the bottom of the pit. But I didn't cry for him.

'I hid my shotgun in the undergrowth and followed the footprints of you and the two Malays. I watched you tie Kim Cheong like a dead pig to a pole and I followed you at a distance until you reached your camp. There I hid and watched from the edge of the jungle. I knew Kim Cheong was dead . . .'

She stopped for a moment and looked at Kim Cheong; Kim Cheong nodded sadly. It didn't show on his face whether he was enjoying the trip into the past or whether he was anticipating the sharp, agonising pain of the knife slicing into his wrists that he sometimes experienced when waking from a sweat-laden nightmare.

Ah Lian turned back to Fylough. Kim Cheong seemed to have taken a back seat in the proceedings; with or without his approval, Ah Lian had taken over as prosecution witness. '. . . I *thought* he was dead,' she corrected. 'But I still fainted when the two Malays cut off his hands. I couldn't believe the barbarity of it. I still can't. When I came to, you were leaving the camp. I saw where you'd buried Kim Cheong and when the last of your men had left I scrabbled in the soil and uncovered his face. All I wanted to do was to say goodbye and make sure he was properly buried. I lifted his face and the top half of his body out of the soil and cradled his head against my chest and whispered goodbye. It was then that I

233

realised he wasn't dead. I put my head on his chest and after several seconds I heard it – a single heartbeat. I screamed and nearly fainted again. He must have heard my scream. A sound came from his lips and his eyes flickered open. I don't know what I did then. I think I panicked and ran round in circles, not knowing what to do and looking at this dreadful sight, the bottom half of his body still buried and the top half covered in a blood and dirt paste.

'After a few moments I calmed down, pulled him out of his grave and dragged him into the jungle. I washed him. The heavy mud, caked in lumps at the end of his arms and covering his body, had prevented him from bleeding to death, but I washed it all off and bound his wounds and the stumps with strips of my shirt. Then I took off my trousers and wrapped them round him as best I could. I dug a shallow pit with my hands, pulled him into it and covered him with *atap* fronds that had been used by your people for their camp. Then I filled in his grave, in case you came back that way, and ran back to the camp that we'd abandoned, stopping only when it became too dark and starting again at first light the next morning.

'From the old camp I picked up the escape track to one of the emergency rendezvous. There I found four of our comrades. One of them went to alert the others to put trackers on to your patrol. They found you and followed you until you left the jungle for Chaah . . .'

Fylough shrugged. It was all a long time ago. But he still felt a slight twinge at the back of his neck; he had known the terrorists sometimes kept in touch with a strong patrol, but it irked, even now, to know that he had wandered home with a bandit tail and had not thought to try a small three-man ambush – but as he'd said to himself, it was all a long time ago.

Ah Lian continued in a flat, unemotional voice. 'The other three came back with me and between us we managed to get Kim Cheong into a small escape camp. Our first-aid kit was primitive – it was almost non-existent. We used surrender leaflets as bandages – large wads of absorbent paper dropped from aeroplanes telling us how kind everybody outside was and how well we'd be looked after if we surrendered.' She shrugged. Fylough thought for a minute that she was going to soften her features and smile. But it didn't happen. 'We kept gangrene away and slowly he built up enough energy to come out of the state of *samadhi* that he'd forced

234

himself into. But he wasn't going to live unless we got him to a proper doctor. We thought at one time to take him to the Yong Peng road and leave him there with surrender leaflets pinned to him. But we didn't trust people like you . . .' The slitted eyes widened and the black diamonds behind signalled her hatred. '. . . not to kill him on the spot.'

Fylough refused to feel sorry for happenings in a far-away place over thirty years ago. 'So what happened eventually?'

She debated in her mind whether the next thing she was going to say would have any repercussions and decided, like Fylough, that it was all a long time ago.

'At the rear of the village of Chaah, behind your barbed wire and surrounded by Min Yuen houses, was a dispensary run by an American missionary and his wife and daughter. Ostensibly they were there to gather converts to some sect of the Christian faith and to help those Chinese villagers who had reason not to trust the English with their minor ailments and sickness. Did you know about them?'

Fylough frowned. He did. But he hadn't thought they were helping terrorists. The American had been an embarrassment. A white man living in a Chinese village in the heat of a Communist war was always going to be at least that, particularly if he showed himself to be neutral, which, not only to Fylough, meant anti-British and anti-Establishment. If he'd known what he suspected he was about to be told, the American's feet wouldn't have touched the ground until he was standing on the Singapore jetty with a one-way steerage ticket to his homeland.

'Yes,' he said. 'I knew about him. We thought he was a humanitarian, anti-war – anti both sides. But do go on . . .'

'He agreed if we could get Kim Cheong to him he'd do what he could. Kim Cheong stayed with him, right under your noses,' she said smugly, 'until his wounds were healed. The American even managed to get supplies of penicillin and other rare drugs from the Red Cross and the dispensary run by the adjacent French-owned Oil Palm estate, so, in a way, being under your noses was a form of security for him.' She had had her moment of self-satisfaction, but saw no reflection of humiliation for having been made a fool of in Fylough's eyes; if anything, he probably admired the organisation that brought Kim Cheong back to life.

'It wasn't until 1955, two years after the ambush, that the American decided Kim Cheong was in a fit state to move on. We made our way north, moving from one camp to another until it was arranged that Kim Cheong be shipped to the Chinese mainland by one of the supply junks that used our rendezvous beach north of Kota Bahru. I naturally went with him – it was as simple as that.' She stared at Fylough for a few seconds longer, then looked away. She'd come to the end of her part of the story. She made it obvious by her expression that if there was anything more to be told it was not she who was going to tell it. Kim Cheong gave her a gentle nod and accepted a cigarette and a light from Goh Peng before taking up the story himself.

He spoke with a calm modesty; no boasting, no gloating. Fylough wondered why he was being told of a Chinese bandit's rise to stardom in a hierarchy where banditry was a prerequisite of office. Perhaps for Kim Cheong it was a form of masochistic soul-cleansing, like the victim telling the flogger how much the punishment helped him succeed where others had failed. He told how following rehabilitation in Peking he'd been assigned to the Malayan Liberation Section of the Central Intelligence Office in Bow Street Alley, Peking, until K'ang Sheng, the overlord of Chinese Intelligence, reorganised the Bow Street Alley centre and promoted him to his new External Operations wing of the Department of Special Affairs – the TEWA. It was in this department that the long-smouldering ashes of the Singapore documents were allowed to burst into flame. But he was alone. Other than Ah Lian there was no one he could confide in; everybody was suspect. He was in a dilemma, he told Fylough. He knew of the contents of the Singapore file but not the details; he knew that somewhere in the Party structure a group of American-trained political agents had been infiltrated. It now would be eight years since the ambush; the grass planted by the Americans in 1953 would be lush and fat, they would be well dug in and moving upwards – it was time to bring out the sickle and stone. But there was nothing to guide him. There was no one he could go to for help; he knew they were there, but he didn't know who. He kept the fire fuelled inside him and watched and waited. Nothing showed. When K'ang Sheng died in 1975 Kim Cheong remained as Second Secretary of the Department of Social Affairs – an almost unassailable position. He had only one superior, Tang Shi, the present head of the department, the man third in line to the throne of the People's Republic, the man known as the 'smiling psychopath', everybody's friend – and enemy. Kim Cheong's patron and confidant; the one man he trusted.

He proudly related how his success allowed Ah Lian's loyalty to be acknowledged and rewarded. He sent her to school, then to university and, before the Cultural Revolution released the cords on the bamboo curtain, to London – the School of Economics. This was followed by polishing in Paris and Rome. The frightened little waif from the jungle camp in Johor blossomed into a beautiful, talented woman. Kim Cheong married her – there had never been any doubt about it, either for him or for her – but to the rest of the Party they were still brother and sister, and referred to as such. They should have lived happily ever after – if it hadn't been for a sudden rekindling of Kim Cheong's desire to see again the packet containing the Singapore documents.

Kim Cheong raised his right hook and sucked on the cigarette gripped in its two components. The pause allowed Fylough to glance down at his wrist and with a casualness that he didn't feel, say:

'A fascinating story. I'm glad everything turned out right for you . . .' He lowered his eyes again and stared pointedly at his watch.

Kim Cheong allowed himself a rare smile. 'I'm surprised, Mr Fylough, that you ever found the patience to mount an ambush, let alone occupy it for any length of time. We're supposed to acquire patience with age, not lose it.' He sucked again on the cigarette before lowering the hook back into his lap. 'Don't concern yourself with the time; you're not going anywhere until the negotiation is finished.'

'Negotiation?' Fylough's eyebrows shot up.

'That's right. I charged Ah Lian with the task of bringing us together so that we could lay this gnawing problem of mine to rest.'

'What gnawing problem is that?' asked Fylough.

Kim Cheong ignored the question. 'She enlisted the help of my very able colleague, Goh Peng – Dr Goh Peng . . .' He waved his

237

hook at the Chinese standing by the window and added gratuitously, '. . . doctor of medicine. He traced your Malay, Togom, and together, through Mr Kenning, Mr Bentley, and the inestimable Colonel Dean, we arrive at this little meeting.'

'What gnawing problem?' repeated Fylough.

'I thought that would be fairly obvious by now. I want the documents that were containted in the envelope you took from me in Malaya in 1953.'

Fylough stared into Kim Cheong's face for several seconds, then burst into loud laughter.

'You must be joking!'

The other Chinese in the room stared at him. Their famous inscrutability had slipped. But Ah Lian's hadn't. She didn't look suprised. Her expression remained one of loathing. Kim Cheong waited until Fylough's laugh had run its course then offered him a faint smile.

'No joke, Mr Fylough.'

'Then I repeat, I haven't the foggiest idea where the documents would have ended up once they got to England. You've wasted your time.' Fylough narrowed his eyes; there was something he'd forgotten. He felt his fingers twitch involuntarily. 'D'you mind telling me what the idea was of going through the motions of lopping off Kenning's and the others' hands? Pretty bizarre sort of thing to do, wasn't it?'

Kim Cheong nodded. 'But it worked – you heard about it. It was Ah Lian's idea. Women seem to have a much deeper sense of cruelty than us men. We remove the hands and it's finished – they go through the motions and you suffer two lots of pain – mental and physical. But it doesn't mean they're incapable of completing the job. Her methods brought us together. You'd have ignored ordinary death, as indeed I think you would now, but I'm sure you'll think twice about completing the rest of your life with a pair of these.' Kim Cheong touched his two shiny hooks together. The metallic tink sounded overloud in the room and brought a slight increase in Fylough's breathing rate.

'I still can't help you. I don't know where the file is kept.'

'But you know someone who does?'

Fylough shook his head, then stared, frowning, as Goh Peng brought himself to his feet and leaned over the back of Kim

Cheong's chair and whispered into his ear. Kim Cheong and Fylough exchanged glances before Kim Cheong nodded, without looking over his shoulder, at Goh Peng.

Goh Peng left his side and went to the door. He opened it a fraction and spoke to one of the men outside, returning to Kim Cheong after a sidelong, secret nod to Ah Lian.

Kim Cheong smiled sadly. Without looking away from Fylough's face he indicated with his right hook to one of the men at the door and said in Chinese:

'Stand behind him. Restrain him if he becomes violent.'

The thickset man moved away from the door and stood behind Fylough. Fylough watched him come without moving his head. His only reaction was a slight twitch of the eyebrows; he hadn't taken his eyes off Kim Cheong. Neither did he when he felt the cold metal of the Chinese man's gun rest in the back of his neck. There was no pressure, just the feathery sensation of imminent death which carried more menace than if the weapon had ground painfully into the nerve. But he didn't flinch.

Kim Cheong said to Goh Peng, 'Have the woman brought in and prepare to remove one of her hands.' Then he sat back in his chair and studied Fylough's face.

30

The man leading the team in the flat overlooking Fylough's house was Russell Potter. He enjoyed his job and he was very good at it. He reckoned it was better than working. He took off his jacket and tie, threw them over the back of a chair, and slipped on an old dark blue anorak. He checked the workings of a two-way handset, plugged in two invisible wires, one from the tiny plug in his ear and the other from the button speaker inside the anorak, and slipped the whole thing into the pocket of the anorak.

The dog watched with mournful eyes from the position he'd chosen in the corner of the room. He was a scruffy but trained cross-breed; if he'd had a voice he would have called himself a mongrel, and been proud of it. In front of him, under his nose on a sheet of newspaper, was a large helping of Pedigree Chum, plonked there like a steaming pile of takeaway tandoori by the man who'd brought him. But he ignored it. He saw the signs – he was going to work, he was going walkies.

Russell picked up the lead, hooked it in the dog's collar and slipped out of the back door. He lifted the dog over the neighbours' fence and used their small back gate into the garage area to bring them out into the next road. He turned right, right again, and strolled along the road towards Fylough's house. He waited while the dog peed against the rear wheel of the Chinese men's car parked below the Watcher post and had time for a casual glance inside. He nodded apologetically to the three pairs of flat eyes that watched their every movement. They weren't suspicious. Russell pulled the dog away and crossed the road. The Chinese eyes followed them without interest. There was another car at the corner but with only one man in it. From his side of the road it was too dark for Russell to make out whether he was Chinese or European, but it didn't matter – either way he was part of the act.

Two hundred yards further on Russell turned left and left again. This brought him down the road behind Fylough's house. The houses here all had small, low-walled gardens, most of them with overgrown self-sown bushes growing out of once neatly made squares of concrete. They all had basements.

Russell stopped in front of one that had outside it a skip overflowing with demolition rubbish out in the roadside. A bit of renovation or conversion – to confirm it there was a pile of sand and shingle casually dumped behind the wall, alongside a heap of splintered and broken old doors. He invited the mongrel to crap on the sand while he spoke softly into the small microphone inside his anorak. Within minutes a nondescript car came from the opposite direction, stopped briefly, and then carried on, turning out of sight at the top of the road.

'This way,' Russell told the two men who'd joined him from the car, and led them down the steps to the basement. The sheet of corrugated tin blocking the basement door fell in with the help of a well-placed boot. The three men and the dog made their way to the back of the house and stepped out into the garden. The back garden was more unkempt than the front. It looked like the council tip. Russell pointed out the back of Fylough's house.

'The one on the right has a basement like the one we've just come through. The door belongs to us. The people who own the house can't get into the basement but you can. Inside there's a plaster wall . . .' Russell corrected himself. '. . . it looks like a plaster wall, but it's on a hinge. It swings both ways. It leads into the basement of the target house and that has the same arrangement. Get as close as you can to the talking, but be careful, there are more bloody Chinks in that house than there were on the Long March.'

The senior of the two men nodded. 'My brief,' he said in a low voice, 'is that there is one European who's not to be knocked off by the Chinks, and maybe a woman, also European – but she's expendable.'

'Was your brief from a guy called Woodhouse?' queried Russell.

''Sright.' He sounded surprised that Russell would know where his brief came from. It sniffed of organisation, but he took it in his stride. 'So when the war starts we whistle in and hoick out our man, that's if he hasn't already got an extra hole in his head! You're going to describe the geography of the house, where this guy is holding court, and how we get to it.'

Russell went down on his launches and drew a diagram in the dust.

'I've also been instructed to stand well out of the way if a Chinese wearing a pair of steel hooks comes rushing out. We can shoot, but not with evil intent. If he goes quietly, regardless of whether our man remains intact, we can do a song-and-dance act to make him think we're going to miss his company, but he must be allowed to gallop over the horizon. Does that agree with your brief?'

Russell's teeth gleamed in the growing darkness. 'I'm only Watching. Fisticuffs are fuck-all to do with me. But you're tuned into my station and I'm in direct contact with Herr Gruppenführer Woodhouse, who'll no doubt pass on any other little gems he wants you to know. If anything happens from my side I'll whisper in your ear; you don't have to say a word. Better you don't – they say the Chinks can hear mice farting in the pantry if they put their minds to it. Push off now, while you can still see where you're going.'

Russell waited in the shadow of the partially derelict house until the two agents disappeared into the jungle of the gardens opposite. They made surprisingly little noise and after a good five minutes he decided they were in place and retraced his steps through the house and out into the road.

The streetlamps were on. They'd been on for a couple of hours but their dim circles of light were only now beginning to show. He lit a cigarette and strolled back the way he'd come. There was no change; the two Chinese cars hadn't moved. Inside, however, there were new arrivals in the room overlooking Fylough's house.

'Everything OK, Russell?' asked Woodhouse. Russell nodded as he shrugged off his anorak and stared, without hiding his curiosity, at the Chinese standing beside the window studying the house opposite. Woodhouse followed his gaze. 'Mr Wang Peng Soon.' He didn't elaborate. Wang turned his head and nodded, then went back to his studies. Russell raised his eyebrows, but only to himself. It was getting more like Hong Kong by the minute. He moved lightly across the room to the man by the telephone monitor.

'Anything happen while I was out?' he asked.

'That plastic bundle we saw going in before you took the dog for a walk . . .'

'What about it?'

'It was definitely female. I think she's one of ours. When the conversation went flat she was introduced to the party. Her name's West . . .' He stopped with a puzzled frown.

'Is that it?' asked Russell.

'Not quite. By the sound of it they've done something to her. I think she's being used as leverage. They told Fylough they were going to cut off one of her hands.'

Russell paled. 'And?'

'There weren't any screams. Funny, I haven't heard that girl say a bloody word since she went into the house. Maybe I misheard – maybe they said her tongue, not her hand.'

31

Hilary West had suffered no real physical damage. It had been clean and almost clinical. The two hefty Chinese had come into her bedroom as if it had been an open tent. The doors and their locks had meant nothing. And the fact that she was asleep, totally naked, had meant even less. They were there on a job, it was nothing sexual, and their faces remained blank and disinterested as they woke her and instructed her to dress. They could have been eunuchs.

When she was dressed she tried conversation; it got her nowhere. One of the men pushed her backwards on the bed and promptly got her bare foot thumped into his groin, but as she bounced off the bed to follow up with a stiff arm jab above his pelvis the other man stepped lightly to one side and hit her expertly across the neck with the side of his hand. She crashed back on to the bed, gasping for air, and he was on top of her, spread-eagled, holding her down by the arms and crushing her into the mattress with the weight of his body. She struggled, but half-heartedly, while the other man, gently massaging his bruised testicles, stood above her. There was no spite in his face, no expression – he seemed almost to have enjoyed it. At a brief command the man lying on her moved his weight to one side, reached down and pulled her skirt up over her thighs. She tried to kick out again but the first man gripped her leg between his knees and then she felt a needle thump high into her bare thigh. Before she realised what had happened she was out – totally.

They draped her with the black plastic dustbin liner and while one checked that the narrow, quiet street was deserted, the other skipped down the steps with Hilary over his shoulders, manoeuvred her onto the back seat of the car and got in beside her. They left as they'd arrived – unnoticed.

Hilary, partly floating, partly climbing, made a laborious passage upwards in the cone-shaped shaft that spiralled towards the pinprick of bright light in the far distance. Every so often, when she reached the light and stretched up to grasp the ledge, she slipped back and found herself at the bottom of the tube, where it was pitch-black. She would start climbing again, and this time when she reached the light she didn't slip back but held on. And then she woke up.

It wasn't a return to life by degrees. One second she was unconscious, the next she'd pulled herself over the ledge and was wide awake. No headache, no hangover – everything was as crisp as an apple. She looked around. She was sitting, half-lying on the stairway with her shoulders resting on the junction of the next step and the wall. She pulled herself upright, only to find that her hands were tied lightly in front of her and her feet bound together. There was a cord running between the two bindings which prevented any movement of her feet, and the reason for it was standing a few yards away, leaning against the wall – the man who'd felt her foot in his groin.

He watched her come back to life without expression.

She lay still, unmoving, and tried to work out what had happened. Why was she being treated like this? She was supposed to be on the Chinese side – what had gone wrong? She gave it up; nothing was making sense. The man watching her moved away from the wall and when she straightened up and tried to rub the pain in her thigh he brought out from the back of his trouser belt a small automatic, its barrel distorted with a stubby suppressor, and held it at his side. Then he nodded to another man standing further along the passageway and jerked his thumb towards the door.

When the signal came Hilary's guard stood back and pointed the pistol at her face while his partner untied first her hands and then her feet. He put one hand under her arm, not roughly, gently pulled her up and guided her through the open door. She stood for a moment staring about her, not really seeing but trying to work out what was going on. She hadn't decided when Kim Cheong motioned her sit down.

Only then did she notice Fylough.

'Say noth – ' Fylough began.

'Or you!' snapped Kim Cheong and Fylough's warning died in his throat as the tentative rise out of his chair was halted by the

245

sudden pressure of a steel-like clamp on his shoulder from the Chinese behind him, who with one hand pressed him back into his seat. The snub pistol barrel found a nerve in his neck as a little, unhurried pressure was applied. The sharp stab of pain caused him to tighten his lips but otherwise he managed to keep his feelings, and the sudden chilling between his thighs, to himself. Hilary hadn't been considered as part of the short game; hers was a later, walk-on part. This was not part of the play.

'You know Mrs West, of course,' said Kim Cheong. Not a question, but a statement, slightly sarcastic. 'We thought she was working for us, but Dr Goh Peng has decided that she is, in fact, one of your people. The clever girl fooled us. She has been what you Intelligence people call "doubling".' He paused for a moment, without taking his eyes off Fylough's face. 'And we all know what happens to people who double, don't we?' No answer was required. Fylough didn't give one. He was busily concerned with the added implications – and responsibility. Kim Cheong's eyebrows remained in the quizzical position. 'You're quite sure, Mr Fylough, that you don't know where these documents are kept?'

'I've already told you – ' began Fylough.

'Thank you,' responded Kim Cheong. His expression didn't change, only his voice. 'Goh Peng?' That was all, just the name and a flick of the head; no instruction. He'd lifted his hand off the tiller for a short break and a breath of fresh air; he'd handed over the captaincy. Goh Peng took it without pausing for breath.

They were like two actors acting out a well-rehearsed play.

Goh Peng flicked his fingers at his housebreaker, who picked up his black briefcase and set it on the table. Hilary, after listening to Kim Cheong's damning statement, stared at him without understanding, then with fright, then horror. She thought she ought to say something and managed a quick glance at Fylough. He didn't return it; he was busy attending to the movements of Goh Peng and his assistant.

The case flicked open with two noisy, solid clunks and the man's hand went in. He didn't scrabble about. He knew exactly what he wanted and in which part of the case he'd find it.

As his hand came out he pivoted on his toes and like a man mounting a horse, swung his leg over Hilary's lap, sat down heavily, encircled her shoulders with his arms and pressed forward so that she was thrust into the back of her chair. It was so unexpected and done so quickly she had no time to scream.

Goh Peng had moved round so that he stood behind her. He took her chin gently in one hand and tilted it so that her head rested on the hard wooden back of the chair.

Now came the scream.

But it got no further than the back of her throat. Goh Peng had, like a magician, removed the thing from the Chinese man's hand and placed it carefully into her open mouth. It was a shiny chrome dentist's clamp used for keeping a nervous patient's mouth open and the teeth from biting off the dentist's fingers. Hilary's scream ended as a wet warble. There was nothing she could do except gag. It was all over in three seconds.

Fylough's reflexes were the slowest of all. First he stared in disbelief, then horror and shock, and by the time he tried to shake off the hand on his shoulder and get to his feet the gun had been removed from the top of his neck and thrust into the corner of his eye socket. There was enough pain to send him flopping back into his seat.

'Do be careful, Mr Fylough!' Kim Cheong's voice was low and filled with concern. 'I've seen people lose their eye by that method. Sit quietly and – '

'You dirty, vicious bastards! This is not – '

'Tch! Tch!' Kim Cheong clicked his tongue. 'If you sit quietly you might get another chance to help – you might even be able to save Mrs West any more discomfort. Goh Peng's taken her voice so that her screams won't disturb your neighbours – the next thing he takes will not be replaceable.' He seemed, strangely, as surprised by the event as Fylough, and he looked round at Goh Peng. No words were exchanged, just a look and a slight inclination of the chin. He returned to Fylough. 'In the mean-time . . .' He nodded to the man behind Fylough and said in English: '. . . show Mr Fylough how close he is to losing that eye.'

It was all very conversational, like a host suggesting to the entertaining magician that he show another little trick to the guest of honour. Fylough didn't have time to cringe away, or to appreciate the trick. The Chinese pressed a fraction harder on the pistol and gave it a minute jerk. Fylough's eyeball almost popped out of its socket. He screamed, but the other hand left his shoulder and clamped itself over his mouth. No sound came out.

'Now please sit there and don't make another movement or sound, and don't say anything, or he will finish the job – on both eyes . . .' Kim Cheong studied Fylough's bowed head, as, with both hands covering his face, he tried to stem the agony and the river of tears that gushed involuntarily out of the damaged eye. Kim Cheong then turned his head to Hilary. Other things were happening.

Goh Peng was back beside his case and measuring into a syringe a quantity of clear liquid from a small phial. He raised it, studied the level, and squirted a minute jet on to the carpet. Then he turned to Hilary.

She couldn't see what he was doing – fortunately. With the heavy man sitting on her lap pressing her neck against the rim of the back of the chair, all she could see was the ceiling. The thing in her mouth was agonising, and as her throat filled with saliva she decided she was drowning. She had little time for the other things that were going on. She struggled with her throat and managed to swallow enough to stop her from passing out. The Chinese with his face close to hers didn't seem to be concerned. She tried another scream and attempted to say something to Goh Peng, to cry for Fylough's help, but the sounds bubbled into nothing and nearly choked her. She closed her eyes. The relief was infinitesimal – and short-lived. Her eyes bulged open, unasked, when hands touched her face.

It was the close-up of a horror story: Goh Peng was peering into her mouth, his finger pulling her lips to one side as he inspected the back of her throat. With professional concern he kept the syringe at his side, out of sight until he'd completed his inspection.

After a second or so he reached in past the clamp and eased her tongue out. Then he very carefully worked the needle into the back of her mouth, applied a little pressure on the plunger, withdrew it, checked the level, then stuck it in again and twice more made small injections into different places. Hilary fainted. It was the effect of the strain on her throat, the fear of the needle, the pressure on her body and the horror of the proximity of the two Chinese faces.

The faint was all too brief.

When she opened her eyes the weight had gone from her body. And, luxury, the dreadful thing had gone from her mouth. Her lips were closed. She opened them to scream again, but nothing happened, and the horror started all over again. Her mouth was dead. Her tongue was dead. There was no feeling anywhere in her mouth and although she could swallow she couldn't speak – and she couldn't scream. She appealed with her eyes to Kim Cheong, to her father, to Goh Peng. But Goh Peng was in charge and he wasn't listening to vibrations or watching eyes – he was taking more things from his case.

These had been used before. Two sets of steel clamps, wrist-size, complete with screws. He handed everything to the Chinese who'd sat on Hilary's lap and was now waiting attentively at her side. She suddenly realised she couldn't move her legs. She looked down. They were tied together again, not with blood-stoppingly tight binding, but loosely, just enough to keep her legs together and stop her running, screaming silently, around the room. She watched, unbelieving, uncomprehending, as the Chinese screwed one side of each clamp to the table, placed her unresisting wrists under them, then screwed the other side firmly so that although she could move her hands slightly this way and that she was anchored to the table.

She looked again to Fylough for help.

He was as helpless as she. He was staring with his one good eye, water still pouring like blood from a burst ulcer down his cheek and neck. With a painful effort he shook his head slowly in apology, then closed the eye. She was not comforted.

'What are you going to do to her?' Fylough spoke to the room in general, his head bowed, his voice blurred. The pistol barrel was back in his eye socket, but just resting lightly on the closed lid. There was no pain from it, but the memory lingered on. Fylough sat like a statue; even his fingers, now lowered from his face, were dug into his trousers legs to stop them shaking or twitching.

'I would have thought that fairly obvious, Mr Fylough,' replied Goh Peng. 'We're going to cut off her hand and then ask you the question again about the Chaah documents. If you're still not willing to help, we'll take her other hand off.'

Hilary's eyes bulged and she fainted again.

Fylough wished he could.

'Why her? Why not me?' The voice sounded like somebody else's, it was not his; this one was dry, husky and had an almost pathetic whine to it. It was good acting – except he wasn't acting. He saw the contempt flash briefly in Goh Peng's eyes, then vanish into two flat, black strips.

'You'd be too easy,' he said. 'You'd die like the soldier Dean.' His lip curled. 'You English are all the same; you make a virtue of the grand gesture. You'd be happy with your painful sacrifice and die with your so-called stiff lip – and we'd end up with nothing. That's why her and not you.'

Fylough raised his head and looked at Ah Lian. She was watching him closely. If he was expecting to see consolation he was wildly off the mark. Her eyes were narrowed in pleasure, she was enjoying the torture – not Hilary's – his. He looked at Kim Cheong. Their eyes met. Kim Cheong was strangely subdued, reflective. His head moved fractionally, almost unnoticeably, but he had nothing to say. Fylough swivelled his eye back to Goh Peng.

The doctor had the syringe in his hand again but he'd changed the long, delicate needle for a thicker, stubby one. He filled the syringe up to the 4 ml mark from a squat phial marked *1% prilocaine*. The bottle was now half empty; he'd found plenty of use for the top half with his earlier patients and his skill in blocking the ulnar and median nerves was sharpening with every patient. He made two precise injections into Hilary's wrist, studied them for a second or two, then recharged the hypodermic with another 5 ml from the same bottle, turned her wrist on to its side and eased the entire quantity into the radial nerve. He looked up at Ah Lian and nodded. In a few seconds Hilary would have no sense left in her hand; a couple of minutes and she'd have no hand. Painless.

Goh Peng's fingers went back into the case on the table and came out with a small leather case. From this he withdrew a gleaming six-inch Soligen surgical scalpel. He held it up to the ceiling light to study its edge. His tongue clicked contentedly; it was the first sound of satisfaction he'd made. But there was no need for inspection. The cutting edge glistened like wet glass. He seemed more at home with this than he'd been with the kukri he'd used on Dean and the others.

Everybody in the room watched him; everybody except Hilary,

her head rested on her chest, still in a dead faint. Goh Peng's eyes looked flat and professional; this wasn't going to give him a great deal of pleasure. But it was enough for Fylough.

'Put that bloody thing down,' he rasped, 'and tell me what you want.'

Goh Peng took no notice. Holding the scalpel between his forefinger and thumb he touched it to Hilary's wrist. It must have been like an electric shock. Hilary's eyes shot open and bulged like a frightened puppy as her lips parted in a scream. It was like an early film, the tableau of faces watching the pretty heroine going through her paces with not a word, not a sound. But it didn't last. Hilary passed out again as Goh Peng drew the blade lightly across her wrist, just breaking the skin, the wafer-thin line following it turning miraculously into a neat red liquid bracelet.

'For Christ's sake!' Fylough was on his feet. But only for a fraction of a second. The squat guard behind him, momentarily absorbed in Goh Peng's artistry, recovered quickly and Fylough's shoulder was almost cut in half by the edge of his hand as it sliced into the nerve and sent him crashing back into his chair. Fylough bellowed in pain. He didn't know which to cry for – the pain in his shoulder or in Hilary's hand. It was solved for him when the barrel of the Chinese's pistol ground into the corner of his eye, bringing a different sort of bellow – a scream – which he managed to clench his teeth on to. He brought his head up, eyes streaming, and pointed his face where last he had seen Kim Cheong. 'For God's sake, man!' he appealed. 'Stop him . . .'

Kim Cheong nodded slowly. It was to himself. Fylough couldn't see a thing. For Ah Lian and Goh Peng it was as if Kim Cheong had received full compensation; they knew that at a whisper from him he'd have Fylough on his knees, begging. It was enough. It was recompense for the hands of a young idealist. Kim Cheong looked over his shoulder at Ah Lian. She hadn't taken her eyes off Fylough, but there was no expression in those eyes, no satisfaction, no mercy – Fylough would have been in a bad way if she'd been here running the show alone. She returned Kim Cheong's glance with a slight inclination of the head and a softly spoken instruction to Goh Peng. He straightened up from Hilary's hand but kept the scalpel in his fingers as he studied, critically, the rapidly enlarging bracelet of blood rising from his shallow incision.

'Where are the documents kept?' Kim Cheong worked another cigarette out of the packet on his knees and accepted a light from one of the guards. He didn't offer a cigarette to Fylough.

'In the Foreign Office Registry,' mumbled Fylough. 'I don't have access . . .'

'Who does?'

Fylough didn't reply immediately.

'Mr Fylough. . . ?' No impatience, just a small rebuke, a gentle prompting.

Fylough had vision through the water in his undamaged eye. Hilary was still out; Goh Peng was poised as if about to finish signing his name in the register; Kim Cheong, solicitous; and his sister, cold and unfeeling.

'Let me use the telephone.'

'By all means, but just a moment . . .' Kim Cheong raised one of his hooks to the man who'd entered the house first, the man with the black case, and pointed to the telephone. It took the man no more than a minute to join an extension with an earpiece to the phone's base; this he handed to Kim Cheong.

'Dial your number, Mr Fylough,' instructed Kim Cheong, then sat back in his chair and raised the cigarette to his lips. 'But first, do you want to say anything to Mrs West? She's awake and I think she might now have a voice to help remind you of the seriousness of our intentions.' Kim Cheong smiled lightly at the expression on Fylough's face. 'In other words, don't do anything silly, Mr Fylough.'

He was right. He must have had eyes in the back of his head. Hilary was awake but this time she didn't surface with her mouth wide open and a scream bubbling noiselessly at the back of her throat. The banana in her mouth was slowly resuming the shape of her tongue and she managed to control both the need to scream and the urge to tell Fylough to do exactly as he was told and tell them anything – everything – and that if he didn't, she would. But it wasn't necessary. Fylough was totally subdued; the work on Hilary's hand and the gouging his eye had undergone had given him all the impetus he needed to do exactly as he was told. He squinted the tears from his eye and dialled Morgan's number.

There were no preliminaries or friendly chit-chat. He went straight to the point. 'Do you remember the Chaah documents, Jim?'

'Are you on a clean line?'

'Of course,' snapped Fylough impatiently and looked up quickly into the watching Chinese man's face. Kim Cheong, with the earpiece held gently against the side of his head, nodded approvingly. He looked like a benign undersized Buddha. But Fylough wasn't misled by the expression; he'd seen Chinese like this one, with the same benign expression, charging across jungle clearings with a rifle and bayonet in their hands and murder in their hearts. With the Chinese the expression was only skin-deep.

'What about them?' asked Morgan.

'I need to see them – the originals. Urgently.'

Morgan didn't reply immediately. Kim Cheong stiffened. 'Very urgently,' added Fylough.

'Let me think about this for a minute, Peter.'

'Why?'

'Because this is the second time in less than a couple of hours these papers have been mentioned. I think I want to know a bit more about your intentions, Peter.'

'*Who?*' mouthed Kim Cheong. He was sitting bolt upright in his chair now, the cigarette in his other hook forgotten and smouldering, the smoke spiralling dangerously near his tightly slitted eyes. Fylough stared back. He tried again.

'I said urgently, James. I'll explain in detail later.' He paused for emphasis and added as an aside, 'Who else has been asking for them?'

'One of Woodhouse's men, somebody named Kent, and he wasn't asking about them, he was asking what to do with them!'

'*What!*' Fylough stared at the phone in his hand and then at Kim Cheong. Kim Cheong gestured with his other hook, shaking ash from his smouldering cigarette all over the place. The gesture could have meant anything. But Fylough knew what was required. 'What d'you mean, asking what to do with them?'

'Apparently he's been working on a Chinese angle. He went to Malaysia and came back with a connection to the Chaah ambush and a key to the papers. Somewhere he'd got the file number. The cheeky bastard wriggled his way into FO's Registry and hoisted the whole bloody file.'

'Jesus Christ! What's he done with them? Where the bloody hell is he now?'

'At his home,' said Morgan lightly. 'He's got the papers with him. I told him to wait there and sit on them. In the meantime I'm arranging for a team of after-dinner speakers to go round and talk him into handing them over before he rushes out and makes copies for the *Sun*!'

'I don't believe it!' rasped Fylough and looked up to see whether Kim Cheong did. But Kim Cheong was ahead of them both.

'Get round to Kent's flat,' he snapped at Goh Peng. 'Bring him here. He has the file. I want him alive. Quick!' He raised his hook and stopped Goh Peng at the door. 'Don't look at the papers. They're not for your eyes.' He turned back to Fylough. 'Put the phone down – immediately. Don't talk any more.' Fylough did as he was told. 'Go and sit down and smoke a cigarette.'

Fylough lit up gratefully. 'What about Hilary?' He met Hilary's eyes and nodded encouragement to her. It was more than he felt.

'One thing at a time,' said Kim Cheong. 'We'll decide everybody's future after we've seen how many maggots there are in this apple. I don't think I like it, Mr Fylough . . .' He gave a sad smile as he placed another cigarette between his lips and allowed it to be lighted. 'So sit quietly and allow me to consider this turn of events.' There was a slight suggestion of suspicion in the tone of his voice as he tailed off and turned to face Ah Lian.

Nobody moved in the room across the street.

'Shouldn't we warn Kent to pack an overnight bag?' suggested Potter after he'd listened to the taped happenings across the road and Morgan's apparently indiscreet conversation with Fylough. But his breezy manner had no effect on Woodhouse or the flat-faced Chinese. They'd exchanged glances but had said nothing to each other since their attention had been attracted to Goh Peng's surgical performance. Potter waited for a lead. Woodhouse was running the show – he couldn't be any closer to it – and what was Potter, after all? He allowed himself a wry grin. Nothing but a set of eyes, and he'd rather be here looking than sitting over there in that Chinese temple with the sound of blood dripping all over the place.

'Russell – ' Woodhouse's voice broke into his reverie. He stared at the back of Woodhouse's head; he hadn't turned, he was still gazing through the lace curtains. 'When they bring Kent into the house tell your two men in the basement to move up to the starting line. Get into a position where an outside diversion will allow them to move into the room and extract Mr Fylough.'

'What about the girl?'

'Do as I say. Just concentrate on lifting Fylough out of that room – but not until I give the word. Got it?'

'Got it.'

'Are you still in touch with the rest of the team?'

Potter tapped the small transmitter with his finger, but nobody was watching. He raised his eyebrows at the two heads still peering into the gloom of the street outside, and said, 'Yes. Two – parked in a side street off Grant Road.'

'Armed?'

'Yes.'

Woodhouse went to the other side of the window so that he could see to the far end of Bellamy Avenue. 'That car down there is the one you say has one Chinaman in it?'

'Right.'

'Tell your people to move within spitting distance of him but don't excite him. Stay out of sight, but be ready for a human wave of Chinks – sorry, Wang! – appearing out of that front door and charging up the street. Make sure they know who's to be allowed a free run and who can be left in the gutter.' He stopped looking down the street and turned to face Potter. 'Shortly after Kent's arrival, Russell, there'll be a general exodus from that house. We want it to turn into a confused bolt. We want it to look to the Chinese over there as if the cavalry's arrived with its nose up Kent's arse, so there's got to be a bit of blood here and there. Just make sure it's Chinese blood and not a fee-fi-fo-fum's . . .' Nobody laughed. 'OK. Get on with it.' He turned back to the window in time for Wang's hissed warning.

A new car was moving slowly down the road as if seeking a place to park. Wang had X-ray eyes. 'More Chinese,' he said softly and moved slightly away from the window as the new arrival wriggled itself into a slot three cars away from the vehicle just below the window. 'They're getting ready to move out.'

Two of the Chinese in the first car got out and one walked briskly towards the new arrival and slid in the front passenger seat. The other man paused to light a cigarette. He gazed casually around him, then wandered along to join the solitary Chinese sitting in the car at the end of Bellamy Avenue.

Woodhouse glanced down at the watch on his wrist. 'How long is it since that evil-looking bastard slipped out of the house?' He didn't wait for a reply; he'd worked it out for himself. 'Where does Kent live?'

'Ranger country,' said Potter. 'Victoria,' he added when Woodhouse turned his head and frowned. 'Ebury Square – that sort of thing . . .'

Woodhouse's eyes went back to the road below. 'Long enough for the Chink to stick a chopstick up his arse and bundle him into a car and bring him to Fylough's soirée.'

'I think they'll want to hurt him a bit first,' murmured Wang. 'To make sure . . .' He didn't elaborate. He didn't have to. Woodhouse shrugged his shoulders and moved away from the window. So did Wang. Potter clicked his fingers and when his man looked up he pointed to the window. No words were necessary; Marcel Marceau would have felt at home. Wang sat down and picked up his briefcase. 'Drink?' he said to Woodhouse.

'Of what?' asked Woodhouse without enthusiam.

The solid bolts of the case clicked open and Wang held up a bottle of duty-free Teacher's. 'Mr Potter?'

'Please call me Russell. No thanks, I'll have cocoa.'

'What about your friend?'

'He'll have cocoa too.'

'Thanks!' grunted the man at the window.

32

David Kent was expecting Morgan, or somebody like him.

'Who is it?' he said softly through the door when the knock came.

The voice was indistinct. It sounded like '. . . Fylough'.

He opened the door, more curious than wary. He should have had it the other way round. But it was too late. As if balancing himself, the heavy Chinese grasped the side of the door with his right hand, leaned his weight into the gap and thrust the fingers of his left hand deep into Kent's midriff. Not a word, no expression – nothing – just the whoosh of Kent's lungs emptying themselves of air. His mouth dropped open and his throat closed up like a stop valve, forcing his eyes almost to spin back on themselves and inspect the inside of his brain. And then his legs turned to paper and the floor cracked him across the nose.

Still barking like a sick dog as he fought the stop valve, he felt his collar grasped and he was picked up and half carried, half dragged away from the door, then lowered on to the carpet in the centre of the room. The door closed gently behind him as Goh Peng followed his companion into the flat. The whole operation had taken fifteen seconds.

'Watch the door,' said Goh Peng and leaned over Kent's body. He held a .32 PPK Walther to the side of Kent's neck, but it wasn't really necessary; Kent was still fighting for breath. He'd managed to work the valve to one side but he wasn't getting enough air, not enough to worry about .32s jammed into his neck.

'Where are the papers?' Goh Peng said softly into his ear.

Kent gave no sign that he'd heard – and understood. He was struggling. He wasn't pretending – the struggle was real – but he took a moment off to let his brain take over from his chest. He'd only seen one Chinese – briefly – but there'd be more; they were like salted peanuts, they never came in ones. 'Where are the papers?' was what oily voice had said. *The papers? Jesus! How. . . ?* The voice at the door had said, 'Fylough'. *Fylough?*

What the bloody hell was going on? Morgan had said *he* was coming for the Foreign Office papers . . . *Oh Jesus Christ! But how. . . ?* There was only one bloody way how – Morgan was chopsticking. He was doing a sweet-and-sour for the bloody Peking mandarins and he'd dropped him, the bastard! He wasn't coming for his bloody papers, he'd never *intended* coming. He'd sent the fucking Chinese – he wanted them to have the file, the treacherous bastard! The anger, and the fright, helped him with his breathing; it was getting through and the pain was subsiding. He felt his eyes swivel back into their proper place and managed to blink away the tears.

Goh Peng mistook his actions. He stepped back out of range, moved out of Kent's vision and took up a new station behind him, an arm's length away from the back of his skull. The muzzle of the little PPK parted his hair and pressed hard into the crown of his head. Kent winced.

The voice said, 'Don't move from there.'

From where he was lying Kent could see the feet, legs, and bottom half of the man who'd stuck his fingers into his solar plexus. He was still standing by the door. Kent could see his hands flexing like the grab on a small digger; close up, his fingers looked like the tines of garden fork, and seemed to be getting ready for another dig.

'I asked you where the papers are.' The voice was out of sight. Kent shook his head. It was a mistake. The muzzle of the .32 rasped across the thin skin of his head and the voice said again, 'Move only your tongue. Where are the papers?'

'What papers?' he hiccuped, and wished he hadn't replied. His voice sounded like that of a child just recovering from a bout of tantrums.

'The Chaah papers,' replied Goh Peng patiently. That's what Fylough had called them. It didn't mean anything to Kent.

'I don't know what you're talking about . . .'

'Sim.' Goh Peng didn't raise his voice, and nothing showed on his flat, peasant features; he could have been at the operating table and asking the nurse for the forceps. They must have worked together before; there were no instructions, just the one word, the name. And the name knew exactly what was required. The feet and legs moved away from the door and straddled Kent's body.

Kent clenched his eyes tightly, then opened them and stared up. He felt like one of Gulliver's friends. Goh Peng spoke again.

'Don't kill him.'

They weren't bluffing. Kent blinked and swallowed. Goh Peng had spoken in Cantonese, a private conversation between himself and the other Chinese; Kent wasn't supposed to understand. Sweet Jesus! 'Don't kill him'? Kent quickly tried to change his mind and offer negotiation, but he was too late.

One of the feet came off the ground, hovered over his stomach, and came down with all its force on the spot where the fingers had been rammed home. Kent screamed. But no sound came out. As his mouth opened Goh Peng reached over his head, jammed the PPK deep into his mouth, held it for a second against the back of his throat, then pressed it down on his tongue.

The Chinese above him repositioned himself so that, balanced like an Olympic gymnast, he stood with all his weight on Kent's arm muscles. The seconds ticked by. Nothing was said. It was like a silent movie, the two expressionless Chinese watching Kent writhe in agony.

After a few minutes, when it became obvious that Kent wasn't going to leap to his feet and start throwing his weight around, Goh Peng removed the pistol from his mouth, straightened up and moved across the room to rest his buttocks on the arm of the only decent armchair in the flat. He signalled his helper to stand aside so that he could watch Kent rearrange himself.

Kent had no feeling anywhere. When the weight was taken off his arms they were dead. Totally numb. There was nothing he could do with them. He could still see the legs but he wasn't bothered. The other man was out of sight – that didn't matter either.

In agony, he rolled on to his side and brought his knees up in a foetal position, concentrating on getting his wind back. His mouth felt like an empty banana skin and had a salty taste that threatened to bring the entire contents of his stomach on to the carpet; they were already halfway there. He spat out the mixture of blood, oil and vomit and tried to work his lungs back into life. He had no time or inclination to think about the two Chinese in his rooms, the Chaah papers or the Fylough/Morgan chopstick connection. He heard nothing over the thunder of his heartbeat. He didn't hear Goh Peng issue instructions to the owner of the feet.

'Take the room apart. Look everywhere. A file or large envelope, probably bulky, maybe official . . . Don't look inside it. Just find it and bring it to me.' He allowed his body to slide into the armchair and rested the hand holding the short pistol on his knee. The weapon was aimed at the back of Kent's head. He was taking no chances, even though his prisoner looked more dead than alive. He lit a cigarette and watched the other man wreck Kent's flat.

It took half an hour. All the furniture was piled into the middle of the room. Kent was dragged from one side of the room to the other while the heavy Chinese lifted the carpet, inspected the underside and dropped it again. The few cushions were cut open and their contents heaped like used confetti in the corner of the room. No papers. Nothing like them. The Chinese didn't appear impatient or frustrated; he merely went on to the next item. Goh Peng sat calmly smoking and watching the carnage.

The three pictures on the wall were taken down, their backs inspected and then bounced on the floor so that the frames shattered, spilling the prints and their backings among a shower of glass. No papers. The bed, the mattress, the wardrobe, Kent's suitcase and finally his clothes. The Chinese spread the suits and coats on the floor and ruckled them with his feet – no papers – nothing, not even a five-pound note. Goh Peng stood up slowly and the two of them up-ended the chair he'd been sitting in. The other man pulled off the hessian backing as if it had been made of recycled lavatory paper. Nothing. It was when they tipped back the armchair and Goh Peng settled himself in it again that his self-restraint finally gave way to his baser instincts.

'Bring him over here.' He jerked his chin at Kent and then at an upturned Windsor chair. 'Put him on that.'

Kent was picked up like a baby doll and dumped across the chair's spokes; he was still fighting for breath. Goh Peng leaned forward, grabbed a handful of hair and raised his head.

'Open your eyes . . .' It was like a party game. But there was no mirth; just a cold unemotional voice from a cold unemotional face. '. . . and listen carefully.'

Kent felt stuff dribbling out of the side of his mouth but it didn't worry him. The awkward position, spread-eagled like somebody's old coat across the back of the upturned chair, didn't help his

breathing exercises or boost his confidence enough to make a fight –
verbal, not physical – of it, but the remnants of his pride forced
him to ignore the order. He kept his eyes firmly shut – until the
stubby barrel of the PPK worked its way into the corner of his left
eye and its tiny foresight gouged open the lid.

Through the tears and red mist he saw Goh Peng's unconcerned
features. He blinked twice, three times, and the face came into
focus. '*Don't kill him.*' The Chinese man's earlier words sang like
Mozart's Requiem through his numbed brain. They didn't want
him killed – that was a point in credit! But how long could he put
up with this? He had said don't kill him – but he hadn't said don't
cripple the poor bastard. He had to hold on – it was about time that
idle bugger Mithers-Wayne put in an appearance . . . Maybe he
was waiting outside the door until he stopped crying? *Maybe*.

He stopped thinking and stared back into the slits on either side
of Goh Peng's nose. Goh Peng was saying something – he'd missed
the first part – maybe that had been the bit about '. . . if you don't
stop fucking about, *kwai lo*, you'll find yourself limping down to
the fish and chip shop minus balls!'

'. . . the papers?'

It was the same old story.

'What papers?'

Goh Peng stared into his face for several seconds. It was a pity
Kim Cheong had said not to kill him. Without looking away from
Kent he put one hand in his jacket pocket and removed a scrap of
paper. He held it out to the other Chinese. 'Ring that number,
then bring the phone to me,' he ordered.

Kent stared back, then allowed his eyes to droop while he
concentrated on his private thoughts. Suddenly, Goh Peng let go
of his hair and, taken by surprise, Kent's head bounced on to the
wooden chair frame. For the first time, he lost consciousness.

It wasn't a healthy slap across the face that woke him but Goh
Peng's sensitive doctor's fingers crawling from behind his ear,
down the side of his face and under his chin. It was quite nice,
almost sexual. After the third trip he realised who it was, opened
his eyes and tried to pull his face away. Then he felt the phone
jammed against his ear.

'Speak,' said Goh Peng.

The tinny voice in his ear must have been talking for some time.

261

It had an air of impatience, although not irritation. 'Is that you Kent? Speak up, I can't hear you . . .'

Kent blinked into Goh Peng's eyes. Goh Peng got the message.

'Mr Fylough,' he said.

'Hello . . .' croaked Kent.

'You know who I am,' snapped Fylough. It wasn't a question, it offered no promise of a formal introduction and there was no pause for interruption. 'You've got some papers that don't belong to you. I want them. The man who is with you is acting on my behalf. His name is Dr Goh Peng. I've empowered him to collect the papers and bring them, and you, to my place right away. Now please do as you're told.'

'What papers, Mr Fylough?' Kent felt like an old 78 gramo-phone record. The needle, in the shape of Goh Peng's PPK, jabbed cruelly into his free ear. Goh Peng had the good manners to remove the mouthpiece of the telephone while he suppressed the high notes of the scream. Fylough wasn't sympathetic.

'Listen, you stupid bastard, lives are at risk, so stop fucking around and hand over those bloody documents before somebody gets the bloody chop! I've spoken to C . . .' He paused for a second to listen to Kent's laboured breathing. 'You know who I mean by C?' He didn't wait for an answer or listen to more heavy breathing. 'And he's in full agreement. Produce the papers and get over here right away.' The phone was removed from Fylough's hand at the same time as Goh Peng took the receiver away from Kent's ear and took over the conversation. He spoke in Cantonese. Kent didn't bother to listen – he'd had enough. If Fylough wanted to hand over a thirty-year-old secret to the Chinese, so be it. Goh Peng handed the telephone back to the fifteen-stone gorilla and tapped the side of Kent's head with the automatic.

'The papers, please,' he said politely.

'In the fridge.'

Goh Peng didn't seem surprised. He passed the message on to his man and Kent heard the fridge door open. There was silence for the best part of a minute, then: 'No papers here.'

Kent waited for Goh Peng to translate.

'In the freezer compartment,' he said wearily and raised his head to look across the room. He'd turned the fridge up to its maximum and the tiny compartment door was frozen to the edges. It didn't stop King Kong. He grasped the small handle, put one foot against the side of the refrigerator and tugged. The door came off its hinges as if it were made of newspaper. He threw it across the room and looked inside the freezer compartment. In there it was like Christmas; everything was white. But it was still obvious. There was nothing except two trays of ice cubes. And lying on top of them the property of the Foreign Office Registry, hard and cold and stiff enough to break.

'Handle them with care,' Goh Peng advised his assistant, who'd got both hands in the compartment and was trying to dislodge the ice trays. They didn't stand a chance and came out with a jerk, the Chaah file neatly stuck to the top of them.

'All right, Mr Kent,' said Goh Peng, 'You can stand up now. Slowly and carefully. Don't make any mistakes. We're going to Mr Fylough's house. There's a car waiting outside for us. If you wish to misbehave my companion will step on your legs and break them and we'll carry you to it. The choice is yours.'

Kent made no reply. He knew Goh Peng meant it. He'd heard him tell the other man and seen the glimmer of a smile in the other's peasant face. He'd enjoy breaking legs; he couldn't disguise it. Kent didn't misbehave.

'Car coming!' Russell Potter's assistant widened the gap in the curtains another inch and whispered the warning without taking his eyes from the road.

It was dark, almost pitch-black, and the ancient overhead lamps, their screens dimmed by several layers of unwashed grime, gave a pale, yellowy inadequate circle of light round the base of the standard. There was one directly opposite – sheer luck – that cast its glow over the pavement just outside Fylough's front doorstep. Behind the man at the window lounged the thin and elegantly dressed Evelyn St John Woodhouse; he stretched comfortably in a soft chair and stared at the ceiling while the ever inscrutable Wang Peng Soon sat upright on a wooden kitchen chair beside the electronic surveillance equipment. Wang didn't move. Neither did Potter.

But Woodhouse welcomed the opportunity. Still grasping his coffee mug he uncurled from the chair and joined Potter's tea boy by the window, peering over his shoulder as he sipped Wang's duty-free Teacher's from the heavy mug.

'Doesn't look too good, our boy Kent,' he said conversationally as he watched Goh Peng and the Sumo wrestler look-alike, one on either side, support Kent up the stairs and into the house.

'He didn't sound too good either,' responded Wang but with a little more concern. 'I wonder *why* they've brought him here? He must have done what he was told and given them the papers. They've got Peter Fylough over there, with somebody's foot in his crotch, to confirm their authenticity and young Hilary to add weight their persuasive powers . . . I can't understand why they want Kent as well – it doesn't make sense.' He peered into his empty mug as if seeking the answer in its depths, then, finding nothing, tipped another two inches of whisky into it and looked up at the unresponsive back of Woodhouse's head. He swivelled his eyes towards Potter. 'Anything coming through the pipe?' he asked.

Potter shook his head. He stood leaning against the wall with one earphone jammed against his ear. 'Just the rasping of matches. They're either playing hot-foot with Mr Fylough or smoking themselves into an early grave. They're not talking to each other. Strange . . . Just a minute! Hang on!' He listened for a fraction of a second, then thrust the headset into Wang's hand. 'Now they are, they're talking flied lice – must be take away time!'

33

Kim Cheong turned slowly in his chair and studied the new arrival.

He waved his arm at the Chinese holding Kent upright to order his release and held a hook out to Goh Peng for the file. He stared at it for several seconds, as if steeling himself to open it and touch again the documents he had last held over thirty-five years ago, to feel once again the horror of the ambush and the frightful pain that had followed. He savoured the moment a little longer. Without opening the file he looked up to nod his congratulations to Goh Peng, and then said:

'The aircraft is still waiting?'

'Yes, but not much longer. Air China cargo – the Dynasty flight – Gatwick for Peking Airport. They were loaded yesterday but managed an engine fault. They can't hold it beyond twenty-three fifty-nine without an extension certificate. Shall I tell them to expect us?'

Kim Cheong nodded. 'But just two, the girl and me. Is there a scheduled British flight that can be got on at short notice?'

'Why, Excellency?'

Kim Cheong's expression changed but he didn't explode; the menace in his quiet, cold features was more pronounced than a raised voice. 'Answer the question,' he hissed.

Goh Peng rearranged the look of surprise on his face. 'Nothing's been arranged.'

'Arrange it. A passage for two to Hong Kong, either this evening or early morning.'

'And the two are, Excellency?'

'This man Kent, and Madame Ah Lian.'

Kent frowned at the back of Hilary's head. It was only when he leaned forward that he saw her hands spread out in front of her and her wrists clamped to the table. It was disbelief at first, then total outrage and anger got the better of discretion.

Without looking round he jammed his elbow into the stomach of the man holding him and swung round to finish him off. It was a foolish, not to say stupid act. The Chinese were light on their feet. The man still at the door showed no expression but moved forward on his toes and with an almighty crack brought the hard edge of his automatic down on the soft part of Kent's neck. He followed this up with a tight-fisted punch below his ear. Kent's knees gave way and before everything went red and black he just had time to recognise the other European staring boggle-eyed from his chair on the other side of the room: Lieutenant Peter Fylough from Togom's little snapshot; Mr er-Smith from Evelyn Woodhouse's little gin-and-tonic soirée in the Pig and Eye. Then he hit the ground with a thump.

Across the road Wang Peng Soon translated the conversation to Evelyn Woodhouse and Russell Potter.

Woodhouse digested the translation. 'Why's he splitting up a winning team?'

'Insurance,' said Wang, then frowned and held up his hand. 'Hang on a minute – he's got a bloody mutiny on his hands! Tape that phone call, Russell,' he hissed urgently, 'I don't want to miss this . . .'

Ah Lian moved out of the shadow of the corner where she'd retired to sit and listen. Her face, like that of Kim Cheong, was set in a cold, querying expression, but unlike the good doctor she was not afraid to voice her confusion.

'This is not what we agreed,' she said firmly. 'What does this change of plan mean?'

'I will tell you in due course,' replied Kim Cheong. He didn't take his eyes off Kent, curled on his knees with his head touching the floor in front of him. He looked most uncomfortable, like a British prisoner of war about to enjoy Japanese sword practice. 'I hope for your sake he's not dead,' he told the heavily built Chinese, and wasn't appeased when he received a reassuring shake of the head from Goh Peng.

But Ah Lian wasn't finished. 'I insist on knowing now,' she said firmly.

Kim Cheong swung round in his chair and stared at length into her face as if seeing her for the first time. She didn't wilt. He softened his eyes and relented, then opened the file on his knees.

It was as if he was already familiar with its contents and he showed no surprise as his partly opened hooks flicked adroitly through the papers. They seemed, like the fortune-teller's budgie's beak, to know exactly when to stop flicking. He extracted the photograph that had caused Kent to take a sharp intake of breath. Shielding the picture from the view of the other Chinese, he allowed Ah Lian to gaze on the unsmiling image of a forty-years' younger Secretary-General of the Chinese Communist Party, the second most important politician in the Politburo, the heir to the throne, the man chosen to step into the current, chain-smoking premier's tiny black plimsolls when he finally coughed himself to death. Ah Lian stared. No inscrutable Chinese was Ah Lian – her eyes boggled and, like Kent, the sudden emptying of her lungs caused a sharp hiss of incredulity from between her shapely lips. Kim Cheong allowed the image to impress itself on her mind, then slid the picture deftly back into its place and warned her with a touch on her arm and a frown.

'A British agent?' she began.

'Shhh!'

'I thought . . .'

'Shhh!' Kim Cheong repeated, the warning hardly carrying beyond his lips. 'Now,' he said in a normal voice and tapped the file with his hook, 'do you think he'll allow me to step on to the tarmac at Peking Airport with this under my arm?'

Ah Lian stepped back a pace. She hadn't attempted to recover her disinterested expression and continued to stare at the file in Kim Cheong's lap as if it were a slumbering, malevolent cobra. 'I understand,' she said with difficulty. 'I don't want to know any more.'

'But you shall,' went on Kim Cheong. 'You demanded to know why the change of plans.' He tapped the file. 'That's the reason. May I continue?' He didn't wait for her approval. Everybody was interested. Wang glued his ear to the crisp tones coming through the high-powered receiver.

'I will take the two places on the Dynasty aircraft with Mrs West – no papers, no file, just the elderly director of TEWA and the daughter of an old English friend taking discreet advantage of passage on one of our own TEWA flights from London. Mrs West will be my guarantee.'

'For what?' asked Ah Lian.

'My guarantee that Mr Kent will look after my papers and bring them to me at the border point on the New Territories boundary.' He raised his right hook to forestall her objection. 'It's being arranged. You and Mr Kent will travel British Airways on Hong Kong British passports. As an officer of British Intelligence he will have no trouble passing the authorities at the London airport – it will be in his interest to ensure that there is no trouble. He won't be searched, stopped or questioned, and you will be with him all the time to make sure the game is played according to the rules I shall lay down.'

'Does he know?' Ah Lian glanced obliquely at Kent.

He'd been picked up from the floor and plonked on to a chair. He was barely with it. His breathing was laboured and the pain in the back of his neck was almost rivalling the knife-like spasms in his stomach muscles which were giving his nose and mouth a pinched, greyish appearance. He hadn't followed any of Kim Cheong's and Ah Lian's conversation but he presumed, by her animated expression, that they were discussing the contents of the file on Kim Cheong's knee; it looked like a major upheaval was on its way in the People's Republic. But it wasn't his problem. He glanced at Fylough from under his half-closed eyelids and got no comfort from that direction; Fylough looked almost as unhappy as *he* felt. It was Hilary who was the problem. He couldn't see her face, only the back of her bowed head, and he didn't know whether she was awake. But he did know where *he* would have been if his hands had been spread out on the chopping block – in a dead faint of pure funk! He, after all, had seen some of the effects of similar treatment; Christ knows what was going through her mind. He switched his attention back to Kim Cheong but he understood few of the words Kim Cheong was using.

Kim Cheong smiled into Ah Lian's eyes. 'Not yet,' he said, 'but like most Englishmen he'll put the welfare of a female, particularly one he has a lusting for, before the well-being and security of his country.' He tapped the file again. 'This means nothing to him.' He looked disdainfully at Hilary. 'But she does, so he'll do exactly as I tell him.' And to prove it he raised his chin at the man standing behind Kent's chair. He, in response, touched the muzzle of his automatic to the back of Kent's neck and, grasping a handful of hair, lifted his head. Kent found himself staring into the face of the man with no hands.

'Mr Kent.' Kim Cheong spoke in English. The familiar language brought Fylough back to life. He shrugged aside the gunman's hands resting on his shoulders and dived into his pocket to bring out a packet of Rothmans and a box of matches. Nobody took any notice of him. Even the guard seemed absorbed by the words of Kim Cheong. Fylough put a cigarette into his mouth but didn't strike a match until Kim Cheong was well into his instructions.

'. . . and when you get to Kowloon you will be taken to the Orchid Hotel in Nathan Road and will not move from that hotel until Ah Lian arranges a meeting between us. Is that understood?'

'Get stuffed!'

Fylough took a deep lungful of smoke and slowly trickled it out through his nose. He was much calmer and more relaxed than he should have been. He stared hard at Kent and glanced sideways at Kim Cheong. Kim Cheong, if he had understood the words, was not the least bit put out; his expression was one of mild amusement.

'I presume that means you don't want to help us, Mr Kent?'

Kent stared defiantly into Kim Cheong's eyes but made no reply. Kim Cheong went on as if he hadn't asked a question. 'But you're very hasty, I haven't yet told you the penalty for not wishing to help.'

'The answer's still the same.'

'I wonder if Mrs West would agree with your aggressive attitude?'

'What has she got to do with it?' It was a silly question, and Kent knew it. He knew bloody well what Mrs West had to with the situation. But asking silly questions wasn't going to help. She was here and Kim Cheong was dying to tell him what was going through his mind.

'Oh, didn't I mention it?' smiled Kim Cheong. 'She'll be with me on the Canton side of the border and if you don't appear with this folder . . .' He tapped his hook very gently on the file; it sounded like the rattle of a loose plate on a tap-dancer's shoe. '. . . then Mrs West will be deposited on the doorstep of your flat and her hands will be in a little bag tied to the knocker. She'll be able to smooth your troubled brow with a pair of these . . .' The smile vanished and he clicked the hooks together angrily. '. . . while you congratulate yourself on having made my life a little more complicated. But don't look so concerned – we'll manage with or without you.'

Hilary opened her eyes and stared, unseeing, at her beautifully manicured hands clamped to the table in front of her. Her fingers waggled themselves nervously, without prompting, betraying her thoughts. Without realising what she was doing, she sobbed softly, in fear and terror, and in desperation moaned, 'David . . . Please . . .'

Kent didn't look at her. He took his eyes off Kim Cheong briefly and glanced at Fylough. Fylough's face showed nothing – there was no encouragement, no condemnation. He swung his eyes back to Kim Cheong.

'OK,' he said gruffly. 'When do we go?'

Hilary choked on a sob and on the other side of the room Fylough's shoulders, tense and set back firmly into the chair, sagged in relief – or disappointment.

'I think you've . . .' he began.

'Shut up!' snapped Kim Cheong and the thickset Chinese standing behind Fylough rapped him sharply across the ear with his automatic. Fylough clamped his teeth on whatever it was he had been going to say and turned his head away from further punishment. Kent, more composed now, stared hard at the top of Fylough's head. He was never going to know now whether Peter Fylough had been about to congratulate him on a wise decision or tell him he'd just fucked up the whole bloody operation.

Wang handed Potter back his headset and asked him to switch on the recording of Goh Peng's telephone conversation. It was in Chinese. Woodhouse raised his eyes at Potter and reached for Wang's duty-free bottle as the aggressive, machine-gun-like syllables rattled around the room. There was a long pause – long enough for Wang to reach out and splash whisky into his own almost dry mug – and then a short response from the outside line.

'The Chinese Embassy have pulled rank and arranged two seats on a BA flight to Hong Kong,' said Wang. 'The earliest they could get them on is the first Australian flight tomorrow – stops at Kai

Tak. Can you arrange something for me, Woody? Something that gets to Hong Kong before that one?'

'Don't give it another thought.' Woodhouse smiled gently to himself, then clicked his fingers as if he were calling for the bill and said, 'Pass the phone, Russell, please.' He looked slightly smug – a little, overbearing smugness – but it was only on the outside; there was still a tiny niggle of doubt deep down inside. It was reflected in his voice.

'James?' It was personal-and-private-number stuff, straight through to Sir James Morgan's armchair in front of the box. Morgan was expecting the call. He lowered the sound on *Newsnight* and raised the volume on the handset. 'They're lowering the curtain on the Chinese opera. It seems to have been well received; in fact a great success.'

'Any complications?'

'Nothing of significance. Only Kent, padding in where angels fear et cetera, has been nominated Postman Pat for his troubles. He's taking the package to Honkers for them – he's going to throw it across the border for KC to take home the long way round. They're using the West girl as deposit.'

'I dread to think what interpretation you'd have put on *significant* complications, Woody! Let's hear the details.'

Woody told him.

When, at length, he finished, Morgan said, 'You will, of course, see that Kent waltzes through Heathrow like the good fairy?'

'It'll all be taken care of, James. Wang says the takeaway shop is cobbling together a new passport for him. I hope they're not getting too elaborate – there are some funny buggers hanging around Heathrow nowadays. Somebody may take it into his head to flush him. Shall I tell Special Branch to – ?'

'No, Woody. Let your own people shuffle him through. Send someone with heavy eyebows to wink and flap his arms if anybody starts buggering about. Let me know when the London Chinese population is back to normal.'

'Just a second, James – Wang wants to go to Hong Kong quickly. I think he wants to meet them there and keep his eye on the packet until it reaches the border . . .'

'Let me talk to him.'

Woodhouse handed the telephone to Wang and went back to

271

look out of the window. He didn't listen to the conversation, he had his own little whirly ball of problems to sort into some sort of order. But then there wasn't much to listen to; Wang's share of the conversation was limited mainly to affirmative grunts and short nods of his wobbly chins. When he put down the phone he went and stood by Woodhouse, sharing in silence his narrow view of Bellamy Avenue. It was quiet and it was gloomy; it looked like a backstreet overlooking a cemetery on Hallowe'en night – empty, silent, no movement, but a feeling that something was there and something was going on. Wang broke the spell.

'Morgan agrees,' he said in a soft voice, lowered in case whoever was out there in the street could hear him, 'So, would you arrange to have some unsuspecting paying passenger booted off the next plane going East to make room for an elderly Chinese named Ah Bee Yong, travelling on a Malaysian passport to Hong Kong?'

Woodhouse removed his finger from the curtain and allowed it to drop back into place. He had a set smile on his face. It was more like a death's-head grin. Evelyn St John Woodhouse was never at his best, or his most humorous, when the final card was about to join the other four.

'Did he say anything else?'

'Nothing that would concern you, Woody. He just wants you to get us all off on our holidays – everything else going on around here, he says, is your game. He says you know what to do. Do you?' Wang was joking. But it fell flat. He'd known Woody long enough not to joke when the ambush was about to be sprung. Woodhouse stared at him for a second as if wondering how he'd got there and what he was doing there, then shook his head, slowly.

'Is your passport genuine?'

'Don't worry about my passport,' said Wang, cheerfully. 'What the eye don't see, Woody!' Wang showed Woody his gold tooth; it wasn't a smile, it was a warning not to ask questions. But it wasn't allowed to go any further. Russell Potter held out the earphones to Wang and said 'Something's happening, Wang . . .'

Wang listened for a brief second. 'They're getting ready to move,' he said.

Woodhouse cleared the frown from his features. He looked almost happy. 'OK, Russell,' he said briskly, 'it's all yours.'

*

Kim Cheong nodded contentedly. 'Mrs West and I will go first,' he told Kent, then allowed a little concern to flit across his eyes as he stared at Hilary's bowed head. You're not going to do anything silly are you, Mrs West?'

Hilary didn't look up. She was in shock and in no state to do anything, silly or otherwise. Released from the clamps on the table she kept her eyes firmly on the line of blood encircling her wrist while flexing and unflexing her fingers as if to reassure herself that the hand was still connected and working normally. She was bothered by the taste in her mouth, a mixture of medicine and bile, and her tongue, still swollen, scoured the back of her mouth which was puffy and unreal – but there was no question about it, she was happy to do anything, say anything that would get her out of this room and its atmosphere of surgical horror.

'Of course you're not,' went on Kim Cheong and turned back to Kent. 'And you, Mr Kent, will leave immediately before us. You'll go with Ah Lian – '

'Go where?' demanded Kent.

'There's no need for you to know,' replied Kim Cheong. 'We will all meet, in due course, in a more civilised part of the world.' He smiled gently, a slight parting of the lips, like a gambler whose gamble has paid a better dividend than he bargained for, but it didn't linger. He inclined his head to Ah Lian and moved into a corner of the room. She followed him. The whispered conversation was audible to no one but themselves.

'Don't go to the airport until the last minute. Avoid the Embassy – they have a watch on Portland Place and Lancaster Gate. Go to Chin Xan's flat behind the New China News Agency; it's not on the British list and it's available for emergency. They know about it at the Agency – ring them.' He rested his right hook on her elbow and pulled her towards him. 'Nobody's to see the file until it's handed over to me on the border, and make sure Kent doesn't make contact with anybody. If anything happens to me you are to go on to Peking and hand the file, personally, to Hu Bang – no one else – and explain its history.'

'But – ' she hissed.

He stopped her impatiently, 'No buts. Do as you're told. I shall give you three minutes then follow you out. Your car is on the opposite side of the road. No compromise – get to Hong Kong and

273

don't let the file out of your sight.' He turned away. There was no kissing, no touching of cheeks, no smile or handshake; they could have been two strangers in a foreign land parting after a brief discussion of the awful weather.

He looked at Kent and jerked his head to the door. 'Go,' he said. Kent made no reply. He stood up and stared hard at Fylough, then inclined his head slightly, nothing friendly or respectful, a nod to a stranger. Fylough shrugged his shoulders and lit another cigarette.

Kim Cheong waited at the closed door until he heard the front door close behind Kent and Ah Lian, then stretched his hook out to Hilary.

'What about him?' Goh Peng jerked his chin at Fylough.

Kim Cheong stared for several seconds at the casual-looking former jungle fighter and smiled into his unflinching eyes.

'Kill him,' he said in English.

It all happened like a badly orchestrated exercise; a demonstration on how it shouldn't be done.

Kim Cheong stood on the pavement outside Fylough's front door and waited for Hilary to slide into the back seat of the car. Gently bathed in the orangey-grey circle of light from the streetlamp, he was clearly visible to the Watchers across the road. He was not at ease. They saw him glance in both directions, as if expecting something, and then stare critically at Ah Lian and Kent, already in the car parked just below the surveillance team's window. It was being noisily manoeuvred from between two cars that had, without malice, boxed it in. They should have left the avenue several minutes ago; instead, the painful revving and grinding of the car's gears echoing off the darkened houses made the otherwise silent street sound like the starting grid at Le Mans. The unease showed clearly on Kim Cheong's face.

And then it happened.

With a shrieking and squealing of tortured tyres a heavy Volvo saloon came hurtling around the corner. Going much too fast to correct itself, it rebounded off the parked Chinese guard car, straightened itself up with a supercharged roar, and with its powerful halogen headlights blazing like twin noonday suns came to a skidding stop, half-blocking Kim Cheong's car and disgorging armed men from every door.

But Kim Cheong's driver didn't lose his nerve – he could almost have been expecting it. He jammed his foot hard on the accelerator and, with Kim Cheong half in and half out of the back, the idling engine roared like an angry panther and took off in leaps and bounds, it rear door flapping and swinging like one of Boadicea's scythes as the Chinese driver winged the screeching car through the narrow gap left by the Volvo.

Kim Cheong was thrown in a jumbled heap across Hilary on the back seat. He caught only a distorted vision of one of the men from the Volvo – a hard-faced Englishman, whose bellow of fear and pain rose above the noise of the engine as, caught by the car's front bumper, he was lifted and spread-eagled for a few brief seconds across the windscreen. Stuck to the speeding car like a squashed fly, with one hand still grasping the metal wedge of a stubby machine-pistol and the other thrown up defensively to his face, his expression changed from aggression to sheer terror – but it was only momentary, and even as the fear registered he slid off, only to be scythed down by the freely swinging door. The Chinese driver didn't give him a second glance. He swerved the car back on to its four wheels and gunned the engine down the road.

Kim Cheong recovered quickly. He dragged himself off Hilary's body and, throwing out his arm, its claw groping like a free-thrown grapple, he hooked on to the swinging door and pulled it shut.

The Volvo's headlights lit Bellamy Avenue like a sports arena and as he pulled himself back on to the seat, he glanced quickly through the rear window. Two men were dragging the injured man off the road and on to the pavement. But there was no time for detail. A series of flashes from the kerb behind the Volvo didn't deter the driver as a burst of machine-pistol failed to find its target. He ducked involuntarily, then almost rose out of his seat as his foot thumped for more acceleration; but there was nowhere left for the pedal to go – it was already flat against the floorboards. Kim Cheong turned his head to the front; he had no time to worry about gunfire.

They skidded on two wheels, just avoided ramming the parked car with the two Chinese bodyguards and scraped past a heavily built van hurtling at them without lights from the opposite direction. They avoided it by a coat of paint as it slammed across the path of the stationary car and two men hurtled out of the back, automatic pistols pointing menacingly into the interior of the car. Kim Cheong had seen enough. He ducked out of sight.

'Gatwick Airport!' he yelled at the driver, the howling engine drowning out normal conversation. 'Get on to the main road quickly. Then slow down – take no risks!' The driver didn't acknowledge; there was no need. With his eyes glued to the wing mirror he studied the road behind, gradually slowing down and gliding into the sparse night-time traffic. Within seconds the car was swallowed up.

After several miles he looked into the rear mirror and met Kim Cheong's eyes.

'Followers lost,' he said.

Kim Cheong glanced round briefly, studied the road behind, then turned back and nodded confirmation. He settled back in his seat. He didn't look the least bit surprised that there was no British Intelligence presence in their wake.

He glanced for the first time at Hilary. She was still on the floor. He helped her gently back on to the seat.

'Are you all right, Mrs West?' His voice was strangely solicitous – not the voice of the man who had ordered, and calmly sat and watched, the preliminaries to a double amputation by the ugly, squat Chinaman with the black bag.

She didn't reply.

At the other end of Bellamy Avenue Ah Lian's driver, with a mouthful of Chinese invective, gave up attempting a gentle manoeuvre out of the box he found himself in and, jamming his gear into reverse, rammed an extra few inches for himself by grinding into the vehicle behind him. He then did the same to the car in front, and with his headlights adding to the early sunrise effect from the Volvo, he bounced his car on to the pavement opposite, narrowly missed a concrete lamppost, reversed again, and with a squeal of burning rubber hurtled down the road, followed by wild bursts of machine-gun fire and the crack of automatic pistols, none of which hit the swaying car.

Kent, once he'd recovered his balance, and without thinking, took advantage of the confusion. He grabbed the offside door catch and got ready to throw himself out of the car and into the road. But the door refused to open. He slammed his elbow against the window. It didn't even bend. He tried again, and over the squeal of the car's brakes managed to subdue the bellow of pain from the agony that shot up his arm to his shoulder and neck. He hardly noticed the sharp dig into his side.

'Sit back!' Ah Lian's voice was high-pitched from fear or shock – it was the first sign of animation she'd shown, and to follow up the instruction she jabbed hard into the soft flesh under his armpit with the barrel of a squat .32 automatic.

'And don't move. Take your hand away from the door and put it between your legs.' She read his mind. 'Don't try. You'll die before you break your neck on the road.' She wasn't being funny deliberately – fear was breaking up her normal crisp use of the language. She pulled herself together. 'Have you already forgotten the danger you have placed the West woman in?'

Kent straightened himself out and tried to move away, fractionally, from the weapon grinding into his armpit. It moved with him.

'I said don't move!'

The warning hissed into his ear. She was right, he had forgotten Hilary West's new problem. Sitting bolt upright, stiff and still, he was grateful for the darkness of the interior that kept his feelings from the Chinese woman at his side as the car sped out of Bellamy Avenue.

He blinked away the memory of Hilary's last anguished expression and concentrated on the present and future. What had brought the troops on to the scene? Too bloody late as usual. He risked Ah Lian's trigger finger and turned slightly to look over his shoulder. They'd turned the corner and left the battlefield. He'd seen one man on the deck but no sign of Kim Cheong and Hilary. They must have got away. He turned his head back. Now they were in the clear, slowing down into the rest of the traffic and moving east. There was only one other problem. He stared at the silhouette of the Chinese driver's stubby head and wondered what had happened to Peter Fylough.

The main Chinese backup team had drifted out of the room and disappeared in the wake of Kim Cheong and Ah Lian so that only one other Chinese remained as support to Goh Peng. Fylough wasn't considered a threat; Fylough was a dead man. But as Goh Peng took a step towards him the dead man stood up.

Goh Peng jerked his chin at the other Chinese, who moved behind Fylough and touched the side of his neck with the muzzle of a heavy Belgian Browning automatic.

Fylough did as he was told, trying to watch both men at the same time. It was difficult. Goh Peng moved sideways across the room to come in behind him. Fylough knew there was nothing he could do about it. Except go down fighting? He tensed his leg muscles and lifted his heels off the floor. Goh Peng moved from behind him and into the corner of his eye. He thought he caught the dull gleam of Goh Peng's snub-nosed Tokarev coming towards the side of his head, but as he turned fractionally to meet it, the squealing of brakes in the street below and then a burst of muffled machine-gun fire stopped Goh Peng dead in his tracks.

Fylough relaxed his body, but it didn't show. His eyes glued to Goh Peng, he was unable to see the man behind him. But he sensed him.

Fylough forgotten for a second, Goh Peng turned his head, quickly swung on his heel and peered down into the street from the window. The other Chinese momentarily released the pressure of the automatic from Fylough's neck as his eyes followed Goh Peng's movements.

Neither the Chinese nor Fylough saw the door quietly open.

Potter's men had worked it very carefully. The leading man, his earphone buzzing with Potter's instructions, waited until the noise below reached a crescendo before walking into the room. He looked in a bad mood. It must have been the long, uncomfortable wait in the damp cellar. He stood in the doorway, raised his arm, and pumped two quick shots into the head of the squat Chinese standing behind Fylough.

The noise of the bullets hitting bone – the crack of the tenderising mallet slapping the unyielding steak – brought Fylough to his feet. A quick glance at the man by the door – a white face, ordinary eyes – one of ours! He threw himself across the floor at Goh Peng, but he was on a hiding to nothing, and he knew it.

Goh Peng had it all ways. Fitter, younger, quicker, his brain took it all in and froze it like a photo-flash: the roar of the automatic; his partner, still on his feet, swaying, with two bullet holes in his face; the man in the raincoat by the door; and Fylough hurtling across the room at him. And he was ready.

Fylough hit him awkwardly – for Fylough, that was – and bounced off the solid Chinese obstructing the raincoated man's aim. He didn't hear the stream of obscenities directed at him as Goh Peng dropped on to Fylough's wiry frame, partially covering himself as he brought his automatic into a firing position. Fylough was helpless. Goh Peng was the first to recover. As the man at the door danced into the room, seeking a clear shot, Goh Peng found his balance, went on one knee and squeezed the trigger. Too quick. The bullet thumped harmlessly into the wall and before he could fire again the second man was in the room.

He slid behind raincoat and crouched almost double, looking for a shot past Fylough's flailing arms and legs. Edging along the wall, he came in at the two men on the floor from behind. Goh Peng tried to throw himself on his back, but too late. The new arrival's full-blooded kick behind his ear almost lifted him off the prostrate Fylough and the pistol dropped from his fingers.

The new man took a step to his right, looked down at the crouching Chinese for a couple of seconds and casually cracked the edge of his hand sharply across his unprotected neck. Goh Peng gave a throaty cough and dropped flat on his face like a dead bullock.

'You took your bloody time!' Fylough's words of gratitude fell on deaf ears. The backup man smiled cheerfully as he dragged the dead Chinese to the centre of the room and laid him alongside the unconscious Goh Peng. He stuck the toe of his shoe into Goh Peng's side and, satisfied he was not dead, reached down and turned him on to his back.

He stared into Goh Peng's face. 'Jesus! There're some ugly buggers about!' he said to Fylough. 'I don't think I'd like to sit down to a bowl of noodles with him!'

Fylough wasn't amused. His nerves were beginning to react to the adrenalin build-up he'd given them which now had nowhere else to go. The MI5 man understood. He nodded in agreement and removed the smile from his lips.

'One of you keep your eye on him,' snapped Fylough, 'and if his eyelids as much as flicker give him another hard one where it hurts. I've got quite a lot to say to the bastard when I've caught my breath.' He pulled himself to his feet, gave a nervous, ineffectual brush to the knees of his trousers, then lit a cigarette and inhaled luxuriously; it was as if he were starting a completely new life.

'Who's directing you?' he asked.

'Russell Potter,' answered the man with the earphone.

'Never heard of him.' Fylough picked up the phone and began dialling. He didn't get far.

'Having fun, Peter?' Woodhouse's voice broke in over the clicks. 'You weren't phoning me, by any chance?'

'Your timing's all to cock, Woody . . .' Fylough's breathing was almost back to normal and the acid from his disturbed stomach was settling gently, taking with it the burning, stinging sensation from his chest. But he still wasn't right. '. . . and I've left my sense of humour on the carpet with this fucking Chinaman who's been trying to drag my bloody eyes out of their sockets and reshape the back of my bloody neck with a loaded Browning – so tread gently, Woodhouse!'

'But apart from that you're all right?'

There was no solicitude in Woodhouse's voice. Fylough ignored the question. 'Have you got a crazy, inefficient bastard over there named Potter?'

Fylough's voice was coming through the laser line as clear as a bell – clearer than the phone held delicately against the side of Woodhouse's head. Woodhouse almost smiled at the stereo effect. But not Potter. He blinked at the machine, then grimaced at his new Chinese friend, Wang Peng Soon, who, still lounging against the wall by the window, grinned toothily in return. Everything seemed to have gone very well; Fylough was just letting off steam. It was a normal reaction after an interrogation party – Wang had often heard high-pitched giggling coming from the unpadded cell part of his 'shop'. Woodhouse stared at his two companions but his expression remained unchanged and unconcerned. 'Yes, Russell Potter's directing the show, Peter. D'you want a little word with him?'

'No, I don't want a fucking little word with the bastard – I want to cut his bloody throat! He should have had those clowns in this room ten minutes before the idle buggers finally strolled in. There could have been blood all over the bloody place!'

'All's well, Peter, that ends – '

'Don't give me fucking platitudes, Woody!' Fylough had got it all off his chest. 'What's the state of play?'

Woodhouse told him what had happened in the street, then asked, 'Did they buy it?'

Fylough suddenly felt very tired. He was feeling his age. It depressed him. He flopped down on the chair recently vacated by Kim Cheong. It was still warm. 'It was like feeding sweets to a bunch of kids. Everybody played their part and Kim Cheong's gone home to Peking with Hilary on his arm and a happy smile on his face.'

'And the file?'

'That's going to join him somewhere between Kowloon and the first takeaway on his side of the border. Now, about this bloody man Kent – '

'A slight aberration,' interrupted Woodhouse.

But Fylough wasn't interested; he went on as if he hadn't heard. It was something he wanted to get off his chest while the irritation was still there. 'He bloody nearly ballsed the whole thing up. He wasn't supposed to be in this far – how the fucking hell did he get his fingers on the file?'

'A long story, Peter. Some other time, eh? Anything else?'

Goh Peng lay still. He lay like a dead man. But he wasn't dead. He wasn't even unconscious. He kept his eyes closed, controlled his breathing and let his brain and ears do the work. His hearing was acute; without straining he could hear the minute complaining of the floorboards under his ear and the almost silent squeak of leather as the man standing above him moved his weight from one leg to the other. He judged his position within inches and knew exactly what he was going to do. But first . . . He took in the significance of Fylough's words: the British had intended from the start that the Chaah documents be put in Kim Cheong's hands. But why? Goh Peng almost gave himself away as the audacity of their plot thundered into his brain, but he remained still. He cursed silently and began gently to flex his muscles. His mind wouldn't let go of it. How had he – they – allowed the British to make fools of them? Even Kim Cheong had swallowed their tricks! He must be warned, he and Ah Lian – particularly Ah Lian – but how? Goh Peng wished he could hear the other end of the conversation. But this was enough. He tensed himself.

Fylough said, 'Well, that interfering fucker Kent's in it up to his bloody hocks and there's bugger-all else we can do now. We've just got to pray that he doesn't fuck us around any more than he's already done. Just so long as he continues playing the innocent dick . . .'

'He shouldn't have any difficulty doing that,' murmured Woodhouse, 'he is an innocent dick.'

Fylough shrugged him aside. 'All Kim Cheong has to do now is collect the file from Kent, take it to the man who lights the Chairman's fags and let events take place. All in all, apart from your bloody "aberration", a good day's work well done, as they say. We've out-KGB'd the bloody KGB, Woody – we've made our own man head of a foreign government . . .'

'Not yet we haven't,' cautioned Woodhouse with a sidelong glance at Potter and Wang, 'Kent's got to play his part yet.'

But Fylough wasn't put off. 'Kent has nothing to say in the matter,' he said briskly. 'He knows bugger-all. He's the only fellow in this game playing a straight role. The poor sod can't get off now – his bike pedals won't stop turning until he crashes into the wall at the end of the road. He either hands the file over to Kim Cheong or he tries to be smart and gets his head kicked in and somebody else hands it over. Kim Cheong doesn't give a bugger who sticks it into his claw provided it gets there. And speaking of which . . .' He looked over his shoulder at the unmoving, apparently dead body of Goh Peng and blew a whistle of smoke in its direction. '. . . is there any backup in Hong Kong to make sure Kent doesn't win?'

'Wang Peng Soon's going. He knows what to do.'

'Wang. . . ?' He got no further.

Goh Peng timed his kick perfectly. The edge of his solid leather shoe caught the MI5 man standing above him a graunching cut an inch below his kneecap. His leg collapsed and with a bellow that deafened the listeners across the road, he crashed to the floor.

As he fell his finger tightened instinctively on the trigger of the automatic he held at his side, cocked and ready for the unlikely necessity of a stopping shot on an unconscious Chinaman. The single shot roared out but missed Goh Peng completely and thudded into the wall beside Fylough's head. Fylough ducked, and in doing so turned his back on Goh Peng, who bounded up like a cloth snake released from its box. A second kick nearly took the MI5 man's head off his shoulders and as he regained his balance, Goh Peng's hand reached down and snatched the automatic from the agent's unresisting fingers.

'What the fucking hell's going on over there!'

Woodhouse's voice bellowed tinnily out of the dangling earpiece of the telephone, but he didn't wait for the reply. He threw the instrument at Potter and lurched across to the window, barging Wang out of the way and ripping aside the curtains. The scene in the street was unchanged. Under the dim yellow light three men grouped round one of the cars stared, like him, at the window of the first floor. They'd heard the shot too. Woodhouse glared through the dirty window. Everybody in the bloody street had heard the shot and those idle buggers hadn't moved an inch. And then another shot boomed out, hollow in the confined space, like an empty blown-up paper bag being exploded for fun. And then, after a short pause, two more shots in quick succession.

'Jesus!'

Moving quickly, Goh Peng lunged, feet first, at the man in the raincoat as he came charging back into the room. Both feet caught him full in the chest and pushed him by force backwards until he crashed against the corridor wall. He was given no time to recover. Goh Peng bounced upright, steadied himself against the opposite wall and again rammed both feet into the disabled man's crotch. It was as if he'd been hit by a pair of fifteen-pound hammers. Another hard kick to the head stopped the dreadful scream that echoed up and down the stairs and out into the street.

Goh Peng swung round to look into the room.

Fylough was still on the floor where he'd dropped. Goh Peng moved quickly and stood over him. He had to make time for it. A question of honour. Reaching down he grabbed one of Fylough's arms and hauled him on to his back, then slapped him hard across the face.

'Open your eyes!'

Fylough stared up at the ugly Chinaman. He had all the time in the world. He knew what was going to happen and he didn't flinch. It had been a long time coming.

Goh Peng raised the automatic away from Fylough's face so that he could see exactly what was happening to him. It was unnecessary, and disappointing – there was no fear in Fylough's eyes for him to gloat over. Fylough almost shrugged as he turned his face away from the weapon just as Goh Peng squeezed the trigger.

The heavy bullet tore into the side of his face.

He died immediately.

Another shot into his head, then, without a second glance at Fylough's shuddering body, Goh Peng threw himself out of the door and tumbled down the backstairs towards the kitchen and, he hoped, the back door.

'Jesus Christ!' Woodhouse repeated the blasphemy. 'Peter! Are you all right? For Christ's sake somebody tell me something!'

A voice croaked down the line, but it wasn't Fylough. It didn't make sense.

'Bloody-well speak up!'

The voice tried again, 'The Chinaman's got away . . . killed Fylough . . .' and then gurgled into silence as the half-unconscious MI5 man's head hit the floor again.

'What d'you mean? What d'you mean – what the bloody hell are you talking about! Wake up you dozy bastard!' He stared at the silent box for a second, then losing his temper, bellowed into the handset; 'WILL SOMEBODY FUCKING-WELL TELL ME WHAT'S GOING ON!'

But he didn't wait for a reply. 'Potter!' He turned his head; he'd been staring across the road trying to pierce the darkened window of Fylough's house. Even in his imagination he couldn't understand what the hell had gone wrong over there. Shots! Shouting! Screaming. Running Chinamen . . . Fylough killed . . . Christ Almighty!

But Potter had good reflexes and had gone – he knew how to spell cock-up, and he knew in whose ear the cock was likely to end up. He was already out in the street and halfway up Fylough's front steps before Woodhouse realised that apart from Wang he only had Potter's number two and his dog to vent his frustration on. And the dog wasn't all that worried. He raised a doleful eye, outstared Woodhouse for a few seconds, then allowed his lids to droop again.

Woodhouse turned back to the street. Potter had dispersed his

284

men. The only sign of movement was the injured man who'd been knocked down by Kim Cheong's car. Partially wrapped in a blanket, he was now laboriously dragging himself, and his blanket, out of the orbit of the overhead light and out of range of any mad Chinese who might come running down the steps with a grudge and a loaded automatic.

'Another fucking cock-up!' said Woodhouse lightly to Wang. Wang nodded sombrely. His inclination was to smile an embarrassed smile, but looking at the side of Woodhouse's hard-set features he decided the gesture might be misinterpreted, so, instead, he kept his lips tightly together and allowed a little snort of agreement to escape through his nose. It was a waste of sympathy; Woodhouse was interested only in what was going on across the road.

Goh Peng had found his way to the carelessly left-open cellar door, out into the back garden and across the rubble and debris negotiated earlier by Potter's two agents. He had a watery moon by which to pick his way to the derelict houses and through the frameless windows of these, like eyeless sockets in a dead face, he could make out the grimy yellow streetlights beyond. He stopped for a moment in the shadow of the front garden and listened. Silence. He waited a few precious seconds longer. It was a wise decision. A door banged behind him, followed by a muffled oath as somebody tripped and fell amongst the rubble. A voice said 'Shut up!' – a voice of authority – and then a torch flickered as if a hand had been placed across the lens. But caution was a luxury – the hand was removed and a beam as broad as a wartime searchlight flashed a huge circle against the wall of the house sheltering him.

'That's the one . . .' said a hushed voice. The searchlight lingered for a few seconds while the two men took their bearings, and was then subdued again.

Goh Peng moved out of the shadows and on the balls of his feet ran several hundred yards down the road. Then he stopped and darted into another garden. This one had a solid wall. The house was occupied. He waited. He was just in time. A car screeched round the top corner and stopped, headlights blazing, outside the house he'd just left. Three men got out and took up positions on either side of the entrance while one man stretched himself across the roof of the car and steadied a pump-action shotgun aimed at the door Goh Peng had just gone through.

A voice called out in a stage whisper from one of the upstairs windows: 'He's in here somewhere, the bastard. I caught a glimpse of him before I went arse over tip. Bob's moved into the next house, just in case. Make sure you have a bloody good look who you're shooting at before you pull the trigger on that bloody wall of steel you've got pointed at us!'

'Get on with it!' said one of the three men. 'And don't make so much bloody noise. Do the downstairs next and then leapfrog Bob to another house. The outside's covered – you can hurt anybody you find in the four houses to your right.'

Sitting behind the wheel of the car Potter stared moodily through the windscreen as he listened to the whispered instructions passing between the concealed men around him. The headlights cut a swathe into the pit-like blackness of the deserted street and made eerie shadows out of neglected overgrown bushes that hung here and there over as yet undemolished garden walls. Nothing moved. He peered beyond the periphery of the lights to the junction of the road some three hundred yards away. There was life, things were going on. The traffic light at the junction of the road clicked from red and orange to green – it hardly showed at this range. Beyond his headlights, where the blackness dropped back into place, a police car, its ice-blue tit flashing silently, shot past with dipped headlights, on the orange, and as he stared, a bus, lit up like a Caribbean cruise ship gliding on a black horizon, moved slowly across his vision. He sat up abruptly. The small black handset was already close to his mouth.

'What're you doing, Willie?' he said without lowering his voice.

'Minding this bloody dog,' came back a crackling voice. 'Everybody else has buggered off!'

'Mr Woodhouse?'

'Yes, and the Chink – they've both gone over the road to give the kiss of life to Fylough. Woodhouse pulled out the plugs before he went – he said it was private.'

'OK. Look, drop everything and get up to Shepherd's Bush and put yourself somewhere near the tube station. If a Chinaman comes bustling along follow him into the Underground and let me know what train he gets.'

'Which one?'

'What d'you mean, which one?'

'There are two bloody Shepherd's Bushes – one up the top here in Uxbridge Road and the other one at Shepherd's Bush.'

'Bloody hell. OK – take the nearest one.'

'What about the dog?'

'Sod the bloody dog!' Potter dropped the handset on the seat beside him and poked his head out of the window. 'Carry on here,' he said to the man with the shotgun. 'I think the bastard's bolted, but carry on looking. I'm going up to the top – I'll be near the bus stop. Buzz me if anything gives.' He didn't wait for a reply. He dipped the headlights, started the engine and moved speedily up to the top of the road. He parked the car in a side street and walked briskly past the traffic lights into the main road.

It was light and bright, most of the shop windows a blaze of burglar prevention, and the overhead lamps, unlike the road he'd just left, lighting the place up like a motorway service area. He found a fish and chip shop next to the nearest bus stop, stepped in, bought fifty-pence worth of soggy chips and stood by the steamy window popping them into his mouth as he studied the passers-by. There was every nationality on the move tonight – everything except Chinese. The bus stop remained naked; no queue, no bus. Maybe they'd gone on strike. He looked at his watch. Half-past eleven. Did buses run at this time of the night? He looked at the greasy man behind the imitation-marble counter, then raised his eyes and studied the clock above his head. The man's head swung up and looked as well. He looked worried. There was nobody else in the shop; maybe he thought it was a hold-up. 'What time does the last bus go?' asked Potter.

The man raised his shoulders and parted his lips to show a row of teeth the same colour as the chips he was cooking. But no sound came out.

Potter repeated his question.

He got the same response.

'Don't you speak English?'

The man gave another nervous smile. 'Only fish and chips, pliss.'

Potter left his half-finished packet of chips on the counter and went back to his car. As he slid behind the wheel his hand radio crackled into life.

34

'That was an exercise in total indiscretion,' said Woodhouse to Wang. 'Total – bloody – indiscretion! What on earth induced him to prattle on like that with a Chinaman lying on the carpet taking it all down in bloody shorthand?'

Peter Fylough's body had been taken away in a dark grey heavy-duty plastic zipper bag, the dead Chinese too. It seemed strange that all the dead men – theirs and ours – ended up in the same colour bag. But to Wang this was only a momentary thought. He'd looked at the dead Chinese without interest and pronounced him as 'just a leg-breaker of no consquence'.

'Can you save it till some other time please, Woody?' asked Wang. He put his empty glass on the side table and stood up. Woodhouse frowned in annoyance but it went over Wang's head. 'The fellow with the thick head was quite sure that it was Goh Peng they had on the floor here?' He looked down at the carpet as if making sure he wasn't still there. 'He'd had his head almost kicked off – he couldn't have made a mistake?'

Woodhouse nodded his head and reached for the rapidly emptying whisky decanter. 'He was quite sure,' he said. 'Fylough had told him who he was and ordered him to watch him like a bloody snake. It's a pity the idle bastard didn't. It's also a pity it wasn't him with the bullets in the face and not Peter!'

Wang was noncommittal; lapping up spilt milk was not part of his character. When they'd gone, they'd gone, that was his philosophy. 'OK,' he said. 'So we have to consider Goh Peng, on the run with his head full of Peter Fylough's revelations, as the worst possible scenario and do something about it. Immediately.'

'What, for example?'

'He's got to be killed – and very quickly.'

'I agree, but I think it's too late,' said Woodhouse without emotion. 'I reckon he was out of the back door, up the road and into a phone box before we even got that bloody front door bashed in.' He stared into the dregs of his glass; there was nothing there to lighten his load. 'The whole bloody shebang's gone up in a puff of smoke. I think we'd better accept we've just tossed away six months' hard blanket work and the chance to readjust the Chinese Politburo at a stroke. Morgan's going to have to tell his puppets in Peking to put on their running spikes. He's not going to be well pleased with this little effort, I can promise you . . .' He refilled his glass from the decanter and managed a bleak effort of a smile.

It was Wang's turn for the decanter. He took it grimly. As he poured whisky into his glass he said, without looking up, 'Who're you expecting Goh Peng to phone?'

Woodhouse's smile disappeared. He looked at Wang as he would an idiot child. 'The Chinese Embassy of course. Where else would he ring to blow a scheme like this sky-high?'

'Wrong,' said the unsmiling Wang. 'Goh Peng is Kim Cheong's liegeman. Apart from that he's not going to expose him to bringing the game into disrepute because he'll be the one to go down. That's the way TEWA does things; if the master craps on the pavement the dog's the one that gets kicked up the arse. The master usually gets away with only a bollocking.'

'What does that mean?' asked Woodhouse.

'It means,' explained Wang. 'that if Kim Cheong wanted to play nasty buggers Goh Peng could well find himself stuck against the wall for allowing the balls-up to occur.'

Woodhouse had forgotten his drink. He ran Wang's words through his mind again – and liked them. 'I think you may have a good point there.'

But Wang didn't need encouragement. 'He'll try to get to Kim Cheong before he leaves Gatwick – and he won't manage that, will he?'

Woodhouse took the hint. He picked up the telephone and spoke to the Duty Officer at Curzon Street. He looked a lot happier when he turned back to Wang.

'The Air China freight plane is on the runaway at Gatwick and cleared for take-off. Apparently they've been given ten minutes' grace to wait for two special additions to the cargo.'

'Kim Cheong and Hilary?'

'Right,' confirmed Woodhouse. 'And there's no outside tele-phone connection with a revving 727, or whatever, on a Gatwick runway. So that's closed that little peepy-hole.'

'What about Heathrow?' asked Wang.

'Same as every other exit,' replied Woodhouse smugly. 'Top national security screen.' He glanced down at his watch. 'They're calling it a timed emergency exercise. Nothing looking like a Chinaman goes out without a fairly serious grope from . . .' He stared at the second hand on his watch until it jogged into its slot, then looked up with a gleam of triumph in his eye. '. . . a quarter-past.'

Wang automatically looked down at his wrist. 'It's a quarter-past now,' he said.

'That's right.'

'What about diplomats?'

'Don't look so bloody sceptical, Wang,' drawled Woodhouse. 'I said nobody goes out without the head to tail, that includes Chinese Embassy people.' He relaxed back in his chair. 'OK, that's solved that one. Where does that leave us?'

'He'll try Ah Lian,' said Wang. 'He'll try to get her by phone and if that doesn't work he'll try and wriggle past your security screen at the airport and make his way to Hong Kong or Peking to try and block the pass.'

'Why Ah Lian first?'

'Convenience,' said Wang. 'A word in her ear and the whole thing's blown at source. She's the fanatical one and she's holding the dice – don't forget that. She won't betray Kim Cheong to anyone here in London or Peking but she'll stop the game and discuss his atonement with him in the privacy of their Peking penthouse.' He paused and gave it a little more thought; his expression didn't change. 'Or, if she really wants to be unpleasant, in a dungeon in the Tsao Lan-Tze.'

'What's that?' asked Woodhouse suspiciously.

Wang hardly paused for breath. 'They call it the "grass basket" – it's Peking's jail for political prisoners. But I don't think it would come to that. If Goh Peng did get to her ear and whisper the outline of what he heard, she'd stick a knife in Kent's ribs and scrawl across the file in dark red lipstick: "We've been had!" And then take it to Shenzhen and hand it over to Kim Cheong herself!'

Woodhouse shook his head doubtfully. 'That's your theory, Wang. Are you quite certain he won't try the Embassy?' He wanted to believe, but he wanted more assurance.

Wang tried to give it to him. He parted his lips and gave a full gold-frontal. 'Woody, weren't you listening? I've just explained how the Chinese deal with team cock-ups. Put yourself in Goh Peng's Y-fronts. Would you go for a knife job on somebody else's balls if you knew that immediately afterwards yours were going to be nailed to the board and measured for the same treatment? Relax, Woody. I'm that certain.'

And then he spoilt it.

'But I wouldn't discourage you from putting a couple of marksmen within shooting range of the Embassy gates, just in case he's fed up with the tone of his voice!'

The look of happiness faded from Woodhouse's features as he picked up the phone again.

'And don't forget Lancaster Gate – the Commercial Centre also has CELD tentacles.' Wang emptied his glass of whisky and stood up. 'One more thing before I go, Woody,' he said as he placed the glass on the sideboard. 'Is there anyone else apart from Goh Peng who knows that we've changed the colour of this puppy we're sending to Peking?'

'You mean apart from Kim Cheong?' asked Evelyn Woodhouse.

35

Goh Peng kept his head well down as he watched Potter's car headlights dip and disappear up the road. He'd already marked the three agents covering the road side of the houses. They'd been a worry to him but the removal of the car's headlights had left them with only the glimmer of overhead lights and the vague backdrop of lighted shop windows and passing traffic to silhouette his movements. Even so, he decided against that route.

The MI5 man's Browning felt heavy and reassuring in his hand as silently, not quite on his knees but crouched double, he picked his way cautiously through a gap in the wall to the next house along the road. It was occupied. He moved along to the next and found it to be another partially converted derelict. He eased his way through the temporary corrugated iron basement door and felt his way through to the back, and there, crouched on his ankles at an open doorway, he listened.

He didn't have long to wait. Silhouetted against the red reflected sky of London's million lights and touched by the struggling three-quarter moon, appeared a head and shoulders. Goh Peng moved his head slowly and stared out of the corner of his eye. The definition sharpened. He held the black outline steadily and watched it joined by another; then the heads parted and vanished into the shadow of the houses. He waited a few minutes longer. His hunters were good. There was no noise.

He moved out of his doorway, and slid over the wall of the house backing on to the conversion, then picked his way silently to the back door. He ran his fingers over it. It was locked with a Chubb. He stretched and pressed the top of the door, then bent and did the same with the bottom. It moved fractionally. He could feel them – top and bottom bolts. Nothing doing here.

Noiselessly he backed away and went over the wall to the house next door. Staying in the shadow, he studied its structure. A conversion. He stared at the windows: curtains drawn on two of the landings and chinks of light escaping through the cracks. He felt the back door as he'd done with the previous one. It wasn't a smile that creased his features; it was a contemptuous sneer. He was in the communal garden, standing at the communal door; a simple lock with the key on the inside, and the last man in hadn't bothered to lock it! He opened it fractionally and slid through into a bare, echoing corridor that turned into a small, shiny, tiled hall. Flat number 1 was on his right, its door firmly closed for the night, and the stairs to the other flats were dimly illuminated by a guide light on the wall. By this light he could make out the heavy front door a few paces in front of him. He opened it a crack. It buzzed noisily as if somebody upstairs had pressed the unlock button, but nobody took any notice. He squeezed through the crack, closed the door behind him and waited in the shadow on the top step of the entrance.

He poked his head out and looked down the road towards Fylough's end. He watched the tail lights of a brightly lighted ambulance some two hundred yards away crawl silently round the corner. No emergency. The chap with the broken legs was at last lying on something soft and enjoying his free shot of morphine. Goh Peng brought his head back, waited a few seconds, then looked again.

A police Granada was double-parked outside Fylough's house. Without straining he could hear its radio crackling, indecipherable and eerily reflected off the silent houses. He tucked the Browning into the back of his trousers, walked purposefully down the steps, turned right and moved briskly but unhurriedly towards the main road. He didn't look round. He knew in his mind what had to be done. Wang Peng Soon had predicted his thought processes as if he'd been his twin brother.

Russell Potter hadn't been too far out, either.

'Willie here, Russell . . .' came the tinny voice from the handset on the passenger seat in Potter's car. There was suppressed excitement in Willie's voice that even the poor reception couldn't conceal. He sounded breathless. 'A Chink in a hurry's just bought a fifty-pee ticket at Shepherd's Bush and is waiting on the southbound Met line platform . . .'

Potter was already moving fast into the Wood Lane/Shepherd's Bush stock-car circuit. He picked up the set. 'What's the next station?'

'Goldhawk Road. You might just make it. Where are you?'

Potter squealed over the second set of red lights and turned left. He caught a partial glimpse of the road sign. 'Turning into Bush Green – is it – ?' he yelled.

'You don't want that!' Willie controlled the urge to bellow but couldn't keep the panic out of his voice. 'Go right, quickly! Then right again. Carry on and you should come back to Shepherd's Bush Road. Turn right at the junction and look for Goldhawk Road. You'll have to get a move on – the bloody train'll be here in a second.'

'Hang on! What's this Chink look like?'

'Squat, black hair, slitty eyes!'

'Thanks, Willie! How many people on the platform?'

'Just him and me.'

'You armed?'

'No.'

'He is. Don't upset him. Just keep your eye on him.' Potter roared past another set of red lights and his eye caught the name of the road: Uxbridge Ro – 'Too bloody far!' He skidded to a halt, U-turned with a squeal of brakes and watched the only cruising Panda in the outer reaches of West London screech out of a side street and into his path.

He jammed on his brakes.

They took their time.

The two heads turned to look over their shoulder but nobody moved. Potter switched on the interior light and gave them a few seconds to see he looked respectable, then met them halfway. They were two big lads, not a bit worried about one wild-looking white man breaking the law. They let him out of his car and eased him against the back of their Panda while they studied his card by the light of a torch. One of them wasn't happy about it, the other was. The other one won.

'Where're you going?' he asked.

'Goldhawk Road Underground,' snapped Potter. 'Security matter – and I'm in a bloody hurry! I want to meet a train – '

'Jump in! Leave your jamjar where it is, we'll look after it.'

'Just a sec . . .' Potter removed the keys and handed them to the policeman, then opened the back door. He pulled away the panel

295

concealing the seat-belt mechanism and withdrew from its hiding place a squat, three-inch-barrel Webley .38 revolver.

'Jesus Christ!' one of the policemen swore as he bundled him into the back of the patrol car. 'I hope you've got a licence for that thing!'

'And I hope that's a bloody joke!' growled Potter, who wasn't in a mood for jokes. 'Can you make this bloody thing move a bit faster?'

The police car screeched to a stop outside Goldhawk Underground station and Potter and his friend leapt over the barrier rails and into the station.

'You go on,' urged the young policeman. 'Metropolitan line. Up there, on the right! I'll clear it with the ticket people. Good luck, mate!'

Potter was already halfway up when he heard the train squeal into the station and hiss to a juddering stop at the platform. He just made it as the doors closed with a thud behind him. He'd arrived in the first carriage. All the seats were taken.

He looked over the heads of the people standing in the entrance and through the small window at the end could see the next carriage. There were people standing in that one as well. Potter recovered his balance and looked around him. No Willie in sight. And no Goh Peng at this end of the carriage. He worked his way out of the small crowd congregating around the door and moved towards the other end. Two Chinese sitting uncomfortably upright, shoulder to shoulder, in one of the four-seaters met his eyes briefly before returning to meet the gaze of the blank-faced West Indian who sat opposite with his hand on his white girlfriend's bare knee.

He stopped at the next entrance bay and frowned up at the printed poem next to the Underground station guide. It didn't make any sense – the poem and the two bloody Chinamen! Where the bloody hell was Willie? He hung on to the strap and leaned back slightly to study the left-hand bank. Just like the right bank of seats – everybody looked at home. But just a minute . . . He glanced again. Everybody, except one . . . He straightened up. Another bloody Chinaman. What the bloody hell did he do now?

He swayed with the movement of the train and looked again.

There he was! It had to be him. A heavily built Chinese. Flat peasant face and broad nostrils. An ugly bugger, but a well-dressed ugly bugger, with a shirt and tie and light grey suit. The suit looked as though it had been hard at work. Nothing wrong with that.

How the bloody hell did he tell?

As if he'd sensed the scrutiny, the man suddenly turned his head and looked directly at Potter. But there was no suspicion in the tightly slitted eyes – why should there be? Potter looked away and read the poem in front of his eyes again; it was unavoidable. And then it clicked. The shoes – the bloody shoes! He leaned back on the strap again and, shielded by a small Indian's oily head, looked along the line of feet.

Got you, you bastard!

There they were – a pair of little black shoes with a half-inch rim of mud and builders' sand around the heels and discolouring the outer edges of the shiny uppers. Like somebody who'd been crawling around the backyards of Bellamy Avenue? Potter looked down guiltily at his own.

'Got you, you bastard!' he breathed again.

The brakes squealed underneath him and he readjusted his balance as the train hissed into Hammersmith. Everybody was moving and shoving as if the train was on fire or hovering on the brink of a precipice. Potter hung on and watched the dirty little black shoes move towards the small door at the end of the carriage.

Potter let go of his hanger and went out onto the platform with the rush. He hung back and at one time found himself shoulder to shoulder with the flat-faced Chinese. He let him go ahead, and then felt a finger jammed into his back. It was Willie. 'You cut that a bit bloody fine,' Willie murmured out of the corner of his mouth.

Potter didn't turn his head. 'Is that your Chinaman just ahead there? The one with the light grey jacket?'

'That's him.'

'OK, put your skates on and dash up in front of this bloody mob and grab the first telephone you come to and ring this number.' He gave Willie the number of Fylough's house. 'Speak to Woodhouse. Tell him I've got Goh Peng on a chain and does he want me to bring him back there or pop him in somebody's nick for collection later. Meet me somewhere at the top – '

'I don't think you've ever been down here – ' began Willie, but Potter didn't give him a chance.

'Fuck off, Willie!'

Potter moved slowly behind Goh Peng, just keeping him in sight until they came to the escalator. He settled about eight steps behind the dapper Chinese and stared at the advertisements as they crawled up another level. When they got to the main entrance Goh Peng made straight for the bank of telephones. Potter moved into position and studied the Underground map, watching out of the corner of his eye as Goh Peng counted the coins in his hand. Potter hoped he'd got enough. Four telephones away Willie replaced the receiver. His normally amused expression was sombre as he turned away and caught sight of Potter. He took the roundabout route and came up alongside him.

'Have you lost the Chink?' he asked.

Potter shook his head. 'He's over there using the phone. What did Woodhouse say?'

Willie didn't look at him. He stared at the Chinese man in the telephone booth. 'He said you're to kill him . . .'

'Stop fucking around, Willie! What did he say?'

Willie didn't look happy. Slightly sick, he couldn't take his eyes off the man in the phone booth. Like Potter, he wasn't into fisticuffs. Blood-letting? Definitely not.

'He said he's got to be killed,' he repeated.

Potter swallowed. 'Christ! Anything else?'

'Yes.'

'What, for Christ's sake?'

'He's not to get near a telephone. He's to be killed before he can phone anybody.'

Potter stared at him. His nerves were bubbling up towards his eyes. 'You stupid bastard!' he exploded. 'Look at him – what the fucking hell d'you think he's doing now? *Come on.*'

He gripped his hand to stop it shaking and eased the short .38 out of his waistband and tucked it into his trouser pocket. He kept his hand round the butt which stuck out. He managed to control the tremor in his voice. 'Do exactly as I say.'

Goh Peng dropped a handful of coins into the slot and dialled the Chinese Embassy. 'Give me the number of the New China News Agency,' he demanded. There was no query from the operator. He recognised the voice; he knew the accent. He gave him the number without hesitation. The NCNA night operator was a member of CELD; he hesitated and asked for identification. It was a mistake. After ten seconds of Goh Peng's voice hissing in his ear he felt the rope tightening around his neck. Goh Peng demanded once more the number of Chin Xan's flat and got it immediately. Ah Lian answered the phone, guardedly.

'I must talk with you,' said Goh Peng urgently. 'It's about the file – '

'Ssh!' she hissed. 'Don't say anything more. This is not a clean line. Ring . . .' There was a slight pause.' Ring 62 – '

'*Excuse me . . .*'

Goh Peng turned in annoyance and scowled at the Englishman who touched his shoulder. He didn't see the other man come behind him. He tried to turn back when he felt the muzzle of the Webley dig gently into the small roll of fat just below his left shoulder blade, but the first man was now gripping his shoulder and forcing him against the wall of the booth. The man was sweating and gritting his teeth. He looked as though he was about to be sick and refused to meet his eye. He heard Ah Lian's voice; she was still warning him. '. . . it's a protected phone,' she said. Behind him the man pressed into him. One arm blocked the downward passage of the hand holding the telephone while the other ground the sharp object into his back. The first man, shaking, hung on to his other hand. 'Hold him still!' grunted the man behind him as Goh Peng filled his lungs to shout, and then there was a muffled bang, like a heavy telephone directory being dropped to the floor. The shout gurgled wetly in his throat.

For a long second his eyes boggled into Willie's sweating, horrified face and nearly shot out of their sockets, then his jaw slackened as the red mist bubbled darker and darker until it turned inwards and told his brain he was dead. Everything went black and all his weight sagged into Willie's arms.

Russell Potter debated whether to squeeze the trigger again but decided against it. Goh Peng was dead and slipping to the floor of the booth. Willie was trying to hold him up. 'Let go of him, you silly bugger,' he hissed, 'and get out of it. Go home. Leave this to me. Go on, quick – fuck off!'

The telephone, bouncing like an elasticated yoyo, tapped him on the side of the head as he stooped down. He took it in his hand gently and held it to his ear. A hollow silence; there was somebody there, listening. He held it for a brief second then hung it back on its hook. His hand had stopped shaking; excitement had over-shadowed the fear and he stared closely into Goh Peng's dead face. 'I hope to God you're the right bloody Chinaman!' He lifted the Browning from the back of the dead man's trouser belt, straightened up and grabbed the first person to walk past. 'I think this man's having a heart attack,' he said excitedly. 'Will you watch him, please, while I go and get help?'

The samaritan didn't give Potter a second glance; all his attention was on the sick man. He was a resourceful person. 'Off you go,' he snapped. 'I'll see to him – I've had first-aid training . . .' He was already pursing his lips, getting ready to kiss the dead man back to life. He didn't look up as Potter vanished out of the station.

Sir James Morgan and Evelyn St John Woodhouse sat in comfortable armchairs in Morgan's flat overlooking Regent's Park. A quarter to five in the morning and they were both very tired. But they kept their tiredness at bay with large stubby, dimpled glasses of Macallan's eighteen-year-old whisky. Wood-house had more troubles to lay to rest than Morgan. He chain-smoked, unusually, pausing only to draw heavily on his glass of half whisky, half water.

'You've got to take your hat off to Russell Potter,' drawled Morgan. 'Considering he's not programmed for letting blood he made a damned good job of putting your Chinese friend in the dustbin. Very professional, no mistakes.'

Woodhouse didn't see it that way. 'It was unprofessional and full of bloody mistakes, James!' he rasped. Too much smoking had dried his mouth out; the Macallan was losing the battle. 'Killing the bugger wasn't enough. He should never have allowed him within spitting distance of a bloody telephone. Taking the bastard's tongue out was the reason he went after him – he should have shot him dead in the train and taken his chances. He'd have got away with it too – nobody gives a bugger about the odd killing on the London Underground. A Chink with a hole in his head wouldn't have got a second look at that time of the night!'

Morgan stared at him over the rim of his glass. There was

nothing to show whether he approved or disapproved of Woodhouse's theories. Woodhouse stared back with red-rimmed eyes and took a very large mouthful of whisky. He wasn't looking for approval. When he lowered the glass his lips were set tight. 'What I want to know is what he said down the bloody phone. And who was on the other end. Was it Ah Lian? And if it was does she now know she's carrying a dead puppy back to Bow Street Alley?'

'We'll have to wait and see,' pronounced Morgan. He hadn't moved his glass from his mouth and it still rested on his bottom lip, bouncing gently up and down as he spoke. 'But we will know, of course – won't we?'

'How?'

'If she turns up at Heathrow on her own without a file of a delicate pale blue hue under her arm we'll know the whole bloody game's been well and truly pissed on – and young David Kent'll be sitting on his heels propped against a wall in a dark corner somewhere between here and God know's where with his throat cut. That's how.'

'I couldn't give a bugger about Kent!' said Woodhouse uncharitably. 'The bloody streets outside are crawling alive with soldiers looking for the chance to get off the parade ground and earn some money. What I'm worried about is all this bloody work going up the jacksie!' He stubbed out a half-smoked cigarette and lit another. Then he looked at his watch.

It was as if it was the cue the telephone had been waiting for.

The two men stopped looking at each other and stared at the buzzing handset on the coffee table beside Morgan's chair. Morgan picked it up, extended the aerial and put it to his ear. He listened guardedly without interrupting, then, with a curt 'Thank you', switched it off and pushed the aerial back into its housing. His expression hadn't changed. He picked up his glass, took a good swig and swirled it in and out of his teeth as if it were mouthwash. Woodhouse watched until his patience ran out.

'Anything interesting?'

'A Madame Ah Lian accompanied by one David Kent has just passed through Immigration en route to boarding an aircraft for Hong Kong.'

There was no elation in Woodhouse's manner, only mistrust. 'Where'd he get his passport?'

301

'The Chinese Embassy made him a new one. They needn't have bothered. Our man at the X-ray bench said Kent's sole baggage was a plastic shopping bag. All he had in it was a new shirt, underpants, toothbrush and shaving gear, and . . .'

'What about the file?'

'. . . and a blue, official-looking file. Kent didn't try to hide it and there were no questions asked. After they'd gone on board a fat, elderly Chinese named Ah Bee Yong, travelling on a non-stop London to Hong Kong flight sidled through Immigration . . .'

Woodhouse's lips parted in the semblance of a smile. It struggled for a second for recognition, then faded; it never got anywhere near his eyes. 'That'll be Mr Wang Peng Soon.'

Morgan nodded tiredly. It was all catching up. 'So, it looks like we're still on course – thanks to Potter.'

'Potter be buggered, James! It's bloody luck we've got to thank.'

36

David Kent settled back in his seat and watched the port wing try and shake itself off the fuselage as its two ridiculously huge Rolls-Royce engines thrust it ponderously along the runway. When it began to fly he continued to stare, mesmerised, until the wing settled back on its rivets; then he closed his eyes. It was the easiest way of avoiding contact or speech with the lady sitting next to him.

Ah Lian didn't object. They hadn't exchanged more than ten words since leaving Fylough's flat late the previous night. She preferred it that way. It seemed they were ideal travelling companions. But she had one thing to say to him before she tucked herself into her shell.

'Where is the file? Is it safe?'

Kent didn't open his eyes.

'Safe enough.'

He knew what she wanted; she wanted the file tucked in her knicker leg, somewhere where she could see or touch it. She'd tried before, as they boarded the aircraft, as if he'd completed his contract by bringing the file through the British airport security screen and was no longer part of the game. Nothing doing! But there was nothing to gain by losing his rag with her. Better save the adrenalin for the bastard with the hooks.

He kept his head turned towards the window, but he couldn't sleep. It wasn't the headache, or the torn and battered muscles from the gentle Dr Goh Peng's ministrations, it was the continuous nagging at the back of his mind that he seemed to be the only person in this game who was getting any of the pain, and the only one who hadn't got a bloody clue what was going on! He wasn't enjoying his pre-slumber thoughts, but you weren't allowed to sleep on BA until you were told to.

'Would you like a cup of coffee, sir, or orange juice? Breakfast will be served in fifteen minutes . . .' The stewardess hovered solicitously over their seats. She'd already received an unsmiling shake of the head from Ah Lian, but nothing showed.

'No thank you.' Kent opened his eyes and straightened up. He knew what he wanted, and it wasn't orange juice, it was sleep, but if he couldn't have that he wanted something to still the aches. She almost got away. 'But I'd like a large whisky and water, please.'

She kept the shudder under control and brought it to him camouflaged as a glass of something else. She didn't want to put her other customers off their breakfast. But she took a long hard look at Kent before she moved on.

Kent sipped his whisky contentedly. He hadn't been to sleep since his hiding from the Chinese Sumo but the whisky was doing its job: the pain, and the need for sleep, were both receding into a comfortable, heavy-eyed throb. He was on his third mouthful when the aircraft broke through the dark, smoky clouds that lived permanently over England and an electric sun thrust its rays through the round porthole. He refused breakfast and asked for another whisky and water. The stewardess was now definitely worried, and the disapproval showed in her eyes. Ah Lian remained inscrutable. She breakfasted on a plain croissant and a cup of unsugared black coffee.

When everybody had settled down to their eggs and sausages and mushrooms and bacon Kent stuck the *Telegraph* into the pouch in front of him and under Ah Lian's watchful eye samba'd along the swaying aisle to the toilets with his shopping bag. He stopped for a smiling chat with the stewardess before sliding through the narrow door and slamming it.

He undressed and stared at his bruises in the mirror. But he didn't dwell on them – there was nothing that could be done about the colour scheme of red, purple, blue and several shades of black. He wondered for a second what the stewardess would make of the sight. One look and she'd probably dash off and bring the bottle and join him. He shook his head and began to scrape the blade across his chin as his brief and temporary feeling of euphoria faded. It needed no special effort when he returned to his seat to rekindle for Ah Lian an expression of surly, forced co-operation on his scrubbed and newly shaved face.

But there was one more thing to be done. The reason for his trip to the toilet and his chat with the stewardess.

From his plastic bag he took the large thick envelope – courtesy of the ever willing, every worried stewardess – then, under Ah

Lian's startled gaze, he inserted the pale blue file, gummed down the flap and with his hand shielding it from her eyes, wrote across it in thick letters:

> DAVID KENT
> C/O AMERICAN EXPRESS
> NEW WORLD TOWER
> QUEEN'S ROAD CENTRAL
> HONG KONG

In the top left-hand corner he printed: HOLD FOR PERSONAL COLLECTION BY ADDRESSEE and underscored it three times. Keeping his hand over the address he showed Ah Lian the instruction.

'This is not agreed,' she hissed. 'You were told to carry the file on your person. Where are you sending it? You realise that by doing this you are jeopardising the life of Mrs West? I can't be responsible . . .'

'Never mind where it's going,' responded Kent. 'Just remember that it'll be somewhere where you can't touch it until I've seen her, spoken to her, and counted the number of hands she's got.' If his voice sounded flippant it didn't reflect on his face. 'So, you'd better make up your mind now about responsibility. No Hilary West, no file.' He reached up and rang for the stewardess.

'Coffee, sir?'

He pulled a face and held out the envelope. 'No thanks – but I wonder if you'd mind dropping this in the aircraft's mailbag for posting in Hong Kong?' He smiled and half stood as he worked his hand into his trouser pocket and raised his eyebrows. 'How much?'

She smiled back. He wasn't half the problem she thought he was going to be.

'Have it on the house, sir.'

'Thanks. And whilst you're up and about perhaps another large whisky?'

Her smile vanished.

The 747 came in across the bay, dipped dangerously low over the towering concrete blocks and teeming streets of Kowloon and dropped anxiously into Kai Tak airport. The collective breaths went out, and then sucked in again as the huge aircraft, squealing like a startled pony and jinking from side to side every time it saw its reflection in the dark muddy waters of Kowloon Bay, finally rattled into a frightened canter and then stopped.

37

The taxi sped, unnecessarily fast, down Nathan Road and skidded to a stop outside the unprepossessing entrance to the Orchid Hotel. It wasn't the smartest hotel in Kowloon, but somewhere between the lower end of the scale and the bottom. It wasn't teeming with eager customers.

Ah Lian didn't move.

'Your room is booked.' She didn't look at Kent or the hotel. He wondered how she knew; she hadn't left his sight since leaving their cosy flat at the back of the Xinhua – the New China News Agency – office in London. And then the question became academic. 'The hotel, Mr Kent, belongs to TEWA.' As simple as that. 'Do not leave it and do not use the telephone. You will be contacted tomorrow. I leave you with a warning. The safe delivery of the documents is entirely your responsibility. You may think you have been clever in concealing them, but while you are congratulating yourself remember what the penalty is for default; there is no second option. No documents and you take back with you to England a cripple. Think on it, Mr Kent.'

Kent made no move to leave the taxi. He looked into Ah Lian's flat eyes for several seconds but said nothing. The taxi driver was becoming impatient as he looked around at a million potential customers and muttered under his breath. Ah Lian used it as an excuse to turn her head away from Kent's gaze and two sharp words sent the taxi driver's face back to where it should be – staring blankly down Nathan Road. She turned back to Kent.

'You have something to say?' She was cool and collected. She was on her home ground – almost – with not much longer to wait.

'Yes,' he said. He was surprised at the steady, even confident, tone of his voice – it was surprising what holding the combination to the safe could do for a man's esteem. 'As I said on the aircraft, I shall want to see Hilary West standing on her feet, smiling happily and waving to me before you even see the file again. If she doesn't appear, no deal – you can kiss it goodbye. Tell that to your friend, and tell it to him before he invites me out for a walk across the bridge.'

'That might not be possible.' No apology, no regret.

'Then no file.'

Kent didn't wait for her response. With his plastic bag gripped in his hand he stepped out of the cab and walked, without looking round, into the foyer of the hotel.

They'd been waiting and watching. They'd been briefed. Two men, both squat, peasant-type Chinese, detached themselves from either side of the door and fell in beside him. Wordlessly they escorted him to the fourth floor, where one of them opened the door to number 87 and showed him round the room like an attentive estate agent. Still no words.

It was a medium to large room with two single beds, a good-sized wardrobe and a quite luxurious bathroom and shower. One of the men, speaking halting Hong Kong English, explained to Kent that he and his friend would be staying there with him until the message came from Madame Ah Lian. He would have no contact outside the room and any request for service of any description would be made through him or his partner. The window would remain shut and the air-conditioning on. 'Understand?'

Kent understood. He went into the bathroom, stripped, took his time over a long shower, and with a towel draped around his waist came back into the room and threw his clothes on one of the easy chairs. He knew that was what they wanted. Again word-lessly, the two Chinese agents picked up every item, inspected them, turned out the pockets and then, incongruously, folded them neatly and replaced them on a chair.

'You want this washed?' One of the men held up the dirty shirt.

'No,' grunted Kent and flopped onto the bed. They watched him until he closed his eyes, then one of them left the room and leaving both doors open, lay down on the bed in the room opposite. The other man sat himself on a chair against the wall, crossed his legs and arms and, like a meditator, fixed his eyes on a spot just above the headboard of Kent's bed. But it didn't worry Kent. Everything had caught up with him at the same time. He'd gone to sleep even before his head had hit the pillow.

*

On the opposite side of Nathan Road, indistinguishable from a thousand like him, a young Chinese wearing a crisp white shirt, tie, dark trousers and shiny black shoes stepped out of a car and waved the driver an airy 'thank you' before disappearing into the dark cool of a noisy bar.

But he went no further than the coloured string curtain that hung between the entrance lobby and the bar itself and stood there, in the shadow, with his arms crossed, and staring across the traffic at the entrance to the Orchid Hotel.

His companion in the car watched Ah Lian's taxi swing round in an illegal curve on an intersection and when it gained speed up Nathan Road he tagged on, along with another thousand cars, in its wake. When they stopped at the lights at the Jordan Road junction he rested his telephone on his knee and glancing down at the number scribbled on a scrap of paper, tapped it into the keyboard. He was heavy-handed with his new toy; it sounded as if he were slapping down a winning hand of mahjong tablets on a marble tabletop. He didn't seem to be enjoying himself.

Wang Peng Soon answered him before the lights changed.

Wang had just taken his shoes off. He was sitting on the edge of a not very comfortable bed in a not very comfortable hotel where he'd been dropped very abruptly by the driver of the car. Fortunately, and as usual, he'd had the foresight to buy himself a bottle of duty-free Teacher's; it was already open and in use. His choler was improving with each mouthful.

'She dropped him off at the Orchid Hotel in Nathan Road . . .' The voice was distorted and hollow. 'It's a shithouse of a hotel. Sonny Chew's watching the traffic in and out but don't expect too much – it's a front for both TEWA and Guojia Anquanbu. They go in and out like drunken sailors. Even the dhobi girl's got rank.'

'What's Guojia Anquanbu?'

'After your time, sir? It's the motherland's latest high-power Intelligence Board – a little bastard by Gonganbu out of Shehuibu's Section IX. They all learned how to wear shoes and break arms in the same place – Nanyuen.'

'OK,' said Wang impatiently, 'I'll read it up on the plane home. You telling me we can't make contact?'

'I wouldn't recommend it.'

'What *do* you recommend?'

'Keep a watch on the hotel and if there's any movement try to have a word with him.'

'OK. But don't push it. Where's the woman now?'

'The taxi's done a wiggly and come back to Gascoigne Road – ' The conversation stopped. There was an indrawn breath and a thump as the handset was dropped on to the seat, and over the atmospherics and the sound of the car's engine Wang heard a stream of ripe Cantonese invective. He held the phone away from his ear and drank whisky while he waited. It didn't take long. 'She's got this bloody driver standing on his head doing silly buggers! OK . . . Got 'em! They've pulled off Chatham North . . .' The crackling and hissing took over for a minute or so, then: 'This must be it. She's home. The taxi went up a drive and it's come out empty. Big house – she's got rich friends!'

'Can you see the house?' asked Wang. 'Can you watch it?'

'Sure. What am I looking for?'

'Maybe they're not going to the border. Maybe he's changed his mind . . . Christ! Don't tell me the buggers are going to do it here in Kowloon!'

'What's that?'

Wang frowned into his nearly empty glass and shook his mind off speculation. 'I was thinking aloud. OK, watch out for a guy with a couple of hooks for hands and a tall, good-looking European woman. Are you in contact with your man outside the hotel?'

'Not exactly. He'll ring me on the car phone if anything happens.'

'And you'll ring me?'

'Right.'

Wang replaced the receiver, slipped off his shoes and wriggled his toes luxuriously as he subsided back on to the fluffy pillows of his bed and closed his eyes. Within seconds he too was fast asleep.

Detective Sergeant Sonny Chew remained standing in the lobby of the bar opposite the Orchid Hotel until his legs ached. He'd been there nearly two hours and nobody had given him a second glance. He walked up Nathan Road with his head swivelling like a Japanese tourist, and then down again with his eyes glued to the hotel entrance. After three hours he decided it was going to be a very, very long night. He stepped into one of the small, 'short-time/long-time' café/hotels that dotted the Golden Mile. It was dead opposite the Orchid. And it was full – so she said. Either that or the older-than-her-years, puffy-faced and over-made-up guardian of the reception counter smelled policeman. The next one didn't smell policeman and had a room: 'Short time? Long time? No problem.' But there was a problem – there was nothing overlooking the Orchid Hotel. He moved further along Nathan Road and on a corner found what he was looking for: the Wai Lee Suan Massage Parlour. He booked a long session and with it a cubby-hole of an attic room and a window on the noisy side. 'No thanks – no massage, no girl, just a drink and I'll take that little window all night . . .' And that's all it was, a clean towel-covered table, hard, and just long enough for a five-foot-six slim-built Chinese to lie on with his legs stretched out. A girl with normal-sized tits and one of them would have to hang out of the window.

Sonny Chew stretched out on his stomach on the tabletop and with his chin cupped in his hand he sipped a cold San Miguel from its stubby brown bottle and struggled to keep his eyes open as he watched the horde below milling up and down the noisy, brightly lit street. At 3 a.m. he dragged himself upright and went downstairs to the front room. He could still see across Nathan Road, but with difficulty. He dialled the number of Inspector Tan Siew's car. 'If I was a local bobby I'd be very suspicious about the Orchid Hotel,' he told himself in an undertone as he waited for Tan to answer.

The massage parlour was far from dead; it was very much alive and buzzing, and it wasn't only perfumed oil being smoothed over taut muscles. The proprietress, dressed in a bright red cheongsam with a split that stopped just below her armpits, sat, chubby legs crossed, on a high stool beside a rickety formica-topped bar, behind which her mate, dressed only in a white singlet and cotton drawers, leaned on his flabby bare arms and gnawed little bits of quick from one of his fingers as he stared across the room at Sonny Chew's back. It was not curiosity; he'd already made his assessment: 'He's queer,' he said without moving his lips or taking his finger from his mouth.

'I don't think so,' replied the woman.

'Of course he bloody is! No girl, no massage . . . And haven't you noticed the way his toes point inwards?'

'It takes one to tell one! I think he's a copper.'

'Copper be buggered! He's a bloody poofter and he's ringing up a pair of hairy legs!'

At that moment Sonny Chew turned his head, and the woman winked at him whilst her husband suspended his manicure to hold up another bottle of San Miguel. Sonny nodded, then turned back to the phone and said to Inspector Tan, 'The front windows on the fourth floor in the Orchid are lit up as if the place was bulging but there's nobody in the rooms. I've seen three lots of couples with their legs crossed go in and three couples still with their legs crossed come out – they're not letting rooms in the Orchid tonight.'

'Don't let it worry you, Sonny. Keep your eyes open for the Englishman. Can you see the entrance clearly?'

'Sure. The foyer light's gone out – they're not welcoming the happy tourist tonight.'

'What about the rear?'

'I've checked. It opens into a closed yard and the only way out of that is up a side alley that comes out on to Nathan Road.'

'Good. Now listen, Sonny, I'm staying here until the woman moves again. There's no real cover and I'm fairly exposed so don't ring me again unless something moves at your end, OK? Can I ring you there?'

'Sure,' Sonny read the number off the base of the telephone. 'Ask for the guy in the top front room, the one without a girl! See you . . . Bye, bye.'

Tan switched off the phone, gazed idly around the dark, dead street for a moment and studied the unmoving silence. He opened the window a couple of inches and flicked out a half-smoked cigarette. Even that died without a whimper. He switched on the phone again and dialled the number of Wang's hotel. It took a long time to answer. The sleepy voice of the night porter grunted the name of the hotel. He wasn't very happy to be woken at three in the morning.

'Take a message for Mr Wa – ' He remembered just in time Wang's Hong Kong name. 'Ah Bee Yong.' His voice sounded hollow, artificial and overloud in the confines of the car. He almost looked over his shoulder, not with fear, but a slight touch of the self-conscious. 'Don't wake him specially, when he appears will do. Tell him to contact Sonny Chew if there's any change of plan.'

'OK.'

'Just a minute! What d'you mean, OK? I haven't finished yet! He's in the Wai Lee Suan, a massage shop on Nathan Road, on the opposite side to the Orchid Hotel, and . . .' Tan stopped.

'Yes?' the grumpy voice was awake now.

'You can say "OK" now.' Tan clicked his phone off without waiting for a reply. He threw the set on the seat beside him, rubbed his eyes, contemplated lighting another cigarette and immediately abandoned the thought. After another glance round he slid down low in the seat so that only his eyes and the top of his head were visible from outside and allowed himself a controlled snooze.

The next three hours were long, cold and miserable. Nothing happened; nothing moved. Tan reached out to switch on the radio for company, then changed his mind. Instead, he eased his cramped body to another cramped position and watched the new sun claw its way through the leaves of the trees lining the drive to the house across the way. He lit his fourteenth cigarette and prayed for movement. He wound his window down fractionally to clear the smoke, flicked the ash through the gap and turned back. His eye caught movement. He stiffened and stared at the end of the road. Nothing. But not quite – a jogger was turning the far corner and lolloping towards him.

The jogger was taking his punishment seriously. Wearing a light grey tracksuit and dirty white trainers, he skipped on his toes along the wide, dawn-lit road and his hands, dangling loosely by his side, flopped with every pace as though they were held on to his arms by strips of elastic.

Tan acknowledged his wave with a slight movement of his head as he passed and followed him in the wing mirror.

The jogger stopped, trotted backwards until he was level with the front door and, at a standing jog, jabbed his finger at the rear end of the car. Tan frowned but didn't move. The jogger smiled, hunched his shoulders, mimed a few words and grimaced. Tan's lack of interest didn't dampen his enthusiasm; he continued jabbing and pointing. Tan swore, tightened his lips, then stretched across the passenger seat and wound the window down about four inches.

'What is it?'

The jogger, somehow, had filled one of his elastic-driven hands with a heavy 9mm Browning. All Tan saw was the bulbous end of a suppressor as it came up and centred on his face. The frown of surprise was still in place when the heavy bullet snapped his head back and threw him across the driving seat to smash him against the far door. The jogger slid his hand and the gun through the gap in the window and staring through the glass, fired again, this time into the dead man's heart. It was quick and it was efficient.

But the jogger hadn't finished.

He stood straight and looked quickly up and down the silent road as he tucked the automatic out of sight into his trouser belt under the tracksuit top. Another quick glance. Still nothing moved. He raised his hand and brought it down on top of his head, then without looking round or waiting, he moved smoothly to the driver's side of the car.

The signal had been received.

From the drive that Tan had been watching, concealed by the ornamental bushes, came another man, also tracksuited, who squeezed his hand through the passenger window and opened the door. There was no exchange of words, no gestures; they were like a trapeze duo, everything done in tandem, automatically. They were a highly skilled assassination team and this wasn't their first job. Tan hadn't stood a chance. The second man slid into the car and disentangled Tan's legs from the controls while the first man, with a quick jerk, flopped Tan's body on to the pavement and dragged him to the rear of the car. The killer already had the boot open. It was a large boot. Tan wasn't all that big – his claustrophobia wouldn't have bothered him – and he fitted in comfortably with plenty of room to spare. Nobody saw, or if they did they didn't care about a car with two men in tracksuits heading for an early jog in the unused crystal mountain air of Tan Mo Shan.

'He's been removed,' the killer of Inspector Tan told Ah Lian. 'He was Special Branch.' He placed on the table before her Tan's revolver, a Royal Hong Kong Police identity card, his wallet and other possessions.

They were of no interest to Ah Lian; she barely gave them a glance and waved her hand in dismissal.

'A moment . . .' The man sitting beside her, an elderly, benign-looking Chinese dressed in an ill-fitting suit that appeared to have come from a 1950s liberated Shanghai charity shop, peered at the man in the grey tracksuit through large, thick lenses that made him look like a myopic, slightly bewildered, pensioned-off accountant. Or, with his short, spiky, steel-grey hair and gaunt, pallid features, a survivor of a lifetime in the Laogai – the Tatamutu Gulag.

But Hu Bang was none of these. He was the former bodyguard and close friend of Mao Tse-tung; he was also one of the co-formers of the TEWA, and in his younger days, its foremost assassin. After a lifetime of political murder and intrigue he had survived the post-Mao purges and was still a close friend, confidant and adviser to his former colleague in the Central Military Commission and now the most powerful man in China, the immovable but ailing Chairman of the People's Republic. Hu Bang was a man to be feared; a man to be listened to; a man whose judgement went unquestioned by the Chairman. Some called him the kingmaker; he didn't dispute it.

Behind the glasses the eyes stared unblinking into the face of the man in the tracksuit. 'Where have you taken him?'

The man tried not to stare back and found a spot to focus on just to the right of one of the old man's ears. His answer was not precise. It wasn't required of him; the fact that the breach of their anonymity had been rectified was sufficient. Later would come the retribution for the lapse in security; in the meantime . . . He addressed Ah Lian: 'There will be no comebacks, Excellency.'

She nodded absently. Like the old killer she'd already lost interest in the activities of a nosy policeman. The inquest would come later. In the meantime what made the policeman nosy? *Who* made the policeman nosy? She glanced sideways at her companion as if bestowing on him the right to dismiss the servants. But it was already being done.

No word, no gesture, just two creased eyelids like old parchment dropped behind the thick lenses in a blink. The man had been dismissed. Before he reached the door the old man's voice rasped: 'Get rid of that stuff, then leave us alone. Make sure we are not disturbed – in here or outside.' The threat was left hanging in the room even after the door had closed.

He turned his head to Ah Lian and with the cold, lifeless fish's eyes staring at her from behind their magnified windows, he said, 'Who is the stupid one, Ah Lian, the person who allowed herself to be followed, or the one who followed and died of ignorance?'

'It was not – ' she began.

He stopped her with a frown. 'You can make your excuses later. What I want to hear now is more of this strange story you whispered in my ear. Miss nothing out . . .' His voice gained strength with use; it was a gravelly, husky voice, the voice of a man who'd spent a great deal of his life speaking in conspiracy. It was a voice suited to intrigue. 'Tell me about this proof you say you have that concerns the loyalty of the Secretary-General of the Communist Party. Tell me how you can accuse the chosen successor to the Comrade Chairman of being a British agent? And be careful, madam, it's very often the accuser who ends up with the needle in the ear.'

Ah Lian shuddered inwardly but didn't wilt in front of the old grey man. Like the bodyguard in the tracksuit, she avoided a direct confrontation with his eyes.

'Would you like tea?' she suggested. It was almost as if she wanted to delay playing her cards. But it didn't work.

'No – talk.'

Ah Lian relaxed into her chair. She sat primly, her knees covered and pressed tightly together, and centring her gaze on a point just below the bridge of the nose, told him of Kim Cheong's first suspicions. She started to outline his activities in Malaya and the incident in the Chaah ambush, but Hu Bang, his hands resting lightly on his thighs, raised the fingers of one hand in a dismissive gesture. She stopped in mid-sentence and waited politely.

'I know all about that,' he rasped. 'Go back to his suspicions about Lee Yuan's origins.'

Ah Lian reformed her thoughts and continued. She told the old man of how with Goh Peng she had traced the Malay, Togom, in Pontian and how from him they'd obtained the names of the people who'd been responsible for removing the CIA documents from Kim Cheong's body. She outlined the process that had led to the tracing of three of them to locations in England. The eyes behind the almost opaque lenses glistened with interest when she explained the method employed to lead them from one to the other – pyscho-amputation of the hands. He nodded sagely as she continued. His methods would have been more direct, the hands would have come off, but he granted the advance the young generation had made in appealing to the brain for information rather than the body. She explained how the first two had contributed to the search for the leader of the party, the man who'd held the secret to the whereabouts of the documents, and how the trail had died with the death of the third man. She dealt briefly with the involvement of the British Security Service and how she and Goh Peng had manoeuvred the British agent, Kent, into working on their behalf. She told of his trip to Malaysia and how the titbits of information that had been fed to him had eventually led to identifying the leader of the ambush party.

'The documents?' murmured Hu Bang when Ah Lian paused for breath. 'Talk about the documents.'

But she was not to be pushed out of sequence. She touched on Hilary West's part and then detailed the events following the invasion of Fylough's house in London, leading up to David Kent and the arrival of the file. At this Hu Bang sat up in his chair, took off his glasses and after breathing heavily on the lenses, wiped them with a crisp white linen handkerchief. Deprived of their shield his eyes strained out of their sockets like those of a startled gecko and liquid – not tears; his eyes hadn't shed tears since he'd suckled at his mother's breast – ran down both sides of his nose. He dried his face with the handkerchief and settled the glasses back on the bridge of his nose. He was suddenly wide awake and fully attentive; there was nothing wrong with his thought processes.

'Is this man Kent a senior officer in the British Intelligence Service?' he asked with deceptive casualness.

'No, very junior – a rank and file operative.'

The unblinking eyes pinpointed her. She was like a butterfly about to have her wings opened out and pinned down, and there was no escape – she was impaled. She stared back.

'How did this rank and file member of the British Intelligence Service discover the whereabouts of these elusive papers and then, without authority, remove them from their highly secure resting place?'

That was all.

Two simple questions.

Ah Lian fought the claustrophobic effect of his eyes and breathed deeply. Her voice remained steady, controlled. 'First,' she said evenly, 'he had access to old police records in Kuala Lumpur, that's where his lead began – '

He stopped her. 'You also had access to Kuala Lumpur records. Why didn't it set you on a shorter route?'

'As I explained, we were using him. Goh Peng gave him a lead in Malaysia and with that he made a connection between Kuala Lumpur and Hong Kong. We are certain that it was there he discovered the link that led him to the Chaah file.' She emphasised that certainty by tightening her lips and adding, 'He had access to the Hong Kong Police Registry.'

It didn't work with Hu Bang. 'Our people also have access to Hong Kong police records,' he said and closed his eyes to consider it. It was a relief to Ah Lian. But he didn't stop talking. 'Were they approached to check exactly what it was that sent him back to England?'

'No,' she admitted. 'That's what he was there for – to find these things for us. Our plan was to point his nose in the right direction, follow him, help him when he stumbled and collect our reward when he'd unravelled the ball of string.' She raised her eyes to frown into the two slits under the magnifying glasses. 'May I ask why you – '

He didn't allow her to finish. In the middle of her question the slits flicked open like spring-loaded shutters and the eyes were boring into hers again. Yet there was no angry animosity; even at seventy-six Hu Bang hadn't yet lost his awareness of an attractive woman, and sitting deep into her chair, her eyes reflecting her disquiet, Ah Lian was at her most attractive. Hu Bang enjoyed the still robust movement within his loins as he brought his eyebrows down in the beginnings of a rebuke to this woman who made no pretence of the difficulty she was having in curbing her impetuosity.

318

'Why?' he asked wetly. 'You ask why! Have you not considered the possibility of the British arranging this matter for you? Do you not find it unusual that a simple British operative can discover in a short time things you, with all the strength of the Department of Special Affairs, the TEWA, the Ministry of State Security and the Guojia Anquanbu at your disposal, could not find?'

Ah Lian let him have his head. She allowed a short, polite pause, then, in a sugary voice, explained. 'But the whole point in our being able to use this man Kent dispels any possibility of collusion. Fylough knew nothing of the man's resourcefulness until he was confronted with the fact that he had the documents in his possession. I don't even believe Fylough knew the man. Furthermore, it was I who recognised Fylough as the man who took the documents off Kim Cheong, and it was Kim Cheong himself who, already suspicious of Secretary-General Lee Yuan, instigated the recovery of the papers so that they could be put in the proper hands – yours.' She stopped for a brief pause and thought over what she had said. Hu Bang's eyes were no longer static orbs; they were moving behind their bubble windows, searching her face, but showing nothing of the way the mind behind them was working. She waited a second. He said nothing. Encouraged, she continued. 'The entire operation was started from Peking by us, not the British.' She became bold. 'But, all that apart, why would the British want to betray their agents, these long-time sleepers in the People's Republic? What could they gain?'

Hu Bang didn't answer. It was as if he hadn't heard a word. 'Have they made any effort to recover the papers?'

She thought briefly. 'We were attacked by a large force when we left the house where we'd interrogated Fylough and the others.'

'And?'

'I don't know. I'm sure Kim Cheong got away with the woman, otherwise you wouldn't be here.'

'He did.'

'Goh Peng rang me at Xinhua's safe house in London, but he said nothing. I presumed they killed him.'

'They did.'

'There you are then! Surely if they were trying to plant a set of false documents they wouldn't have put obstacles in our way; they

319

wouldn't have attempted to kill the very people they needed to carry out the operation?'

'It depends. Now, this Englishwoman. . . ?'

Ah Lian allowed the corners of her mouth to twitch. It was never going to grow into a smile but it was an improvement on the rock-hard expression she'd maintained since the arrival of the Old Executioner. For his part he saw the woman emerge, only briefly, but enough to raise a complaint again from his unresponsive groin. A tiny senescent dribble of saliva escaped into the corner of his mouth, otherwise his face remained totally blank.

'She has no alternative.'

'And this Englishwoman is of such value to the British Secret Intelligence community that they are prepared to exchange the lives of not only their own agent but also American CIA people in highly placed sensitive positions in the People's Republic for her return? Is this possible?'

Ah Lian bridled at his mocking tone. 'The deal is nothing to do with British Intelligence. It is a straightforward arrangement between Kim Cheong and agent Kent. It won't be the first time an Englishman has chosen sentiment before duty!'

Hu Bang didn't respond immediately. He studied the workings of his mind for several long silent minutes. Ah Lian left him to it. Without asking permission she stood up and pressed a button on the wall beside a large silk tapestry.

Tea arrived on a gaily decorated black papier mâché tray. Ah Lian poured two bowls and placed one of them in Hu Bang's gnarled but thinly elegant hand. He didn't look down but allowed his well-manicured fingers to close automatically round the thin bowl and carry it to his lips.

'The British sometimes give the impression of total stupidity,' he observed. 'That is usually the time to beware of them . . .' He sipped from his bowl and gave a little inward sigh of pleasure. 'This thing is wrong somewhere.' He sipped again. 'You were followed here.'

She didn't deny it.

'Which means the man with the documents was also followed. If the Special Branch man reported to his masters before he was killed this place would now be surrounded. It isn't. Why haven't they walked into the Orchid Hotel and recovered their file?'

320

'The woman?' suggested Ah Lian.

Hu Bang shook his head slowly, then stopped to sip more tea. Ah Lian went on the offensive.

'They don't know the documents are in Hong Kong.' She sounded surprised at the statement. She'd only just worked it out. 'The only people who knew what Kim Cheong planned, apart from the woman, West, who is with him now, and the agent Kent, was Fylough. Kim Cheong was going to instruct Goh Peng to kill him.'

'How can you be sure he carried out his instructions?'

'He could not have failed. There was no one in the room to stop him. Shots were heard coming from the house we had just left. Goh Peng risked his life to ring me – it would have been to confirm Fylough's death. Nobody else knew we were coming here.'

The old man showed no appeasement. 'So why did Hong Kong Special Branch follow you and maintain watch on the house?'

Ah Lian wasn't going to be put off. 'Routine?' she hazarded. 'The wife of a senior Chinese official stopping the night with an old friend in Kowloon before catching the morning express to the People's Republic? Or perhaps they followed *you* here from Shenzhen?' It was a dangerous assertion, but he didn't take offence. Perhaps he hadn't heard.

'Have the Englishman brought here,' he said. 'With the documents. I'll make an assessment when I've spoken to him and opened the file. You might be right – we could have on our hands the material to avert a grave crisis in our country's political future. Nobody is too high, or too mighty. If Lee Yuan is what you claim him to be, he must be talked to, then moved to one side and examined.'

Ah Lian shuddered delicately. But Hu Bang didn't notice, he was busy mentally 'examining' the leader designate of the People's Republic, the traitor designate, Lee Yuan. Then, absently, he said, 'You know, of course, who must take Lee Yuan's place beside the Chairman?'

Surprised, she answered carefully. 'Tang Shi?'

He nodded.

She knew more than most about Tang Shi; he was, after all, Kim Cheong's closest and most senior associate, his patron, no less. But in Ah Lian he inspired fear rather than love. She wasn't alone.

Tang Shi was one of the wave of younger Chinese political arrivistes to find a position of power in the present Chairman's wake. No choker-necked coolie smock, no canvas slip-ons and flat, peasant-type soldier's cap, the elegantly attired Tang Shi was the antithesis of the traditional Long Marcher-type leader of the People's Republic. Neither did he wear the usual unemotional, non-smiling, coldly inscrutable expression; he could have taken his place alongside any of the grinning, gesturing leaders of the other world. But under the smile and the smart suit was a gentleman devotee of the Heinrich Himmler school of charm. Tang Shi had arrived from nowhere borne on the shoulders of the Chinese security services of which he was the 'Supreme Co-ordinator', a title bestowed by his mentor, the Chairman himself. As Supreme Co-ordinator of the Social Affairs Department, the Shehuibu, he had at his fingertips the largest security force in the world and controlled the myriad factions and branches that made up the entire Intelligence network at home and abroad. A very powerful man, but still only second choice as future supreme head of the Chinese Republic to Lee Yuan, a younger man without the power but who had the support of the majority of the slower moving and more orthodox thinkers in the Zhonnanhai – Peking's Kremlin. There was no doubt that once he lowered his bottom on to the throne of China, Lee Yuan would be at the head of the Chinese Communist Party for ever – and ever is a very long time in Chinese Communist terms. Tang Shi would be the oldest man in China if, under normal circumstances, he was going to have to wait for Lee Yuan to join Mao, Deng and the other stuffed ex-Chairmen in the Peking waxworks, the Zhonnanhai mausoleum.

But these circumstances weren't normal; Kim Cheong had changed them. And it was no coincidence that the man who stood to benefit from the changed circumstances was Kim Cheong's patron and master – and when the master mounts the steps to the throne there's always room on the corner of the dais for the loyal servant who helped put him there . . . As umpire, Hu Bang was not entirely unbiased. His had been one of the few voices raised against the appointment of Lee Yuan. It seemed providential that doubts could be raised and proven against Lee Yuan's pedigree, even at this late hour, because once he was in position nothing would shift him . . .

Hu Bang stopped nodding his head and refocused his eyes on the woman sitting primly opposite him. It seemed that the little warrior, their lord and master, was doing them all a favour by hanging on to life and power – provided, of course, that these documents the woman was talking of were as solid as she said. He would have liked to have had a longer talk with Kim Cheong, instead of yesterday's guarded conversation which had brought him on the long, anonymous journey to Kowloon, but Kim Cheong had been nervous, and rightly so. One whisper in the wrong ear and friend Kim Cheong would end up with a couple of iron feet to go with his tin hands.

His voice jolted Ah Lian out of her trance.

'Let us not waste any more time,' he said harshly. 'I want to see these documents this morning.'

'I don't think that's possible,' she replied. 'The Englishman posted the file from the aircraft. He's the only one who knows where and the only one who can collect it. He won't budge until he sees that the woman is safe. It'll take a little time.'

Hu Bang was not displeased at that. He made a rumbling noise in his throat; this was his line of business. Take the spy; keep the hostage; recover the documents; give nothing in exchange. The thoughts didn't take long to crystallise. 'He doesn't know where the woman is?'

'No.' Ah Lian stood up and gently removed the empty bowl from the old man's fingers and refilled it. When she gave it back he carried it to his nose, breathed in its perfume then replaced it on the tray.

'It's not hot enough,' he said gruffly. 'Get some more.' She did as she was told. By the time he had the new, scalding bowl in his hand he'd worked it all out. It was simplicity itself.

'Contact him. Make an arrangement. Let him look at the woman, first from a distance, and when he insists give in to his demand, reluctantly, that he be allowed to talk to her and touch her . . .'

'Is that wise?'

The look he gave her sent a chill into Ah Lian's stomach. She clamped her lips together and lowered her eyes. Hu Bang continued as if there'd been no interruption. He could have been talking to the wall.

'The man sounds like a simpleton. If handled correctly he will come to a rendezvous with the file in one hand and his other hand held out to gather in his woman. When the exchange has been made they can both be killed. In that manner our problem is kept within our own walls and there are two English less knowing of our private affairs.' He studied her air of uncertainty. 'The responsibility for the recovery of the documents remains with Kim Cheong; the responsibility for the elimination of the two English will rest with you.' To Ah Lian the message was clear. David Kent and Hilary West must die – if they don't, you do. She shuddered and lowered her eyes submissively. He was not longer interested in that part of the operation. He'd finished with the man Kent and Hilary West – they were dead. 'Start the recovery process immediately,' he said finally, and sat back in his chair to resume sipping the hot, green tea.

38

Wang Peng Soon removed his head from under the pillow and sat up in bed. He gave up trying to recapture the deep, death-like sleep from which he'd been catapulted at dawn by the sonic boom of the muezzin's amplified bellow from the minaret of the mosque in Kowloon Park which had informed the Moslem community that it was time to unroll their mats. It wasn't too far away from Wang's bedroom window. It sounded as though it was outside in the hotel's car park. Wang rubbed the glue out of his puffy eyes and stuffed a pillow behind his back. It was time for roll call. But first . . . He ordered tea and told the chambermaid to stand by for a breakfast order. He noted she had strong arms. She was going to need them; Wang Peng Soon had woken up with a substantial appetite. Having sent her off, he dipped two garibaldies in the sweet tea, sucked them in and washed it all away with the sweet, thick tea, then peeled a large banana and held it in his hand while he dialled Inspector Tan's car-phone number.

No reply.

He ate half the banana and dialled again. Nothing. He ate the other half, tossed the skin on to the tray and dialled again.

Still no reply.

His face showed no expression. Sitting cross-legged on the bed he looked like an overweight Buddha, his eyes, puffy from a disturbed sleep, slitted into two black cotton lines as he tapped his finger several times on the receiver rest. When the reception desk answered he said, 'Look up the number of Police Headquarters, please – Arsenal Road.'

'I'll call you back.' It was a female voice, not tired like his but chirpy and bright, happy she'd had a good night one way or the other. 'Er . . . there's a message here for you, Mr Ah Bee Yong.'

'Pardon?' Wang's eyes opened a fraction in surprise – who the bloody hell was Mr Ah Bee Yong? Then he remembered. 'Send it up with my breakfast.'

'Right away. I'll send the phone number you asked for as well.'

'Forget it. I shan't need that now.' Tan had come out of the bog, or woken up and phoned in on the public system. His phone was on the blink . . . Wang sorted out Tan's problems for him as he peeled another banana, then sat back on his crumpled pillow and waited for his breakfast.

He read the badly scrawled note as he lifted the tin lid off his plate. Without touching its contents he replaced the lid gently and moved the tray on to the side table as he slid out of bed. The look of anticipation with which he'd greeted the arrival of the tray had vanished; in its place was the nearest thing to a perplexed frown as Wang would allow to show. There was the smell of something wrong and he didn't hang around. He splashed water on his face, cleaned his teeth and dressed rapidly. Shaving wasn't necessary, there was not a hair on his face and never had been; a razor would have been on unexplored territory. He slipped the small auto-matic into his trouser band and covered it with a lightweight cotton jacket. Within ten minutes of reading Inspector Tan's message he was on the pavement outside the hotel.

The Orchid Hotel stood out quite clearly on the opposite side of the road – if you were looking for it – but where the bloody hell was the Wai Lee Suan knocking shop? Within view of the Orchid, had said the message. His short stumpy legs moved quickly up Nathan Road. He gave no impression of haste, nothing like an undignified scamper, barging into and darting round the already milling masses. It was a controlled urgency, it kept people out of his way and brought him quickly outside the Wai Lee Suan. He wasn't surprised to find his helpers spending the night in such exotic surroundings – he envied them the ability.

'You've got a Mr Chew taking the waters here,' he said to Madame. She was still sitting in the same place, same chair and looked exactly as she had the previous night; possibly a new layer of *maquillage*, certainly new lipstick and eyeliner, but her clothes hadn't changed, nor her willing manner. Her husband wasn't propping up the bar, not that it would have made any difference to her answer.

'Who wants to know?'

Wang's eyes narrowed and he sent his hand to the inside pocket of his jacket. There was nothing in it, but she didn't know – it allowed her to see the butt of the small automatic. It was enough. She no longer wanted to know who wanted to know. She tried a smile but it dislodged some of the make-up so she turned it into a sort of kissing pout.

'He's gone,' she said. 'My husband thought he was a fairy. I reckoned he was a copper.'

'Did he say where he was going? Did he leave a message?'

'You're a bit old for this game ain't you?' She tried another smile.

'Madam, I'm going to piss all over you if you don't quickly answer my question.' Wang didn't raise his voice, but she looked for the first time into his eyes and what she saw there disturbed her; he looked as though he meant it. She turned her head away quickly, uncrossed her flabby thighs and pointed at the door with her chin. 'He didn't say where he was going. He turned left. I think he's gone for something to eat.'

'When did he go?'

She turned her head again and studied the clock mounted in a star-shaped mirror on the wall. ' 'Bout twenty minutes ago. If you want my . . .'

But Wang had gone.

This time he was in a hurry and darted without caring whether people got in his way. His waters were breaking – there was definitely something wrong.

He found Sonny Chew standing in the open under an awning with three different baskets of *dim sum* on a table and half a shrimp dumpling in his mouth but with his eye still on the entrance to the Orchid Hotel. Sonny carried on eating as Wang sidled up alongside him. He debated saying good morning but Wang took the decision away from him.

'Have you tried to get in touch with Inspector Tan?'

Sonny Chew swallowed what he had in his mouth, took a sip of hot, sweet tea and swilled it around before answering.

'He rang me last night and said not to bother him as he was exposed. I rang this morning to tell him nothing was happening across the road and I was going to eat. But I couldn't get him. How did you find me?' His hand hovered over one of the baskets and picked out a crispy *chun kuen*. 'Want one?' he asked.

Wang had lost his appetite. He shook his head. 'Tan left me a message last night saying where I could find you. I've been trying since dawn to raise him, but nothing.'

Sonny had taken a large bite from his spring roll; it took a second or two for him to clear it before he could speak. 'Let's try the phone in there.' He jerked his head at the shop behind them. 'Maybe he'd gone for a pee?'

Wang stared at him, unimpressed. 'Go and ring the number. I'll pay for this while you're doing it. Be quick!'

Sonny reached out for another *chun kuen* and took it into the shop with him. He came out shaking his head. 'It's ringing, but no answer. Where was he when he rang you?'

'I don't know, he didn't say,' said Wang grimly. 'He was watching the woman. She'd gone to ground somewhere. I want to know what the bloody hell she's up to and who she's seeing. But I want an eye on Kent as well. Does Tan have a tracing code on that phone?'

Sonny nodded. 'Let's go back to my knocking shop, it's quieter. Perhaps you'd watch the Orchid while I make a few calls.'

When he returned he said, 'They're working on it. It'll take a bit of time. We'll probably find the bloody thing's U/S and he's sitting outside somebody's house pissed off because nobody's ringing.' But he didn't believe that. Neither did Wang.

39

David Kent drank three cups of tea and smoked five cigarettes. That was breakfast out of the way. Then he showered.

The two Chinese had alternated throughout the night, one on, one off. Between them they'd had slightly more sleep than he'd managed. It had been a tossing and turning night, of visions of Hilary holding out her arms to him with nothing on the end of them . . . If he'd had the energy he'd have woken with a little scream, instead of a startled, wide-eyed awakening and a thankful turning over on a crumpled, sweat-drenched pillow. It had all been a dream. Until the next one. He was kissing her and she was responding enthusiastically, bringing her hand from the back of his neck to stroke his face. Only it wasn't a hand; she was stroking his face with a bloody stump . . . This time he had sat up with a groan still gurgling in his throat, which had died abruptly when the light went on and he saw the Chinaman standing over him, his eyes slitted out of sight with suspicion. There was no question of more sleep, not for him or his guards.

He had greeted the dawn and the thin light that came in through the curtained window like a long-lost friend. It was only when he had sat up and smoked his first cigarette that he realised he hadn't had a single nightmare about the poor bastard who featured in the file. But that had been his own fault – if he wanted to play spies he could find his own nightmares. Hilary was something different.

The telephone call came while he was still in the bathroom.

It was Ah Lian.

She sounded like a platoon commander briefing the patrol. 'The two men with you have been instructed to accompany you to wherever the file is deposited and when you've collected it to bring you to a place where I shall be waiting. You're to give them no trouble and make no attempt to contact anybody. Is that clear?'

Kent's mood was a reflection of his nightmares. 'Wrong,' he said.

'I beg your pardon?'

'I said, wrong. Nobody's going anywhere until you produce Hilary West and she's within touching distance of me.'

There was a long pause. Too long. Kent replaced the receiver, lit a cigarette, but stayed within reach of the phone. He didn't touch it when it rang again. The second Chinese had entered the room and stood agressively against the wall by the door. He seemed to have scented mutiny. He nodded to the other man to answer the phone.

It was placed in Kent's hand.

'That was a stupid thing to do Mr Kent,' said Ah Lian. 'I think you've forgotten that we hold a considerable security against the surrender of those documents. And we've changed the rules. The file is to be brought here for inspection. If you refuse, Mrs West will be handed over to Department 5 and taken to the Laogai at Peking and executed.' Ah Lian's toneless voice scraped on Kent's eardrums like a scalpel, but he kept his feelings off his face, and out of his voice. She gave him a few seconds to think about it, then added, 'Where is the file?'

Kent looked into the two expressionless faces staring at him from different parts of the room. He wondered what their orders were, and then realised it didn't make any difference. He turned his back on them and spoke into the phone. 'You've just over-estimated the strength of your position, madam. I've had a change of heart – I've decided that the file should go back to London Registry. A telephone call will redirect it, if not, it'll stay where it is. One thing is certain, you're never going to see it. I hope Kim Cheong has faith in your judgement and that he hasn't got too much of his hard-earned capital riding on the outcome. Goodbye.' As a bluff it was pathetic. It all depended on how much of the corn he'd strewn around was needed to make the loaf. As soon as she spoke he knew.

'Just a minute. You're being very stupid. Don't put the phone down . . .'

He lit a cigarette to hide the relief that threatened to take his breath away. If the two Chinese hadn't been in the room he'd have gone down on his knees.

'You're prepared to sacrifice Mrs West?'

This was the sum result of the murmuring he'd tried hard to decipher through the hand she'd held loosely across the phone's mouthpiece. There was a tiny element of disbelief in her voice. Thank God there was a man directing her; she, with her instinctive feminine knowledge of a man's weakness, would have called his bet, but she would do as she was told.

He didn't reply.

'What do you propose?' she said with difficulty.

'Let me speak to Kim Cheong.'

'He's not here.'

Kent smiled grimly to himself. Kim Cheong was looking after Hilary. Hadn't he said in Fylough's flat '. . . we'll meet on the border'? *Let's try it*.

'I'm handing the file only to him. Where is he?'

'It's not poss – '

'Don't say it's not possible – make it possible. Where is he?'

Ah Lian's hand went over the mouthpiece again but the mumble was short; the instructions given to her were even shorter. 'Stay where you are, then, Mr Kent,' she said between her teeth, 'and Kim Cheong will phone you.'

'No – not good enough.' Kent looked at his cards again; they were worth another raise. 'Call him, wherever he is, and tell him to stay by the telephone until I get in touch. Bring the number with you when you come to the Orchid Hotel.'

'I beg your pardon!'

'You heard. Ring Kim Cheong, give him my message, then get yourself a little red taxi and come to the hotel – alone.'

'But – '

'No buts. Do as I say. First, though, talk to one of these apes and tell him I shall be coming down to the foyer to meet you – I don't want to have to break their legs to get past them. Here.' He crooked his finger at the man by the door and held out the telephone. He didn't wait to find out whether Ah Lian had accepted his invitation or whether he'd overcalled on a low pair; but he kept his legs slightly crossed as an insurance.

He needn't have bothered. Ah Lian was following her orders to the letter. She didn't have to agree with them, she had no choice – Hu Bang's nodding head at the repetition of each demand was as emphatic as a bullet in the back of the neck if she offered the slightest risk of losing him the chance of changing China's direction. Hu Bang had taken over the galloping horse; all she could do was hang on to the stirrup until Kim Cheong's friend was sitting comfortably on the throne and Hu Bang had returned to his retirement hut on the edge of the *padi* fields.

She excused herself and went to her room. By the time she returned the taxi was waiting at the front door. She was dressed in a full skirt, blouse and a fawn-coloured, lightweight cotton jacket. On her way out she called in for last-minute instructions from Hu Bang. He was still sitting where she'd left him. He hadn't moved, not even his head.

'I'm not surprised the Englishman has lost interest in the woman's welfare,' he mused. He was impervious to Ah Lian's air of urgency. 'Few woman are worth a nation's secrets.' Ah Lian said nothing. 'But as she's still part of our bargain it's imperative that he be persuaded to do what I suggested earlier – it is still possible to use the woman to recover the documents. Don't forget, he wants you close by as a guarantor of the exchange, but he must be killed when the documents are brought into the open and there is no longer a risk of their destruction or return to London. That is clear?'

Ah Lian nodded. 'Quite clear. Will you pass on the message to Kim Cheong? He must ring . . .'

'I know, I know!' snapped the old man testily. 'Get on and do your work. Do everything the Englishman asks; refuse him nothing, lull him into a sense of security. Just make sure the file is delivered. Go now.'

'Will you remain here?' Ah Lian refused to be hurried. She wanted to know where the troops would be stationed when the battle started.

'I shall be with Kim Cheong and the woman at Shenzhen.'

The taxi honked its horn, flashed its indicator at the last minute and slid to an awkward angle right outside the Orchid Hotel.

When Ah Lian stepped out of the taxi and disappeared into the hotel, Wang turned quickly to Sonny Chew and snapped, 'You've got a Department taxi on call?'

'Sure,' said Sonny. His eyes were all over the place. 'Where d'you want it?'

'Make it two,' demanded Wang, abruptly. 'One pointing that way, and one that.' He jabbed a stubby finger, first down Nathan Road towards the harbour and then in the opposite direction.

'When you've done that, nip across the road and book a double room in the Orchid for your uncle who's coming from London. While you're doing it have a good look round – see what sort of conference the woman and the Englishman are having. But don't hang around; don't make yourself conspicuous. Book the room, see how many she's got in her team and come back here.'

Kent's two warders stood apart, one by the reception desk, one covering the lift and stairs. Their eyes never left his back.

Kent sat perfectly at ease at one of the small tables dotted around the reception area and watched the front entrance. When Ah Lian stepped out of her taxi he moved to the door, where without actually leaving the foyer, he could study the immediate surrounds of the hotel and the street outside.

When she walked past him he didn't acknowledge her, nor she him. He watched her taxi leave, then leaned forward and glanced up and down Nathan Road. The movement of traffic was continuous; nobody was paying off taxis and making a meal of it and there were no uncomfortable-looking drivers staring at the hotel entrance, nobody stopping dead and looked into the shop next door when his head appeared round the door. Ah Lian was playing the game. She was on her own – he had to believe it.

He turned away from the entrance, walked straight past her and, ignoring the open door of the waiting lift, took to the stairs.

Halfway up he could hear the heavy breathing of one of the guards who, on his toes, moved rapidly to keep him in sight. Kent stopped and looked over the rails. The man behind him stopped also and put his hand under his coat, then, sheepishly, took it away and stood uncomfortably watching. Kent ignored him and stared down. Ah Lian and the other gunman were just mounting the stairs. Kent waited until they were on his flight, then continued at a leisurely pace, turned into the corridor, walking straight through the partly open door of his room, and sat down on the edge of the bed. The man who'd kept pace with him on the stairs came in and waited, staring at him until Ah Lian and her bodyguard arrived, then, without a word, edged out of the room and took up his position on the other side of the corridor.

Kent looked over his shoulder and jerked his chin at the remaining guard.

'Get him out of here,' he said to Ah Lian. 'And shut the door behind you,' he added in Cantonese to the Chinese, who, without changing expression, shifted his eyes to Ah Lian's face and waited. After a moment's reflection she inclined her head in the briefest of nods and the man backed out of the door and closed it behind him. But he wouldn't have gone far; he'd probably be leaning with his back to the door and his ear cocked for the summons to come crashing in and break Kent's arms. Kent was surprised it had been so easy; perhaps he had better have another look at the cards he was holding. But first, a cheeky look at hers.

In the silence of the room the match Kent rasped on the box sounded like gunfire. She walked towards the window, probably to get away from the smoke of his cigarette, and stared down at the rubbish in the hotel's backyard. She kept her back to him while she surreptitiously glanced at the tiny watch on her wrist.

'I have left a message for Kim Cheong to ring me here,' she said, staring out of the window. Kent said nothing. She didn't look round. She heard the bed-springs creak and a gentle blowing as he exhaled a mouthful of smoke. 'I hope you realise that you've probably signed the West woman's death warrant. I've been instructed to tell you that if there's the slightest hint of trickery there will be no hesitation – she will be killed.' She turned her head sideways, not to look at him but to make sure he heard and understood what was coming next. 'And so will you.' It gave her some solace to say it, and, more than solace, a feeling of satisfaction, knowing that they were not just words. She turned so that her back was against the window and studied the effect. It wasn't reassuring.

Kent was comfortable and at ease. Their eyes met and with the cigarette smouldering between his lips he swung his feet up on the bed, propped his back against the headboard and, with his hands behind his head, looked her up and down.

She didn't wilt.

He brought one hand from behind his head, held it out and said, 'Your bag, please.'

'I beg your pardon?'

'You heard me.'

She stared back at him for several seconds and then, surprisingly, surrendered. She slipped the strap of her handbag from

334

her shoulder and, moving only her arm, swung it in his direction. Her aim was bad. It thudded on to the floor beside the bed. Kent didn't have to move to pick it up, but when he did he knew he was wasting his time. He went through the motions all the same. He pulled open the zip and, without ceremony, emptied the bag's contents on to the floor. She watched without interest. Her normally attractive mouth had vanished into a thin line of controlled anger, but she remained calm and made no comment as he leaned over and stared at the jumble on the carpet. He touched nothing, just looked at the pile of women's things, and then picked up the bag again, inspected its interior, shook it up and down and dropped it back on to the floor.

'Have you finished?' she asked. There was a certain dignity about her as she took a step forward and went on her knee to retrieve her belongings. Perhaps she shouldn't have asked.

'Not quite . . .'

Their hands were close and on the same level and as her eyes came up to meet his he removed the cigarette from his mouth. The question remained unasked on her lips.

'Take your clothes off.'

She remained kneeling, as if carved in ivory, her eyes, almond-shaped, staring back into his as if she hadn't heard or had not understood, and when it finally went home, they widened in a sort of innocent disbelief. The tableau lasted only seconds, then, in outrage, her eyes widened into black marbles and her lips tightened in anger.

'I beg your pardon!'

He ignored the indignation. 'And I suggest before you do you go and lock the door, unless you want your two night soil collectors to stroll in and get the wrong idea.'

'I absolutely refuse!'

'Fair enough. Close the door on your way out – and take those two with you when you leave. Goodbye.'

But she didn't move. Her mind was working with the speed of a survivor as, on her knees, with Hu Bang's final words still fresh and crisp in her mind, she worked out the odds. Kent had stopped looking at her but it didn't help. He was gazing at the ceiling, watching a gentle, waif-like wisp of smoke flatten against the cornice in search of a non-existent passage out of the room. Ah

Lian's eyes lowered away from his face. Survivor or not she knew she'd run full pelt into the brick wall at the end of the road. She tried to recover some dignity.

'You lecherous English bastard!'

He ignored her outburst. 'Don't take too long,' he said comfortably.

'Pig!'

Kent said nothing.

'You filthy bastard!'

'Don't start that again.'

Ah Lian's high cheekbones stood out like pink whiplashes across her porcelain features as, overcoming her humiliation, she kicked off her tiny high-heeled sandals and then draped her coat on the back of one of the chairs. Her blouse and skirt followed, leaving her standing in a thigh-length split petticoat and an ethereal white lace-work brassière that revealed more than it concealed or supported. She lifted her head and stared at Kent through cold, narrowed eyes, then held her two hands at her side, palms outwards.

'Have you seen all you want, pig?' she said quietly.

Kent brought his eyes down from the ceiling again, turned on his elbow and stubbed out his cigarette. He looked up from the ashtray and studied the length of her body, lingering on her flat stomach before raising his eyes and meeting hers. She didn't submit. She stared back.

'Take off the rest,' he said.

She shrugged her shoulders. 'That won't be necessary.'

'Yes it will.'

She should have known. This wasn't a pink-cheeked English gentleman, this was a man who'd done the Hong Kong street-corner scene; he'd been a policeman, he knew what it was all about. She gave in and turned her back on him.

She clasped her hands round her back and unclipped the bra. Then she eased the petticoat over her slim, almost non-existent hips and allowed it to slither to the floor. She wore no panties. She was naked. Well, almost.

'Turn round.'

She did so, modestly – and guiltily.

Ah Lian had a lovely, unspoiled body. Everything appeared to

336

be brand-new, unused. It was firm and beautifully proportioned. Her breasts, although small, were perfectly shaped and full with two erect rosebud nipples pointing hard in his direction, out of her control, swollen in the mistaken sensation that this was sexual.

Standing with her thighs pressed tightly together she suffered his raised-eyebrow scrutiny without flinching. She didn't bother watching his reaction; she knew exactly where his eyes would be and she knew the expression on his face would not be lascivious but cynical. She was right.

Kent crooked his finger. 'OK. Not original, but bring it over here.'

Her eyes went down her naked body to the join between her legs where instead of the lush triangle of silken down snuggled blushingly a pudendum as hairless as a baby's and as plump as a ripe peach; but, as excitingly feminine as it was, it wasn't this that Kent wanted. She looked up contemptuously and began to unknot the thin strap that encircled her waist.

'No – I said bring it here!'

'It' was a thin silk pouch that hung from the strap round her waist and fitted snugly where the dark triangle should have been. It was held lightly in place, like a gunfighter's low-slung holster, by two thin lace straps running from the point of the pouch and fastened with little bows round each smooth, hard thigh.

From the tiny pouch's opening peeped the butt of a small automatic pistol.

'Don't be shy,' counselled Kent.

She lowered her head.

'No, leave it where it is.'

She took her hand away.

Her embarrassment had evaporated; anger had taken its place. Kent was inching his way along a very fragile branch, and he knew it, but it was a branch that wouldn't support him on a return journey. 'That's it. Now bring it over here – pouch and all.'

She walked on tiptoe across the room. For a Chinese she had very long legs, with slim calves in the right proportion – it must have been all that running about in the jungle as a young girl. When she reached the bedside she lowered her heels and stood in front of him submissively, remaining statue-still when his finger and thumb went into the pouch and extracted the tiny weapon from its cosy hiding place.

It was warm and from it came a gentle hint of perfume as he held it up in front of his eyes and admired its workmanship. It looked naughty – and sexy – and it was lethal. It was too small to fit into his grip and his forefinger was too large to enter the trigger guard, but, like Ah Lian's body, it was beautifully put together. He recognised it; he'd seen one before, though not from such a nice home. It was an American weapon, a Bauer .25, made in stainless steel, with its pretty mother-of-pearl butt holding a magazine of six nickel-coated .25 lead bullets. It weighed only ten ounces, was less than three inches high, and was more than enough to kill him, and anybody else who got in her way. He glanced critically at Ah Lian's hairless pelvis where its tiny holster hung and he felt himself getting angry. 'You can get dressed now,' he said sharply and allowed the magazine to drop out of the butt and into his hand.

She didn't move.

'I'd like it back please,' she said politely. 'You can keep the magazine.' She seemed no longer to have inhibitions about standing in front of Kent without a stitch on and only a tiny silk pouch protecting her femininity. Kent stared at her. Maybe it had been the gun that had made her shy and coy.

'Don't be bloody stupid!' He lit another cigarette and rolled off the bed and onto his feet. As he walked across the room to the bathroom he tossed the silver automatic from hand to hand, like a bowler with a cricket ball on his way back to his mark. She hadn't moved. She seemed mesmerised. 'I said get dressed.' He stopped at the bathroom door. 'And go and get rid of your two keepers. Clear them out of the hotel – and I don't want to see them hanging about Nathan Road either.' Kent's feeling of superiority was almost overwhelming. A proud and coldly domineering woman reduced to girlish submissiveness? He was right – somebody must have well and truly put the fear of God into her about the recovery of the documents. He tried not to let it go to his head. 'When Kim Cheong rings,' he said, 'answer the phone and tell him to give a number that I can call back . . .' He studied his watch. '. . . in an hour and half – exactly.'

Ah Lian had slipped her petticoat over her nakedness and the empty little pouch and was filling her firm breasts into the flimsy brassière. She didn't stop; she didn't look up.

'I shall want to talk to Hilary West,' Kent continued, 'and then – only then, tell him – will I make arrangements for the exchange.'

He didn't wait for Ah Lian's acknowledgement. He backed into the bathroom, closing the door behind him, but leaving a sufficiently wide gap for him to hear any change in the atmosphere in the other room.

After a leisurely wash he opened the door fully and stood drying his face with a towel. Nothing had changed.

'No call yet?' It was an unnecessary remark and she knew it. She didn't bother answering, instead shrugging her shoulders and continuing to repair her make-up. But he'd drawn her attention. He held up the Bauer for her to see, and with her eyes following him through the mirror he reached into the bathroom, removed the cistern lid and dropped the tiny weapon in it. It made a healthy splash and then a heavy clunk as it hit the bottom.

'You can come back later and fish it out,' he told the back of her head, 'when we're all nothing but a bad memory to each other.' She'd stopped looking. She didn't appear to be listening either. He emptied the magazine of its six shiny rounds, flicking them one by one into the water. Then he tossed in the empty magazine, dropped the lid on to the cistern and returned to the bedroom.

Just then the telephone rang.

40

Outside, Kowloon was getting into its stride and the sun was moving the shade of the crowded buildings and spreading its warm glow down the length and breadth of the already crowded and bustling Nathan Road.

Earlier, Wang had strolled across the road and found himself a cup of sweet tea in a shop almost next door to the Orchid Hotel. He washed down a prawn dumpling and a chopped pork roll with the dregs of the cup and ordered another. It arrived just as Kent and Ah Lian came out of the hotel.

Kent played the clever game. He stood in the shade of the hotel's entrance and watched several empty taxis jink into position when they saw a European fare, and jink out again when he ignored them.

Wang looked across the road at Sonny Chew, who nodded discreetly and moved towards the taxi he'd posted a few yards up the road with its meter running and its engine ticking over.

Sonny took his time. He had other things to watch, and he'd seen what he was watching for. So far he'd made it two two-man teams of stocky young Chinese making themselves look inconspicuous. They were good at their job. Sonny marked them down: Gonganbu, no question about it. No question either that they were the Guojia Anquanbu annexe, the Hong Kong specialists, the advance party nicely installed in time to direct the traffic in 1997. He climbed into the back of his taxi and accepted the two-way radio from the driver. He stared at Wang through the window. Wang hadn't moved, and there was nothing Sonny could say to him until he had hauled his ample frame into his own taxi and clicked on his radio. He leaned forward and spoke to the driver, then looked back at Wang.

He was just in time.

Wang was standing in the shadow of the shop waving. There was an air of the frenetic about Wang's attempt at discretion, but Sonny got the message. He leapt out of his taxi just as Wang's

340

windmill stopped and his finger pointed to the taxi he'd just left and then held an imaginary telephone to his ear. It could have meant anything but Sonny made a guess, and took a chance. He stuck his head back in the taxi window. 'Are you on my wavelength?' he asked the driver. The driver nodded – he too was watching Wang's signals.

'OK,' snapped Sonny. 'Watch me. Don't take your eyes off me and move quickly when I give the word. Are you switched on?'

'Yeh.'

'See that fat man over there?'

'The one waving his arm?'

'That's him. He's the boss – he gives orders too. Listen out for him, his name's – ' Sonny had to think for a moment; Wang changed his name as other people changed their shirts. 'Oh, bugger it! Wang – call him Wang if the occasion arrives. OK?'

He didn't wait to see whether the police driver had worked it all out. He cut diagonally across Nathan Road and sidled into the shade beside Wang. Wang hadn't moved. Kent was still studying his surroundings, Ah Lian standing slightly behind him. She looked cool and composed and gazed straight ahead; she'd already spotted the Chinese cover crew.

'D'you see that taxi?' Sonny Chew said to Wang. Wang didn't turn his head. 'Two Bow Street people are arguing the price. Both, plus the driver, are covering Kent and the woman.'

'Any more?' Wang's eyes swivelled fractionally, took in the scene and returned to Kent.

'Fellow on a scooter, wearing a black and silver helmet, blue shirt . . .'

'Got him! Did you bring a set with you?'

Sonny tapped his pocket. Like Wang his eyes were on swivels and as he pulled them away from the man on the scooter he saw out of the corner of his eye Kent suddenly dart into the road and whistle at a cruising taxi going up Nathan Road. The taxi driver liked what he saw. Almost doing a wheelie he honked his horn optimistically and without looking right or left nipped through the gap in the central island, pulling up within inches of David Kent's toes.

Wang's measured tones removed the panic from Sonny Chew's face.

341

'Quickly now!' he hissed. 'Speak into your thing and tell my taxi to cut in front of those three clowns to pick me up. Tell yours to dart across the road and accidentally block theirs tightly into a . . .'

But Sonny Chew had anticipated him. His back turned to the road, he was already speaking urgently into the small transmitter.

They were very good. The two police taxis moved like a duet in a ballet troupe. Sonny's taxi, over-enthusiastic, instead of sidling in front and blocking it, caught the Chinese agents' vehicle a heavy blow on its front bumper. In spite of the hand-waving and the 'It doesn't matter! Just get out of the bloody way!' Sonny's man got out of his cab and with a great deal of teeth-sucking and head-shaking made a laborious inspection of the damage to both vehicles. It was too much for the team leader of the Bow Street Alley men. Detaching himself from the excitement, he pushed the taxi driver aside and without any attempt at subtlety elbowed his way through the gathering crowd. Grabbing the spare helmet from the pannier on the back of the scooter, he leapt on to the pillion of the already moving bike.

Wang, with Sonny in the back of his taxi, stared out of the rear window just in time to see the scooter gather speed. His look of satisfaction faded.

'Reverse!' he bellowed.

The taxi driver reacted like a frightened snake. He jabbed his foot on the brake, made a clean clutch and without grinding the gears, threw the taxi into a rapid reverse.

The scooter, already moving at speed, met the reversing taxi head-on. There was no squeal of brakes, no skid, just the thump of a head ramming into the back of the taxi and the sound of a thousand empty tin cans falling onto the road as the scooter's front wheel vanished into a shapeless mass of shiny aluminium and rubber. The driver hadn't a chance. Like his passenger, he hurtled over the handlebars, thumped head first into the back of the taxi, slithered under its rear wheels and died without a murmur.

Wang didn't give him a second glance. 'Move!' he told the driver, and when they'd nipped smartly into the stream of traffic he tapped him on the shoulder and said, 'Did you get that taxi's number?'

'Yup.'

342

'Follow him – and watch that the passengers don't nip out at a light.' Wang settled back in his seat and let Sonny help the driver with the watching.

They hadn't got very far down Nathan Road before the driver sucked air through his teeth and touched the brakes. 'He's turned down Gascoigne Road,' observed Sonny. 'They're going to the station.'

Wang closed his eyes.

'No they're not . . .' Sonny perched forward on his seat and rested his arm on the driver's shoulder, shaking his head as they went down the Chatham Road underpass. Kent's taxi, some four or five cars ahead of them, came out of Chatham and jostled into the right-hand lane. With the driver nodding agreement, Sonny said emphatically, 'The tunnel . . . They're going to Hong Kong.'

Sonny was right. They sped into Hong Chong Road and for a brief moment at the toll gate Sonny and the driver lost sight of Kent's taxi, but then, as they sloped down into the fluorescent tube, the driver spotted them again and latched on a comfortable four or five cars behind.

He closed up as they burst out into the scorching sun of the Island and whirled round the noodle junction before taking off in close pursuit up Gloucester Road. The driver and Sonny rapidly put on their dark glasses but Wang used his eyelids. He didn't stir. Sonny stared at him for a moment to make sure he hadn't died in the tunnel, then took up his observation post again, on his knees just behind the driver. He continued his commentary.

'He's taking her for a strip-search in the dungeons!' They were approaching Harcourt Road but the grin vanished as the taxi filtered through Arsenal Street, passed Police HQ on tiptoes, and joined the flow of traffic in Queensway. Wang opened his eyes and turned his head. For a brief moment he gazed out of the rear window, but it was brief – very brief – and he swung back and stared through the gap between the two heads in front of him as if he didn't trust them to keep in touch with Kent's darting red taxi.

'Has our friend from Arsenal found us yet?' he asked the driver. Sonny had booked another police taxi to replace the decoy they'd left behind in Nathan Road and it was he who answered.

'He's locked in two cars behind us. He picked us up as we came

343

past the AA. He's going to be discreet until we stick a finger out for him.'

'That was clever of you, Sonny,' observed Wang and sat up to look out of the back again. 'You said that without looking behind us!' Wang smiled to himself. He'd spotted the backmarker. 'You must have eyes in the back of your whatnot!'

Sonny had missed Wang's smile. He took his eyes off the quarry for a moment and turned on his knees, saying seriously, 'He's on the wireless – we're all hooked up.' But Wang's moment of humour had passed; all Sonny got for his trouble was a blank stare. He turned back to Kent's taxi, content that Wang Peng Soon's eyes, were sharing his problem, even if his forehead wasn't yet, like his, creased with anxiety!

On Cotton Tree Drive they veered left and accelerated past the Hilton Hotel and into Queen's Road Central. Following Sonny's instruction the driver overtook the car in front of them so that they were only two cars behind Kent. But Sonny was too slow. His anticipation was just seconds late as the traffic lights flicked into amber and, with hardly a pause, into red. The driver of the car in front of them stood on his brakes. Kent's taxi made it. And Sonny had a fit.

The second police taxi pulled up in the lane alongside and the driver glanced across and winked at them. Sonny stared at him. He got the message and quickly turned his head to the front. But Sonny wasn't appeased.

'You stupid bastard!' he said to his driver. 'You've lost the fucker! Now what?' He daren't turn his head to meet Wang's eyes; he gritted his teeth and waited for the outburst.

But nothing came. At least no outburst – not even a gentle rebuke. 'When the lights change,' Wang said to the back of the driver's head, 'pull into Duddle Street and wait on the edge of the car park.'

'Why don't I go in? It'll keep us out of the way?'

'Did you ever see a taxi parked in a car park? Do as I say and be ready to move quickly.'

'Just a minute! What's happening?'

Sonny had been too busy having a heart attack to notice what was happening on the Queen's Road side of the traffic lights. But Wang hadn't. Neither had the driver. He didn't turn his head.

'They've pulled into the New World Tower,' he said. 'The two passengers are getting out.'

'New World Tower?' Wang sat forward in his seat and balanced himself with an arm on Sonny's shoulder. 'Quick, Sonny! What happens in there?'

Sonny didn't have to think. 'Ground floor, American Express. First floor – '

'That's enough.' Wang's eyes creased contentedly. 'He's gone to pick something up. What's American Express got there? Bank? Travel? Come on, quick, Sonny!'

'All of those.'

'OK.' He punched Sonny's shoulder. 'Get in there, quickly. We'll wait here. Take your walkie-talkie and let us know what's going on. Go on, bugger off!'

Sonny jumped out of the taxi, walked briskly to the Queen's Road and disappeared round the corner. Wang leaned forward and picked up the driver's handset from the front seat. 'Is this in touch with the other car?' he asked.

When the driver nodded he flicked the switch and said 'Come in . . .' to the hiss and crackle. A voice said something incomprehensible. He stared at the machine and began to swear until the driver half-turned his head and deciphered it for him.

'He's in Ice House Street. He said he can see us but he feels exposed.'

Wang didn't look sympathetic. He held the set to his mouth and said loudly, 'Stay where you are. If anybody tries to bugger you about tell them you've got an American lady tourist who's shopping for rhino horn! Keep your radio open and listen out for Sergeant Chew – he's treading water with the target in the New World . . . Did you get that?' The driver winced at Wang's radio telephone technique and waited for the other car's acknowledgement. Nothing came. He was about to turn round when the set, crackling and hissing, arrived on his shoulder and Wang said, 'You talk to him next time. Put me in contact with Sergeant Chew.'

But before the driver could answer the set came to life again. It was as clear as a bell. It was Sonny Chew, even Wang recognised his voice.

'Your English friend's at the enquiries counter. His girlfriend's by his side – she's like glue. Hang on – ' The set died in Wang's hand, but only briefly, as if Sonny had moved out of sight or out of range, or even tucked his head under his arm, and then it came back, even stronger: 'You were right about Amex. He's shown his passport, and something else, probably his Amex card. I swear she said "That'll do nicely, sir"!'

Wang took the set from his ear and stared at it. 'I wish he'd cut out the bloody cackle and stick to what he can see,' he muttered. But Sonny was still talking and Wang jammed the machine back to his ear.

'They've handed him a large envelope . . . Just a sec – ' the phone went dead again, then: 'He's ducked into a phone drome. She's squeezed in with him – looks ever so sexy!'

'What's the number?' asked Kent.

'I'll do it,' she replied. 'Give me the phone.'

'The number,' he insisted.

She told him.

He raised his eyebrows. 'China code?' He wrote the number down on the flap of his cigarette packet. 'Where in China?' He smiled crookedly at her tightly drawn lips. 'Surprise me!'

'Shenzhen.'

He dialled the code and number, listened to the response in *putonghua* and handed the receiver to Ah Lian.

She spoke rapidly. When she made a brief pause he butted in. 'If you mention where you're calling from I'll walk out of here and the deal's off.'

She gave no indication that she'd heard what he said other than an undirected look of contempt, then she carried on talking into the mouthpiece in a soft, urgent voice. Kent thought he detected a note of relief in her manner. But he wasn't given time to reflect on it. The phone was thrust into his hand.

'Mr Kent?' It was Kim Cheong. He recognised the voice. Kim Cheong spoke in English. He didn't wait for Kent to identify himself but went straight into his act. 'Let me pass you Hilary West.'

Kent strained his ears for the clashing of steel on plastic but the pass over was smooth and immediate.

'Hello, David . . .' There wasn't much else Hilary could say.

'Are you all right?' Kent felt strangely shy and awkward, like a teenager confronted with the long-awaited realisation of his bedtime fantasies. But he managed to keep the uncertainty off his face. He avoided catching Ah Lian's eye but he knew she was studying him closely and analysing each word. He tried the light-hearted approach. 'Can you still count up to ten without taking your shoes off?'

'That's not funny, David!' He could almost hear her shudder, and agreed with her, it wasn't funny, but it brought the conversation to a head, 'Have you got the things Kim Cheong asked for?'

His eyes dropped instinctively to the plastic bag in his other hand and he was surprised to note that his knuckles were white with the tightness of his grip. Ah Lian followed the direction of his eyes but, like Kent, kept her feelings to herself.

She allowed herself a gentle survey of the area around them and wondered where the team of watchers she had organised had placed themselves. She had taken it for granted that she and Kent had been escorted to the New World and had had to fight the temptation to stare out of the taxi's back window. She turned her eyes back to Kent's face; they were slightly troubled eyes. Surely Hu Bang would also have people? She glanced sideways again and knew instinctively that she was alone – and it worried her.

She turned back and listened to Kent. His voice was soothing, encouraging and although he seemed reluctant to cut the fragile contact with Hilary his tone was one of impatience, as if he wanted to get the business over and done with.

'Everything's all right,' he told her. 'You have nothing to worry about and nothing's going to go wrong – trust me.' He gave her no chance to reply. 'Let me talk to Kim Cheong again.'

'If you'd like to bring Mrs West to Kai Tak Airport,' said Kent when Kim Cheong picked up the receiver, 'we'll make the exchange in the main hall.'

Kim Cheong's response was exactly what he expected.

'In our short association, Mr Kent, that's the first sign of humour you've shown!' Kim Cheong gave a short, hiss-like chuckle. To Kent it was like a nerve being pinched. 'But, let us not be funny – or stupid.' The chuckle was coughed out of existence and replaced by a voice crisp with authority. 'Will you make a sensible suggestion, or will you listen to my proposal?'

'Let's hear your proposal,' said Kent grudgingly. He had no

347

doubt to whose advantage it would be. But, he reminded himself, he had no choice, no real argument, unless he wanted to be haunted for the rest of his life by the spectre of Hilary's hands being hacked off at the wrists and, probably as bad, Ah Lian's threat to have her placed in the care of the Gonganbu's hairy masseurs. Yet why? Why either of these? They wanted the documents that would allow them to rearrange the seats around the Chairman's dinner table – they didn't want a stray English girl, with or without hands, pegged out in the Peking Laogai and being bounced on by a team of Kim Cheong's Sumo wrestlers. That would turn her into a liability, not an asset. So where did that leave them? Kent's brain almost stopped. It left them with a possibly spiteful bastard who was saying *we've* nothing to lose – if you don't want to give us the wherewithal to shift your cuckoo's arse from the second-highest shithouse in the land then somebody'll have to pay for our disappointment . . . Somebody? Hilary West was the one wrapped up in the butcher's apron. Kent was in a slightly different frame of mind when Kim Cheong outlined his proposal.

'We'll meet in the customs shed at Lo Wu. You will hand the file to me and I will give you Hilary West and two first-class tickets on the next train to Hung Hom. Then – '

'No,' cut in Kent, 'I don't cross the bridge. Lo Wu station, OK. But our side.' His belligerent manner belied the feelings of doubt he'd just talked himself into. It surprised him. Kim Cheong continued the bargaining.

'Out of the question. Lo Wu is surrounded by British Army watch-towers and there's a Security Force OP within its confines – the risk would be entirely ours. Surrounded by military and police personnel you would be able to walk away with the girl – and my documents.' Kim Cheong's voice betrayed his impatience and he seemed to have credited Kent with powers of contact and influence which were, due to his own arrangements, patently non-existent, if only he had stopped to consider the situation. Kim Cheong had let his imagination cloud his advantage. In an unusual – for him – state of anxiety the unflappable had flapped. He had overlooked the fact that Kent had been totally incommunicado since Goh Peng had picked him up from the safe house in London and that he'd had Ah Lian with him ever since to make sure he stayed so.

Kent sensed Kim Cheong's indecision.

'OK,' he agreed, 'I shall wait on the platform at Lo Wu station – the Hong Kong section. Ah Lian will stay with me. I will ring you at this number and you will send one person across who is empowered to make arrangements. We'll do it face to face. Do you agree?'

'We will want to see the file before any decision is made. The documents must be checked first.'

'Then make sure the person you send across knows what to look for. Just the one person – no more.'

'Very well. What train will you catch?'

'I didn't say anything about trains,' snapped Kent and grabbed the initiative presented to him. 'I said I'd ring you from Lo Wu station. Don't make any arrangements until I ring – you may find you've gone to a lot of trouble for nothing.' He replaced the receiver without waiting for Kim Cheong's reaction.

'And you'd better make sure,' he said to Ah Lian as they left their space capsule, 'that you get word to any of the spiders you might have crawling around Hung Hom station to keep their hands – and their noses – pointed in the other direction.'

She made no comment. The first person she'd spoken to at the Shenzhen number had been Hu Bang. If he was in on the handing-over act the chances of this man Kent returning to Kowloon were extremely remote. She allowed herself an invisible shrug of the shoulders. Why bother arguing with a man who was already dead!

When he spotted them getting ready to leave the phone bubble Sonny Chew moved out of the building and waited in the shadow of a huge imitation-marble pillar. He flicked on the handset and spoke urgently to Wang.

'Can you change taxis – quickly!' His voice was barely above a whisper. He didn't allow a reply; there was no time. 'The other driver doesn't know the target, yours does. Clear the cab as quickly as you can and get him ready to move when Kent sticks his hand out. Don't acknowledge . . .'

Kent held open the door of the American Express Office and followed Ah Lian out into the hot sun. After twenty minutes in

American igloo-style air-conditioning the heat rising from the open concrete piazza in front of the New World Tower hit Kent like a furnace blast. Almost immediately his shirt clammed wetly to his back and as he walked across the concourse towards Queen's Road he stuck his hand out half-heartedly at a cruising empty taxi. He was lucky. Taxis in Queen's Road Central select their own customers, at their own convenience, and this one, perversely, jumped like a startled pony and cut from an outside line to the kerb as if the fare was going to be the saving of his life.

'Oh, Jesus Christ! What the bloody – ' Sonny stopped in his tracks. The taxi was a stranger. How the bloody hell had he got into the game? Sonny broke into a sweaty, worried gallop and threw himself into the body of the strange taxi inches in front of Ah Lian.

'Drive on!' he hissed to the driver. 'I'm in a bloody hurry!' He managed a snatched look out of the rear window as the cab, with a startled screech of tyres, charged into the moving traffic. He was in time to see Wang's empty taxi just pull in to the kerb in front of Kent, who stood scowling, his hand still outstretched as if to open the door of the departing cab. 'Oh, please, God, don't let the silly bugger lean out and ask if anybody wants a taxi!' prayed Sonny.

But Ah Lian had seen it and her hand went out almost into the police taxi driver's face as he slid into position just short of her fingertips.

Once Kent and Ah Lian had settled in and the taxi was in the flow moving along Queen's Road, Wang, sitting in the backup taxi, ordered his driver to move out of Ice House Street, and after a little argy-bargy with the other traffic, they settled in some four or five cars behind. He was just beginning to worry about Sonny Chew when the radio coughed, spat and crackled and Sonny joined them loud and clear.

'I've got them covered,' he said. 'I've dropped back so that I'm just behind the target vehicle. Our driver's giving plenty of warning so you can keep out of the way if you like and leave it up to me.'

'Roger,' said Wang. He wasn't in a conversational mood.

Five minutes later Sonny's voice crackled into the cab again. 'Close up . . . He's going back to Kowloon.'

'Roger,' said Wang again.

They were cruising at speed along Harcourt Road. Kent had instructed his driver to do several rights and lefts – just in case – but, as Sonny said, he hadn't really got his heart in it and gave it up before it became serious. Sonny's bonafide taxi driver had entered into the spirit of the game after he'd been allowed a fleeting glance at Sonny's ID card.

'Close up,' appealed Sonny to Wang's taxi. 'I want to change cars, but I don't want to lose the friends. Collect me just before he gets into the cross-harbour tunnel system. I'll be on the road-side . . .'

'Roger,' intoned Wang.

The taxi with Kent and Ah Lian on board crawled into Hung Hom railway terminal. It was a slow turn-off but not slow enough to excite Kent's suspicion, and the driver's eyes, careful to avoid contact with Kent through the rear mirror, were glued to his wing mirror until he spotted Wang's taxi, several cars away, turn in behind him.

Kent and Ah Lian got out and vanished into the crowd, but not before Sonny Chew had darted out of his still moving vehicle and slid after them. Wang, a later starter, used the calculated guess method and ambled slowly towards the booking counter. Sonny spotted him from a distance, worked his way towards him and, taking him by the arm, pulled him away from the crush.

'He's just bought two returns to Guangzhou; they're already sitting in the train.'

'The through train?'

'That surprised me too! No, they've joined the slow train to China!' Sonny's face split in a wide grin. But he got no response from Wang. The grin vanished. 'I reckon they're only going as far as Shenzhen – probably getting off at Lo Wu and walking the bridge.'

'Why d'you reckon that?'

'Because the fast train doesn't stop – not even at Lo Wu. It goes straight through and into Shenzhen proper. I don't think your man wants that. I think he'll want to play this game on home ground. Wouldn't you?'

But Wang wasn't really paying attention; he'd got other things on his mind.

'I've just remembered,' he said with a scowl. 'Kent's got a cobbled passport – he'll have a China visa in it – sure to. I've got bugger-all. What have you got?'

Sonny grinned again. 'A brother in HM Customs mobile unit.'

Wang's scowl vanished. 'Don't tell me. Your brother – '

Sonny finished it for him. 'Travels regularly between here and Lo Wu. Lucky couple of buggers, aren't we?'

'Don't bloody stand here grinning, then,' barked Wang. 'Go and kiss him, or whatever brothers do to each other!'

41

Lo Wu station was like Petticoat Lane on a Sunday morning, only more people.

Kent hung on to Ah Lian's arm as they disembarked from the train. It was like falling into a fast-moving, in-spate stream as the crush pushed, pulled and dragged them into the vortex of the covered iron bridge that spanned the Sham Chun river. This was the way into China and the noise of several thousand wooden flip-flops clattering across the bridge echoed hollowly from the arched tin roof and drowned out the incessant chatter of the human tide. It suited Ah Lian. She was going in the right direction: halfway across was the People's Republic, a little further on and there stood, in New China basic architecture, the long, featureless and cold Customs sheds, already resounding to shouted instructions from members of Gonganbu dressed up as customs officers. But it didn't suit David Kent.

Like a drowning man, he pulled himself to one side of the main flow before he was swept into the covered bridge with no possible hope of fighting his way back until they were disgorged like stampeding cattle into the waiting corrals of the Customs and Immigration channels. With Ah Lian neither helping nor obstructing, and with his back to the filter wall, he inched his way into the backwater of the platform. When the crowd had thinned he found a long wooden bench, unoccupied. People didn't come to Lo Wu railway station to sit on wooden benches and admire the scenery; the bench was a legacy of the British habit of making all colonial railway stations replicas of Tunbridge Wells station. He sat down gratefully.

Wang and Sonny Chew's brother Rodney sat in a carriage at the rear of the train while Sonny hung out of the door and plotted Kent's progress. It was with relief that he was able to report that Kent and the woman had survived the disembarkation. Before the crowd thinned to a trickle, the three of them left the train and slipped across the platform into the Hong Kong Customs complex, from where, through a venetian-blind-protected window, Wang was able to see Kent and the woman quite clearly.

He was still watching when Kent, after a casual survey of his surroundings, strolled back along the platform to one of the enclosed telephone kiosks.

'I don't suppose,' remarked Wang gloomily, 'there's any way we can listen to what he's saying? And who he's saying it to?' He didn't have to look around for an answer; he could almost hear the two heads behind him shaking.

Then Rodney said, 'Why don't we ask him?'

'Don't be bl – ' Sonny stopped in mid-expletive as he watched Wang stiffen and slowly turn.

'What a bloody good idea!'

'How?' asked Sonny.

'Tell him,' said Wang.

Rodney came and joined Wang at the window. With his finger he gently lowered one of the blind's segments and gazed up and down the, for the moment, almost deserted platform.

'When they finish with the phone and go back to their bench I wander along and ask them what they're doing sitting around making the station look untidy.' He turned round and gazed innocently at Wang. 'Something like that, Mr Wang?'

Wang smiled cherubically and nodded to Sonny. 'Thank God your father was given the good fortune to produce at least one intelligent son.' He continued to beam. 'I want to talk to him, Rodney, but out of sight of the woman. How about checking their passports and finding something not quite right with them?' He didn't tell Rodney Chew that there was nothing right about them in case Rodney suddenly remembered where and what he was. 'She could be taken to the women's section, pending verification. And he . . . well, you don't need me to teach you how to peel the skin off a banana, do you, Rodney?'

Rodney didn't. 'Leave it up to me.' He started a running commentary. 'Look – they've finished in the phone box. Will they go and sit down or continue into the People's Paradise? They're sitting down again. He's looking at his watch. They've arranged something.'

'Go and do your stuff, Rodney.'

*

Rodney stood outside the door marked CUSTOMS OFFICIALS ONLY until the heads of the two people sitting on the bench turned to inspect him. Then he walked purposefully towards them. Their eyes broke contact. Rodney would have had them on that alone.

'May I ask why you haven't gone across the border?'

Rodney spoke in English to Kent but at the same time studied Ah Lian. She looked straight ahead. This was exactly what she didn't want. She smiled, but before it could take effect on the questioner Kent growled, 'I'm not sure it's any of your business.'

Kent's aggressive attitude was unnecessary, and it was too late for her to repair the damage. She exhaled slowly, just loud enough for Kent to hear, but he wasn't interested in Ah Lian's exasperation. Rodney's good manners remained intact. He took his hand out of his pocket and with finger and thumb held out a small plastic-covered card. There was no need to study it; it was official and it had Rodney's photograph in one corner.

'Customs department,' said Rodney, and after a pause during which he outstared Kent and nodded gently at Ah Lian, added, 'and Immigration. It is my business, so may I see your passport please, sir? Thank you. Yours madam?'

Rodney accepted the two passports but didn't immediately inspect them. He juggled them absent-mindedly, like a card-sharp preparing a fixed deal, first one on top, then, with a flick of the wrist, the other, at the same time staring casually into Kent's face. There was no aggression in his manner. Rodney Chew was a perfect, and well-trained, customs officer and Sonny's boss, Wang, had said to make it authentic – more for the woman's sake than the Englishman's.

'Perhaps I can ask you again, sir – why are you waiting here?'

Kent mentally cursed himself. A simple answer would have sent this persistent little bugger back to his tea and *dim sum*, instead of which here he was, his arse itching with power, about to put him on the rack. He blamed it on jet lag. Blame everything on jet lag! Let's hope he doesn't put those bloody passports through the system. He put on a reasonable, respectful expression. 'We're waiting to meet a friend who's taking us through Shenzhen and then on to Shanghai. We're going for a holiday.'

Rodney nodded encouragingly. Kent smiled sadly.

'But he's been delayed. We thought it more pleasant to wait

here than in the sheds over there.' Kent nodded towards the bridge and the new Shenzhen skyscrapers towering beyond. 'He's going to be about another hour.' Kent looked beyond Rodney, measuring the angle between the telephone box and the door from where Rodney had emerged – he could have been seen – and decided to elaborate. 'I rang his home a few minutes ago. He said about an hour . . .'

Rodney smiled contentedly and glanced down at the two passports in his hand. He opened the top one, Kent's Portland Square forgery, glanced at the photograph, at the page behind it, flicked the pages over, studied the visa for entry to the People's Republic of China, then did the same with Ah Lian's.

'Oh, come on, for Christ's sake!' hissed Wang from behind the venetian blind. 'What's your bloody brother up to?' he said, without looking round at Sonny. 'Does he think he's auditioning for a fucking *wayang*? Why doesn't he get on with it and bring them in here?'

Sonny Chew smiled at the back of the fat Chinese's head. 'That's what you have to put up with, Mr Wang, when you're dealing with the intelligent member of the family! He's forgotten we're bouncing sticks – he thinks it's the real thing.'

'Shhh! Here they come.'

'I think . . .' said Rodney, not looking up at Kent but speaking to his slightly fuzzy Instamatic image on the first page of the passport. '. . . that I'd like to have a longer look at both these.' Before Kent could object he flicked it shut and closed his fingers over the two passports. But the game had to be continued. 'You can ring your friend in Shenzhen from my office if you like, just in case he gets worried if you're a bit late yourself.'

'I don't think that'll be necessary, thank you.' Ah Lian, tight-lipped, decided to take over the public relations. She didn't look at Kent. She wanted to spit.

Rodney took them into a bare, hardboard partitioned waiting room. There was nothing in it except a table, four collapsible chairs, a calendar on the wall and a dog-eared poster warning of the consequences of border violation which looked as if it had been there since the reopening of the frontier in 1979.

'What about your luggage?' asked Rodney.

Kent held up his plastic bag. Ah Lian told him she had a wardrobe in Shenzhen. Rodney didn't pursue the matter.

'Please sit down,' he told them. 'I shan't be long.' And then they were alone.

It wasn't necessary for Ah Lian's finger to brush delicately across her lips. Kent had no intention of conversation. He was still cursing his impatience and stupidity in putting up the back of the man who'd gone to expose two interesting passport forgeries. They sat in silence. But not for long.

Rodney returned. Wherever he'd been it hadn't taken five minutes. But Kent wasn't suspicious. Ah Lian might have been but she didn't show it, though her eyebrows rose when a muscular Chinese female in a khaki skirt and a tunic with shiny silver-metal sergeant's stripes on one arm followed him into the room.

'Would you go with the sergeant, please, madam,' said Rodney. It might have sounded like a request but Rodney gave Ah Lian no chance to test it. 'There are certain formalities.' He stood aside for Ah Lian to study the sergeant. She was a big woman for a Chinese, and the peasant stock shone through her glowing, healthy but cold and friendless face. 'Please take . . .' Rodney glanced down, unnecessarily, at Ah Lian's passport. '. . . Madame Ah Lian to the ladies' section. I'll join you when I've finished with Mr Kent.' He turned back to Ah Lian and smiled sympathetically. It was genuine. Rodney Chew was very much an older-woman man, and beautiful elegant ones figured prominently in his unfulfilled fantasies. He'd got it all here. Pity it was a wrong 'un! 'It will be more comfortable there, and there's a ladies' room,' he added, overdoing the solicitude.

'Is all this absolutely necessary?' Ah Lian had locked into Rodney's soft spot. There was a lot of promise in her question – it amounted almost to bribery – but Rodney didn't respond. 'I'll be with you in a moment, Sergeant,' he said and closed the door behind the two women. 'Now, Mr Kent,' he said, 'will you come with me, please?'

Kent followed Rodney along a corridor and, accepting the young Customs officer's invitation, stepped through the door he was holding open. An office, this one, a direct contrast to the box he'd just left, solid and by frontier standards comfortable, with, sitting in an overstuffed leather armchair, a thinner, younger version of the man who'd brought him here.

There was another man in the room.

This one sat with his back to the window on an uncomfortable wooden straight-backed chair, and through the window the sun, obstructed only by the open slats of the venetian blind, cut a halo round his head, blanking out his face. But there was no mistaking the rest of him. Kent tried not to show surprise.

Wang stood up and moved to the other side of the room so that the sun was now in his face.

'Sonny, close that blind, there's a good chap, and I suggest you go and have a cup of tea with Rodney. I'll see that Mr Kent doesn't run away!' There was a titter of polite laughter and the two young Chews left the room.

'D'you want a drink, David?'

Kent continued staring at the fat Chinese.

Wang wasn't put out. Whisky all right for you?'

There was a thermos jug of water on a small table positioned on the visitor's side of the desk and on either side of this was a chair. It was very cosy; you could sit and touch knees as you chatted. Wang poured two measures from his inevitable bottle of duty-free Teacher's, then came round and lowered himself into one of the chairs and began to unscrew the thermos.

'Water, David?'

Kent nodded and sat down, watching as Wang measured water into the two glasses. When he was satisfied with the quantities Wang pushed one across to Kent and said, 'Evelyn Woodhouse is very cross with you, David.' He sipped his drink and pursed his lips in approval. 'You pinched a file from the Foreign Office Registry. Everybody's jumping up and down – apparently it's quite irreplaceable – "Y" box, duck-egg blue, Top Secret and all that! Very naughty, David. They – that's Evelyn and his friends – think you've turned Cambridge and are going over the bridge. Either that or you're selling and going to retire in Tasmania.'

Kent stared at Wang's invisible eyes. He didn't know whether to laugh, scream or run out onto the railway track and empty the sudden overfill of his bladder. Instead, he sat still with his hand grasped round the thick tumbler and then shook his head. It was an effort to remain calm. But he did.

'Fuck off, Wang!' That helped a little bit.

'Pardon?'

'I said, fuck off. There's no money involved – it's a straight swap.' He'd got over the shock of seeing Wang Peng Soon running the Lo Wu Customs Service and the fright Rodney had given him over the passport. Now he was angry – and felt a different sort of fright. He drank his glass of whisky and water in three gulps and slid it the short distance to Wang's side of the table. Wang automatically poured a measure, slid the glass back and pushed the water thermos so that it stood beside it.

'And you know it,' said Kent as he poured water into his whisky. 'And so does Fylough, or whatever he calls himself when he's not doing theatrical tandems with Woodhouse. He was there, in the room, when it was set up.'

'Fylough won't be able to help you out, David, he's dead.'

Kent wasn't particularly concerned. He didn't even pause for a moment's requiem. 'They've got Hilary West over there.' He waved his glass in the direction of China. 'And I'm buying her back.' He took another large swig of whisky and stared defiantly at Wang. 'Simple as that.'

Wang shook his head sadly. 'Sorry, David. Hilary West doesn't meet the value of the missing file. That's top brass assessment. Woody's not too pleased with you, and he's sent me to relieve you of the Foreign Office's documents and take them back to London.'

Kent didn't laugh outright. 'D'you mind getting to the point, Wang, and telling me what the bloody hell you're doing here at the arsehole of the Empire with those two Katzenjammer kids? And please don't say coincidence.'

Wang fixed him with an apologetic smile. It went on for quite a long time, but it didn't embarrass Kent; he concentrated on studying the contents of his glass of whisky until Wang let out a heavy sigh. 'I followed you here, David, because I felt sorry for you. I think you've taken too much on to yourself, but I've developed this soft spot for you – I'm like that, I make these quick assessments of people. It's a flaw in my character, I know, but I don't think it's letting me down in this case. I like you David . . .'

'Whatever bit of bullshit you're trying to put across, Wang, would you mind getting on with it and getting to the point?'

Wang didn't take umbrage. 'I was hot-headed like you when I

was your age – OK, sorry, I know, you're in a hurry! Look, I think Woodhouse and his friends have used you; in fact, I rather think they've dropped you in the shit, and Hilary too, and I've got a soft spot for her as well, so, as I don't agree with nice young people being dropped in the shit, I'm going to help you get the best of both worlds.' Wang emptied his glass and placed it gently back on the table. It seemed that cocktail time was finished for the day, or at least for this part of it. Wang looked as though he was about to pull on his boiler suit and pick up his bucket and chamois. 'It's not going to be easy. We've got to satisfy Mr Woodhouse so that he'll call his Rottweilers off you and at the same time bring Hilary over here so that she and the pale blue file can board the train to Hung Hom on the same side of the bridge.'

Kent glanced sharply at Wang. 'That's what I had in mind.'

'And how were you going to do it?'

'Christ knows. I thought I'd cross that bridge when I came to it.'

Wang shook his head. 'Very professional! Very English!' He wasn't being insulting. 'Those people over there, waiting to see how you play chess without first studying the board, didn't learn their manners on the playing fields of Eton. You go strolling on to that bridge and you'll wake up lying on your face in the Customs shed with a Shike 51 shoved in your ear. Once they've got their hands on that file they'll let you sit up and watch them toss Hilary in front of the next through train to Guangzhou.'

Kent's expression didn't change. 'Well, they're not going to let her stroll across the bridge. I'm going to have to go one way or the other.'

Wang shook his head.

Kent did the same but with a different meaning. 'There's no point sitting there wagging your chins at me, Wang. You haven't seen a copy of the contract. I have, and right at the bottom, between the signature and the first line of small print, it says that unless this file . . .' he jerked his chin at the small plastic bag, '. . . with its contents – originals untouched – is handed over to one Kim Cheong, Hilary West will be sent over on the last through train tonight and her hands'll come on the first one tomorrow morning.'

Wang smiled kindly. 'We Chinese love the dramatic gesture, David. Nobody's going to chop anybody's hands off.'

'Somebody chopped off Kim Cheong's.'

Wang's expression didn't change. 'That was different – that was war.'

'Go on!'

'If you ring your friend Kim Cheong again and say "Sorry, old boy, the deal's off, no file, we're all going home", the worst they would do with her is stick her in the "grass basket" in Peking and we, er . . . I mean Woodhouse and his friends, would negotiate a swap.'

'Nothing doing!' Kent downed the last of his whisky and skidded the glass across the small table where, with a noisy clink, it came to rest alongside the water thermos. 'I wouldn't trust Evelyn St John Woodhouse, or any of his friends, to negotiate a passage across a zebra crossing for me. And if you don't mind my saying so, I don't think this is any of your bloody business! Why don't you bugger off?'

Wang still didn't take offence. He reached down and brought his briefcase up to the table. He opened it and took out a newspaper-wrapped packet. There were traces of oil just beginning to smudge the paper; it looked like a bundle of fish and chips. But it wasn't. He dropped it on the table with a solid clunk and without a word pushed it across to Kent.

Kent didn't touch it.

'Unwrap it,' said Wang.

Kent leaned forward. It was a Hong Kong newspaper – yesterday's. Definitely not fish and chips. He opened it slowly. It was a lightweight, short-barrelled .32 Special. He looked closer without touching. It had been messed about. He picked it up and studied it: an adapted S&W, no number, no name, no pack drill! Definitely anonymous – untraceable. He flicked open the cylinder. It was full: six rounds. He clicked it shut, tucked it into his belt and closed his jacket over it. Nothing showed. But his satisfaction was only skin-deep. The weapon was a small advantage, which advanced him nowhere. It improved the position – slightly. But it didn't solve it.

'You're going to need that.' Wang studied Kent's face for several seconds as if debating in his mind his next line of argument, then decided. 'OK, David, if you're determined to go ahead and try a double-cross on the bridge I'll help you.'

'Why?'

'I've just told you – I like you. I must also be moving into my second bloody childhood! Right, first of all, if you're going to play cards with Peking Chinamen you'll need backup. You're going to need not only somebody covering your back but someone with his arm round your shoulder and his hand in your pocket to stop them lifting your wallet. D'you know how many you're dealing with?'

'Kim Cheong said just him – and Ah Lian, who'll be over here with me.'

Wang sighed and shook his head. 'You can multiply that by ten. And if you wait until the next vegetable train disgorges and watch from here you'll see what I mean. There'll be a thousand Chinese wandering about out there. Try and count how many are on your side and how many queue up outside the back door of Gonganbu's Dong Chanon Avenue entrance for their wages! You rang Kim Cheong from over there?' Wang didn't indicate where over there was; there was only one telephone on this side of the track. 'I presume he was in Shenzhen?'

'That was the number he gave me when I was in Hong Kong. Incidentally – '

Wang forestalled him. 'Yes. I had you covered in the Orchid, and looked after your rear when you went to Queen's Road. But we'll discuss the wheres and whyfores some other time. In the meantime, what arrangements have you made so far?'

'I'm to wait on the platform until after the next non-through train has cleared its passengers and I'll be joined by a man who will call himself Bang.'

'Just Bang?' interrupted Wang. 'Nothing else?'

'That's all he said.'

'Go on.'

'This Bang will inspect the contents of the file and if he's satisfied that they're authentic he'll suggest a hand-over formula.'

Wang glanced at the clock on the wall, then at his wrist, as if doubting one or the other, and said, 'I reckon that gives us about ten minutes to get ourselves organised. Keep that gun of yours out of sight. What we need is something else for him to look at to show that you're not a boy who's just tasting his first banana. Stay where you are for a second.' He lumbered to his feet and opened the door. There was somebody just round the corner. One of the Chews was taking no chances. 'D'you know Sergeant Sonny

Chew?' asked Wang of the unseen guard. 'Good! Go and get him. Quickly, please.'

Sonny sidled into the room, but he didn't sit down. The conversation he had with Wang was rapid, one-sided and on his part limited to affirmative grunts and nods of the head. When he'd gone Wang sat down and looked longingly at the bottle of Teacher's, but fought the temptation. He didn't have to fight long. Chew came back within a few minutes and placed, gingerly, on the small table between Wang and Kent, a white, green-striped cylindrical grenade. Beside it, but not touching, he placed with equal delicacy its U-shaped fuse. Then he stood back out of the way. For once Sonny Chew didn't look happy.

'Paint's still wet,' he informed Wang. 'But it's quick-dry – give it five minutes and it'll be bone dry.'

'Thanks,' said Wang and dragged his eyes away from it to smile at Kent, who'd instinctively pushed himself back into his chair to put a few more inches between his face and the grenade. 'It's a little bit over its sell-by date,' he said unconcernedly, 'but I think it's safe enough. It's Chinese Army, coloured for phosphorous, which is banned, as I'm sure you know.'

Kent didn't. And he didn't like the sound of it, or its proximity. 'But it's not what it seems. It's smoke – heavy, dense smoke on a three-second fuse – just in case you need to duck out of trouble. Hopefully, your Mr Bang will know all about phosphorus grenades. Tell him you'll pull the pin and throw it and the bag on to the railway track. He'll know what phosphorus'll do to the contents of that bag – it'll turn it into ashes – not to mention what it'll do to his facial hair!'

'Or mine,' suggested Kent.

'It's only smoke,' Wang reminded him, 'but if he does start on the arm-bending stuff it'll give you the wherewithal to get out of his way. The important thing is that you make sure he gets a good look at its markings, which'll banish any thoughts of his shooting you and wandering off across the bridge with Woody's papers.' He smiled cheerfully, and allowed the smile to reach his eyes. 'But whatever you do, make sure your cheerful lady companion doesn't get a sight of it. We don't want her wondering what sort of company you've been mixing with while she's been answering questions about her passport, do we? Get her out of the way, tell

363

her to go for a walk before you start flashing things under Mr Bang's nose.'

Kent reached out and touched the grenade. It was still tacky, but drying rapidly. He looked much happier. He stuck his little finger in the ring and twisted the grenade round, studying it from different angles.

'And I go along with anything he proposes?'

Wang's smile vanished. 'Within reason, David, within reason. I wouldn't like to see you vanishing across the bridge in front of Mr Bang with his hand thrust between your legs! Listen to his proposals while you twirl this around from its ring, and then tell him – whatever he suggests – that you want half an hour to consider your feelings over the matter.'

'What if he doesn't agree? What if he wants the change-over there and then?'

'You tell him to get stuffed.'

'What about Hilary?'

'Stop worrying about Hilary. This file's worth more to them than she is: in fact she's worth bugger-all to them. She'll be there, so don't give it another thought.' He reached out and touched the body of the grenade. 'That's nice and dry now. Marvellous stuff this modern paint.' He picked it up, unscrewed its bottom and without fuss manoeuvred the fuse into its bed. He tapped it lightly, pressed it home with his finger and screwed back the base. He held it in his hand for a second as if judging its weight, then, without warning, tossed it to Sonny Chew. Sonny juggled it for a few seconds and, slightly white-faced, hugged it to his bosom. 'Jesus!'

'Rub it against something, Sonny – distress it. It looks as though it's just come out of the joke shop. What's the matter? You not feeling well?'

Ah Lian had been treated with the utmost courtesy. But she was angry. Fortunately. The anger blanked out any suspicion she might have had about the way they'd been plucked off the platform, the separation from Kent, and the interminable wait with this fat lump dressed as a policewoman while her false passport was checked for flaws. The wait seemed never-ending. She heard the next train pull in and the cacophony of noise that followed it and then the uncanny still and silence when the mass

364

had cleared the platform. It was during this silence that the Customs officer returned and handed her back her passport. She waited for the caution, the raised eyebrows and supercilious smile, and the arrest. But they didn't come. A polite smile, an apology and the big peasant sergeant held the door open for her and accompanied her along the corridor to the room she'd been sitting in earlier with Kent.

He was still there, and in front of him, on the rickety fold-up table, was an ashtray that hadn't been there before. It held several half-smoked cigarettes and one still smouldering, its thin blue cotton-like thread bending ever so slightly off the perpendicular as she entered the room and disturbed the still air. She said nothing. Neither did he until they were back sitting on their lonely bench on the main platform.

'Did they ask you any questions?' Kent said out of the corner of his mouth.

'They took my passport – they asked me nothing. Incompetent fools!' She seemed quite happy with her escape; happy was better than doubt. She turned her head away and set her lips in their normal hard line. When she turned her head back to watch the bridge Hu Bang was standing beside her. He'd appeared as if from nowhere.

One minute they were sitting, two unfriendly strangers thrown together in a foreign railway station, the next they were three.

Hu Bang looked through her. His attention was directed at Kent alone and without invitation he sat down beside him and gazed across the river of unmoving steel lines, then said casually, 'My name's Bang. Yours is Kent. You've already spoken to Kim Cheong.'

Kent looked first at Ah Lian. 'Go for a walk,' he told her. 'This is private.' She didn't move immediately but looked at the old man. He nodded his head slightly and, ungraciously, she stood up and strolled to the far end of the station. Only when she'd left did Kent turn and study the new arrival. He didn't know what he'd been expecting but it was certainly not an eighty-year-old pensioner. He allowed his surprise to show, but there was no rebuke from Hu Bang. He wasn't interested in the reactions of messenger boys – from whatever Intelligence agency.

*

But Wang Peng Soon was.

His eye, peering through the thin slit of the venetian blind, narrowed with interest as he studied Kent's new companion.

'D'you know who that is?' he asked Sonny Chew standing beside him.

Sonny widened the crack slightly. 'Mao Tse-tung's great-grandfather?'

Sonny Chew's humour ran off Wang's back, but he didn't rebuke him. 'It's Hu Bang, one of the last of the Long Marchers – one of the few left who can remember what it's like to eat boiled worms on toast for breakfast. The great survivor. He had to be, didn't he? He killed most of the other poor old buggers.'

Sonny's interest was aroused. 'Why?'

'He was bodyguard to Mao Tse-tung and then chief assassin for the old schemer's TEWA. You've heard of Pol Pot?'

'Who hasn't!'

'Compared to old Hu Bang, Pol Pot is about as nasty as a milk monitor in a girls' boarding school.'

'What's he doing on Lo Wu station?'

'You might well ask. I hope young Kent doesn't try to take any liberties with him.' But Wang didn't have the expression of a worried man; if anything, he looked almost contented – just short of smug.

Hu Bang stared into the plastic bag held open by David Kent. Through his milk-bottle bottoms he studied the grenade, minus pin, held with the lever pressed against the side by Kent's hand.

'It's phosphorus,' Kent told him, and with his hand still in the bag turned it over so that Hu Bang could study the markings on its side. He watched the old man's reactions closely. He needn't have bothered. There were none.

'You're right,' said Hu Bang when he raised his head. His English was rusty but not without quality.

'Nasty stuff, phosphorus,' Kent reminded him, 'and this one's on a three-second fuse. The file would go up in ashes and you wouldn't get as far as the bridge entrance . . .' He left the threat unfinished. Hu Bang merely shrugged his shoulders and looked back into the bag.

'Show me the file.'

*

Kent remained seated as he watched the old Chinese amble back along the platform and disappear across the bridge.

'Who is he?' he asked Ah Lian when she rejoined him on the bench.

'It's none of your business who he is,' she retorted. 'He's important, that's enough for you. What did he say? What arrangements has he agreed to? How are you going to hand over the file?'

Kent didn't look at her. 'It's none of your business.'

'Where are you going?' she hissed. Kent had stood up. He looked down the track at the twin lines that disappeared into the sky, and then glanced at his wrist. 'Telephone,' he told her. 'Your grandfather took the number of that phone over there. He's gone to discuss arrangements with Kim Cheong. You'd better come with me – I think the people here must be wondering what the bloody hell's going on. I don't want that stupid, drooling youth to come around again with his silly questions, so stand in the phone box and make it look as if you're talking to your missing relatives in the *padi* fields.'

But there was no need for her to pretend. The phone rang once, just as they reached it.

Ah Lian spoke briefly, then handed the receiver to Kent. He told her to wait further along the platform. She seemed on the point of mutiny but after a few seconds' stand-off moved out of earshot and stood under the shade of the station awning where she studied the Hong Kong Tourist Board's latest offerings. She'd read them all and committed them to memory when she saw Kent leave the phone box and look at his watch again.

'Are we going across the bridge?' she asked hopefully.

He shook his head.

'What then?'

'Do you know a man named Fang Longzhen?'

'No. Why, should I?'

'He's a Customs official, he's taking us out of the station. He seems to be one of your people – planted. You sure you don't know him?'

'Quite sure. What then?'

'That's all you need to know. Go and wait in there.' Kent pointed to a brightly lit but unpatronised self-service cafeteria. 'I'll be with you in a moment.'

She didn't move. Her eyes flashed suspiciously. 'Where are you going?'

'Don't ask so many bloody questions.'

'I repeat – '

'I'm going to the bloody lavatory. Now, get in there and wait for me. Act natural, if you can. Drink a cup of tea . . .'

'Are you going to be long?'

Kent didn't answer. Under her suspicious gaze he walked briskly along the platform. As he passed the window with the slatted blinds he gave a slight nod of his head. He didn't look directly at the window; he took it for granted that Wang would be glued to the position.

He was right.

Wang sidled up alongside him and undid his flies. For a Chinese lavatory it was clean, bright and had an overpowering smell of raw antiseptic. Things would be going rapidly downhill from here on in.

'You meet the most interesting people in Lo Wu pisshouse,' said Wang, without a smile, and told him what he'd told Sonny Chew about Hu Bang. Kent's interest was nominal; he was being polite. But he was in a hurry.

He broke into Wang's story without apology. 'Mr Bang was very interested in the contents of the file.'

'He said so?'

'No. But he took a long time studying them. He particularly liked the photograph and the *This Is Your Life* folder of Lee Yuan, the future Chairman of the Communist Party and Leader of the People's Republic. He couldn't put it down.'

'Did he invite you to go to China with him?'

'Sure. But I didn't fancy it. He suggested a hand-over midway on the bridge, but I turned it down.'

'Why?'

'You've seen that bridge? It's as straight as a bloody rifle barrel. In fact it's like being *in* a bloody rifle barrel! There's nowhere to hide. All it needs is some "careless" bloody pongo to "accidently" let off his T56 and that bloody funnel would be showered with thirty unfriendly rounds of copper-nosed 7.62.'

'Very instructive, David. Did you show him your "phosphorus" bomb?'

'Yes. He didn't seem terribly interested. He didn't wee himself either.'

'So how did you leave it?'

'I kept my legs crossed and kept saying no until his final option.'

'And that was?' Now Wang was getting impatient.

'An outside rendezvous. Do you know Muk Wu?'

Wang shook his head. 'But Sonny will – so will Rodney.'

Kent allowed himself a little smug satisfaction. 'Muk Wu's a dead-end crossing that everybody turns a blind eye to, provided the crossing's being done with an official nod and wink – on our side, that is. As a secret crossing place it's about as inconspicuous as Checkpoint Charlie. It's like a major freeway, but nobody notices it. Mr Bang said he'd clear his side but ours would have to be shifty. He said not to worry because he could arrange for Ah Lian and myself to clear the station and move across the "closed area" and through the wire.'

Wang stared down between his legs and asked, 'How was he going to do that?'

'A Hong Kong Customs officer named Fang Longzhen is going to arrange it. He was going to be contacted by Kim Cheong, who would then ring me to confirm the arrangements. He's just done that. I've now got wait for this Fang Longzhen to come and whisper his ideas into my ear.'

Wang bent his knees and did up his zip. 'Go along with everything he says. I'll get Rodney to make sure there are no hitches. We'll let Mr Fang think he's sitting on feathers for the time being and Sonny can sort him out sometime in the future. You're going to hand this file over in Chinese no-man's-land and bring Hilary back under your arm. Is that it? Have you got any plans for bringing back the file as well?'

Kent shook his head. 'I'll play it by ear. You'll be there, of course?'

Wang smiled. 'Of course. Play straight with them when the times comes. Make sure you've got Hilary on the firm ground on our side, hand the file over and leave the rest to me. Push off now and meet your new friend. Don't forget, do as he tells you – and don't keep looking over your shoulder!'

369

42

Another time and under different circumstances Kent would have enjoyed the drive through the rough countryside. It was drawing towards dusk and a huge orange-coloured sun, still and shimmering, touched the horizon, and then suddenly, as if it had had enough of that day, began to drop with alarming speed into somebody else's dawn. The road, straight and featureless, stretched into the darkening distance and behind, nothing – except a swirling brown dust that shielded another, slower moving, unlighted Land Rover.

Rodney Chew kept the Customs and Excise vehicle just in sight.

There weren't many roads it could turn off and the thick, penetrating cloud of slow-settling dust and laterite eased the need for concentration and allowed him to watch his rear with more attention than he would normally employ. But he could relax; there was nothing on the road behind them. Wang, by his side, was quiet, contemplative. He was contented with his thoughts and sucked gently on a newly lighted cigarette. Sonny, lounging on the sack seat coughed his discomfort, but it had no effect on Wang. Wang was in limbo, somewhere where everything went according to plan. He wasn't sure it was here – but it was a good substitute.

'Don't strain your eyes, Rodney,' he murmured. 'There's no need to break the Lo Wu to Muk Wu record. Give them time to get there and settle down. Slow down a bit.'

Rodney did as he was told.

Like Wang, Kent also lit a cigarette. He didn't offer one to his driver; it wouldn't have gone with the uniform. Neither would he have accepted it.

The Customs officer wasn't happy to have his cover exposed to the *kwai lo* – the white man, the Englishman – the enemy. Fang Longzhen was a true son of the revolution; he didn't fraternise. And he didn't talk. He sat driving carefully, watching for the signs of ambush.

He continued past the junction leading to the Man Kam To border with its solidly manned police post and carried on for half a mile before taking the left fork to Muk Wu. He skirted the built-up area, slipped into a dead-end gravel road and turned right, following the road as far as he could go. It deteriorated into a track.

Fang stopped the Land Rover and switched off the engine. He pointed through the windscreen and said in English to Kent: 'Three hundred yards is the border fence. Don't make a sound – there are soldiers every mile or so in ambush positions.' He waggled his finger up and down nervously. 'Through there is a gap in a section of the wire that has had its sensor bypassed. There will be somebody in the grass near the gap to open it for you. He will take you to a quarry on this side of the river. Kim Cheong will be waiting there. Those were his instructions. In half an hour it will be dark. I will wait until then to take you back.' He looked over his shoulder and said in *putonghua*, 'Will you go with him, madam? Will you come back here, or stay with Kim Cheong?'

'Don't ask stupid questions.' Ah Lian's disposition remained ugly. Nobody was exempt.

Wang eased back the side window and dropped his spent cigarette on the edge of the road.

'Why have we stopped, Rodney?' he asked as he peered about him. In front was a large fish pond, the trailings of an unsurfaced road to the right, and not a soul in sight.

Rodney didn't look round. He stared straight ahead, whilst from the back of the Land Rover Sonny came forward, crouched on his knees, spread his arms across the backs of both front seats and, like his brother, surveyed the road before them.

'The road finishes round that bend.' Rodney lowered his voice automatically to a harsh whisper. 'Then there's a track that leads to the fence. The same track continues into the People's Republic. There's a quarry not too far inside – I reckon that's where your friend's breaking the law.'

Wang didn't speak for a moment. He stared straight ahead, as if trying to see round the corner, but he'd thought about it – and decided.

'How far up the track will that other Land Rover get?' he asked Rodney.

'It won't,' replied Rodney instinctively. 'It'll be parked just round that bend. D'you want us to move up behind it?'

'No, not just yet. Sonny, go and have a look – see if the Customs man's anywhere about. He may not have gone with Kent and the woman.'

'And if he hasn't?' Sonny was already climbing out of the Land Rover. 'Shall I bring him back here for you to talk to?'

'No.' Wang looked sharply at the young man. 'Attend to him.'

'All the way?'

'All the way,' repeated Wang. 'With extreme prejudice!' Wang chuckled as Sonny waggled his finger through the windscreen. He stuck his head out of the side window and hissed, 'Silently!' The chuckle still lingered on his lips as he followed Sonny's progress up the road, then he said out of the corner of his mouth, 'You don't mind if a vacancy arises in the Lo Wu branch of HM Customs and Excise, do you, Rodney?'

Rodney wasn't concerned about vacancies. He said, 'What does "extreme prejudice" mean?'

Wang didn't answer; he was concentrating on the bend in the road.

Sonny reached the bend and went down on his knees and peered round the corner. The Customs Land Rover was about eighty yards away, not parked but stopped where the road deteriorated into a dusty, heavily rutted track. He could see the driver's elbow resting on the open window and every so often a head half-turned and a little puff of cigarette smoke wheezed out of the window.

Sonny slid the short-barrelled Police Special from its small holster on his belt, eased back the hammer, and lined himself up with the back of Land Rover. A quick, instinctive glance over his shoulder, and on the balls of his feet he tiptoed the short distance to the parked vehicle.

The driver didn't hear a thing until Sonny's warning hissed into his ear.

'Don't move!'

There was nothing wrong with Fang's nerves. He didn't go through the roof. He sat like a statue, a smoking statue, the cigarette being carried to his lips held unwaveringly by the two fingers of his left hand just short of its objective, sending an erratic stream of smoke into his eyes. But he didn't flinch, he didn't blink – the only thing that moved were the stinging tears from his smoke-choked eyes. A little more pressure and the muzzle of Sonny's revolver pressed harder into the soft spot behind his right ear.

Then Sonny hissed again: 'Lower your hand. Drop the cigarette.' Sonny stepped back, the pistol at the end of his straight arm pointing at the Customs officer's face. 'Turn your head. Look at me.' Fang did as he was told. 'Open the door – slowly. Get out. Turn round and put your hands against the side and spread your legs.' Fang expected to feel hands run over his body and prepared his counter-attack. It didn't happen like that.

Sonny, with the pistol still at arm's length, still pointing at the back of Fang's head, moved round the Land Rover, opened the door, groped with his hand in the back and removed one of the cushions from the rear seat.

'Stand still,' he whispered and moved to within two feet of Fang. He stopped. Fang remained still, rock steady, his legs apart and arms outstretched, but his eyes alert and his ears straining.

Without moving, Sonny leaned forward, held the cushion up in line with Fang's head, jammed the muzzle of the pistol into it and squeezed the trigger.

The cushion took most of the sharpness out of the explosion. The thump was loud, but not loud enough to carry more than a hundred and fifty yards.

It was loud enough for the sound to reach Wang and Rodney.

Both appeared almost immediately. Wang with a pistol held loosely at his side, Rodney unarmed, staring with a mixture of horror and fascination at his younger brother preparing to give the dying driver another shot. But it wasn't necessary. Sonny straightened up and lowered the hammer of his revolver. He replaced the round he'd used and tucked the weapon back in its holster. Rodney was amazed. It was the first time he'd seen his little brother at work – Sonny's hand wasn't even shaking.

Wang wasted no time on the body by the Land Rover. He nodded his approval to Sonny and put his arm round Rodney's shoulder. He pointed at the crumpled heap on the floor.

'That's what's meant by "extreme prejudice",' he said.

Kent, with Ah Lian close behind, slid down the crumbling slope and came to a stop beside the huge chain-link, barbed-wire-topped curtain.

'Wait here,' he whispered and moved a few yards to his right. He studied the wire closely without touching. It was taut. There was no gap, no gate – not in this spot. Nor a smiling guide from the People's Republic. He waited a few seconds, listening to the silence and the overture to the frogs' evening performance, then moved back to his starting point.

'What's the matter? What's happening?' hissed Ah Lian. For once he detected a note of anxiety in her voice. But it didn't help him. He felt exactly the same. He didn't answer, but inched his way in the opposite direction another five or six yards, and waited again.

'Psst!'

The sound came from just beside his ankles.

He stared into the undergrowth, and after a moment his eyes picked out the broken silhouette of a soft-capped head. The wire near the head opened on concealed hinges. A man stood at a half-crouch, holding back the almost invisible gate for Kent to duck through. 'This way,' he murmured and allowed it to flip back into place. He spoke in Cantonese.

The track was well defined and the wooden bridge over the river was solid and steady. They made no noise as they crossed and then, like a disturbed ghost, the guide disappeared. Kent stopped dead and reached for his revolver, but before he could bring it from his belt the man's head reappeared, this time at ground level. He'd slid over the lip of a gravel quarry, still in use except for the narrow ledge on which Kent stood, where undergrowth had been allowed to re-establish itself. To his right, full of the reflection of the darkening dusk clouds, the sprawling expanse of water collected in a man-made lake shimmered with a gentle breeze that nipped over the lip and whispered to the edge where the gravel rose in an unintended barrier.

Kent stopped dead again, and remained still. He tried not to stare as he searched for the source of the single brief reflection that had flicked across his eye. It had not been from the water.

On the rise to his right he could just make out the flat top of a vehicle. Carelessly hidden, it should have been parked another three feet away to have made it completely invisible from his side

374

of the quarry. But the damage had been done. He caught the reflection again in the corner of his eye. Windscreen? No. Binoculars? Not quite . . . There it was again. Now the corner of his eye sharpened the image: the last glimmer of the dying sun was being reflected from a pair of spectacle lenses shaped like a couple of milk-bottle bottoms and pushed up on to a stubbly grey head. Hu Bang was studying the killing zone through military binoculars.

And who was going to do the shooting? Kent followed his guide another few yards, then stopped. A new angle. He crouched and retied his shoe lace, then glanced again – and there it was! Lying at the old man's feet like a football waiting for the kick-off was the round shape of an uncovered head. And just below that, the miniature black matt pyramid of a telescope unit mounted on a sniper rifle. He could almost feel the cross-hairs on the side of his face.

'Wait here . . .' The Chinese guide continued to walk towards the edge of the quarry, where it began to slope upwards to the unexploited scrubland. Before he reached it, two figures detached themselves from another car. This, a saloon, black or dark blue, was parked without attempt at concealment.

One of the figures was a woman. She wore trousers but her hair, long and luxuriant, flowed as she walked. When she saw Kent standing on his own in the middle of the pit she almost broke into a run but one of Kim Cheong's hooks darted out and clutched the crook of her elbow. She gave a tiny squeal – not pain, but the shock of the hook digging into her soft skin.

And then they were only yards away.

Kent tore his eyes away from Hilary and Kim Cheong and, without moving his head, glanced quickly again at the rise. The rifle was rock steady, still pointing directly at him. He turned his back, innocently, on Hu Bang and the gunman and, with his left hand shielded by the plastic bag, grasped the grenade and gently eased the pin out of its housing. He let the pin drop into the bottom of the bag and turned sideways so that the gunman could see his face again. He also made sure Hu Bang could see the grenade in his hand, hovering over the open bag.

'David. . . ?' Hilary's voice was well controlled. He couldn't tell whether she was glad to see him or furious that he'd allowed things to get this far. She took a step towards him.

'Just a moment . . .' Kim Cheong held out his other hook. 'The file, please.'

Kent transferred the bag to his right hand and kept the other hand by his side. He held the bag out to Kim Cheong, straight, his arm level with his chin, and angled it so that it came between his head and the cross-hairs on the telescope. Kim Cheong let go of Hilary's arm and extended his hook for Kent to hang the bag on.

He must have read Kent's eyes.

For a man in his sixties there was nothing wrong with his reflexes. Shouting a warning at the top of his voice he grabbed the bag and threw himself on the ground. He was just in time. Kent loosened his grip on the grenade and the lever flew upwards with a sharp, .22 cartridge crack. He held it for a brief fraction of a second then released it and sent it flying over his head. It wasn't the best throw he'd ever made, but it was good enough to travel about fifteen yards to thump solidly between Kim Cheong, Hilary and himself, and the gunman on the rise. He'd been counting. Three seconds had already gone.

He grabbed Hilary by the waist, dragged her round to his safe side and threw her to the ground. Her scream was only halfway to her throat before the wind was knocked out of her and her eardrums bent inwards.

C-ERACK – WHOOF!

The top exploded off the grenade. It was instantaneous. An eye-searing flash and a complete wall of white, soot-streaked smoke was gushing upwards and outwards like a geyser gone mad. From the other side of the smoke came a clean crack and a bang – almost together – and a lump of sharp gravel detached itself from the ground near Kent's eye and gouged into his cheek. Then another shot – a gentler, more refined crack of a pistol from the same direction. There was nothing wrong with the aim even if it was guesswork. This one whistled between his head and Hilary's shoulder. It was good shooting. Hu Bang had joined the range with a long-barrelled Luger, and he could still shoot. Then a wild shot from the rifle sliced through the thickening cloud of smoke, bounced off a stone and winged into nowhere.

Kim Cheong was the first to recover.

Scrabbling on his knees and clutching the plastic bag he made a dive for the protection of the smoke. But too late. Kent was with him. Dragging himself over Hilary's prostrate body, he launched himself wildly at the disappearing man's shadow. He made contact and hung on, bringing him crashing to his knees. But Kim Cheong was wiry and moved like a sprinter; it was like clutching a newly landed trout. He kicked out and struggled to release himself from Kent's grip, scrabbling with both hooks to find purchase in the gravel. The bag broke and he had no time to get a hook into its other handle, but, with a wild, feet-together double kick and a jerk from his knees, he felt Kent's weight shift from his legs and, twisting his body round, he was almost on his feet again. He reached triumphantly for the bag. But for the second time he was too late. Kent got to it first.

He snatched up the bag, turned, burst out of the fog, and thrust it into Hilary's hand. She was on her knees. He picked her up bodily, turned her in the direction of the wire and shouting in her ear to crouch, pushed her forward out of the smoke. He was a yard behind her and doubled forward, his hands outstretched, urging her on, when, for a fraction of a second, a freak gust of wind blew a hole in the screen.

It happened in a flash. Hu Bang's man was good at his job. His eye was still glued to the sight – it was what he had been waiting for.

BANG!

The heavy bullet slammed into Kent's thigh, shattering the bone and almost splitting him apart as his leg shot out from under him. He had just enough time to stare down at the grotesque angle of his leg before the second shot hit him high up in the right of his chest. The third shot was snatched. It smashed into the gravel by his head, hit a stone, and whined away into the darkening sky. And then, mercifully, the smoke was back, swirling around his head, breaking up his silhouette until stilled, it dropped around him like a blanket.

But he didn't die.

He stared, helpless, at Hilary's shocked face. '*Go!*' he screamed. 'Run! For Christ's sake! *Run!* Get out of it!' But she didn't move; she stood transfixed, with the plastic bag dangling and flapping from her hand, outstretched towards him and shaking like a flag in the wind in time with her uncontrollable nervous reflexes.

377

There was nothing he could do. He began to shiver and his teeth chattered. It was shock. No pain yet, not real pain, but it was on its way. He blinked, but nothing happened. He tried to wipe away the tears with his right hand so that he could focus over her shoulder, but his arm wouldn't move. And then, for a brief lucid moment, the red mist that was taking over his eyes cleared and he saw the other figure in the background. It was closing in rapidly.

'Oh, Christ! Hilary, for God's sake run!'

But it was too late.

Ah Lian, barefooted, ran like the peasant girl she had been long ago and, within ten feet of Hilary's back, launched herself feet first at her unmoving target. She caught Hilary just below the shoulder blades, recovered herself, and, still moving fast, swung her outstretched hand at Hilary's falling body, catching the side of her head with a vicious karate chop. The sound, like a butcher cutting chops, echoed around the smoky pit and Hilary lay where she had dropped, lifeless.

'Oh, Jesus!' He wanted to faint, to sleep – he could feel the warm, beckoning finger and closed his eyes. Then forced then open again. *Not yet. Christ, no! Not yet!* Ah Lian had picked up the bag. *No! Not yet!* He struggled through the oozing pain and got his fingers hooked round the revolver tucked in his belt. Left-handed – unnatural . . . *But you've only got to point it and squeeze the bloody trigger – you're not on the bloody range. Aim between the tits! No time. Aim anywhere!* He did that.

CRACK! CRACK!

Nowhere – she didn't even flinch. And then the pistol, covered in blood, slipped out of his hand. But he wasn't finished. Ah Lian doubled towards him and reached down for the bloody revolver. It was a mistake. She should have picked up her skirts and run.

With a superhuman effort he flung out his left arm, caught her round the neck and locked on. She screamed. He dragged her down across him, still tightening the strangle grip. She struggled and kicked but still he hung on, pressing her face into his chest, ignoring the pain, covering her with his blood until her screams turned to gurgles. He opened his eyes.

He couldn't believe what he was seeing.

Barely visible, little more than a heavy shadow in the dying light, Wang Peng Soon was ambling across the quarry. It was a fast

378

amble, a sort of controlled trot where the feet never left the ground. *Bless you, Wang!* He kept coming and as he closed in Kent could see in his fist the twin brother of the short-barrelled S&W now fallen out of Ah Lian's limp grasp. *Good old Wang!* He raised his head and tried a smile. Wang was almost on top of him. His jaw was set – he was serious. He slowed down and changed step and with perfect balance swung his foot and caught Kent a vicious swipe on the side of the head. Kent's head snapped back and then forward as if his neck was made of rubber, and he stared open-mouthed, the welcome grin for the saviour engraved on his lips. The kick should have finished him. It did – almost. His neck refused to continue and his head dropped into the gravel. He lay on his side and wondered if this was the end of the nightmare – and please could he wake up now?

He opened his eyes and found them level with Wang's dusty black shoe.

Wang reached down and picked up the plastic bag with one finger. For a brief second their eyes met. In Wang's there was no pity, no mercy – nothing. Then Kent looked beyond the black shoe. Wang had timed his entrance perfectly, invisible from the killing crew on the higher ground and unnoticed by Ah Lian, who was on her knees, her face inches from the sandy soil, with whatever she'd had for dinner last night making a little pool in the gravel in front of her. She was in trouble, and there was still more to come as her body heaved and racked. Kent swivelled his eyes back to Wang.

Wang was busy, he had things to do – no time for his friends. He glanced briefly at the woman on her knees; he gave her no more time than he'd given Kent. He turned his back on the two of them and with the bag hanging from one of his chubby fingers, disappeared into the billowing smoke.

But Kent's growing-up pains weren't finished.

He stared uncomprehendingly at the spot where Wang had disappeared – and it happened again. Another brief swirl made a gap in the fog and through the cloud-like screen he could just make out two shadows. Wang and. . .? The evil bastard with the Himmler glasses? No, it wasn't. The smoke swirled again and through the dark grey light not yet entirely banished by the inrushing night, he saw a momentary gleam as a shiny steel hook snaked out from the thinner shadow and grasped firmly the plastic bag held out by Wang. And then the smoke swallowed them up again. He turned his head away and tried to pull himself to his knees.

He wished he hadn't.

Ah Lian was dragging herself towards him. Her face, half covered with red gravel, was distorted and ugly with anger and in her hand was grasped the wet, sticky revolver. She stopped and stared at him, but for only a second. She was trying to tell him something – something not very nice. And when she saw he was watching, and that he was aware of what was happening, she clasped her other hand round the butt of the pistol, pointed it at Hilary's still body, and, with her eyes now locked on his anguished face, pulled the trigger. The gun roared and kicked. He bellowed at the top of his voice – it sounded like an animal in pain. Then he screamed. She pulled the trigger again.

With her eyes still locked on his she continued to crawl towards him, the gun held in front of her, pointing at him. He closed his eyes – he was no longer interested. He knew what she was going to do.

He heard only one thunderous roar in his ear. But he felt no pain. He didn't hear the second explosion.

43

Alone now, Wang stood still, careful not to attract attention to himself until the last of the smoke had vanished to join the dark clouds hanging above his head. His ear was cocked, listening, his expression untroubled.

He heard first the vehicle on the slope to the right start up. Its driver ground the gears like a novice and after a doubtful, skidding reverse it roared round the track on the lip of the quarry to pull up alongside the car from which Hilary and Kim Cheong had earlier emerged.

Without straining his ears he could hear a quick, guttural conversation, with on one occasion the high-pitched voice of Ah Lian joining in. She sounded slightly hysterical and a gruff command silenced her. Then both vehicles moved away in convoy, quietly and without fuss. Nobody had seemed the slightest bit interested in the two bodies lying in the quarry.

As soon as the sound of the vehicles died away Wang moved. And he moved quickly.

First he stooped over David Kent and turned him onto his side. He stuck four chubby fingers into his neck beside the jugular and cocked his head, as if not only feeling but listening for a pulse. After a few seconds he removed Kent's belt and fashioned a tourniquet round the top of his thigh, then, stripping off his bloodied shirt, he made a rough but effective bandage for the gaping wound. It slowed the bleeding, but didn't stop it. He glanced quickly at the chest wound and wiped the blood away with his handkerchief. In the fading light it looked uncomplicated – a clean bullet entry hole into the fleshy part of his upper chest. He pushed the handkerchief into the hole with his finger as far as it would go, then stood up, took off his jacket and draped it over the apparently dead man. As he moved towards Hilary his foot stubbed the little revolver thrown down by Ah Lian as she'd rushed into the enveloping smoke. He stooped down, picked it up by its trigger guard and slipped it into the jacket draped over

Kent's body. He turned and knelt beside Hilary and, with his arm round her shoulders, lifted her to a sitting position. She moaned. It moved something in her throat and made her cough, wakening her. Her eyes opened and she began to scream but Wang's hand clamped lightly over her mouth.

'It's Wang,' he said softly, in case she couldn't see who it was. 'Don't make a noise. We're not out of the woods yet. I'm going to take my hand away from your mouth – don't scream, just lie still.' He took his hand away and she gasped in pain, but kept the scream at bay.

'David?' she hissed.

'Don't worry about David . . .' Wang's hands were gently probing her back. When he reached her shoulder she couldn't control a groan of agony – it came out with a whoosh and the tears gushed. 'Not too bad,' said Wang, partly to himself. 'I think you've got a busted collarbone.'

'Oh, is that *all*!' she gasped through clenched teeth. 'Bugger you, Wang!'

'And two burn marks, one on your neck, from a close-range revolver shot.'

Her eyes closed. 'Do something, Wang! Please!'

'I'm going to pick you up. It'll hurt at first, but try not to make a noise. Here we go . . . OK?'

'Oh, Jesus! Oh, Christ!'

The two young Chews had taken up ambush positions at the end of the track. Wang had expressly forbidden Sonny to make a move towards the fence, regardless of what he heard. Sonny Chew knew better than to go against Chief Superintendent Wang Peng Soon's instructions. But with the shooting and bellowing and screaming which had followed the muffled explosion of the grenade it had taken all his willpower to stay where he was.

'Somebody's coming!' whispered Rodney.

'I hope it's not the bloody Gurkhas!' Sonny silently eased the hammer back on his pistol and moved, at a crouch, onto the edge of the track. But Wang had seen him.

'It's me,' he said hoarsely and fended them off when they rushed forward to take Hilary from him. 'Both of you, get down into that quarry quickly! On a straight line from the gap in the fence you'll find the Englishman. He's been badly hurt – shot . . . Watch his leg, it's in a mess, and he's got another in his chest. But he's alive. Get him up here – and don't make a bloody noise! Just a minute!'

The two Chews stopped in their tracks.

Wang looked over his shoulder at the dead Customs officer lying by the Land Rover's front wheel. 'Take that with you and dump it near some of Kent's blood. I want them to think they've shot him as well – by mistake. Go on! Get on with it!'

They lay the unconscious Kent carefully on the floor of the Land Rover and covered him with their coats. He could have been dead. He probably was in his mind, but at one frame in the nightmare, when the two slightly built Chinese hauling their difficult load through the wire bumped him on the ground, a groan broke through his lips. It was a groan from deep down, and when he opened his eyes briefly and saw nothing but darkness to go with the swaying of his body he relaxed and went to sleep again, knowing that he was eleven years old, on holiday, and on the roller-coaster at Yarmouth with Uncle Teddy. Only he wished he hadn't eaten so much candyfloss and coconut ice because he felt sick and could feel it coming up . . .

Rodney Chew said there was a police post on either side of them: one at the major frontier crossing post at Man Kam To and the other on the upper slope of the Ping Yuen Ho river. The second one was the more accessible, he told Wang, and possibly nearer. But Wang had other ideas. Lo Wu's Customs staff had been penetrated, not scratched. Fang wasn't a peon, he wasn't somebody who'd been slipped on to the shelf at ground level. He was a Customs officer with rank who'd been there some time, and if they could do it with one they could do it with more. And they could do the same with the police . . . Wang wasn't as bright-eyed as some over the purity of the Royal Hong Kong Police . . . A wounded Kent and a damaged Hilary West was not information he wanted being shot across the border on the end of flaming arrows.

'Who's looking after the fence in this area?' he asked Rodney.

'Gurkhas. And there'll be a half-section sniffing around that fence now. They have unscheduled ambush positions every mile or so. They don't make a noise those buggers, and you don't get a lot of notice of their presence. A razor-sharp kukri at the back of your ear is your first indication that they're in amongst you and curious!'

'They'll have been briefed,' murmured Wang enigmatically. 'Where's the nearest tower?'

A brief smile of understanding and Rodney said, 'About a mile beyond the river. I'll lead in our Land Rover, you bring up the rear in Fang's.' He'd read Wang's mind.

The road was never going to get acceptance as a grand prix circuit but it didn't put off Rodney. Hilary complained bitterly. Wang reckoned that was a good sign in a sick woman, but Kent was ominously silent – not even a groan – and by the reflected light from the Land Rover's headlights his face had taken on a pasty, grey, sweaty look. Hilary wanted to do something, but she was stuck in her place by Wang, and with a shoulder and arm that shrieked in concert with every indentation in the road she realised very quickly that the best place for her was out of everybody's way.

When they arrived at the watch-tower a young lieutenant, with three poker-faced but watchful Gurkhas, took charge. The lieutenant, a boy of twenty-two with a man's experience, inspected first Kent's leg, then his chest before slowly straightening up and looking down into Wang's eyes.

'Is this anything to do with the shindig I've been listening to coming from over there in the People's Paradise? I was ordered to take minimum notice. D'you know anything about that?'

'Tell you later,' responded Wang. 'Can I get to a phone while you're dabbing those cuts with iodine?'

The young officer stood his ground. He'd already instructed his medical orderly to take over and out of the corner of his eye Wang could see the other Gurkhas lifting Kent out of the Land Rover and placing him on a stretcher. 'You won't need a phone,' the young man said belligerently; he was no Sinophile. 'But you might need a bloody good lawyer if instead of telling me what you want, you start telling me what the bloody hell's going on.' He stopped and looked over his shoulder, cocked his ear, then raised his chin at a Gurkha with corporal's stripes on his arm standing by the door.

A few words of Gurkhali were exchanged, and then the officer, in English for Wang's benefit said, 'I can hear it. Thanks, Tulbahadur.' He turned back to Wang. 'That's a helicopter. The two Europeans will go to BMH in Hong Kong and you and your two friends will stay here with me and my friends until somebody with a little more than this,' he tapped the two pips on his left shoulder, 'tells me whether to shoot the three of you or lock you in our downstairs shithouse. Now, tell me – '

He stopped short and watched Wang's hand shoot round his back and extract from his trouser pocket a worn leather wallet. Wang opened it, pulled out a dirty grey plastic-covered card and offered it to the young officer who studied it without expression. Wang had rank for all occasions. The officer looked up into the slits of Wang's eyes and smiled sheepishly. 'Let me find that phone for you, Colonel . . .' He relaxed visibly. He looked even younger now that he knew he was among friends, but there was no subservience, even though he realised the size of the barrel he'd been offering to lock in his shithouse. 'In the meantime, would you like a cup of tea?'

Wang refused. He was now in a hurry, although he did stop and peer over the verandah into the arc-lit area below where a hovering helicopter, like a glass in a shaky hand being lowered onto a coaster, was being directed by a stocky Gurkha in jungle green.

'Is this a scheduled visit?' asked Wang.

'No – I ordered it the minute I saw that guy in the back of your Land Rover.'

'Do you have a schedule of helicopter visits?' persisted Wang.

'Good God, no!' said the young officer. He looked shocked at the suggestion.

'So, if the Chinese were listening or watching they'd find nothing unusual in this one dropping in?'

'Nothing at all. This one, by the way, came from just up from Brigade at Sek Kong.' He pointed to the south and dipped his finger to indicate the other side of a hilly crest somewhere on the dark, unseen horizon. He frowned in recollection. 'Funny – they didn't seem surprised, and they're not usually this quick. They could almost have been waiting . . .' He shrugged when he got no response. 'D'you want to go into town with it, or are you driving back?'

Wang nodded. 'Forget the phone, I'll go with it. First, though, I'd like a word with my two men. But one thing . . . erm, who are you by the way?'

'Tenth PMO,' said the young officer, then misinterpreting Wang's frown, added, 'Princess Mary's Own.'

Wang's frown disappeared but for another reason. 'Can I ask you not to mention any of tonight's events over the wireless until I've spoken to HQ in Hong Kong? I promise I'll do that the minute the chopper lands in the BMH compound. It's important.'

Young Gurkha officers are not stupid. 'I've already reported shooting and a minor explosion coming from the Red side of the border, sir. They'd have been very surprised if they hadn't heard our views on that. You can bet your life they're tuned in to our frequencies and waiting for more.'

Wang touched the young man's arm briefly. 'I reckon you'll be a general before you reach my age!'

The lieutenant didn't laugh. He didn't even smile. 'Thank you, sir,' he said – he was terribly well brought up. But there was no more time for banter; the helicopter's blades were struggling into the horizontal and the dust, liberally dampened down, was still loose enough to swirl as viciously as a sandstorm, splattering chippings and gravel like little bullets against the tiny Gurkha's legs, sending him scampering out of range, a grin as big as his kukri splitting his dusky features.

Wang and the lieutenant went down the steps to the waiting helicopter. Wang branched off and headed towards Rodney and Sonny Chew. He took Rodney to one side. It was difficult to hold a conversation with the racket of the helicopter's motor thudding the air and he had to shout. He put his mouth close to Rodney's ear.

'Rodney, I can't thank you enough. But I've one more favour to ask you.'

Rodney was willing. But he also looked tired: the work he'd done today was a little more energetic than even an officer in the mobile Customs unit was used to. He held his hand over the other ear and shouted hoarsely, 'Ask away Mr Wang.' From a distance they looked like an ivory netsuke tableau locked in an eternal conversation.

'I want you to forget entirely today's happenings,' shouted

Wang, 'particularly the events of this evening. Any talk of Special Branch activities, of fat Chinamen, of crossing borders, killing Chinese spies . . .' He paused to dampen down his throat. '. . . and wounded European civilians being flown out by helicopters will endanger not only the whole meaning of the operation we've just carried out but will put a direct threat on Sonny's life. Can I count on your discretion?'

'When are all these things going to happen, Mr Wang?' asked Rodney with a quizzical expression.

'Good man! Goodbye, Rodney.' They shook hands briefly and Wang went back to Sonny Chew.

'Sonny, follow Rodney back to Lo Wu in the other Land Rover and then take the first train back to Kowloon. OK?'

'OK. Have a nice trip, boss.'

'I haven't finished yet! I want you out of Hong Kong first thing in the morning. Get yourself to Kuala Lumpur, and don't talk to anybody. If there are any explanations to be made, I'll make them. OK?'

'OK.'

'See you in KL. Take care, Sonny.'

'And you, boss.'

The Gurkha lieutenant helped the Wessex Loadmaster heave Wang into the body of the helicopter, then leapt in easily behind him. He studied Wang's mouthed queries for a moment then shook his head and pointed to his ears. Wang stared sharply at him and moved into the body of the helicopter while the crew manoeuvred the door shut.

Hilary sat in a bucket seat looking very unhappy. Her arm was bandaged into a sling and another tight, straight-jacket-type dressing kept her shoulder and back from moving. A dampened army field dressing had been roughly applied to the burns on the back of her neck, forcing her chin up into the air so that she had to look down her nose at Wang. She looked like a scruffy Oxfam-dressed Lady Bracknell at a village amateur dramatic performance. But there were no feelings of grandeur in Hilary's mind. Every time she closed her eyes to blot out the horror all she could see was David Kent screaming at her to run. And when she opened them the reality was there, lying at her feet. David Kent, dying. Which brought another wave of nausea and another battle to stop the tears from flooding. She wondered whether it had all been worthwhile but was unable to come to a conclusion. Finally she gave up and closed her eyes – and mind – to everything. She didn't want conclusions, or decisions – all she wanted was a painkiller, a bath, a crisp clean bed, and half a dozen Mogadons . . .

David Kent was lying in a deep stretcher. His hands were outside the heavy army blanket and seemed to be the only part of him not covered in blood. His eyes were closed and his face grey, wet and lined with pain. The globules of sweat that trickled erratically from his forehead formed into tiny rivulets and rushed hurriedly down the side of his face, cutting a channel through the caked red gravel of the quarry and collecting in the pit of his neck. They all looked at him but nobody wiped the sweat away. He'd had an ampoule of morphine, but there was no sign on his face that it was giving him a pleasant trip.

Wang stepped gingerly towards him and grabbed the side netting as he struggled to keep his footing in the rapidly rising and turning helicopter. The lieutenant got there before him and held his hand out to help him cover the last yard.

'Thanks!' he bellowed and the young man nodded and stared down at Kent.

The shouting must have jogged something. Kent's eyes were suddenly open. Not focusing; just open – looking.

Then he saw Wang.

His eyes opened wider. He was trying desperately to work things out. Where was he? What was all this bloody racket? Who was this soldier? And – Jesus Christ! Wang? There was a taste of blood in his mouth – and bile. He spat and it went over his shirt. In a haze he followed Wang's outline as he came closer and knelt beside him. Wang's face was blank; he was just looking. The lieutenant joined him and wiped Kent's mouth with a snowy white handkerchief, but he pushed it away, his face tightening so that his cheekbones stood out like red knuckles. And then he shouted at the top of his voice – but it came out only as a gravel-loaded hoarse whisper that was rendered almost incomprehensible by the noise of the thundering rotors.

'You bastard! You dirty, fucking bastard!' He tried to force himself up but succeeded only in grabbing Wang's shirt. It tore with the sound of sawing wood but, hanging on to it, he managed to push his face within an inch of Wang's. 'You bastard! You treacherous bastard! *Why?*'

Wang took hold of Kent's clenched fist firmly with one hand and broke its grip from his shirt. He made no defence as he gently eased Kent back on to the stretcher.

'You bastard – you let that fucking woman kill Hilary . . . You're going to die for that, you Chinese bastard!'

Wang didn't turn his head away. He looked totally unperturbed and continued to stare into Kent's face. But Kent was suddenly silent. He'd emptied the bile from his mind and his brain had gone dead. He'd forgotten what else he wanted to tell Wang; he'd forgotten what he was doing and where he was going. He felt a warm dizziness creep up from his stomach as he tried to outstare Wang, but it couldn't last. Something inside him crawled up to his eyeballs, reached out, and dragged his eyelids down. He didn't fight it; he didn't struggle. It was much nicer this way.

'I don't think he likes you very much, Mr Wang,' shouted the young Gurkha lieutenant. He looked quite serious. There was no smile in his eyes.

Wang tried a smile for the lieutenant but it didn't work. 'Did you bring my jacket?' he asked. The lieutenant handed it to him. It was too light. He jabbed his hand in the right-hand pocket and the voice beside him said in his ear:

'Is this what you're looking for, Mr Wang?' It was the blood-covered revolver in a handkerchief. The lieutenant held it out with the handkerchief draping round his hand; it was still bloody, mucky and gruesome.

'Break it open,' ordered Wang.

The young man did so. There were six rounds in the cylinder, each with a tiny indentation in its cap. The lieutenant studied them for a moment then, reflectively, eased the ejector pin forward and dropped the spent cartridges into his hand. He looked down at them, picked one up and studied the crimping at the discharged end. He did the same with another, then another, and then he looked into Wang's eyes, puzzled, and raised his eyebrows.

'Blanks?'

Wang nodded. There was no expression on his face. He jerked

his chin down at David Kent. 'Are you going to the hospital with him?'

'Would you like me to?'

'Yes please. And will you return his gun to him when he wakes up?'

'With these spent rounds?'

'Would you mind?'

44

Wang paddled out of his bathroom, draped himself in a big fluffy towelling robe and lowered himself into his bed. On the table beside him was a bottle of Highland Spring water, the remains of his Teacher's and a glass waiting for something to be put in it.

He half-filled the glass and showed it to the bottle of Highland Spring. It tasted very nice, thank you. He looked at his watch on the table. Half-past midnight; half-past four in London. Evelyn St John Woodhouse would be just dipping his third custard cream into his afternoon cup of Lapsang suchong. He took another gentle swallow from his glass and dialled Woodhouse's Curzon Street number.

He heard the bone-china cup clink into its saucer.

'Hello, Wangy.' Woodhouse cleared the biscuit crumbs from the corners of his mouth and swallowed the harvest. 'Nice of you to ring and let us know what's going on out there! I've had an expensive chat with DSO. Hong Kong and he told me lots of things but nothing that I wanted to hear. Are you clean?'

'Yes, thank you, Woody – I've just had a nice hot bath.'

Woodhouse wasn't amused. 'Don't bugger about, Wang, these are serious matters.'

Wang smiled to himself; Woodhouse was so predictable. 'I'm in a Hong Kong hotel room, Woody, they don't bug places like this on spec. D'you want to know about the chicken?'

'Careful, Wang!'

'It's gone home to roost.'

In London the cup clinked in its saucer again and tea was sipped while Woodhouse analysed this. It didn't take more than two brisk sips.

'With all its implications?'

'Only time will tell. Hilary did her stuff and David Kent played the innocent idiot. He got hurt – so did she, but not as much.'

Woodhouse ignored the casualty list. 'The Defence Security Officer mentioned trouble on the border. The Army had to help out, he said. Doesn't that compromise the format?'

'A statement issued to the press by the Hong Kong Police stated that following a skirmish in the border area two bodies were recovered. No further details were released. This is normal practice. Nationalities are never revealed; it's normally accepted that people killed up there are Chinese – ours or theirs. Xinhua – the New China News Agency – picked it up. They would have been highly suspicious if the release had said two Europeans, a man and a woman, were killed.'

'This was in accordance with your scheme of things – the business about people getting killed? I presume you want the aunts and uncles in Peking to assume that two principal players have been removed from the list of those who know?' Woodhouse's questions obviously didn't need replies – he didn't wait. 'How bad was Hilary West hurt?'

'Scratches and things. Kent's the one with the problems; he nearly got his leg blown off. But don't worry about it, Woody.' Woody wasn't. Woody was holding his Royal Worcester out for a refill. Wang gave him a few seconds to comment but when nothing but the clink of porcelain came he continued: 'I think he ought to be told the story; I think he has a right to know what being a pawn in international intrigue is all about. It'll help him understand when he's limping down to the post office to collect his pension.'

There were no tears in Evelyn St John's eyes. 'Get him out of Hong Kong,' he ordered. He must have looked down at his wrist to see whether there was enough time left today. There wasn't. 'Tomorrow. The army'll help – they have things flying this way all the time. And, no, Wang, definitely N.O. He's not to be told any more than he already knows – other than he's to keep his mouth shut until I've had time to recite to him specific sections of the Official Secrets Act!'

'Can I offer him anything on your behalf?'

'Like what?'

'A job, Woody. David Kent's supposed to have been killed. People saw it happen. If you're going to put him back above the shop watching the Chinese Embassy in London and he's rumbled it's going to make those people wonder exactly what the bloody hell's going on. They're going to regurgitate that bloody chicken and stick the bits and pieces under the microscope again. He ought to be somewhere in the sun – how about a nice little sinecure in, say, Fiji?'

'You worry too much, Wangy. Leave all that to me. All you have to do now is get the bugger home here and then go back to your little hut in the jungle in KL. And, Wangy?'

'Yeh?'

'Thanks. You've done a grand job.'

Wang dropped the phone on its rest and finished his glass of whisky. It had been a long day. He took off his towelling robe and pulled a thin sheet over his body, then switched off the light. He rocked his mind to sleep by wondering how David Kent was faring under the arc lights in the British Military Hospital operating theatre, where he'd been since ten o'clock. He was still there, the security wing told him, and the surgeons had ordered their breakfast to be sent up at 7 a.m.

Wang was fast asleep before his brain had time to register sympathy.

Hilary had had her bath and her Mogadons and her sleep. She looked much better, her hair was shining, but her eyes weren't as bright as a healthy girl's should be; maybe she'd been giving too much thought to how fragile a thing is life . . . Wang heaved himself onto the edge of the bed and looked down at her. She was sitting, somewhat uncomfortably, in an armchair by the open french windows. Her arm was still bound across her chest but it was purely nominal – a healthy young SAS corporal attached to the bone unit had jumped up and down on her shoulder and, miraculously, cured it. Nevertheless it was still painful.

'You're being flown to the UK this afternoon,' Wang told her. 'I'm afraid you're going to have to dye your hair and wear dark glasses for a time.'

'How long?' Her voice was flat and listless.

Wang was noncommittal. 'Until Ah Lian forgets she stuck a couple of .32s into the back of your neck. She thinks you're dead; it was all part of the show. When the excitement dies down you can come back to Kuala Lumpur; we'll change your name. Maybe you could get married . . .'

'Perish the thought, Wang! I've got enough problems on my

mind without some bloody man mooning around in the background.'

Wang shrugged his shoulders. So much for the ancient Chinese art of matchmaking.

'I'm going to see David,' he said after a lengthy silence. 'I think it might be a nice gesture if you popped in later and asked him how his leg is.'

'How *is* his leg?'

'Fairly rough. They spent all night and the best part of this morning screwing the parts together. Woodhouse said he'd supply him a pair of callipers and a mahogany walking stick, but I don't think we'll see him up with the leaders in the next London marathon.'

'I'll go and see him now.' Hilary's look of concern was genuine. Wang thought there might be hope yet.

'No, not just yet,' he said carefully. 'I've a bit of explaining to do. It might take some time. It might end up with him beating me to death with the bedpan. I'll send for you . . .' He thought about it for a moment, then changed his mind. 'Better still, come and wait outside his room – I might need you as evidence.'

He slipped off the bed and peered round the corner of the door. A young man in slacks and a cotton bush shirt was sitting on the ledge of the window at the end of the corridor. He said he was a hospital orderly but he looked anything but – far too healthy, far too fit, and the way the bush shirt hung awkwardly over his left hip produced a bulge far more substantial than a hypodermic syringe or thermometer.

He approached warily when Wang inclined his head.

'I'm going to spend half an hour with Mr, er . . .'

'Jones,' volunteered the young man.

'. . . with Mr Jones,' repeated Wang. 'Would you, in a few minutes, bring Miss . . .' He waited.

The young man came in on cue. 'Smith.' He didn't smile. Neither did Wang.

'. . . Miss . . . er . . . Smith to his room and wait in the corridor until I give you the word? Perhaps you could find her a chair?'

A second young 'hospital orderly' standing outside the unmarked door in the isolated contagious diseases annexe stood to one side when Wang approached. The system was working.

Wang opened the door quietly and went in.

Kent was lying flat on his back, staring up at the ceiling. There were no bed-covers on him – even with the air-conditioning it was still too hot – but it didn't matter, there was more bandage and plaster visible on Kent's body than bare skin.

He gave no sign that he'd seen Wang enter the room.

'Have you got everything you want, David?'

'Fuck off!'

Wang smiled wryly, closed the door quietly behind him and walked across the room. There was a deep armchair beside the low-slung bed. He lowered himself into it.

'Glad to see you're feeling better,' he said. 'D'you want a cigarette?' He laid a packet of Rothmans on the edge of the bed, took one out for himself, lit it and blew the smoke in the direction of the closed windows. The air-conditioning unit sucked at it and coughed throatily. 'I'll light you one if you want?'

Kent turned his head slowly on a pillow and stared stonily at the Chinese man. Wang returned his inspection with a slow nod. He'd left the cigarette in his mouth, dead centre, his lips crimped round it as if he was sucking sherbert from a yellow packet through a liquorice straw, and each little nod stuck a kink at regular intervals in the thin spiral of blue smoke that crawled up past his eyes to take on the cold air nearer the ceiling. Wang seemed unperturbed by the Englishman's blank stare.

'I'm going back to Kuala Lumpur this afternoon.' He followed the smoke with his eyes up to the ceiling for a second, then came down again. Kent's expression hadn't changed. 'I spoke to Evelyn Woodhouse late last night, after we got you in here. I told him there were things that I thought you ought to know, but he said the only things you needed to know were certain sections of the Official Secrets Act.' Wang didn't smile, but he finally took the cigarette out of his mouth and flicked the ash on the clean, shiny floor. He studied it for a moment, then put his foot on it. 'So, in the gratifying knowledge that it'll upset him, I've decided to tell you exactly what you got yourself into . . .' He paused for a second. 'But perhaps you've already worked it out for yourself?'

Kent winced as if in pain and turned himself on his back again.

'Leg hurting?' There was no solicitude in Wang's voice; he could have been asking if the coffee was sweet enough.

'No,' Kent spoke finally. 'It's my head. Some fucking little Chinaman stuck his boot in my bloody face. It's given me a headache, and it's not helped when that same fucking Chinaman is sitting within hitting distance and I haven't got the strength to do anything about it!' But there was interest in his voice. 'What d'you mean – *exactly* what I got myself into?'

'Do you want that cigarette?'

Kent nodded and Wang lit one and held it out to him. 'You were set up, David. You were set up from the day Woodhouse arranged for you to be put on the Watch on Portland Place, and everything you've done since has been plotted and jiggled around by him, Peter Fylough, and Sir James Morgan – with a small walking-on part for me.'

'Just a minute . . .'

Wang knew what was coming. He wondered why it had taken Kent at least five minutes.

'Hilary?'

'Oh, she's up and about. Not quite a rubber ball – but bouncy.' Wang jabbed his cigarette at the six spent cartridges lined up like little soldiers on the bedside table. 'Like you, she was "shot" with a couple of those.'

'Why?'

'I'll tell you in a minute. Shall I go on?' He didn't wait for Kent's approval. 'Woodhouse had you brought into the Portland Place Watcher team because you were the only man he could lay his hands on who could tell the difference between a Chinaman and a tomato sandwich. The game was for you to pick up the satchel of torn up bits of paper and run like mad, spreading them around so that everybody could follow you. It's that silly English game called hounds and something or other. But this game you bloody nearly buggered up. The bits of paper were the Chaah documents and the object was to get them out of the London Registry and into the hands of Bow Street Alley's murder team for onward transmission to the Peking conspiracy. They were supposed to think they were doing all the running. You ought to get a medal – or an Oscar – but all you're going to get is a walking stick and a threat to have your tongue taken out if you ever dream of talking about it, or if anyone catches you reading *Spycatcher*! Let me tell you what happened . . .'

Kent handed his unsmoked cigarette back to Wang and told him to stub it out. Then he closed his eyes. But he wasn't sleeping.

'You read the documents in the file,' went on Wang. 'You know what they were about so there's no need for me to go into them in any depth. Our man – '

'China's future Chairman,' mumbled Kent, 'Lee Yuan.'

Wang shook his head. 'No. Lee Yuan is the man in the picture. Our man's name is Stanley Booth.'

'Stanley Booth! Who the bloody hell is Stanley Booth?'

'He changed his name. He's now known as Tang Shi – Supreme Co-ordinator of the Chinese Intelligence Services, third in line to the chairmanship of the largest nation in the world.'

'But *Stanley Booth*?'

'Found on the doorstep of a Salvation Army mission in one of the eastern provinces in 1925. China was crawling alive with Christian zealots in those days. They named him Stanley for Christ knows what reason and Booth after their leader. They got out in front of the Japs in '37 and they brought young Stanley with them. He took our shilling.'

'*Our* shilling?'

'British, and by 1953 was a highly thought-of agent operating out of Hong Kong. He was very good – a natural – and wherever he was going to be employed he was going to reach the top. He was the one James Morgan slipped across the border into the hands of the American team already in place. The fact that the Yanks had done all the groundwork and had been installed for over a year was neither here nor there – we were in, and Stanley was off to a flying start. And it's worth noting that he was a sleeper in the true sense of the word – in all those years there wasn't a single word exchanged in either direction.

'But to go back to what I was saying. In his new capacity as a vice-premier, Stanley Booth was leading a delegation to stir up a bit more hatred in South Africa when, on his way home, he stopped off in Paris. It was a legitimate stop, it raised no eyebrows – the Chinese and the French have always recognised each other as blood relations in matters of perfidy. At that time I was also in Paris. It was 1985 – October. The tenth. A good date – the tenth day of the tenth month – the double tenth – very auspicious to us highly superstitious Chinese! Our man, Stanley, had done better than well. He was the rising light of the Chinese Communist Party and that year had been made a vice-Premier. He was already the Co-ordinator of Security Services, with everything that that implies. You could say that in controlling the direction of the largest Intelligence organisation in the world he was, after the Chairman, the most powerful man in the People's Republic. Except that he wasn't. There was somebody in the way.

'Anyway, while I was enjoying my bowl of rice in a restaurant in one of the streets behind the Champs Élysées, I was given a note by a waiter. It had written on it a Paris telephone number. All the man said was "Ring it", and then carried on serving the rest of my meal. It was good, by the way!'

Wang stubbed out his cigarette and, unusually, lit another immediately. He didn't offer one to Kent.

'I rang the number and was invited to name a rendezvous to meet a man who, it was claimed, "had wandered across my path in Malaya during the Indonesian confrontation". Intriguing! I arranged to meet him in a little café behind the Boulevard St Germain, on the Left Bank. It was safe. It was owned by a relation of mine. I didn't recognise the man, but then recognising him wasn't the object of the exercise. He was very edgy and had chosen a table in the darkest corner of the café. He sat without taking off his raincoat and kept his hands jammed in his pockets. I got the feeling he was holding a gun in there somewhere. He didn't eat. I did. And what we discussed was quite interesting. It resulted in your getting your leg nearly blown off . . .' Wang stopped talking and peered into the face of the man on the bed. 'You haven't gone to sleep, have you?'

Kent grunted but didn't open his eyes.

Wang changed the position of his legs and flicked more ash on the shiny floor. 'His method of laying his credentials on the table was to tell me that I was a member of the British Intelligence community and to detail what my role in that organisation was. I didn't like that. I liked it even less when he told me he was a senior executive of the TEWA, the supreme organisation of the Chinese Intelligence Service. But it meant we could look each other in the eye.

'He was in Paris, he told me, with the Tang Shi delegation. Tang Shi, he said, is a British Agent. Just like that! No easing into it –

398

the Supreme Co-ordinator of Security in the People's Republic of China is a British Intelligence agent!

'I carried on eating. I wasn't sure whether he expected me to faint or leap on the table and shake my rattle or what, so I did what came natural to me. I ate. He stared at me for a moment, then carried on. Tang Shi, he said – he was whispering now – had shared his cover a couple of years ago with his closest friend and adviser, the man he'd raised literally from nothing to Second Secretary of the Bow Street Group, one Kim Cheong . . .

'So why hasn't he been shot? was my immediate reaction. My informant shook his head. Kim Cheong, he said, owed everything to this man. And there was more to come. Apart from material gain, loyalty and friendship, Kim Cheong had discovered how narrow is the bridge that crosses the divide between devoted Communist and rabid anti-imperialist and devoted capitalist and co-conspirator. So, my informant told me, Kim Cheong kept quiet and covered Tang Shi's back. Very cosy, I remarked, and commendable, so why were we sitting there talking about it?

'You have heard, he asked me, of the recent appointment of Lee Yuan to the position of Secretary-General of the Communist Party and Vice-Chairman of the Military Affairs Commission? I had. I told him so. That makes him undisputed successor to the Chairman, he said. Immediately behind Lee Yuan in the order of succession is Tang Shi. This is Tang Shi's problem. Lee Yuan is only fifty-eight; the Chairman of the People's Republic is eighty-four and likely to drop dead at any minute. If Lee Yuan steps into his shoes he'll be there for ever. And when he does lower himself on to the throne the first man to have the wire put round his neck will be Tang Shi, then, presumably, a few minutes afterwards, Tang Shi's friend Kim Cheong.

'I was beginning to get the signals, but surely this man wasn't building up his case to invite an elderly Malaysian Chinese to go and kill Lee Yuan? Tang Shi, or rather Stanley Booth, would only have to raise his eyebrows and he'd have ten thousand willing assassins queuing outside his lavatory door eager to take on the job. Oh, no – too easy for the devious Chinese mind. What Stanley wanted was the State to remove Lee Yuan – and the State to call on the reliable subordinate Stanley Booth to quieten the country down in the aftermath. This was where his friend Kim Cheong sprouted horns.'

During the latter part of Wang's recital Kent had opened his eyes and laboriously, and in obvious pain, turned himself onto his side. Wang didn't help him; he'd never been very good with sick people.

'Christ, David, you look bloody awful – d'you want a cigarette?'

'You haven't got a drink, have you?' Kent's interest in Wang's story had, for a moment, helped him forget the kick in the face and the rest of the Chinese man's peculiar behaviour.

'A glass of water?'

'Don't be bloody silly!'

'It just so happens . . . .' Wang reached into the little bag at his feet. Then stopped. 'Is whisky all right with a chest wound?'

'Just pour the bloody stuff! And, yes, light me a cigarette too.'

The strictly sterile room rapidly took on the atmosphere of a planter's bungalow. 'So did this fellow ever tell you why Stanley Booth wanted you to know all this?' asked Kent. His voice was improving with the alcohol; it was now almost normal and caused Wang to glance cautiously over his shoulder at the closed door.

'I'm coming to that,' said Wang in a lowered voice. 'Kim Cheong had, of course, told his master about the Chaah documents. That was the first Stanley Booth had heard of them. Morgan, apparently, when he cobbled Tang Shi together in 1954 to take his place alongside the Yanks, hadn't said a word about this. All Stanley knew was that he was on file somewhere in England and that his curriculum vitae was that of a man of the same age, same build, same background, who, naturally, was dead when he took his name. The thought of details like this, even though they weren't his, being stuck in a bag and tied round a boy's waist for a trek through the jungle must have put him off his chicken soup for days, but he had faith in Jimmy Morgan – as well he might. Morgan knew what he was doing. He'd made an uncrackable cover for Stanley and buried it so that only he knew where to dig for it.'

'Uncrackable?' grimaced Kent. 'Is anything in this bloody business ever uncrackable – or untraceable?'

Wang ignored the last part of Kent's sentence. 'No trouble about building a life story for those days. It was a fortunate age in that respect. In China there was that enormous grey area of time between the risings and the final taking of power by the

Communists where proof of birth, of living, or even of having died was non-existent. Documented life, at that time, began only when a man joined the Party. In Stanley Booth's case the documentation was already done for him when he took Tang Shi's identity. Although there was a small difference in age between the real Tang Shi and Lee Yuan, their origins were similarly obscure, and if anybody thought they remembered the beginnings of either of them Stanley had had them buried.' Wang pulled a face; it was hard to tell whether he agreed with or just envied the simplicity of such methods. 'Kim Cheong had suggested to his friend Stanley Booth that the documents that had been taken off him in the jungle should be brought to Peking, but with an addition, or rather, an inclusion – Stanley's 1954 file. Stanley got the picture. As neither he nor Lee Yuan could prove their origins all they had to do was replace Stanley's picture with one of a thirty-year-old Lee Yuan and alter the details, without harming the orginal documents, so that they fitted Lee Yuan.

'But it was necessary to give the file an unimpeachable pedigree. And the only way to do that was to have Kim Cheong's documents disinterred and placed in the hands of a reliable neutral for examination. They settled on the old gangster and deviate exterminator, Hu Bang. It wasn't an indiscriminate choice. Hu Bang was in the Tang Shi camp, and he also liked Kim Cheong. He didn't like Lee Yuan. His credentials were therefore impeccable!'

'Wasn't this going to jeopardise the American agents' position?' asked Kent.

'Yes.'

'Dangerous.'

Wang shook his head. 'Kim Cheong would arrange for them to get out before the documents arrived in Peking. They would be quietly shuffled out of the country following an arranged student riot. It happens all the time. They'd be out of the way by the time the serious head-rolling started.'

'It wasn't quite what I meant.'

'I know. But you have to think of the size of the snowball. What you had in the offing was the future Chairman of the People's Congress of the Republic of China, Tang Shi, alias Stanley Booth, and his Co-ordinator of intelligence, Kim Cheong, holding down their positions by grace of Sir James Morgan and Evelyn St John

Woodhouse. A couple of old American agents were very small beer. Anyway, the decision was made that Stanley should break his thirty-year cover and re-establish contact with James Morgan. They chose their moment – and their man. Me.'

'Weren't Stanley and Kim Cheong a bit naïve employing a third person to come and spill the beans to you?'

Wang looked up from pouring himself another whisky. He knew the hospital routine well enough; he kept the bottle in its little bag and introduced the glass to it without it seeing daylight. 'That's exactly what I thought, David – until we parted. When I held out my hand to shake his hand he brought his from his pocket for the first time. He didn't have one!'

'A hook?'

'Yes. And the other one the same – the one I thought was a gun. It was a serious business; they were keeping it in the family.

'I brought all this to London. The three wise men, Morgan, Fylough and Woodhouse, put their heads together and decided that we'd kick off with Morgan and Fylough's joining the Queen's entourage when during her China trip she was taken to X'ian to see the flowerpot soldiers. They met secretly with Kim Cheong and it was on his suggestion that it be in Ah Lian, now one of the Party's great faithful and a dedicated and respected member of the National Committee for Defence, that the seed of intrigue be sown.

'Briefed by Kim Cheong, she accepted the task with alacrity. Nobody's head would be safe with Ah Lian once she began the quest. She was empowered to recover the documents by any means, and given unlimited resources to do it. Given that the documents would reveal treason in the highest quarters, and bound by her loyalty to Kim Cheong, she consented to say nothing until the documents were finally laid at Hu Bang's feet.'

'Isn't all this a bit complicated?' Kent held out his empty glass. Wang hesitated. Kent waggled it. It was half filled – no water. 'Why not just dig the file out of its coffin and hand it to Kim Cheong to give to Hu Bang?'

'Christ, David! I thought you understood the Chinese mentality.' Wang topped up his own glass. 'Nothing freely given can have any worth – or, as Deng Xiaoping's official published thoughts advise us: "*Only trust information that is stolen, or*

*obtained by means; information given is suspect automatically
. . .*" And you ought to know that Chinese Intelligence hold
Spycatcher as the definitive bible of British Military Intelligence
activities purely because of the fight the British Government put
up to suppress it. The fact that that fight cost millions of the British
taxpayers' money proved to them that it was authentic stuff. So,
the Kim Cheong, or Chaah, papers had to have a similar passage.
They had to be got the hard way: a bit of murder, a bit of theft, and
above all, difficulty and complication – that would be the seal of
authenticity. The murders of Dean, Kenning and the others were
considered acceptable casualties by Woodhouse and Fylough
when weighed against the file's potential. There was no hedging or
pussyfooting by Woodhouse. He allowed Ah Lian, and her hand-
picked lieutenant, Goh Peng, to make the rules, and went along
with them. It was only when the action lagged, after Dean's death,
that you were brought in as Judas goat – or the innocent agent – to
lead them back onto the rails.'

'Why didn't Woodhouse tell me?' there was no hurt in Kent's
voice, just curiosity.

'You would have found it difficult to play as you did. Your
innocent patriotism was the one thing that was needed. It
convinced Goh Peng and, above all, Ah Lian that everything was
on the straight and level. You couldn't have acted the role – you'd
have betrayed yourself. Even so, it nearly went wrong.'

'How?'

'Woody and Fylough underestimated your tenacity. Your part
of the action was scheduled to be faded out when you were given
details of the ambush at Chaah and shown the photograph of
Fylough. Having got all that down on your slate you were
supposed to return to London and jump up and down in front of
Peter Fylough and demand an explanation – thus pointing him out
to the Goh Peng recovery crew. It wasn't intended that you go to
Hong Kong and start rummaging around like a dustman in the old
Registry at Police HQ . . .' Wang stopped for a moment and
looked sharply at Kent. 'What did you find there by the way?'

'Somebody had left the combination to the safe – it must have
been overlooked or slipped into the files by mistake. It told me
where to find the Chaah documents in London.'

Wang looked askance. 'I'd actually had somebody in there

cleaning up. Under normal circumstances I'd have the bugger's balls for tomorrow's breakfast, but as it is, he did us a favour.'

Kent still wasn't happy. 'What would have happened if I hadn't recognised Fylough? It was after all a scruffy little picture and thirty-five years can play havoc with some people.'

'Woody made a point of letting you have a good look at Peter Fylough in London. He was fairly certain the face would stick. And if it didn't, we had contingencies.'

Kent was becoming quite animated; the talk was doing him a lot more good than lying on his back and just staring up at the ceiling.

'I'll have a drop more of that stuff in your bag, if you don't mind,' he demanded. 'I'm not sure I can stand all this excitement!' The whisky was certainly doing something to him: his face had lost its grey hue and had taken on quite a cheery, feverish, pinky-red colour. But his eyes still looked dull; maybe the glass Wang now handed to him would do something for them. 'Tell me about these contingencies,' he said.

'Hilary West – did you know she was Peter Fylough's daughter, by the way? You didn't? Never mind, it doesn't matter now, does it?' Wang shrugged callously into Kent's startled eyes but didn't give him time to comment. It would be something he could think about when the lights went out and the effect of the Teacher's gave way to the pain of a shattered thigh. He continued. 'Hilary was our contingency. She went back to London with you as a sort of second string. Once Goh Peng and his agents had made your association in Kuala Lumpur the time was ripe for her to come back and be brought into the action. If you hadn't got together with her they, or we, couldn't have moved her into the game without suspicion.'

And talking about suspicion. A nasty line had appeared on Kent's forehead. Suspicion and scepticism. 'What had Hilary to do with this?' he asked, ominously.

Wang felt perfectly safe. 'She'd been lent to Woodhouse. Peter Fylough was her case officer, but actually she was a Morgan woman, MI6. She'd been sent to China as a student some time ago, with orders to get herself into trouble and be recruited by Chinese Intelligence. She succeeded – clever girl our Hilary! She settled in Malaysia as a double TEWA sleeper, but she was actually a non-active member of my MI5/MI6 conglomerate. Goh Peng woke her from her slumbers and instructed her to lie alongside you and report that you were as genuine as you appeared. My instructions also – almost to the letter. She did. How did you get on with her, by the way?'

'That's none of your bloody business!' Kent fixed Wang with a baleful stare. 'Are you telling me that that performance in Fylough's flat was a put-up job?'

'It started that way, then it all went wrong. And that was your fault. You hadn't been programmed to worm your way into the Foreign Office Registry and swipe confidential documents. What should have happened, and would have happened if it hadn't been for you, was that after a bit of persuasive but unproductive argy-bargy on Fylough, Hilary would have been brought in and threatened – only threatened, mind you – unless the file was produced. Fylough would have reluctantly phoned Morgan, who would have reluctantly produced the file, after going through the motions of asking for asylum for our agents at risk in Peking. It was all authentic stuff and would have satisfied Goh Peng. Kim Cheong would, naturally, have refused this request but, regardless, the file would have been handed over. Hilary would have been released and Fylough sent on his way with a slapped wrist. That was Kim Cheong's plan.

'It was also part of his plan that Ah Lian should take the file to Hong Kong and that Goh Peng should travel under separate cover to Peking to give Hu Bang a blow-by-blow account to substantiate Kim Cheong's report. Everything was nicely sewn up – everything was hunky-dory. And then along came David Kent, and the whole bloody thing was splashed all over the ceiling. They lost their chief independent witness, Goh Peng – some silly bastard shot him on Woodhouse's orders, the reason is unimportant. But, strangely enough, your marching in and buggering up the works was, I was told by Kim Cheong on the battlefield, one of the deciding factors in establishing for Hu Bang the veracity of the whole business. He was there. You probably didn't see him – he was organising the shoot! I've also been told since the battle,' and Wang touched the side of his nose as he spoke, 'that the fact that both you and Hilary were killed by Ah Lian put any doubts, if there had been any, straight out of the window. Thank you, David!'

'Get stuffed!'

The two men looked at each other for several moments as they drank their neat whiskies. 'I'll have another cigarette now, please,' demanded Kent and while Wang was lighting it for him he focused his eyes over the top of his glass at the little row of six spent cartridge cases. 'What about those? Why did you go to the trouble of giving me a gun loaded with blank ammunition?'

Wang took the cigarette from between his lips, checked that it was alight and passed it to Kent.

'I knew you'd only check that it was loaded. Nobody flips bullets out of a revolver to make sure that they really are bullets, do they? That's why it was a little S&W. I couldn't have done it with an automatic.'

'I wasn't asking that. I said *why*?'

Wang smiled shyly. 'I had visions of Kim Cheong and Ah Lian being gunned down by you and the bloody file arriving back in London. I gave you the gun to stop you looking for some other means of destruction. You'd already shown us what a resourceful bastard you are – I couldn't take a chance. Anyway, it saved your life. And Hilary's.'

Kent frowned, then, surprisingly, smiled – it even got as far as his eyes. 'I think, Wang, I'm just about ready to forgive you!'

Wang looked embarrassed. 'D'you want to shake my hand or something?'

'Don't be bloody silly. Where's Hilary?'

'She stayed. She refused to go back to London unless you went with her,' he lied cheerfully. 'She wants to be with you – she feels guilt.'

'And do you?'

'A kick in the face, David? I could have done worse – my gun wasn't loaded with blanks.'

'Forget it, Wang. What happens now?'

'You and Hilary go under cover in the bush somewhere and stay quiet until the rumblings in the People's Republic die into little tremors. When our man Stanley Booth starts making their world a better place you can both come back and sit round the fireside with us. Woody'll find you something interesting to do.'

'Like what? Watching Portland Place?'

'Wouldn't you prefer being Hilary's kept man? You're not going to do a lot of steeplechasing for some time – and she seems to be showing very friendly tendencies.'

'Do they have tok-tok birds in this bush you're thinking of sending us to?'

'It could be arranged!'

'I accept.'

'She's outside. I'll send her in. Be gentle with her – she's got a sore shoulder!'

But Kent didn't laugh. Wang stood up and gathered together his few belongings. Kent was staring at him.

'What's the matter?'

'I was just thinking, Peng Soon . . .' It was the first time Kent had used Wang's first names.

Wang beamed, it pleased him. 'What were you thinking, David?'

'I was thinking that if you ever see me coming along your side of the street, get out of the bloody way – or duck!'

He could hear Wang's laughter echoing down the corridor even as Hilary walked through the door, smiling.

CHINA'S NEW
GUARD SETTLES
SUCCESSION

By Dennis Wombell
in Peking

The death has been announced of Lee Yuan, who resigned last year as Secretary-General of the Chinese Communist Party and Vice-Chairman of the all-important Military Affairs Commission. He was 59. No cause was given for his death although at the time of his sudden resignation, and in the absence of an official explanation, it was generally believed that he was seriously ill. Lee Yuan had been officially recognised as successor to the Chairman and designate Head of State prior to his resignation as Secretary-General.

The succession was the subject of intense interest among delegates attending a special meeting of the National People's Congress, China's Parliament, at which Tang Shi, Co-ordinator of Intelligence and a vice-premier was chosen to replace Lee Yuan as successor to the ailing Chairman.

Delegates who feared a period of uncertainty or a power struggle are now relaxed, certain that Tang Shi's election will have a calming influence among the younger and more radical members of the politburo.

He is succeeded in the powerful and important post of Co-ordinator of Intelligence by his deputy Kim Cheong, an appointment welcomed by the delegates, and a position which carries promise of election to the country's select leadership committee.

Here follows an extract from George Brown's
next novel, **Pinpoint** now available in hard-
back from Century:

1

Paris 1961

FROM THE SHADOW of dead ground at the back of the
car bay, where the inadequate strip of neon built into the
underground car-park ceiling failed to meet its neighbour, two
darker shadows, shapeless, indistinct, waited, unmoving.

'Philippe, this is a waste of time – he's not the one we want,
he's insignificant, small stuff. We should be going for Big Nose,
not the bloody street cleaners!'

The whisper barely reached but it was enough to earn a quiet,
warning 'Shhh!' A hand shot out, grabbing the shorter of the
two shapes, cautioning silence. It wasn't enough. The whisperer
was uncomfortable, he was dying for a cigarette. He was dying
for anything to alleviate the tension of waiting.

'And we don't even know that he'll come,' the whisperer
continued, slightly louder, as if having broken the hour-long
silence it didn't matter any more.

But the other man's voice stayed on the lower key and hissed
into the crouching shadow's ear: 'For Christ's sake shut up! If
you don't keep quiet, I'll stick my boot in your mouth!' The
speaker rolled up the sleeve of his thick sweater and strained his
eyes at the faintly luminous dial of his watch. The hands
appeared not to have moved since his last check. *When was*

that? An hour ago? He stared hard, in disbelief, then brought the watch slowly up to his eye. *Jesus! Only five minutes ago!* The slight movement brought a tiny reflection of light from one of the silver buttons on the cuff of the police uniform he was wearing; it startled him for a moment and he stared into the shadow beside him for a similar give-away. But there was nothing, the gleam was insignificant, nobody standing a metre away would have seen anything to break the shadow. He gave a fractional nod of satisfaction and this brought another slight but duller gleam from the shiny visor of the uniform kepi jammed on his head. Half-past ten. He allowed his wrist to drop slowly to his side.

He controlled the doubt in his own mind with a hoarse whisper: 'Lucienne won't let us down.' It was for himself; he needed the reassurance. His crouching companion had already given up. 'Listen,' he hissed, 'don't let go. Anything could have held them up. She'll keep her word . . .' *She had better!* he added under his breath. But she was three-quarters of an hour late. Something had to be wrong, and his instinct told him that if it started wrong it would end wrong. He had great faith in his instincts, but he stood his ground. 'We'll give it another ten.'

'It's a waste of time!'

'Shhh!'

A revved engine in neutral gear echoed from the concrete dungeon walls and a car's headlights bounced erratically from ground to ceiling as it negotiated the ramp, out of sight of the two waiting men, before turning the corner. The two men pressed themselves hard into the wall behind them and froze rigid as the car's wheels squealed impatiently, then shot off to the far end of the garage and disappeared down the slope to one of the lower floors. The standing man relaxed and touched the arm of his companion, who rose slowly to stand beside him. The machine-pistol he held across his body touched the wall with a dull metallic thud, causing the taller of the two men to hiss urgently, 'Shut up, Paul! I'm not going to warn you again. Be careful with that bloody thing and don't make a bloody sound!'

4

The warning had barely left his lips when the lights of another vehicle bounced off the wall, briefly illuminating the empty bays and lighting up the sign warning that the landing was reserved for special-permit holders, Government and VIPs. The lights steadied for a second, then gave a double flash on high beam and dipped again.

'That's ours!' The taller of the two men nudged his partner. 'Don't forget, the eyes of those in the second car'll be on me. I'll let them see the uniform. It'll calm them down. You look after the Minister. Shoot him in the leg if he argues, but that's as far as you go. I want him alive, not on a bloody slab! And Paul—'

'For Christ sake!'

'Make sure there's room for Lucienne to make a bolt for it.'

'Jesus! We've been all through this, there's no need to keep on repeating things — I'm not a bloody idiot.'

'That's debatable . . .' He raised his voice from the whispered hiss and spoke normally: 'The second car'll be full of pros, so don't distract me. Just do as you've been told, and nothing else, OK?'

The second man made no reply.

'I said, OK?'

'OK, OK!' It came reluctantly. But he wasn't perturbed. He was quite a few years younger, less experienced in the gun game, and he had a younger man's excitability, but the excitement was well controlled and the adrenalin was pumping healthily. 'Just stop worrying about me. Do what you have to do. I can look after myself.'

The tall man, Philippe, took the machine-pistol from him and quickly checked that the magazine was firmly home before easing the bolt out of its safety recess. It was a serious killing tool: a Schmeisser P40, 60 × 9mm in a double magazine, the stock removed for ease of movement. He handled it like an old friend. The barrel fitted comfortably in the crook of his arm whilst, with one hand lightly grasping the pistol grip, he remained in the shadow and watched his companion step out into the path of the Peugeot. Its lights dipped as it bounced over the ramp and crawled towards him.

Ten metres behind a second car bumped gently in its wake and fractionally scraped its sump on the ramp.

'Philippe!' Paul's warning barely carried. His uniform clearly visible, he was now standing in the full glare of the Peugeot's lights. He hissed again out of the corner of his mouth, without moving his lips, 'Philippe! Four – probably five in the second car!' In the car nearest to him, silhouetted against the other's lights, he could see only two heads.

The Peugeot stopped. The second car continued moving at a snail's pace until it was four metres away, then it, too, stopped and waited. Without moving from the passageway, Paul held up his hand and pointed his finger at it. There was no response from the driver or the front-seat passenger, who stared back with indifference. The three men on the back seat appeared to be asleep.

The policeman shrugged his shoulders and approached the driver's side of the Peugeot and peered into its interior. A girl's white face peered back at him. He lowered his head and studied the man in the passenger seat.

Heavy-featured, his lips thick and wet, the passenger ignored the policeman and stared straight ahead. There was no acknowledgement, no greeting; he wasn't interested. The policeman took his eyes off him and glanced down at the woman's lap. Her short skirt was rumpled around her hips and the passenger's hand was firmly between her slim thighs.

'Gautier,' the passenger grunted after a moment. It was a condescension; a command to get your eyes off and get on with your job. He didn't remove his hand. He didn't look at the policeman. 'You know who I am?'

The policeman touched the peak of his kepi. 'Yes, Minister, I know who you are – and what you are.' The Minister was too preoccupied with the working of his fingers to notice the lack of servility in the policeman's response. Paul stared at the side of his sweating face for a moment, then touched the girl's shoulder and pointed to an empty bay further along on the left-hand side of the garage. 'Please park there where I can keep watch on you. Are these people behind with you, monsieur?'

'Yes, of course they bloody are – idiot! Get on with it!' The Minister's preoccupation didn't extend to the common gendarme. Whatever he wanted to do, he was in a hurry to do it.

The policeman looked briefly at the back of the Minister's hand, attracted for a moment to its sinews, raised like cords as his fingers worked and probed between the girl's legs. He glanced openly at the girl. The probing and feeling was having no effect on her; she was upset, nervous, and it wasn't the Minister's hand making her so. The policeman turned his eyes briefly back to the Minister. He wasn't concerned about her feelings. There was only one person who concerned him. And his wrist was beginning to ache. 'I said get on with it – and get your bloody eyes off!'

The girl glanced shyly into the policeman's face. She didn't smile. She eased the Peugeot forward into the space the policeman had indicated and switched off the engine. The second car moved up.

The windows were down. The driver didn't give the policeman time to speak. 'The Minister's bodyguard.' He flicked his half-smoked cigarette out of the window. 'His little friend wants to eat couscous. We all know what he wants to eat!' His snigger was echoed from the loaded back seat. The policeman didn't join in the mirth. He bent from the waist and peered into the car at the grinning faces. 'Would you mind putting on the interior light, please?' he asked politely.

The driver stopped grinning and reached above him to switch on the roof light. It was a normal request, he didn't argue. The policeman glanced unconcernedly at the automatic in a shoulder-harness revealed by his arm movement and turned his head to study more closely the three men bunched on the back seat.

The driver said, 'Come on, get a bloody move on!' and raised his arm again to switch off the light.

'Leave it on.' Philippe's voice was calm and authoritative. It had an instant effect. Nobody had noticed him move out of the shadow and into the artificially lit tunnel. He moved back slightly

7

and stood by the offside wheel where they could all see him. All heads turned, but nothing else moved. The driver's hand remained just above his head.

When he'd got their full attention, Philippe showed them the Schmeisser. But they'd already seen it. He moved it gently to the left and then to the right so that they each had a good look down the short barrel. They stared like so many rabbits caught in a car's headlights and, paralysed, sat stiff, rigid, careful not to move their hands from where they'd rested them while talking to Paul.

'Go and get the Minister and take him to our car,' ordered Philippe. He didn't look at Paul; he didn't take his eyes off the men in the car. 'Be quick!'

Paul didn't acknowledge. He turned quickly on his heels, the heavy police 9mm MAB automatic out of the holster on his belt and in his hand as he sidled up to the passenger side of the parked Peugeot. The Minister glared round in anger when the police uniform filled his side-window again. His hand remained between the girl's legs, but was locked, unmoving – and then he saw the pistol as Paul brought it up from his side and rested its barrel on the open window-ledge. It took a second to register, then his stomach dropped on to his bladder, threatening to burst it in terror as he stared first at the automatic, pointing directly at his head, and then at the no longer familiar or reassuring sight of the dependable French gendarme. But the paralysis lasted only seconds. He came to life and started to move his hand away from the girl, then stopped dead as Paul raised the MAB and touched its muzzle to the side of his temple.

'What do you want?' There was no more arrogance there; no more the Minister. He was a man very afraid. But Paul gave him no time to consider the situation. He squeezed the trigger and part of the Minister's head splattered over the girl in the driving seat. She screamed and dragged his hand from between her thighs and tried to open the door on her side. There was another ear-shattering explosion as Paul fired again into the shuddering body beside her. She went out of control. It wasn't supposed to be like this. She opened her eyes to the sudden silence and then her scream rose higher when she became aware of the horror of the mess that had hit her and, beside her, thumping up and down on the ridge of the dashboard, the rest of the Minister's exploded head. She stopped struggling with the door handle and closed her eyes and stuffed her knuckles into her wide-open mouth, but still her screams built up, a white searing crescendo of noise.

'What the . . . !' bellowed Philippe, and for a fraction of a second turned his head towards the Minister's car. It was only for a second. One of the men on the back seat thought it was long enough and his hand shot under his arm. But it wasn't. Philippe recovered as quickly as his attention had lapsed. He stroked the trigger. Three rounds thumped into the man's chest as his hand reappeared with a cocked automatic. Two of the others thought they too had a chance. The Schmeisser thudded again, this time a longer burst, and all three men on the back seat tumbled together like three old bundles of washing, their bodies jerking like puppets as Philippe emptied the first of the magazines into the back of the car.

He reversed the magazine without taking his eyes off the twitching bodies. None was alive. Neither was the front-seat passenger, who, in his panic to get out of the car, had managed to get the door open, only to catch on his way out two bullets from the edge of the burst, both in the neck, one just below his ear. There he stayed, half in and half out of the car, one arm hooked over the window-ledge, his shoulders shuddering with the shock as his life dribbled out of the two holes. Just one more: the driver. Philippe dare not take his eyes off him.

'*Paul*!' he bellowed again, his voice rasping with the inhalation of blow-back cordite fumes and his ears ringing with the explosions.

'*What the fucking hell's going on? For Christ's sake! What the bloody hell are you doing?*'

There was no answer.

Paul leaned into the car and touched the girl's head with the muzzle of the automatic. 'Shut up!' he rasped urgently.

9

The screams died in her throat. She opened her eyes and stared with horror into his face. But the tableau lasted for only a second and then she half turned and jerked her shoulders against the door as, once again, she struggled to get it open. But her shaking hands kept slipping. 'Help me . . .' she hiccuped, and then choked: 'Please! Please! Get me away from here! Where's Philippe? Quick, help me get out . . .'

She turned sharply in her seat and stared appealingly into Paul's cold eyes. The MAB hadn't moved. Rock steady, it was still only two inches from the side of her face.

'Sorry,' he murmured. 'They'll tear you to pieces.'

She didn't have time to register his words. Without flinching, he squeezed the trigger once. The explosion sounded even louder this time as the bullet tore a passage just below her ear lobe and ploughed downwards. It was a careless shot. He cursed silently to himself as her head crashed on to the steering-wheel. But she wasn't dead. He leaned across the Minister's dead body, rested one hand on his shoulder, and placed the muzzle against her temple. She was making a barking, coughing noise like a dog with a piece of bone stuck in its throat and her shoulders were jerking up and down, making a clean shot difficult. He pushed himself further through the open window and reached out with his other hand and grasped her hair to steady her head. Then he fired. Everything stopped. He picked up her handbag, wriggled his way out of the window and backed away.

Without taking his eyes off the driver, Philippe moved back until he was almost level with the Minister's car. He gave a quick glance over his shoulder.

'What's happened? Where's the Minister? Where's Lucienne? What the bloody hell . . . !'

'I'll tell you in a—' He elbowed past Philippe. 'Watch it! There's one still there!' He pointed his automatic at the windscreen of the car and looked in. 'Jesus!' Then he stared at Philippe. 'You've killed the whole bloody lot! God, what a fucking game! I'm enjoying this!'

Philippe turned to stare at the bodies in the Minister's car. For a second he was speechless. Then he exploded in a cold rage.

But Paul was not listening. The younger man's blood was thudding behind his eyes; he was unstoppable.

'Forget it, Philippe – it's bloody war! Come on, get out of it. I'll tell you all about it later. Finish that bugger off and let's go.'

The tall man stared grimly at his companion for several seconds. 'But why Lucienne?' He swung the Schmeisser round, ominously, so that it was pointed at Paul.

Paul wasn't perturbed. He shook his head. 'I said I'll tell you about it. Quick, you go. I'll cover you in case anybody here moves.'

Philippe hesitated for a second, but time was running out. He growled something incomprehensible, then turned and walked briskly into the depths of the car park. He didn't look round.

Paul poked his hand with the MAB into the window and tapped the crouching driver's hands. The driver came to life. He seemed to know what was expected of him. He wrapped his hands round the steering-wheel where they could be seen and began to plead incoherently for his life. He had only seconds in which to do it. Their eyes met. 'Please . . .' His hands and wrists jerked uncontrollably. He was swarthy, with tight, pock-marked cheeks, sallow skin, jet-black crinkly hair – Corsican – but the normal hard cruelty of his face was softened by the fear-driven quivering of his facial muscles. Paul squeezed the trigger twice and the dark face disappeared under the force of the two 9mms.

Philippe halted in his tracks and began to turn back. A bellow from Paul stopped him. 'Duck, Philippe!' He went down on one knee and saw the younger man, with a grin splitting his face, toss a small object through the window of the car and then, at a crouch, double towards him. A second later the grenade exploded with a whoof, and a whoosh of hot air funnelled towards him as the bodyguard's car disappeared in a ball of white, then red and black oily flames.

Paul shot past him. 'Come on, Philippe! Let's get the bloody hell out of here!' He had to shout to make himself heard over

11

the roar of the flames, but he didn't wait for his partner and pounded into the gloom at the far end of the car park.

The taller man followed at a slower pace, a gentle trot, turning every so often to study the carnage they'd left behind them. When he joined the younger man he handed him the Schmeisser and, grim-faced, took the automatic from him and tucked it into the back of his trouser-band. The anger showed through his drawn expression. There were a lot of questions to be answered. A simple kidnapping, a well-organized, bloodless exercise had turned into a bloodbath, and the reason for that bloodbath stood grinning at the roaring flames and the crack of exploding pistol ammunition from under the cremating Corsicans' armpits. Paul was enjoying himself. And he wasn't finished with the killing. The adrenalin was still coursing.

'What about them, Philippe? Do we kill them?' The blood-lust showed in his red-rimmed eyes as he pointed the muzzle of the Schmeisser at another recess in an empty bay where, kneeling side by side, their hands tied behind their backs and their faces pressed against the cold concrete wall, two uniformed gendarmes shivered with fear. One had given up. The other, less experienced, strained to turn his head to see what was going on. He stopped straining when he heard the sentence of death.

'No. There's been enough killing, you vicious bastard!' Philippe turned his back to the two policemen and his partner. 'Come on. Leave them as they are.'

'They'll recognize us.'

'I said leave them!' His anger burst. 'Just do as I bloody say for once, will you! Without fucking argument!'

The young man's face showed nothing. He shrugged his shoulders, but continued staring at the heads of the two bound gendarmes. The adventurous policeman had stopped trying to see what was going on. He'd heard enough. He didn't want to see anybody's face; he didn't want to recognize anybody.

'Come on!'

Paul shrugged again and moved away.

There was no look of relief on the policemen's faces, now highlighted by the gushing, roaring flames of the torched car.

They weren't going to be shot – but they could just as well be burned to death. They could feel the heat already, here in the bowels of the car park, and even deep in one of the bays, with the flickering of the roaring flames reflecting off the concrete walls around them, it felt like the approach of hell. They began to scream, and the new fear showed in their bulging eyes as they stared at each other. It was like a silent horror film with their screams reduced to gurgles of terror behind the thick wrapping of plaster that covered their mouths and lower part of their faces. Their plight didn't worry Paul as he left them behind.

Still in their bogus uniforms, Philippe de Guy-Montbron and Paul Vernet descended at a trot to the lower floor, and then, more casually, to the sub-basement. Above them the Boulevard St-Germain, after a period of shocked paralysis, was beginning to react to the sound of muted gunfire and the dull thump of underground explosions, and the sirens were converging from all directions. But the two men didn't panic. They stopped by a nondescript, old-model brown Renault and with controlled haste stripped off their uniforms and tossed them on to the back seat of the car. The Schmeisser went in last of all. They opened the boot and dressed themselves in their everyday clothes. Philippe removed the magazine from the butt of the MAB, threw it on to the clothes in the car and replaced it with a full one. He cocked the weapon, applied the safety, tucked it into his belt and pulled his sweater down over it.

'Wait for me over there,' he snapped, and jerked his chin at the upward slope and a door marked 'Emergency Exit'. He was finding it difficult to talk to his companion. He kept his words to a minimum, turning his back and then leaning into the boot of the Renault. He shifted an old sack and inspected beneath it the packet flattened over the petrol tank. He ran his hands over it and checked that it was firmly in place, then compared the time on the small clock attached to the packet with the dial on his wrist. Nothing registered on his face. He looked tired. It was the aftermath of battle. He brought the two loose wires together and twirled them into a join, studied the packet for another second, then dropped the boot and joined Paul Vernet at the exit.

They surfaced at street level on the opposite side of the car-park entrance. Avoiding the confusion of police, ambulance, fire and emergency services they walked, without hurrying, away from the chaos. They passed no one. The few cars they saw were all hurrying to the party to add to the confusion and nobody had time to give the two men a second glance. Without exchanging a word they walked up the Rue de Rennes as far as the inter-section with the Boulevard Raspail.

'We make a bloody good team, Philippe!' Paul broke the silence. He was impervious to the older man's silent anger. 'We'll show the bastards, won't we?'

Philippe stared at him. This wasn't the time – or the place. He didn't reply. Finally he nodded in the direction of Montparnasse. 'Walk to Montparnasse and take the Métro. Go straight home and have a bath. Wash your hair. Keep your head down and don't go out for two days. I'll be in touch – usual manner – be there.' He watched as the younger man turned away towards the Métro. 'Paul,' he called, softly.

'What?'

'Why did you kill Gautier?'

Paul smiled. 'I didn't like his fat face. And the bastard called me an idiot!'

'You killed him because he called you an idiot? Jesus Christ!'

'It wasn't only that – he was going to be awkward. He'd never have gone with us, and it was my life on the line as well. I reckoned it was the easiest way out.' The younger man's face took on a look of truculence. 'I still think kidnapping the old bastard was a silly idea. This was much easier – it'll make a much bigger splash.'

Philippe kept his temper. 'Even though all my planning and instructions were that he remain alive? Didn't you think, for one idiotic minute, that there was a reason for that? If I'd wanted him killed, don't you think I'd have said? Christ! Was that too much for you to understand?'

14

Paul shrugged his shoulders and again turned to go, but Philippe gripped his arm. Paul didn't try to pull away. 'Philippe, what's done's done. I reckon we're better off this way.'

Philippe let go of his arm. It was a waste of time. 'Why'd you kill Lucienne?'

'Because you'd have been too soft to do it yourself. It's all very well telling her to run and forget, but what would have happened when the *barbouzes* shoved her up against the wall and started knocking her about? D'you think she'd have stood there shaking her head and saying she knew nothing about it? D'you think she'd have whistled with joy as they were breaking her arms and asking who's the bastard who killed the Minister? She bloody wouldn't have, Philippe. She'd have screamed at the top of her voice it was Philippe de Guy-Montbron and Paul Vernet who did it, and this is how you can find them . . . !'

'What happened afterwards was none of your business,' said Montbron with as much control as he could muster. He might as well have saved his breath.

'My life is my business.'

'Then it's time you packed your bloody bag and buggered off back into the mountains.'

'No can do, Philippe. You need me. There's no one else.'

He was right. Philippe studied him for a moment and tried hard not to shake his head in exasperation. There wasn't much else he could say, or do. He said, tamely, 'There was supposed to be no killing tonight. Next time . . .'

But Paul was on firm ground; he was still riding the blood trip; the adrenalin was still coursing. He grinned into the older man's face. 'They were only fuckin' Corsicans!'

Philippe de Guy-Montbron shook his head sadly. His unhappy features were a permanent legacy of an unpleasant profession. 'You're a mindless young bastard,' he said through his teeth.

'Yeh, I know – but I'm still your brother.'

Whatever else he was going to say was cut off by the sound of a muffled subterranean thump. There was a faint rumble, a vague movement under their feet. The old Renault had disintegrated, exploded under a two-kilo wad of PE. Nothing drastic

15

– just enough to blow the thing, and everything in it, to tiny pieces, and give the forensic people an interesting hour or two before they shook their heads and went home.

The two men looked at each other. No more words. Montbron stood in a shop doorway and watched the younger man until he disappeared up the Rue de Rennes towards the Boulevard Montparnasse. He waited a few minutes longer, then crossed the road, skirted the Jardin du Luxembourg, cut through a side-street and then joined the Boulevard St Michel. He glanced casually around him. He knew nobody had picked him up, but he wasn't relaxed. Nobody was relaxed. It was like wartime, and as in wartime, the best-laid plans go wrong. As this one had. He found his car where he'd left it and sat at an adjacent café and drank a small glass of beer while he studied his surroundings.

The car had no watcher, but it had a ticket for overstaying its welcome. He'd have been very suspicious if it hadn't.

When he finished his beer he changed to coffee and cognac and waited another three-quarters of an hour. There was plenty of life about. The Boulevard St-Michel was at its most vibrant and the tall, slightly balding man in his early thirties sitting outside the café with his back to the wall, sipping cognac and coffee, caused no interest. Montbron suited the Left Bank. Clean-shaven, with a firm chin and grey eyes that with a trace of mockery, gazed at the thronging mass without interest. He looked the part. A dark roll-neck sweater and rust-coloured suede jacket kept his appearance within the bounds of mature student/youngish lecturer. The fact that he was sitting alone might have raised an eyebrow, but it would have been nothing more than that and it didn't seem to concern him. He glanced down at his watch. The minute hand was creeping towards ten-past twelve. Unhurriedly he tipped the remains of his cognac down his throat, swirled the coffee-cup absently and drained it as he picked up the little tab, stood and squeezed his way past his neighbours through the café to the bar. He paid his bill and bought half a dozen telephone *jetons*, then, after a brief glance through the café door at the spot he'd just vacated, he strolled to the end of the café and locked himself in the phone booth. He looked at his watch again. One minute to quarter past. He began to dial. It was a Metz number on the Army network.

The phone rang three times before it was picked up.

Montbron listened for a second, then said, 'Diderot.'

'I've just heard the news,' said the voice at the other end. It didn't sound too pleased. 'What went wrong?'

Montbron told him.

'A simple kidnap turns into a bloodbath – that's going to take some explaining at the end of the day. Who's this mad bastard you've picked up as a partner?' The voice didn't wait for an answer. 'You're supposed to be on your own. If you need backup, I'll supply it, but that wasn't in the drawing. What happens now, Philippe?'

'You want me to abort the programme?'

There was a longish pause. Montbron coughed lightly to show he was still there, then pressed another *jeton* into the slot. It wasn't necessary; the phone came to life again. 'No. Pick the cards up again and carry on – but I repeat, get rid of that bloody maniac. They'll have your head in the bloody bucket if it happens again. Is that clear?'

'Yes, sir. I'm sorry about Gautier.'

'It's not as bad as it seems.'

'Even so—'

'Forget it.'

Montbron waited for a few seconds longer with the receiver jammed against his ear. But the line was dead. No goodbye. Nothing. He put the phone down and went outside, ordered himself another cognac, no coffee, then sat down and watched his car for another ten minutes before getting into it and driving away.